i     **Gutter**

ii     **Editorial**

001    Digitalis Lust
       **Olufemi Terry**
006    Extract from the novel *This is Where I Am*
       **Karen Campbell**
012    The Correct Recipe for Bleached Bones
       **Lara S Williams**
017    A Scottish Cent(o)ury
       **Rob A Mackenzie**
020    Henry Lord Darnley, syphilitic
       **Andrew F Giles**
020    Plangent
       **Julian Colton**
021    The F word
       **Kona Macphee**
021    The questions that go at fi...
       **Kona Macphee**
022    Aurora
       **Kona Macphee**
023    Show Me A Man's Teeth
       **Andy Jackson**
024    Fuji Rock and Ever After
       **Iain Maloney**
028    Please
       **Wayne Price**
034    Excavating The Heaney Machine
       **Dearman McKay**
035    This Is Not A Translation
       **Dearman McKay**
036    The immaculate speech
       **Nick Brooks**
036    Post-Revolutionary Poets of the Future
       **Andrew McCallum**
037    Women's Secret Language in China
       **Tessa Ransford**
038    Hum Int
       **Andrew Philip**
039    Look North (and North Again)
       **Andrew Philip**
040    Tae a Lousy Piper
       **Andrew Philip**
041    I was like, oh my God, I was literally
       **Gordon Legge**
048    After the Dance
       **Carl MacDougall**
052    Knife
       **Andrew McCallum Crawford**
057    Extract from the novel *Ramshackle*
       **Elizabeth Reeder**
062    Watching Wild Parrots in San Francisco
       **Brian Docherty**
063    Summer
       **Julian Colton**
064    Sour Jewel
       **Andy Jackson**
065    Dignity
       **Andy Jackson**
066    Extract from *Buddha: A Novel*
       **Kevin MacNeil**
070    Windows
       **Alison Irvine**
073    The Umbrella
       **Regi Claire**

074    Edwin and Federico: A Fable
       **Andrew McCallum**
075    Hero
       **Andrew F Giles**
076    The Songs of Kirilov
       **Niall Campbell**
077    After the battles of Camulodunum, London & Verulamium
       **Andrew F Giles**
07?    Odradek[2]
       **...tteridge**
       ...rds
       ...ou want to talk to me?
       ...egor
       ...m II
       **Ross McGregor**
089    Poem III
       **Ross McGregor**
089    Poem V
       **Ross McGregor**
090    At Balmaha
       **AC Clarke**
091    Extract from the novel *The Year of the Whale*
       **Simon Sylvester**
100    El Café de l'Opera
       **Cat Dean**
104    Sandra Alland
       **Air**

183    **Reviews**

119    The Classification
       **Li San Xing**
122    Critic's Corner
       **Alexander Hutchison**
126    Extracts from the novel *Claustrophobia*
       **Graeme Williamson**
132    The Quadrangle
       **Michael Owen Fisher**
137    all the time billions
       **Chris Powici**
137    Graviton love
       **David Eyre**
138    Nothing
       **Lindsay Macgregor**
139    You can see light. What's it like?
       **Nuala Watt**
139    Sometimes I forget
       **Stav Poleg**
140    Returns
       **Judith Taylor**
140    Tinderbox
       **Jim C Wilson**
141    Apple
       **Christopher Crawford**
141    Last Night
       **Jim C Wilson**
142    A Modern Melodrama in V x 53 words.
       **Penny Cole**
143    Holding A Cord
       **Patricia McCaw**

# Contents

144 Earthquake
   **Deborah Moffatt**
145 Dundee wedding
   **Deborah Moffatt**
146 The hour lost
   **Stav Poleg**
147 Extract from novel *Wider than the sky*
   **Pippa Goldschmidt**
153 A Walk Before Santa Soledad
   **Conan McMurtrie**
157 Viewing the Emperor
   **AC Clarke**
158 Chimera
   **AC Clarke**
159 Scrogs on a bush
   **Bridget Khursheed**
160 Knife?
   **Stewart Sanderson**
160 Wet Day
   **Stewart Sanderson**
161 The gift from Cairo
   **Rizwan Akhtar**
162 Disaster diary
   **Rizwan Akhtar**
163 No me importa la lluvia
   **Andrea McNicoll**
168 Bertolt Brecht in exile
   **David Eyre**
169 Autumn in Lahore
   **Rizwan Akhtar**
170 Lavender
   **Graham Brodie**
171 Visiting Winter: a Johannesburg Quintet
   **William Bonar**
173 Uptown New Year Transition
   **Nicholas YB Wong**
174 Privilege of Morning
   **Nicholas YB Wong**
175 neues Deutschland II
   **Fiona Rintoul**
176 Auld grulsh, efter 'the poetry reading'
   **Alan Harkness**
176 Sunstruck
   **Mary Wight**
177 Behind the Carpathians
   **Svenja Herrmann**
178 My Father And Fishing
   **Gordon Meade**
178 Reality Check No. 1
   **Anita John**
179 Four Kinds of Death
   **Andrew Ferguson**
181 Life of Brian
   **Graham Fulton**
182 The Optimist
   **Graham Fulton**
182 Slow Down
   **Larry Butler**

183 **Contributor Biographies**

Gutter Magazine

# *Gutter*
# Editorial

Older readers may remember Channel 4's cult comedy *Absólutély*. Our favourite sketches featured Stonybridge. In one, the small Scottish town, run by tweedy, moustachioed, provincial worthies, decide to bid to host the Olympics. A promo video is produced featuring the 'stony bridge', the stadium (wasteland), the Olympic Pool (muddy puddles), the Olympic Village (the local hotel) and the Media Centre (a phone box). When one committee member suggests they may be getting ahead of themselves, another says, "Let's bid for the Commonwealth Games instead – it's crap."

In another sketch Stonybridge declares independence. Things fall apart when the committee fails to agree on the allocation of cakes and one burgher declares himself King, annexing the pastries at the far end of the hall. These were outstanding satires on the extraordinary lack of talent in Scottish public office in the 1980s. But Stonybridge also highlighted Scotland's worst failing, the crippling self-doubt at the heart of our national psyche. We recognised the ignorant, petty-minded pigmies in Stonybridge as ourselves.

At *Gutter*, it's our firm belief that independence, or more likely 'devo max' – devolved government with tax raising powers – is now inevitable. Whether it happens in the current parliament, while the Scottish National Party has its all-conquering majority, or in the next ten or fifteen years, is academic.

In its first term the SNP government proved itself politically adept, able to run the country without the calamity that followed each cack-handed Labour administration after 1997. For the first time this has given the electorate evidence that we might be able to run our own affairs. Alex Salmond and his deputy Nicola Sturgeon have been able to create the impression we're finally moving beyond 'Stonybridge'.

Recently Salmond has cemented his reputation as a shrewd operator. Every intervention by those against a referendum has been rebuffed as meddling in an exclusively Scottish debate. Already, the SNP are talking as if Scotland were a sovereign state, getting the populace used to the idea so that when the time comes, a 'yes' vote isn't such a giant leap.

The arguments are predominantly economic. It's hard to disagree that Scotland has always been geographically disadvantaged in the Union, with resources and talent naturally gravitating south. We also seem to be in terminal economic decline. The number of Scottish PLCs quoted on the stock market now is a fraction of what it was even twenty years ago. And we've become economically dependent on the public sector (public sector employment being significantly higher than England) to the extent that entrepreneurship is viewed with suspicion. The suggestion is that we could follow the model of the Irish 'Celtic Tiger' (before it was wrecked by the banks) by reducing corporation tax to attract inward investment from across Europe – but most likely from England. Clearly something needs to be done to kick start the country's economy.

While we seem to be growing up politically the rest of the culture still seems dominated by the spirit of Stonybridge. There's a prevailing view amongst national commentators that artistic output, and in particular literature, that originates in and from Scotland is 'crap'. In other words, interest in Scottish creative work is negligible until someone clever from beyond our borders gives it the thumbs up.

What's the evidence for this? Here are couple of quick examples. First, on BBC Radio Scotland, our national radio station's book programme, the only broadcast content in the country devoted to Scottish literature, shows a remarkable lack of interest in Scottish books, preferring to feature more "mainstream" London titles most of the time. Books that are perfectly well covered by

Radio 4's five separate literature programmes. What a disgrace.

Second, one of our most erudite local critics was asked in a UK podcast interview last summer who he thought were the great new Scottish writers emerging? His response was, "I'm rather concerned that we might be facing an epigonic generation, that wants to imitate the great writers of the 80s and 90s rather than overturn what they did. At my lowest moments I worry that what we're going to get is the Forsyte Saga with Buckfast rather than something genuinely new."

Critics clearly stand or fall on their reputation to identify the good stuff. This critic, who elsewhere in the interview made several compelling, lucid points, was presented with the opportunity to draw the attention of a UK audience to an emerging writer or two but proceeded to drop the ball spectacularly. It was embarrassing. Not even a qualified endorsement of one or two safe names. Again one suspects the cultural cringe – the Stonybridge effect – our inability to praise ourselves in case someone outside disagrees and we're found out, exposed as the charlatans we secretly fear we are.

If we're heading for independence, or the economic equivalent, it is critically important that those with the responsibility of championing literature – our broadcasters, our academics, our critics and our public arts agencies – shed their fears, prejudices and insecurities and respond to the work being written and published here with honesty. It's time to grow up as a nation. Nobody is frightened of debate and disagreement. But if we don't take an interest in our own literature who else will?

Now we are 06. We're delighted that this edition of *Gutter* continues to present a fascinating range of new fiction and poetry by established and new writers alike. The weather outside may be frightful, but between our covers the climate is insightful and varied. We hope you'll find something in here that taps your literary barometer.

We have an exclusive extract from Kevin MacNeil's work-in-progress, *Buddha: the novél*. We've a visceral story from Carl MacDougall, while Dilys Rose and Regi Clare both provide short fiction. We are also pleased to include longer novel extracts from both Simon Sylvester and Graeme Williamson. But *Gutter* 06 begins with a fabulous story by Olufemi Terry, winner of the Caine Prize for African Writing in 2010. It's the first of two stories we'll be publishing by Olufemi, who recently spent several months in Scotland in residency at Cove Park in Argyll. In response to his story 'Digitalis Lust', Karen Campbell has provided us with an extract from *This is Where I Am*, her Glasgow-set novel about a Somali refugee, which will be published by Bloomsbury in early 2013.

We continue to attract poetry submissions of a great standard. The only downside is our inability to publish as much as we'd like due to restrictions of space. Our radar seems well calibrated too: we are particularly proud that three poems in Salt Publishing's *The Best British Poetry 2011* (ed. Roddy Lumsden), by Alexander Hutchison, Andrew Philip and Gordon Meade, first appeared in *Gutter*, and that the names of several other recent *Gutter* contributors also feature.

Production costs aside, there's a bumper crop here. We have Rob A MacKenzie's extraordinary 'Cent(o)ury', a remix of 100 lines from 100 other great Scottish poems. We're delighted to publish three new poems by Kona Macphee, whose latest collection *Perfect Blue* won the 2010 Geoffrey Faber Memorial Prize. While there are welcome returns for the five Andrews; Andrew F Giles, Andrew C Ferguson, Andrew McCallum, Andrew Philip and Andy Jackson, we're also glad to have a number of *Gutter* debuts, from amongst others, Julian Colton, Patricia McCaw, Dearman Mackay, Stav Poleg and Nicholas WB Wong.

...now I am six, I'm as clever as clever. So I think I'll be six now and forever.

# Digitalis Lust
**Olufemi Terry**

HE LOOKS FORWARD to the second Wednesday of every month, and with the same impatience regardless of his libido. On those afternoons, which his colleagues believe have been set aside for playing squash as his Mondays are, he leaves the office at half past four to drive into town, glad to go against the city traffic.

He turns the car away from the ocean road and wends some distance up the mountain. Here, the streets are close, cobbled in places and uneven. In the sunlight of early summer he sees no one walking. The building he is going to is shouldered on one side by a bed and breakfast; its other neighbour is a town house. He's in the habit of parking directly outside or at the opposite kerb, but today finds it necessary to go as far as the next intersection to find a space.

He presses the top buzzer. The door jangles to signal it's unlocked and he lets himself in. On the second floor landing hang etchings of stylised hunters with bent bows meant, he assumes, to connote primitive art. With a short knock at the last door, he enters without waiting for a response. A woman with cocoa brown skin is unhurriedly placing a magazine beneath the bed. In the same motion, she gets to her feet.

'Mr Raymond.' The greeting carries a note of pleased startlement, genuine but practiced. His lips pull into a blank almost-smile, a look of discretion that's part of his ritual for these assignations. Their eyes meet an instant before his slide away. The flowers in the tall thin vase strike him as a peculiar choice; he associates roses with romance. He sets down his case next to the wall before she can take it, but allows her to assist him in removing his jacket.

The small room, with its high, square bed, is cozy rather than cramped and carries a lilyish scent. He sits on the bed to unlace his shoes. From behind comes the stir and clink of her preparations. Atonal music, faintly Asian, plays.

In nothing but grey under-shorts he lies, face in the pillow. The floor squeaks beneath her step and a coverlet, light as lace drops over his prickling skin, draping his body.

Warm, greased palms clasp his shoulders, a readying touch. She begins to work oil into the muscles about his shoulder blades, which are, he thinks with pride, knotty from years of swimming. Once or twice, she's told him he is tense but today she moves without pause or comment to press his lower back. He drowses. In the flexing of small strong hands over his torso he detects a rhythm that keeps time with the music. Against her first touch there, close to the buttocks, he clenches a little.

She crosses to the other side and folds back the sheet to expose calves, hamstrings. With a slow movement, as if from an almost-healed injury, he wipes drool from the corner of his mouth, conscious of his erection.

He is on his back now. He watches her movements through half-closed lashes, a pretense which, deceiving no one, is a form of intimacy between them in this room. She gives no sign she's noticed his excitement, not so much as a glance at the bulge of his shorts. Setting down the bottle of oil, she tugs gently at his waistband. He's grateful for the unspoken arrangement they – he and she – have fixed. He need never demand of her the more purposeful touch that is imminent. This would bring him shame. His arousal, visible, insistent, conveys whether the massage is to continue.

How often does she end a session this way? His mind shies from the thought. Her adroit grip, the warm unguent bring him after a few strokes to climax. He utters no sound, not wishing to embarrass either of them.

She is stanching ejaculate with tissue as one might a flesh wound. In this moment, his body subsiding, surrendering swift heat, he feels vulnerable. He wants a few minutes to himself but forces open his eyes – even now a fresh client might be at the door downstairs.

He sits up, and she brings his shirt, his trousers. Only now that it's done does he permit his eyes to meet hers. She complies in the little game, busying herself with small needless tasks, directing toward him occasional demure glances. At each turn her robe swings open to offer a momentary allure. Even when he does not have a happy ending (the euphemism amuses him) it is a matter of many minutes before he speaks.

'Thank you, Maryam.' He says at last, wary of the false intimacy that might come with near nakedness and the scent of semen. 'How are things?'

Now she will not turn – he cannot see what holds her attention, perhaps she offers her back simply to safeguard his privacy – but says with a kind of shiver, 'I'm exhausted.'

He does not know what his response should be. Instead, too sharply, he stands to pull on his trousers and blood flees his skull. Puffs of white burst and star before his eyes. He shuts them a moment. Swaying, he decides he must tip her more than usual. As if he were not generous already.

But she faces him, arms folded. 'I have a sister. She can't take care of herself, you know, like a vegetable. So we have to do it. My ma and me. But it's work, *ek se*.' Her voice is flat with suppressed anger.

Is it pity she wants?

'I wish sometimes she'd die. It's no life she has.'

'How did she become that way?' His own curiosity surprises him.

'She's always been. She was born like that. I've been wishing she weren't around since I was ten and I had to help wash her.'

'Does your mother also find her a burden?'

'It's her child. From her body, you know. Maybe I'd feel the same if she were my daughter not my sister.' She leans against the table. The robe, which falls as far as her knee, exposes thighs that are paler than her face. Before, he'd put her age at below thirty but he guesses now she's not more than twenty-five. 'But the effort to take care of her, to clean her... sis, man!'

'Have you heard of mercy killing?' The toe tips of his socked feet rest on the floor but he makes no move to put on his shoes. Incomprehension is apparent on Maryam's face. He does not know if he means the question as a joke. The conversation has abruptly become morbid. 'It's for those who'd be better off dead.' He tries to assume his vapid half smile but his cheeks are stiff. A silence has cut between them. Scrubbing a hand through his hair, he ignores the stickiness spreading down his thigh and goes to his coat. From his wallet he removes four notes, trying to conceal that he counts them. He sets the money beneath the pillow and does not look at her.

The next night, he goes to buy Thai food and takes it to Carol's house. Carol is undemanding. Her law career absorbs much of her energy and there's little obligation with respect to sex. He's known her since varsity and although they discussed it idly over breakfast one damp Sunday morning, they do not want to marry each another. They are, he suspects, too alike. Perhaps neither will ever marry.

He watches television. Carol sits close by on the floor, biting her pen, squinting fiercely. She's writing a law brief. At half past ten, she brushes his lips with hers and enters the bedroom. She's already asleep as he ducks beneath the cool tight sheets on her narrow bed. Carol does not like to be held but in the night she rolls against him, snaring his ankles with long feet. Her sibilant breaths do not quite reach the level of a snore. Beside her house stands a forest. The silence is complete. Lying awake, he imagines the trees loom over the little house and peer in with mistrust. He dislikes the quiet and is thankful for the solitary comfort of Carol's noisy exhalations.

Maryam telephones. He is sitting at his desk, the door of his office ajar, and looking at his computer screen. He does not immediately hear, the ring has been turned down very low.

'Hello?'

'Mr Raymond, I'm sorry to bother you, Maryam here.' He shuts the door. How did she get his number? His next appointment with her is a few weeks off.

His voice doesn't waver. 'Maryam.'

'I couldn't.' Her words come to him as from far off. 'I wanted to. I even had the opportunity. My mother was out to the shops. Memla was sleeping, but I couldn't bring myself to do it.'

He interrupts. 'Where do you live?' In her agitation she will say too much. She mutters an address, embarrassed now. He knows the area she mentions only indistinctly. He gives her the name of a coffee shop. 'I'll see you at six.'

Maryam comes dressed as a woman does to meet a man whose intentions she does not know. Jeans, hair tied back, practical unheeled black shoes. Her face is free of cosmetics. He stands up to greet her. She bends toward him, offering her cheek, then thinks better of it and sits. There is, he observes, no place in our interaction for hugs or cheek kisses. She orders red wine and perhaps to cover awkwardness, looks around. He dislikes this coffee shop, which he's chosen for convenience. It's done up to imitate cafes in films about true love in Seattle or San Francisco. The banisters are blond wood and behind the counter rests a gleaming steel machine that presumably makes coffee.

Before him on the table is an untouched mug of decaffeinated coffee. Maryam waits, taking small sips of a house wine he knows tastes of ash. Leaning forward, he says 'You were telling me about... Memla.' The name has a strange taste on his tongue.

'I couldn't do it. My mother loves her too much. But I also thought, she'll know. Ma, I mean. If I did it I'd have to pretend when she came home... Ma, ma, Memla's not waking. I'm not one of those actress girls who can make tears come to their eyes just like that.'

'So what will you do?' This is as near as he can come to asking, 'what do you want from me?' His fingers press a spot beneath the inside lining of his coat for reassurance.

'I don't know.' She twists her mouth, which, oddly, makes her prettier. 'Advice, maybe. You know about these things. Mercy killing, you said.'

'Why? Raymond may not even be my real name? I could be with the police for all you know.' Shrewdness colours her gaze a moment. She says nothing. How often one assumes others are fools because they are poor or uneducated.

Again, he puts his hand inside his jacket. Now, he sets down beside his cup a small plastic canister with a click cap. Without looking at it he says, 'In this bottle there are 40 pills. Digitalis.' He drops his voice to a whisper. The cafe will, however, soon be shut for the night and there are no other patrons. Water sluices down the drain as the server rinses off dishes.

Her eyes are intent on his. Foxglove. The name crowds his mouth but she will not understand it. She darts a brief look at the bottle and then resumes staring at him. Her expression is faintly lascivious. He continues, 'I assume you prepare her food? Good. Today, or tomorrow, grind up one half of a tablet into fine powder and mix it into her noon meal. The taste is metallic but only slightly unpleasant. Every five days, increase the dose by a half pill. If you hurry the process, she... Memla may suffer a sudden, sharp heart attack. Maybe fatal, maybe not. She'll certainly experience pain and hallucinations and, being unable to communicate distress, will suffer terribly. In three weeks, if you follow my directions, she'll fall into a deep sleep and die peacefully.'

Maryam's foot brushes his own and he pauses. The contact, he assumes, is not deliberate. Gulping thin, tepid coffee, he waits to be asked to repeat himself. Again, she says nothing, chewing her lip in calculation. Then she shoves the pill canister in her pocket. She has no handbag. 'Thank you... Mr Raymond.' In her inflection is an echo of doubt. She's begun to comprehend how little they know of one another. He's curious but does not ask if Maryam is her real name. Is she a student? Does she work simply to pay tuition? Rather, he too is silent. Surely she has questions to put to him about autopsies. Post-mortems. But she sits back, incurious, at least about the business of poisoning, for her eyes do not leave his face. Her wine glass is empty.

He gestures to the server, who comes over with the bill. 'Thank you,' Maryam says again, so tonelessly it might be gratitude for a shared drink. Outside, it is light, the sun stands high enough that their seated forms cast shadows like stumps. He follows her out, but does not offer a lift. Driving home, he ponders the white scar on her cheek, which does not quite mar her face.

He cannot wait for the next month; desire is like an itch on his sole that will not go away. On an impulse, after a weekend of which he recalls few details, he telephones to arrange an appointment with Maryam for that very afternoon, although it is Monday. He is successful and this emboldens him. In a lying voice, which he makes no attempt to disguise he dials a different number and cancels his engagement at the squash court.

He leaves in haste a little after half past four. He bumps into Paulsen near the elevator. 'Off for squash?' Paulsen is a physiotherapist with whom he must sometimes consult. Their relationship is amicable but Paulsen's habit of wearing his white coat outside the lab irks him. There is something knowing in Paulsen's look, or so he thinks. He nods and puts his head down to deter further talk.

The traffic goes more slowly than usual. There has been an accident at some bend of the highway. He drives with a patience he does not feel.

At ten past five, he raps at Maryam's door and then waits. She bids him to enter. Here, inside the room, the rituals are unchanged. She takes his case. He attempts to smile properly, not the imitation that is nothing more than a bland spreading of lips, but he's unsuccessful.

No matter, for she turns her eyes from his face. Breathless, he climbs on the bed. Lying on his stomach, hands at his sides, his arousal aches as it presses into the mattress from his body's weight. The secret between them invests the air with a charge. The sheet falls across his body. There is no music and this causes a slight irritation.

Then her fingers clasp his neck and he bites back a shudder. She goes about her work with an unfamiliar delicacy, yet her hands are unconcerned with any stiffness. Instead, her caresses deepen his arousal, as he knows they are meant to, until he feels he must burst. Particular care is lavished on his feet. She chafes each toe, her oiled fingers snaking between so that they tingle when he rubs them together.

Today, it is not by her hand he receives release. He scarcely dares breathe for fear he will whimper. In the moment of greatest intensity and restraint, he opens his eyes. The sensation at the base of his belly is one of physical pain. Once, he calls her name. Afterward, spent as if he's swum against a strong tide, he lies with an arm over his face, wanting the weight of her body on his. He feels no shame.

He looks at his watch. Nearly, two hours have elapsed. Maryam sits on a chair in the corner, her robe cinched about her body. She's watching him but he cannot guess her thoughts. He sits to dress. Maryam neither stirs nor averts her eyes. Darkness is settling but a last glare of sunlight illuminates the mountain above him.

He's already inside his car, about to turn the ignition, when he thinks of Memla. He sits, waiting for Maryam to come out. Perhaps her day is finished. But this is foolishness. He drives through quiet streets to his empty, cooling house, too enervated to think of eating. There's nothing on television to hold his interest and it's years since he read a book. In bed the faint film of oil on his skin sticks to the sheets. He falls easily asleep.

Days pass in which he makes no attempt to see Carol. In turn, there is no word from her. Long silences between them are not unusual. In the laboratory or seated before his computer he experiences sharp, sudden recollections of smooth brown skin, and the crescents of fingernails.

At night, his thoughts turn to Memla. He does not know what she looks like, but imagines a bloated and grotesque form listlessly sprawled in a soiled bed; its breathing comes in harsh gasps. The Memla of his imagination has become more inert in recent days. She sleeps deeply and is not easily roused. Her resting heart rate has slowed, and resembles the gait of an old man. In the heat of the day, she dozes. An attentive caregiver might detect the unwonted coolness of Memla's skin. Death approaches with a stealth and placidity he likens to summer's ebb. Maryam's words reel, again and again, through his consciousness: It's no life she has. His dreams are haunted by Maryam herself. Not since he was a teenager has he touched himself so often.

At his desk, he redoes the calculations on a note pad to be sure. It is certain: the dose of digitalis being mixed into the girl's food must now be very high. As if in sympathy, his own limbs grow heavy, lethargic as the day lengthens. He carries out his duties in a fog. There are moments in which his hands shake as if with palsy. Yet he's too adept to break any vials in the laboratory. For him, there can be no mistakes or accidents.

What he wants, as dearly as the touch of her hand, is to hear Maryam's confidential tones over the telephone. He would give much for an opportunity to murmur in her ear the remembered obscenities that are his dreams. Still, no word comes. He scans the papers but there are no stories of poisoning.

It is the second Wednesday of November. The calm he feels in the morning has dissipated by noon. He fears the worst, that when he opens the door in that house, he will see a woman other than Maryam. He drives too fast, slowing only when in range of the highway speed cameras. His grip on the steering wheel is like the hold of a madman.

In his eagerness, he does not knock and rushes clattering into the room he thinks of as hers. He's arrived some minutes early. He shuts the door and sets down his case. She's standing over the small table by the window, arranging the flowers in the vase. She knows he is behind her but does not acknowledge his presence in any way. Approaching, he experiences a flare of jealousy. Who has been here? He gathers her hair in his hand and pushes it aside to bare her neck. He stoops to kiss the thin skin, taut over the bones of her spine. She bows her head, offering neither resistance nor invitation. Gently, he turns her about. Her lips meet his. Her eyes are tight shut. 'Your sister?' The question burns in his mind, as if Memla is merely ailing. But there'll be time enough for that.

She's steering him toward the bed, her kisses insistent. Her mouth tastes of nothing at all. His hands are beneath her robe as she tries to undress him. His trousers and his undershorts are gathered about his ankles. There is no friction when she straddles him. Her thighs are warm against his groin. The robe hangs from her shoulders like a cape. He jack knifes his body so his head comes to rest on her chest. Her posture shifts to accommodate him. A swelling against which he is powerless gathers at the base of his belly. He struggles to sit back, needing to look fully on her. Maryam is unrecognizable, her face a mask. Her eyes are slitted and she bares small jagged teeth. But, he thinks, and the lucidity of the thought is a shock in itself, I too must look like this, in the writhing possession of some demon. Something wrenches from him so sharply he is incapable of crying out. A sensitivity that cannot be borne invades his entire skin and then over his abdomen he feels a spreading numbness.

He starts awake with a yelp. In his dream a beast with a pig's snout has been gnawing at his genitals. He looks about the room with embarrassment but he is alone.

# Extract from the novel *This is Where I Am*
## Karen Campbell

'KYLE! NO! COME here this minute!'

The lady pulls her little boy away, glowering. Change my mindset, change my mindset. She is frustrated, she is tired. Her look is not directed at me, a lanky black man who has the glazed vision of an addict. What was it Mrs Coutts said? *You're lookin right glaikit the day son. When you stopping they daft pills?*

Soon, Mrs Coutts, soon.

There's no rush.

I hold a copper coin. My thumb conceals the queen-face, my index rests on a feathered plume. Work or college? I can do one but not the other my doctor tells me. Too much will 'overload' me, and it's not fair on Rebecca. He's right, of course. I pretend I have a choice. I haven't officially lost my apprenticeship yet. In fact, Mr Maloney has telephoned me twice.

'We've no filled your place, Abdi. There's no rush, no rush.'

I can't believe that. People are watching my interactions with my child now; they're hardly going to let me loose with knives. Debs says she will speak with her brother-in-law, but I don't want that. I know he must have told Mr Maloney everything already – no person is that accommodating of their own volition.

Not where there's knives involved.

My doctor is right. Accept. Process. I forget the other one.

College will start this month. A warm, dry classroom and searching minds. A crèche for Rebecca – if I lie about her age. (Debs and I are still arguing about this, but I like the notion of Rebecca being in the same building as me.) What is this preoccupation with age? She will learn when she is ready. And Debs will soften when I bring her my gift. I have an excellent idea, you see, to show her my appreciation. For all she does for us, I mean.

I let the coin drop. It is, as they say, a moot point. I enrolled at the college this morning. Higher English and Mathematics, and Intermediate in Italian. I wanted to do a science subject too, but I am not to overload. So yes, the world is oily and slow once more. Nice slow, like Deborah's bath oils. We have a rhythm, where I am threaded to my groupwork and my therapy, to Mrs Coutt's house and the parade of shops and, once a week, to Deborah's house for tea. It's a pleasant web and its filaments give me structure. On one other day Debs takes Rebecca to soft play. They are in a club there, they meet the others, have lunch. And I have a day of drifting. I have not felt strong enough for church, which is strange because I'm praying every day. It is the public nature of it, I think. The sympathetic hands I'll have to shake. My minister understands.

'There's no rush,' he tells me.

No rush at all.

I could go to the Somali Centre I suppose, but it seems so far away. Anyway, do I want to talk about home, over and over again? What is comforting can end up suffocating. When I was very small, I remember huddling with my mother in our aqal. Poles stretched with skin and cloth, light to carry, but it stinks inside when the rains teem down. The air grows foetid and sags and drips until you are desperate for unlidded skies.

After the rainy season is over, the ground

is malleable. And so I think of my days as warm soft mud. When I had signed my name at college, I walked here, to the big supermarket. I've been here a while now, watching the shoppers come and go. Old ladies with wheeled message bags, single men who leave with cigarettes and drink. Smart people in big cars, who load up with their sunglasses tipped onto their heads. As they bend into their boots, the glasses sometimes slip, land awkwardly on nose or ground, and they will scowl to check who has seen. The joke is; it's not even sunny.

I fill my lungs with fresh air, rinse them out. Pick up my coin and my bag, and go inside the supermarket. Mr Maloney is at the fish counter.

'Can I help you – Abdi son! How you doing?'

He grips my hand with two slimy palms, pumping and spilling fishscales. We laugh; I don't know what we're laughing at.

'Good to see you, Abdi. Good to *see* you. Here Cammie, Wullie,' he shouts. 'Away through the front a minute.'

The plastic curtain parts and Cammie takes the stage. 'Abdi! Nice one! Howzitgoin? Let you out did they?'

'*Cammie*! So, what you been up to, Abdi? Cammie, where's Wullie?'

'Eh... he's away for a slash.'

'You mean a fag?'

Cammie assumes a look of innocence. 'I wouldny know Mr Maloney.'

'Um... I have come to say thank you, for your nice cards. Um... and to say thank you for... for all of this. And to bring you this back.' I take the freshly laundered white coat from my rucksack. 'I have ironed it so the little tabs on the pockets don't stick up anymore.'

'So you're no coming back to join us then? Sorry –' Mr Maloney snaps his gaze to the left of me. 'Yes sir. What can I get you?'

I move aside to let a stout man in close to the counter.

'I won't be able to come back,' I say to Cammie. 'I can't... I am going to go to college.'

'Is that right Big Man? Quality.'

Another customer arrives at the counter, a young woman with an exposed midriff. 'Yes, hen?' Cammie reaches for a plastic glove. 'Sorry pal, I better get this.'

'No, is fine. Of course.'

'Gie's a wee bell if you're still on for the football, mind. Wullie was saying.'

'Yes, I would like that –'

He is gone towards the whiting. I wait until he dips back near the till.

'Will I give you my telephone number?'

'Ho, are yous gabbin or servin?'

Another woman is standing behind me.

'Eh... wee bit hectic the now pal. Just gie's a ring at the store, yeah, and we'll sort something out.'

'Sure... It is no bother.'

Cammie nods, makes a reassuring phone-shape with his pinkie and his thumb. Mr Maloney, who is finished with his customer, comes back over and lifts my coat.

'Cheers for this, Abdi. You didny need to come all the way in though.'

'I wanted to say thank you. And sorry. I am very very sorry for all the confusion that I caused.'

'Ach, away. No harm done. I'm only sorry you're no coming back. I mean, don't get me wrong, we'll get another apprentice in – thon scheme's still running – but they're all daft boys, you know? You had the makings of a great wee worker –'

'I'm off to college!'

There is too much brightness to my voice.

'Proper college you mean, not catering?'

I knew it; I sounded like a child. 'For Highers. So I can be a teacher.'

'Well son, I wish you all the luck in the world. Now don't you be a stranger, you hear?'

'Yes.'

He smoothes the folded coat which I have scrubbed and bleached.

'Well. You take care then, son.'

'Yes Mr Maloney. I will.'

We shake hands one final time.

'Here, wait –' He disappears for a second, returns with a polystyrene tray. 'Smoked salmon. Disny even need cooked. You take that for your tea, alright?'

'Thank you. Mr Maloney – can I ask you

something please?'

'Fire away.'

'I want to buy my friend a present. Where is a good place to go? All she likes is old things.'

'Oh, it's a *she* is it? Well, you canny go wrong with perfume – try aisle seven. See down at the bottom there?'

'No. Her house if full of old things. What you call antiques? But I don't have very much money.'

Mr Maloney scratches his head. 'Eh... I don't know. Huvny a clue.'

*Stupid refugee.* Why would I think Mr Maloney should know? He is good enough to give me fish, and I embarrass the man.

'It is no matter–'

'Antiques, Cammie. Where would you get antiques roon here?'

'Up the Gala Bingo!' Cammie is still serving the woman with no patience. She has a face on her that is narrow and foreshortened, a tracery of liver-coloured veins round her nose.

'Cheeky bastirt,' she says. 'Whit kind of stuff you efter, son? Is it furniture and that?'

'I don't know... a jug maybe. For flowers? I have saved up ten pounds.'

'Och, you'll no get much for that.'

Mr Maloney is still trying to help. 'What about a second-hand shop–'

'Naw wait. What day's the day? Saturday? Have you tried the Barras, son? You get all sorts there.'

'Away. He'll get ripped off something terrible.'

'No he'll no. There's a load of right decent stuff–'

'Aye, and dodgy DVDs and stalls wi' jewellery that'll turn your skin black. Oh. Nae offence Abdi, son.'

I smile at Mr Maloney. 'Where is this Barras please?'

'See if you get a 9 bus into Argyle Street. Then head along to George's Square–'

'Naw, naw. When you're in the toon, get a 240. That'll take you right out Parkheid way–'

'Naw. See if you're...'

I glean enough from their argument to know one bus will take me near to the Central Station (I am better with buses now. They do not intimidate me so much).

'Please. From there I can walk.'

'You sure? It's quite a way. Take you a good hour I reckon.'

'Och rubbish. The boy's got big gangly legs on him. Half an hour max.'

'No rush,' I say. 'There is no rush.'

*

What a place is the Barras! It reminds me a little of Dadaab in its confusion, but more gaudy. It is nothing like the markets at home, there is no foodstuffs that I can see, except for a wagon selling burgers and hot do-nuts – which, I admit, smell delicious. If I have enough money left from my purchase, I will buy myself a hot do-nut. People mill without urgency; I feel no threat here, despite Mr Maloney's warnings. Yes, there are charlatans and snakes; all furtive glances and sleight-of-hand: a sensible person knows this is any language.

'Awright, Big Man?' A thin man drags on his cigarette, nods approvingly as I pass his stall. Which is selling prepacked processed cheese and shoes.

I am wondering if, in certain situations, my height plus my blackness may become an asset, in a city which is pinched and pale. The fact of this makes me uncomfortable. And still conspicuous.

'Err yir sportsocks! Threefurapun, threefurapun.'

A jaunty red-metal arch declares the perimeters of the enclosure. I know there is one at either end, for I have walked the length of the market twice. It is how you might read an excellent book – devouring first at a gallop, and then retracing your steps, slower, more reflectively to appreciate the detailed colour, the precision of the piece. And I do. Pillars of sunglasses jostle by bales of towels and rolls of carpets, men at the corners sell CDs and cigarette lighters the way you would sell khat. There are stalls outside and stalls within the collection of long brick buildings and warehouses, spilling clothes and handbags and books and life. I love the Barras! It has a vibrancy that fills your veins. Turning right instead of left, I find another passageway. The smell here is of damp, the lane darker. Pitched on one brick wall I see a line of paintings. Old things. I hurry down. Up close, even I can tell the paintings are cheap imitations. One is of a green-faced lady, and there are several of horses: in fields, with carts, running through spumes of water. The surfaces of these paintings are flat, they are not possessed with the rough real life of the pictures at Kelvingrove. In front of the paintings: trestles piled with artefacts: boxes, mirrors, lots of brass and glass. Some jugs are in amongst this mess, mostly small, mostly chipped. It doesn't have to be a jug of course. A vase would be fine, if I can find one pretty enough.

I pick up a jug made with the face of a black man. Immediately, he is funny, with his fat, beturbanned head and ludicrous gold hoops in his ears. Is this perfect? Will Debs laugh as I give her irony? Could you put flowers in such a thing? I think it may be too wee.

'What is this please?'

'Toby jug. Totally unique, that one. Ba-Bru, so it is.'

'Baboon?'

Well, now I am quite angry at his effrontery. I slam the jug back on the table.

'Naw, ya eejit! Ba-Bru? Fae the Irn Bru adverts? Used to be a big neon one at the bottom of Renfield Street? Naw?'

'I don't know it.' The jug is actually very ugly. I go to walk away.

'So, is it Toby jugs you're efter, pal?'

'No. Just a jug. I want a big jug to put flowers in. And no cracks. There must be no cracks.'

'Ho, Stumpy!' The stallholder shouts at another man across the way. 'Did we no get that stuff in fae Creggans Hoose yet?'

'Aye.'

'So, how's it no oot?'

'Fucking up tae ma oxters here, Jim.'

'I'm sure there were two of they big cream pitchers in wi' it. Gonny have a swatch for us?'

'Whit's a pitcher?' says Stumpy.

'A fuckin' big jug, ya plum.' He shakes his head. 'Just gies a minute and we'll see what we can do you fur.'

I am in no hurry. I leaf through some old books, gone rotten with mildew.

'Like your history, do you?' The man nods at where my hand rests. *Centuries of Glasgow*.

'Some.'

'So, where is it you're from then, ma man?'

'Somalia.'

'Aw, right. Dinny get many Somalians in here. Yous lot are all up the Red Road, aren't you? Sighthill, no?' He blows on his hands. Is wearing fingerless gloves.

'I live in Cardonald.'

'That right? Good for you, pal. That's it started already, then.'

'What is started?'

'Well... I mean, this is where it a' started really. *This* is the heart of Glasgow – no all that Victorian crap roon George Square. You know that, don't you?'

'Where the city began?'

'Naw – well, aye, aye, it did, but I mean all the different folk. *This* is where they came to. You read that book you're hauding. You've got your Irish, your Tallies. Your Jews an' all. A' roon here is where they were punted – Gorbals, the Calton, Brigton Cross. Then they either head back home cause it's shite, or they do no bad for theirsels, move onwards and upwards and the next lot arrive. The toon gets bigger; they spread theirsels a wee bit further out. You've your Chinese in Garnethill, your Asians in Woodlands. And your Somalians in Sighthill. See – you've bucked the trend already.'

'That is good?'

'Oh aye. Stumpy, ma man. What you got for us?'

Stumpy carries a cardboard box, brimming with treasure.

'I didny know whit the fuck a pitcher looked like, so I just brought everything wi a haundle.'

'Good man. Using your *initiative*. Okay pal, have a wee rummage, see what you fancy.'

Already, I have seen it. Not the enamel pitchers the man is pressing on me, nor the tubby milk jugs or the turquoise vase. What I have fixed on is nothing like I imagined. An elegant, lipped urn, made possibly of stone, but lustrous, there are layers of translucent colour which shimmer as the light turns. It

Fiction/009

is green then it is blue and pearl. It is pink and sunset and the sea. The curve of it flares symmetrically, out then in, with two tiny handles at the top, like ears. Gently, I ting the rim with my fingernail.

'Clear as a bell, that. Nae cracks, not a one.'
'No.'
'Totally unique. A lustre-wear ginger jar. You don't get many o them tae the pound.'

I glance up, eager. 'It is only a pound?'
'Eh, naw. Figure of speech, pal. How much you got tae spend?'
'I have...' I stop. 'How much is the bottle?'
'To you... twenty quid.'
'Ah.' I place the urn back in its box. 'I am sorry to have taken up your time.'
'Haw – hold up, pal. Hold up. Look, I could maybe dae it for you for £15? As a favour like.'
'I'm sorry,' I repeat. 'I have only eight pounds that I can spend.' I hold out the ten pound note. 'This is all the money I possess. Eight pounds for the vase and two pounds for my bus fare home.'
'Sorry pal. I canny let it go for under a tenner.'

The hot do-nuts are two for one pound. I wanted to get some for Debs and Rebecca as well.

'Nine pounds, and I must walk home.'
'Done!'

He takes my ten pound note, wraps the urn in newspaper. There is a moment when I am waiting for my change and he has finished wrapping that I think he is not going to give me my £1 back. I hold out my hand and smile. 'My change, please.'

'Oh, right. What was it we said again?'
'You have to give me one pound.' I make my smile bigger. 'Or maybe it was two?'
'No, no. Fair dos. Right you are. £1 it is.'

As I am leaving the Barras, with my one and a half hot do-nuts (the other half is in my belly. Delicious does not describe it. I am thinking that they are better eaten hot. To keep just the one... yes, I chew down the remainder of the first do-nut... yes, I fear it would become greasy if not eaten immediately) anyway, I am passing under the red metal arch, when a voice calls out: 'Big Issue, pal?'

Immediately, I turn, in case it's Decksy, but this man is much older.

'I'm sorry,' I say. 'I have only got my bus fare.'

His focus has already glided; he is monitoring the herd. Seeking the stragglers and the slow.

I touch his sleeve. 'Are you hungry?'
'Eh?'
'I have this, look.' I unzip my rucksack to reveal the salmon. The tray has become a little squashed. 'If you would like some.'
'Fucksake man. That is totally honkin.'
'It is good. Is good fish.'

He folds his hand below his nose. 'Naw, you're awright. In fact, gonny move downwind of me? You're scaring off the custom – and I've a tona these tae shift.'

There is certainly a pile of Big Issues in his hand. More still in the polythene bag wedged at his feet. He has bare feet inside his trainers. Even engulfed in Mrs Coutts's hand-knitted socks, my own toes are cold. I wiggle them, making the blood come alive. Nipping and popping. And I think.

'Do you always work in the same place?'
'Aye. How? Gonny come back wi a fuckin big shark or somethin? Look, I don't want your fish, pal, awright?'
'No. I wondered – do all the people who sell your books have their own place? I mean, if someone was selling books in one street one day, would they be in the same street the next? If you understand.'

'Aye? I'm no a fuckin' numpty. How? You thinking of taking up the noble art of issuing the big?'

'Pardon? Oh – I see... No. I am wondering if you know a man called Decksy. He sells your books too.'

'Dodgy fucking Decksy?'
'Yes!'
'Naw. Never heard of him.'
'Ah.' I hoist my rucksack onto my back. The weight of the urn curves into me. 'I am sorry to have bothered you. Good luck with your books.'

It was a hasty notion anyway.

'Ho!' he shouts. 'See if you're looking for a vendor?'

'Yes?'

'We should of got the new edition on Thursday but there wis something up wi the printers. The depot's only started gieing them out the day. There's a pure wad a folk doon there the now, picking up.'

'Is this depot near?'

'Saltmarket. Straight doon London Road, come tae a fucking great tower in the middle of the road, hing a left and that's you at it.'

'Thank you. Would you like a–'

'NAW!'

'– do-nut?'

'Oh. Aye. Go on then.'

True enough, the Saltmarket is very near. The longer I have been in this day though, the more I am alive. I could lope for very far: I will walk home. Maybe I will run. To feel the strength of my legs, and my heart pump, to surge with breath and be steady, steady, steady in my sway and pound and leap. To run for joy, not fear? Rushing. Yes, that is when you *want* the rush.

Before I reach the depot, when I am only at the *fucking great tower* – which is in reality skinny and truncated – a handful of men saunter across the main road. They have bags and bundles, I quicken but do not run. (The heavy bounce of my rucksack reminds me of my eight pound cargo.) Today, walking quickly will suffice, for it is a boundless day and I *know* he will be in that group. *Haddii Eebbe yidhaahdo*. Otherwise, why else would God have given me this fine idea?

'Decksy!' I shout. 'Hey Decksy!'

The group stop. A small, tight man who is made of wire scrutinises me. Draws himself in. It is Decksy

'How is it going? It is me!' I touch my head. 'Red hat?'

I don't actually know where my hat is: I've rarely worn it since – since we met.

'Aw aye! That's right. On yous go lads. I'll catch yis later.'

His friends trundle on with out him.

'How you doin pal. Ali?'

'Abdi.'

'*Abdi*!' Said like he discovered the name himself.

'I am sorry, I cannot buy your magazine today. I have no more money.'

'Makes two of us, my friend.'

'Business is not good?'

'Fair tae shite, I'd say. Put it this way, if I don't get this lot puntit, there'll be nae dinner the night. Again.'

'Do you like fish?'

'Whit?'

I open my rucksack. 'Here. Do you like fish? I have some smoked salmon.'

'Fucksake. You rob Marks and Sparks?'

'No, it was a present. Please. Would you like it?'

'Aye. Don't mind if I dae.'

The entirity of my bag smells of sewage. Big fish in an enclosed pocket. Not good.

'So, you like fish?'

'S'alright, aye.' Decksy peels a strip of pink salmon, drops it in his mouth. His teeth chop through it at a tremendous rate, and he delves for more. Begrimed fingers, filthy nails, and he couldn't care less. I wonder if he has ever scrabbled rice grains from a latrine. I wonder if he would like to work indoors.

'That is good that you like fish. And you are homeless still?'

He ceases chewing, tongue still thick with salmon. 'Fuck d'you think?'

'Tell me,' I say. 'How do you feel about blood?'

# The Correct Recipe for Bleached Bones
**Lara S Williams**

IT TOOK FORTY three pieces of wire to put the fox back together.

His body was the only one we collected in its entirety. The first bone was a femur Mum swore blind was from a kangaroo. It was fresh, still embraced by sods of flesh and fur. Marrow glistened in a crack at the knee.

'How did this get out here by itself? There aren't even any scraps.'

'Probably carried by something. Or left behind.' Mum bent to pick it up, the setting sun peaking over her lowered head.

'Left by what?'

'Hunters' dogs I'd say. They're baiting at the moment.'

'Why would the dogs eat it? If it's poisoned?' I spotted a white sliver in the grass and dug at the ground, uncovering a tattered piece of tarpaulin.

'Dogs don't know that. And hunters don't know where their bait ends up, after a fox has had it in them.'

'Do they die?'

'Foxes or dogs?'

'Dogs. If they eat poisoned fox.'

'If they're lucky.'

We drove home on the quad bike, her driving, me with thumbs hooked in the rack over the exhaust. I wore the only helmet and raised my chin until the top swooped over my eyes and blinded me from the pale summer scrub. Without sight I judged our position by the weave of the bike, measured terrain by the rapid vibrations running through my thighs and buttocks. I slouched and swayed easy in my blindness. The bones knocked in the chequered table cloth slung across Mum's chest. She used to carry me around as a baby in the same way. My tiny body had rubbed the material shiny.

There were two dams on our property, both rich in bone. We found cow carcasses every few months but mum liked the smaller animals, trickier to track and almost impossible to find complete. We only took skulls home and painted them with my high school paint set. I nailed them, dark shades radiating to light, on the barn walls and, if we'd found a bull, hung my brown suede hat on the horns.

We decided to do the fox after Dad moved out. He found a rotting sparrow when I was seven and cleaned the skeleton, giving it as a gift on my birthday. I loved the tiny green wires he used to secure the bones released from their clothing of meat and skin. They were like emeralds glowing through cracked white ceramic. Mum said he had chosen green because they matched my eyes.

'It's two measures of water to one of bleach.'

'Water?'

'You have to dilute it.'

'Why?'

She stopped pouring and held the bleach container underneath my nose. 'It's too strong by itself. The bones would burn away.'

'Bleach can make bones burn?' The femur felt solid under my nails.

We soaked all bones for thirty minutes, no matter the size. The bleach would bubble upon meeting dried blood so I often left on bits of meat to watch it dissolve and gasp air into the cloudy water.

After they were clean, Mum poured baby oil over a car chamois and rubbed the bones until my fingers left wrinkled prints where I had prematurely handled them.

When Mum brought home the pelvic bone I couldn't keep my hands away. It curved in and under itself like a collapsing rainbow. There was a nub at the base that, when pressed, bent inward. I could squeeze the nail of my little finger into the indent and feel it fold almost to breaking.

I held it up against my own torso and imagined the many fox pups my own body could contain. It went whiter than other bones and was a stark contrast against my coconut shell skin.

We found all the ribs in one spot but I broke the smallest in the backyard. Bleached paper white, I took it outside and held it to the light. I had a theory that thin bone would turn transparent in direct sunlight. When it didn't I knocked it, frustrated, on our stone water tank and snapped it in half.

'Bleach makes them weak. Why did you hit it?'

'It was an accident. I'll find another.'

When I didn't come home with a replacement within the week she glued the broken bone together and laid it out with the twenty-one already collected.

Mum found the skull on the edge of our property when we were out counting cows. She spotted the nostrils jutting from the low branches of pine scrub and recognised the shape of fox snout. 'Number, what is it, thirty four?' She held it out and I inspected the stab of teeth.

'Looks young.' I looked where she had come from, seeing the bluff backing onto the pines. 'Ah, there's a fox den round there.' I pointed, Mum shaded her eyes.

'Near the fence?'

'Sort of. Further up.'

She pursed her mouth and tapped a finger against her cheek. It made a sound like a hammer on cloth.

'What?'

'We should put bait round here. They're a bit close to the sheep for my liking.'

I glanced back out at the fence. My brow wept with sweat.

'We've got some at home,' she said. 'I'll bring it out next trip to the dam.'

'You can't bait them.'

Mum leant back on the handle bars of the bike and wiped her face. Raised her eyebrows. 'Why not?'

'There are pups. They have pups.'

'All the more reason to. They'll grow up, get chickens, lambs.'

'No!'

She crossed her arms and regarded me from under the brim of her cap. I had bought it for her from an ABC shop. She breathed deeply before speaking.

'We can't have a fox family living in the perimeters. You know that. If there are pups, we have to get rid of them before they grow up and spread.'

'I don't want to kill pups.'

'That's the way this works. We protect our stock.' She turned her back on me and rearranged the bone cloth on her chest. I walked around the bike to face her.

'I'm not killing pups.'

'You don't have to.'

'You know what I mean.'

'How else do you think we get the bones for your animals?'

'That's not fair. I wouldn't kill an animal to get the bones.'

'You wouldn't but someone has to. I'll do it.'

I pushed her shoulder. 'If you do, I'll never forgive you. I'll never forgi–'

'Stop!' She slapped her hand on the bike seat. 'Don't ever say that. You never say that to someone.' She snatched my wrist, jerked me close to her face. I looked away over her shoulder and she dropped my hand like it burned.

I kept my head down all the way home.

When we got back I fed the dogs. Our boxer died of a paralysis tick two months earlier and the two others were sheep dogs, brothers, too old to run the farm. The fourth was a wolf hound Mum found out the back of town with a torn off ear. He had a stub of hair stuck straight up from the wound that perked up when called.

Mum was in the laundry filling the tub. I took off my boots and banged them on the wall to release the caps of dirt and grass. My socks were grimy at the toes and I picked at them, waiting. Mum wet a cloth and threw it to me. 'Clean your shoes.'

I wiped for a moment, put them aside and stood with her at the sink. My shoulder brushed hers and she swayed away.

'I'm sorry,' I said.

She rinsed the eye socket under the tap, reached for the bleach.

'I didn't mean to upset you.'

'Mmmm.'

'Mum?'

She stopped, passed me the skull. 'It doesn't matter.'

'I'm sorry.'

The bleach hit the bottom of the sink and clouded out like dust storms on a flat horizon. She slipped the skull under the water.

'I'm going out baiting. We can't afford to lose any animals.'

'I know.'

'You okay with it?'

'I have to be.'

'You'll forgive me?'

I looked at her as she dug her fingernails into the nostrils of the bone, bringing out dens of dirt.

'I didn't mean that.'

'That was the last thing I said to my father.'

'What was?'

'"I'll never forgive you".'

'Why?'

She sagged heavy over the tub and closed her eyes. 'He didn't come to my communion. He died the next morning.'

I touched the skull and shivered at the slick surface the bleach created. 'How did he die?'

She eased it from my hand. 'Killed himself.'

I let her take it. 'You never told me.'

'It didn't seem important.'

'He was your dad.'

She dropped the bone with a jerk of her hand. 'Sorry.'

'That's okay. I'll finish.'

She smiled and brushed my hair with her lips. I left the skull to soak and followed her into the kitchen. She sat, chin hovering on her palm.

'You want some tea? I kept the bags from this morning.'

She shook her head, waved a hand at the kettle. 'Too hot.'

I sat opposite and put my hands palm down on the table. 'How old was he when he died?'

'Forty-seven.'

'Why did he do it?'

She laughed and shrugged. 'He was unhappy. Mum and he were in separate rooms, he drank all the time, Lesley had left and got married.' She laughed again and pointed a finger at me. 'He got into a fight with John at their wedding.'

'Why didn't you and Nan leave?'

'Go where? Mum didn't own the house. They never owned anything. He didn't want to get into debt.' She paused. 'Actually we did move out. To Great Nanny's for two weeks. I cried the whole time so we went back.'

'Did he work?'

'Off and on. He was as an undertaker for a while. The place was called 'Motor Funerals'.' We sat silent for a long while. I got up to put on the kettle but she called me back.

'You know what my mum used to say? He was the most handsome man she had ever met and from the moment she married him she knew she'd made a mistake.'

'People say those things when they're angry. She wouldn't have meant it.'

Mum looked at me from under her bent head. 'I wouldn't presume to know what my mother meant.'

'Was she upset?'

'Not that I saw. She found him in bed with pills. She wouldn't let me in the room but I looked and saw him lying on his side. His shoulder looked too big under the bedspread.'

I scratched at a tea ring on the table. 'You never blamed yourself, did you?'

She bobbed her head before answering. 'For a long time I did. I thought I'd tipped the scale.' She held out her hand and slowly turned it sideways. 'It wasn't me. It was the drink. I think...' she put the hand to her head to hold in the thought. 'I think we were relieved that he died. Not because we didn't love him. Because there was no more fighting and shouting. I used to go sit with the neighbours until they were finished and Dad would go out to the bowling club and Mum would get on the phone to Great Nanny and cry. It was shit. We were happy it was all over.' Mum wiped her eyes, though they were dry, and stood from the table. I watched her go to her room, heard the creak of the bed as she lay down. It was hot; her hands had left foggy streaks on the table top.

I went to check the fox skull. It looked grey under the water and when I pulled it up it still had black lines around the fissures on the head. Those stains never came up. Upon completion they were the only mar on an otherwise perfect skeleton.

I rode out to the east dam and sat silent on the bike, engine running. The cows had come to drink and I watched their heads bend to touch the water, pause to check their surroundings and drink in great bobbing motions. They looked like dogs when they drank.

Watching them crowd and push one another, I imagined the bones moving beneath their hides. Sharp angles ramming into the skin and scraping on cartilage and joints. I felt my hand run along their backs and encounter jagged peaks of spine and hip, navigate valleys of fat-run muscle and rub the short hair to stand tall.

I listened to their breathy, drinking noises and imagined the day when they would die. Many were underfed and sickly from hunger and there was no rain forecast until mid-autumn. Soon, for some, legs would crumble, faces collapse and stomachs puncture and rot.

Underneath it all the bones would shoot up. After the rain, long grass would entwine around the vertebrae and daisy heads poke out between the rib cage. Petals, dried and falling, would plaster the bones until each separate rib became a patchwork of browning flower.

I went past the fox den on the way home. There was no sign of them but I spotted fresh scat and knew they were close. I considered filling the hole and forcing the foxes to move to a safer spot but I hadn't brought a shovel and for all I knew they were hiding in the bowels of their home and I ran the danger of suffocating them. I wondered which death would be less painful.

A kookaburra rattled in the eucalypts and I revved the bike and turned for home.

The skull had dried and I went to work oiling it until the surface was so smooth I could run a nail along it without catching. The rest of the skeleton was scattered on the tool table in our back shed and after adding the skull I regarded the shape it made.

Mum had already wired the leg bones together. They bent out and back in a freeze-frame of flight and the ribs, including the one glued together, were complete and awaiting wiring. The spine looked too short and I counted the vertebrae; just one missing, at the very base of the neck.

Mum was still in her room. I looked in on my way to the kitchen and stopped. She was rolled on one shoulder, back to me, facing the door to her bathroom. I stepped over the threshold and the door creaked behind me. She didn't move.

'Mum, can I get you anything?' I reached the bed and put my weight on the corner, tipping her body. 'Tea? It's cooled down a bit.'

She was silent and I craned to see her face. I bounced the bed and still she didn't move.

'Mum?' I touched her and when she didn't react I shook her. My throat itched. I was struck by how broad her shoulder was under my fingers.

'What?'

I exhaled and dropped my hand. 'You weren't answering.'

'Sorry. Sleeping.' She raised up on one elbow and rubbed her face, then stopped and stared at me between her fingers. 'I forgot, I found something.' She reached over the side of the mattress into her bedside cabinet. Her hand returned holding something small and brown. She held it out.

I rolled it around my palm and smiled at

the rough hollow at its centre. 'When did you find this?'

'When we came home today. Out by the wood pile.' She sat up fully. 'I think the mutt brought it up. Wasn't there yesterday.'

'The skull is finished. Come have a look.'

'Later. I'm tired. Go put that with it. See the full effect.'

I left her in bed and went back to the shed. The skeleton lay shining in a slant of sunlight. The vertebrae in my hand was unbleached but I put it in place.

Our fox lay sectioned before me in a slip-shod of sizes. Each bone taken from a different animal, the effect was startling. The head, far smaller than the body, looked shrunken and unsure of itself. One leg touched the rim of the table while the others fell inches short. The vertebrae were pebbles on a rocky beach, thrown in line by an eager child building water forts. I thought him beautiful. I clipped strings of wire and placed them between each bone's joint, in preparation for the final step. Next to the white clouds of skeleton the wire looked like patches of clear sky screaming to be let out. There were forty three pieces. Forty three pieces to put it all back together again.

# A Scottish Cent(o)ury
**Rob A Mackenzie**

This is a difficult land. Here things miscarry,
fates get their yarn in a twist,
but greet, an' in your tears ye'll drown.
Jings! But it's laughable, tae,
the permanence of the young men
filled with synthetic joy,
remembering smoke and flowerless slum
lit up like a paper lantern,
their laughter a mist in my ears.
I think, quiet Midnight, that the sun will rise
which lay in a ditch, its mouth full of dying fires
blown in blown out again
cold and luminous like a moon,
a death wha's licht slocks me.
Acquiring is what's easy, relinquishing, what's hard.
A great place and its people are not renewed lightly
in time's grace, the grace of change,
a change of more than silhouette.
O knives, forks and spoons, fulfil yourselves!
History has made you slaves to short-arsed curers
who buy peripheral history to confirm some malcontents in palaces,
put worms to work, and moles to mark
every simple terror of a single brain of fish
as out of the dark they swing:
'OK, you got this far, you passed the test,
au revoir to you ma petite sardine.'
The committee of unthinkable thoughts
are ringing constantly with their questions:
>   how much mystery we need to make a world moment by moment escaping
>   how we undervalue all earlier anxieties.
With habitual disregard for public safety
I twine the past through my fingers –
hits mizzerlessness, da marginalia, da element o winder –
every day its being shifts with
morning's levitation over hills and cold rain.
What should we fly from Scotland's drizzlements?
kilts, skirts, troosers, shorts?
New Gen and their ad men?
sweet gentle modest lightness?
a wee hairy dog with two wee eyes?
murdered fish suppers?
cigarettes, their spent ends?
Let those who can still read, read the signs,
be upstanding. Now: let us raise the fucking *tone*:

somewhere between a tenor and an alto, this rosé voice –
master of the 30-length stanza, Olympian,
blind drunk from politeness –
relapses into patterns of favourite self-pitying sentiments,
plunges into the déjà vu of a phlegm-skied twilight
down some Scottish plughole:
a darkness that grows
ready to hypnotise with drills –
a mouth-watering prospect for the damned.
The road to hell is paved with clichés, friend.
Three goldfish gleam in the pupil appraising
a future lit by bridges and the burning
Big Barn of the Gaelic Resurrection,
all but real for a moment, then
a crumpled heaven,
a furnace made of tiny fishhooks,
a head lickin holes where limbs once were,
a drift of greens and reds that make no sense.
Is that no enough for the Scots Lords tae cry, enuff's enuff,
turn a fresh eye on this outworn frame?
May we make of it something else!
Night downs its curtain on the show:
tar boils out of the toffeed sleepers
and a voice from elsewhere whispers, *He is risen*,
threaded on time
like the continual rain,
the distant Latin chanting of a train.
Time to bite on a spring onion,
botox our frownliness,
eat avocados with apostle spoons.
We stare back over decades
spliced into bars of an old wheel
about to crack the darkness
that sight imposes on the world.
It takes a rare person to look through stones to the other side
believing this compact rolling ball could be restored, maybe, maybe, maybe.
We see nothing but fog,
a struck match,
a spirit released, a loss,
and somewhere, someone singing flat,
'Dinna be glaikit, dinna be ower smert.'
We set our compass tae a fremmit airt,
tour the sodden carbrain underpasses
through the needle's eye
on the far side of the water,
look hard into the deep, unshouldered blue.
And the sea, the sea takes care of everything,
as hungry as the flame below
the years, the tears, the dead;

we dat koort da storm's upstierin
expect deliverance in smoke,
essays of soot,
words that sound each arc of hurt.
We leap bareback through the rainbow's hoop,
not an escape itself but its fine surprise
partly revealed and partly veiled,
our wishes bright against a sullen sky.

Glossary: L14, "...wha's licht slocks me" – ... whose light extinguishes me
L33, "hits mizzerlessness, da marginalia, da element o winder" – its immeasurability, the marginalia, the element of wonder
L85, "...tae a fremmit airt" – ...to a peculiar direction
L93, "as we dat koort da storm's upstierin" – as we who court the storm's beginning

*Generally, the lines and phrases are exactly those used in their original poems, but I have taken a few liberties with some of them for the sake of internal coherence, changing singular to plural, past to present, 'I' to 'we', 'the' to 'its', and vice-versa. I also felt free to add or subtract punctuation.*

Sources: 1. Edwin Muir 'The Difficult Land'; 2. Valerie Gillies, 'We Meet Again'; 3. Hugh MacDiarmid 'The Bonnie Broukit Bairn'; 4. Joe Corrie, 'The Image o' God'; 5. William Soutar, 'The Permanence of the Young Men'; 6. Robert Garioch, 'Embro to the Ploy'; 7. William Montgomerie, 'Glasgow Street'; 8. Eleanor Livingstone, ' The Visit'; 9. Somhairle MacGill-Eain/Sorley Maclean, 'Hallaig'; 10. Iain Crichton Smith, 'Tonight'; 11. George Mackay Brown, 'Hamnavoe Market'; 12. C.F. Dutton, 'clach eanchainn'; 13. Alasdair Gray, 'Awakening'; 14. Christie Williamson, 'Gacela o da Flicht'; 15. Gael Turnbull, 'National Trust'; 16. Edwin Morgan, 'The Second Life; 17. W.S. Graham, 'The Nightfishing'; 18. Liz Lochhead, 'The Grim Sisters'; 19. Ivor Cutler, 'The Purposeful Culinary Implements'; 20. Ruaraidh MacThomais/Derick Thomson, 'Clann-Nighean an Sgadain'/'The Herring Girls'; 21. Peter McCarey, Tantris, part II; 22. Alexander Hutchison, 'An Ounce of Wit to a Pound of Clergy'; 23. Ian Abbot, 'Fishing through a Hole' 24. Andrew Greig, 'A Man is Driving'; 25. Andy Jackson, 'The Assassination Museum': 26. Eddie Gibbons, 'Eric Cantona Meets Frida Kahlo'; 27. Alasdair Paterson, 'On Nomenclature'; 28. W.N. Herbert, 'Hangover Thursday'; 29. John Burnside, 'Annunciation with a Garland of Self-Heal'; 30. Frank Kuppner, 'Arioflotga'; 31. Tim Turnbull, 'It Lives!'; 32. Polly Clark, 'My Life with Horses'; 33. Christine de Luca, 'Nae Aesy Mizzer'; 34. Robert Crawford, 'Crannog'; 35. Ron Butlin, 'At Linton Kirk'; 36. David Kinloch, 'Saltires'; 37. Nancy Somerville, 'The Big Hooley'; 38. Raymond Friel, 'Songs of the Plough'; 39. Meg Bateman, 'Lightness'; 40. Tom Leonard, 'The Voyeur'; 41. Brian McCabe, 'Seagull'; 42. Claire Askew, 'I'm sorry, I'm still in love with my grandmother'; 43. Tom Pow, 'Nebuchadnezzar in the Arboretum by Moonlight'; 44. Don Paterson, 'Prologue'; 45. Brian Johnstone, 'The Man Who Sang to Wine'; 46. Colin Will, 'Entering Your Poem'; 47. Vicki Feaver, 'Teddy Bears' 48. Mick Imlah, 'Goldilocks'; 49. Alan Gillis, 'Down Through Dark and Emptying Streets'; 50. Hugh McMillan, 'Leaving Scotland by Train'; 51. Ryan Van Winkle, 'Necessary Astronomy'; 52. Hazel Frew, 'Corridors'; 53. A.B. Jackson, 'Apocrypha, part II'; 54. Helena Nelson, 'From "Interrogating the Silence"'; 55. James MacGonigal, 'The Eye of the Beholder'; 56. Robin Robertson, 'Crossing the Archipelago'; 57. Martainn Mac An T-Saoir/Martin MacIntyre, 'Faces of a Uist Girl'; 58. Hamish Henderson, 'Second Elegy for the Dead in Cyrenaica'; 59. Kei Miller, 'This Zinc Roof'; 60. Kevin Williamson, 'A Different Kind of Love'; 61. Gerry Loose, 'that person himself'; 62. Andrew Forster, 'Black Beauty'; 63. Alistair Findlay, 'Knox's Theory of Revolution'; 64. Lilias Scott Forbes, 'Turning a Fresh Eye'; 65. John Glenday, 'For Lucie'; 66. Donald S. Murray, 'An Incomplete History of Rock Music in the Hebrides'; 67. Jen Hadfield, 'Towhee'; 68. James W. Wood, 'Byzantine'; 69. Norman MacCaig, 'Summer Farm'; 70. Sydney Goodsir Smith, 'Cokkils'; 71. Carol Ann Duffy, 'Prayer'; 72. Anna Crowe, 'The Pattern of our Days'; 73. Peter Manson, 'For January'; 74. Kathleen Jamie, 'The Queen of Sheba'; 75. Angus Calder, 'Haymarket Sunset'; 76. Jackie Kay, 'In My Country'; 77. Elizabeth Burns, 'The Stranger'; 78. Robin Fulton, 'It Takes a Rare Person'; 79. Richard Price, 'Like a Student Gardener'; 80. Sally Evans, 'Ullapool'; 81. Douglas Dunn, 'The Clear Day'; 82. Jim Carruth, 'A Cairn'; 83. Kate Clanchy, 'Timetable'; 84. James Robertson, 'A Manifesto for MSPs'; 85. Raymond Vettese, 'Prologue'; 86. Colin Herd, 'Cumbernauld'; 87. Margaret Christie, 'Suspended Animation'; 88. Jenni Daiches, 'Psalm'; 89. Andrew Philip, 'Notes to Self'; 90. Kapka Kassabova, 'How to Build Your Dream Garden'; 91. Dawn Wood, 'Her Grace'; 92. Cheryl Follon, 'Drinking Song'; 93. Robert Alan Jamieson, 'Kael-Jaerd'/'Kailyard'; 94. Stephen Nelson, 'The Vital Heart'; 95. J.L. Williams, 'History'; 96. Kona Macphee, 'Self-Portrait Aged 8 with Electric Fence'; 97. Ian Hamilton Finlay, 'Le Circus'; 98. Gerry Cambridge, 'A Winter Morning'; 99. Thomas A. Clarke, 'in the half-light of dusk...'; 100. Roddy Lumsden, 'A Story of Spice'.

# Henry Lord Darnley, syphilitic
## Andrew F Giles

The scots king has a history of disease & a leer
for the past & its face that peers from the stave.
Traitor. Who's to blame for the dark-ended years
& the witchcraft of blood from knave to knave?

When did the boils appear? The pus & the rash?
Was it the chisel-face *seigneur* in the castle park
who kissed so well with the thin moustache?
Was it that forbidden knight back then in the dark

with eyes on an auld alliance? He fell asleep all
night with arms looped tight & suddenly woke
breathing hard boozy medieval breath & hauled
himself up to divine rights, one royal line of coke.

Fill in the gaps. There's a trace of your erogenous zone
on the watchtowers; the signs and symbols burn fire
& one hot sexy mood incubates like death in your bones.
Wild Lord Henry went mad, loopy, they say he was a liar.


# Plangent
## Julian Colton

Walking through the dense undergrowth
I realise it's a word I should know, intimately
But precise definition escapes me
Discarded by gravestone memory.

Later, after looking it up
Associations return, realign themselves
As always, more than a single meaning–
The wailing woman and the 'poet's plangent dream.'

But here in my heart's stained glass window
Imagery resounds, silently
Like a disused church in England
Devoid of pealing bells.

# The F word
**Kona Macphee**

You'd argue that a tended garden
stands as a poor metaphor for a grudge,
citing flowers in profusion, a perfect lawn,
the long days weeding, adoring, on your knees –
and maybe in the clasp of straitened herbage
you miss the measure of my point:
the bulbs banked under frosted soil
like teeth-buds biding their time,
the lily-bed flaring with trumpets
that would wake vengeance, bring down the walls,
the skiting wasp squadrons
flaunting eager stingers, violent stripes,
the fallen leaves, their blades sucked dry
by lust to stoke the ravage of a pyre;
so let that little acre sap your hours,
your juices with its petty seasons
until, exhausted, you'll concede
I'm going to have to let the garden go,
and later, from the stoop, perhaps you'll see
in your tattered plots, my trope's veracity
as some meagre crumb of rhizome takes,
then spreads like knotweed: a wild new green.


# The questions that go at first unanswered
**Kona Macphee**

If I should say yes, will you gloss like a lover,
or look at the face when they draw back the cover,
or steal the long shadow of father and mother,
or fold your arms quietly, one on another?

# Aurora
## Kona Macphee

I
The story opens:
a covenant, a promise?
Green as leaves, princess.

II
Immure your blessings.
Caulk the heart's wild apertures.
Burn the spinning wheels.

III
*One Way. No Through Road.*
(The phrasebook's wild translation:
Eternity Street.)

IV
Mending a rent seam,
you spear your finger; blood wells
from a red loophole.

V
From sleep to waking:
the last bud whispers open;
a sentence begins.

VI
No jury. No judge.
No waiver. No get-out clause.
No mitigation.

VII
A cloudless night sky:
the ache of the unbounded,
this stab of viewpoint.

VIII
The blooms are finished.
Princess, put down that fiction:
the vase is leaking.

IX
A page. Another.
One day soon, the endpaper,
blank as a wiped slate.

# Show Me A Man's Teeth
**Andy Jackson**

and I will tell you who he is, or what.
Don't give me grey forensic finds
but cultured pearls that grow
around a living tongue. Show me
the tilt of their owner's chin,
the rictus that betrays them
like a kiss, the lantern jaw or overbite
that hints at light in-breeding,
the wax-eyed drunk
with two yellowed rotten rows,
who smokes the guns to sleep.
The nervous girl who rolls up
at the shoot, whose agent paid a grand
to get them fixed, whose make-up girl
sends texts and reassures her
as she rouges up her nipples
that they're looking at her smile –
don't you think her every thought
was known the second
that she opened up to show me
her impossible dentition?

At bloodstock sales and selling plates,
one glance into the ring of white
inside the noble mouth
can mark the beast as thoroughbred
or meat. So it is with me.
Fillings are a giveaway,
but gaps between are secrets
held in sleep; the sliding tackle,
the playtime scrap you couldn't hope
to win, the blood, your mother saying
*nice boys don't get into fights,*
the space she used to occupy,
the bridge from milk to wisdom.

# Fuji Rock and Ever After
**Iain Maloney**

I NEED A bath. This is disgusting. Every millimetre of skin is tight, crawling with dirt, hair dry and brittle. I brushed my teeth in the restroom and it just made things worse, like when you write your name on a car and the clear lines just show how dirty the rest is. It feels like decades since my last bath. But it was... well this is Monday and we left Friday so it must be three days. Three days in a field with nothing but wet tissues for hygiene. Ew.

'I can't believe that guy,' Aya-chan says for like the thousandth time. That's what Aya-chan does: repeat herself as if she thinks you didn't hear her the first time, or didn't understand. Like everything is this big drama for her, momentous, and if people don't react like it's the end of the world she'll just keep going until you do or until you tell her to shut up. 'I can't believe that guy.'

It's dark in here which is just as well. None of us look good, not just me. Like zombies or something, cosmetics caked over exhaustion. Try to rest against the wall but the décor in this izakaya is old style, the walls uneven, spiky, hurts. At least it's quiet, being a Monday. A table of boys near the door, university by the look, by the noise and drinking games. Janken-poi. Some salarymen at the counter, drowning though it's only Monday. That's it. Them and us, stinking after three days of dancing, walking and camping. Refugees from my leaving party.

'I can't believe that guy. He actually thought I'd do him. In that tent. In the middle of a festival. With all those people around.'

He had thought that. We all had. And Aya-chan would've after the usual drama. She would've if he hadn't got bored and wandered off to find another girl, one less addicted to melodrama. There'd been about seventy thousand people in that field, so he hadn't had to go far. But she doesn't want us to say that. She wants us to screech in horror and sympathise with her for almost being raped by the bad man, to say honestly, men these days, what are they like? But we don't. None of us have the energy. None of us can see the point. I can't see the point. Not tonight.

The food starts to arrive and, ravenous, we devour it. Little plates dotted along the table, wooden skewers at angles, meaty pincushion. Tsukune, yakitori, asparabacon. Anything hot, anything fast. Is this my last yakitori? It must be. No yakitori over there. Should I take some as a souvenir? The tebazaki chicken is burning and spicy, the grease takes the last of the chill from my fingers. The nights were cold and I didn't pack enough warm clothes. My first music festival and I didn't know what to expect. I'll know better next time. Next time.

Shimo-chan takes a swig of beer and sighs, looks around for the waiter impatient for the next dish. She really needs to diet, but she won't. She's always been like that and doesn't care. None of us understand it. 'So,' she says. 'Same time next year?'

They all nod. No one really knows if they can go next year but no one wants to spoil the campaign mood. The mud, the tiredness, the camaraderie: like returning warriors. We survived, fields and crowds and toilets and buses and now we're lingering halfway between the field and home, unable to admit it's over.

They nod and no one looks at me. They're all thinking it. Sure, we might go, they think, but Kasumi won't. She won't be here. I won't be here next year when they graduate from high school and do something to celebrate, I'll be thousands of kilometres away. By Thursday morning I'll be in America. I mean, while they're in double maths I'll be landing in America. Even now I can't quite believe it.

'It's a great opportunity for us,' Father said, meaning it's a great opportunity for him. He's a liver transplant surgeon, at the top of his game and the only way is up. So he got a job in Athens, Georgia without even discussing it. I've never heard of Athens, Georgia. When he said 'America' I thought of New York and LA. That wouldn't be too bad. All that shopping and restaurants, museums and cafes. Broadway and Universal Studios. There're bound to be lots of other Japanese people there, so I could make some friends. I doubt there will be many Japanese people in Athens, Georgia. I can't imagine what's in Athens, Georgia. I can't even pronounce Athens, the 'th' gets stuck behind my teeth and comes out as either 'se' or 'te'. That stupid English teacher Max-sensei making me say it again and again and again, repeating it like one of Aya-chan's stories.

I don't want to go but apparently I have no say. My voice doesn't count. I mean, I only have one more year of school left, can't he wait? I mean, I've seen American movies. Clueless, Mean Girls. DVDs and nabe on cold winter nights, giggling in the back row of Koronaworld with these girls, popcorn all over the floor. I know what happens to new kids, especially foreign ones who can't speak English well. Ones who aren't blonde. Outcast. Alien. Freak. I'm being sent into exile.

Little brother, Taichi-kun, he can't wait. Nothing in the world for him but baseball and America is baseball so he'll be fine. What can I do? Max-sensei says volleyball isn't so popular except on the beach and he says it in that way where he means girls in bikinis jumping around and is thinking about me in a bikini jumping around. It's so gross. Anyway there's no beach in Athens, Georgia. In the movies all the girls want to be cheerleaders. Not me. The thought of all those people watching me dance is horrifying. That time I went with Father and Taichi-kun to Nagoya Dome, I was embarrassed on behalf of the cheerleaders. Jiggling away in front of all those old men, all with the same expression as Max-sensei.

'Hey, Kasumi-chan, don't be down,' Miho-chan says. 'Come on, drink up. You've hardly touched that.'

True. One sip of my Calpis Sour and then I'd ignored it. Miho-chan is right. I've known these girls since elementary school and I don't want my last memories of them to be miserable. A big drink from my glass and I feel the alcohol enter me, soothe tired muscles the way a hot bath would. Another drink.

'That's the way,' Miho-chan says. 'So, who did you think were the best?'

'Yucca, definitely,' I say. 'Their music is just so beautiful.'

'Yeah, it's nice,' says Shimo-chan. 'But a bit boring. No singing. It's not music without a singer. They weren't as good as Nhhmbase. They were intense.'

The same argument we've been having for years. At least that's something I can take to America, something Father can't make me leave behind. No one in Athens, Georgia will know the bands I like, but maybe there are people who like similar music. In those movies there are always kids in the background who look normal, who look like they know of a world other than sport, cheerleading and popularity. Maybe I can make friends with them. Be with the extras in the background.

The salarymen leave, bumping chairs, leering. The university boys are calm now, settled into conversation. There are four of them in the same Uni Qlo jumpers and Gap jeans, but a fifth is sitting slightly apart, like he's not with them. He looks like something out of Death Note: black fedora, black jacket with silver chains, black trousers cut just past the knee, oversize wallet in the back pocket also with silver chain, black boots, laces loose.

These people, do they dress like this everyday? Go to work, or college like that. Do they dress up like it's Halloween just to go to the

➜

7/11 or is it a special thing? Goths, punks. Lolita girls, Visual Kei. In Tokyo they dress up on a Sunday to hang out at Yoyogi Park but what do they wear the rest of the week?

The guy at the table must be at university to be friends with the others. Does he wear his Death Note look to class? What do his parents say when he comes downstairs in the morning, when he comes home at night? Does his father silently shake his head or does he say something insulting? Does he shout and stomp and talk about standards? Does his mother tell him to tie his laces, to pull his waistband up to his waist? Or does he usually wear Uni Qlo jumpers and Gap jeans?

He looks up before I can look down. Eye contact. Face flush and gulp at my drink too fast, choke.

'What is it?' Miho-chan says.

'Nothing. Went down the wrong way.'

Face burning. Why? Because a guy looked at me? Ridiculous. I keep my eyes on Miho-chan, try to think of something to talk about. Nothing. There's nothing there. I feel like a puppet with its strings cut. No energy. I just want to hide. A bath, sleep. Sleep forever and ever, like some princess in a fairy story. Centuries of dreamless sleep, centuries pass until I'm woken by the kiss of some Prince Charming. By themselves my eyes shift back to Death Note. Some Prince Charming. No Prince Charming in Death Note. Still the connection is made and the idea of kissing him screens itself in my head.

He noticed me looking again, I can tell, but he doesn't make eye contact. Instead he leans forward. He looks quizzically at the most preppy boy.

'What? What is it?' he says.

'This,' Death Note says, leaning over and pulling a cigarette from his nostril.

'Ohhh, amazing!' says Aya-chan. Everyone else is looking too. I must have zoned out and they saw, followed my sightline.

No, now there's a link, a connection between our tables. There's only custom to stop it turning into contact, and how many people care about custom these days? Certainly not Aya-chan.

'Do another, show us another trick.'

'Can you make Aya-chan disappear?' says Shimo-chan.

Death Note is writing something on a chopstick sheath. He crumples it into a ball, picks up three sake cups and, oh no, he's coming over to us. He sits directly opposite me. I can feel the dried sweat, the mud, the knots in my hair and the stink coming off me. I half expect him to stand up again and back off. He doesn't.

'What's your name?'

'Kasumi,' I say in a voice stronger than I feel. 'What's yours?'

'Ryu.'

'My name's Aya-chan,' says Aya-chan. He ignores her. He shows me the three empty cups and the ball of paper. I nod. He places the ball on the table, covers it with one of the cups and shuffles the three around. Another trick. I watch his hands move smoothly over the table, rings catching the light.

'You've been to Fuji Rock.'

'Yeah. How did you know?' I say.

'He's magic!' says Aya-chan.

'You're still wearing the wristband.'

'Did you go too?' Miho-chan says.

'No. I had to work. I wanted to go.'

'What do you do?' I ask.

'I'm a hairdresser.'

'Do you always dress like that?' I say the words before my brain can stop me. I blush, but he doesn't look angry. Shimo-chan laughs.

'Usually. Not when I visit my grandmother. She doesn't like black. Says it reminds her of funerals. But then she's eighty seven. Everything reminds her of funerals.' He stops shuffling the cups. 'Which one is the paper under?'

I haven't been paying attention. 'Um, the middle one.'

He lifts it. Nothing.

'Left?'

Again nothing.

'So must be right.'

Nothing.

'Eeeeeeh?' screeches Aya-chan. 'Where is it?'

'Disappeared,' he says. 'Gone.' He stands up. 'See you later,' he says looking at me.

026/Gutter Magazine

Casually waves at the boys on his way past, then he too is gone.

'Weird,' says Miho-chan.

The Gap guys are looking over, but none of them has the guts to do anything more than look, and no one is interested in guys with no guts. It seems like a good moment to call the weekend over. We pay up and head outside for tearful farewells.

Everyone else lives within walking distance but I have to get the train two stops. I hate goodbyes, even though I've never had to say goodbye like this, and I'm glad they all go in other directions. Dragging it out over many minutes and many corners would've killed me. My face must be quite a sight by now with all that crying.

I wait at the lights, watching the red dashes count down, waiting for the green man with his jaunty hat and jaunty step to appear. I'll miss the green man when I go. He always seems so happy, on his way to meet his girl, all dressed up in his fedora like Death Note from the izakaya. I used to imagine he was on his way to propose and that's why he was looking so smart, so sharp. A ring in a box inside his green jacket, hopeful smile and a million thoughts buzzing in his head. Good luck, I tell him when he appears. I hope it all works out. I cross the black and white in front of one of the new hybrid buses, a girl in a black K-car, dashboard crowded with soft toys all looking this way, like some muppet festival. I can learn to drive when we get to America, Father says. I'm old enough there. But they drive on the other side, everything opposite. When I come home I won't be able to drive here. I'll be like a foreigner in my own country. Turn right in front of the bank and step through the light and music of the gyoza restaurant. I look in and everyone looks out, curious. Smells good. I'm not hungry but I almost stop, I've got to do everything because every time is the last time now. Past the hotel, businessmen bowing, past Family Mart, Sukiya, MacDonalds, Ogaki Kyouritsu Ginko, Big Echo, get a leaflet for an izakaya which I'll never get to use, cross under another green man on his way somewhere and into the Meitetsu station. I've still got nearly fifteen thousand yen on my fare card. How am I going to use that by Wednesday? What a waste of money.

The train is quiet; a fat middle-aged man in a Tigers cap, a guy in a suit, not much older than me, asleep with his mouth open, a woman in a long flowery skirt reading a book hidden behind the bookshop's wrapper. All the usual adverts. Sugiyama's terrifying legal grin, like a crocodile. Inuyama castle surrounded by cherry blossom, map of a hiking trail. Beat Takeshi looking at an ECC teacher, bored. Their slogan is 'why not?'

See you, Takeshi.

Bath over and time for bed. Mama wants those 'disgusting clothes' so she can wash Fuji Rock out of them. Already the weekend is disintegrating, disappearing, another memory. The dirt has gone, the tangles. Once the clothes are neatly folded into my suitcase and my Converse – 'These are disgusting, beyond redemption' – dumped in the bin there'll be nothing left but the wristband.

I empty my backpack on the floor, pushing washing into one pile, not washing into another, adding them to the mound already in the washing machine. Check the pockets of my jacket. Some money, keys, rubbish. Something makes me look down as the rubbish falls into the bin. A ball of paper, a chopstick sheath rolled into a ball. How had he got it into my pocket without me noticing? He must have thrown it or something. I mean, surely I'd have noticed him leaning over the table and reaching a hand out. Am I really that tired, that distracted? I pick it out the bin and unfold it. 'Kasumi,' it says. 'Give me a call, Ryu.' And his phone number. He knew my name before he came to the table. He'd been listening to us talk. That trick, the whole performance had been simply to give me his phone number.

The clock moves into Tuesday. It's too late to call now, and on Wednesday, tomorrow now, I'll fly away. That still leaves one night. I put the paper in my purse and climb into bed. I've said goodbye to the girls, I've nearly finished packing. Every time is the last time now.

Fiction /027

# Please
## Wayne Price

FOR A MOMENT, his mind numbed by the jostle and hubbub of the crowd, Phelps thought someone had draped an arm across his shoulders and he twisted away from the unexpected touch. Then the snake's dark, lipless head rose up drowsily to meet his face and *Jesus!* he yelped, shrugging to buck himself free. But the long, hanging body was too heavy and weirdly inert, and the owner's hands were already fixed on it, holding it there across the back of his neck.

Photograph? the middle-aged Berber grinned.

No, Phelps snapped. Get it off me.

The handler, laughing now, lifted the snake away and draped it like a bolt of cloth between his skinny arms. He began to speak but already Phelps had turned and was concealing himself again in the swirling crowds of the *Djemaa*.

It was getting dark and he had lost Rachel completely. Music from a gang of trance dancers whirling in their blue silk robes just to his right drowned out all but the nearest voices. He raised himself on his toes to scan the heads passing by and it was then that she tapped his shoulder.

What happened there? she shouted over the din, turning to watch the dancers before he could begin to reply.

Nothing, he shouted back. He wanted me to pay for a photograph.

You're an easy mark, she called over her shoulder. They can tell.

He frowned but said nothing. All day they'd bickered like this and he was sick of it. Anyway, he said, watch out for that. Don't stand too near the snake charmers.

She was swaying in time with the dancers but stopped to shrug. What makes you think I'm afraid of snakes?

Phelps shook his head. Fine, he said. A group of local girls jostled by them, joking and giggling amongst themselves as they threaded quickly through the crowd. He watched them pass like a loose conga line, trailing a faint vanilla perfume in their wake. Their high spirits made him vaguely sad. I think they drug them anyway, he added, though he knew he was talking more to himself than to Rachel and she didn't give any sign that she might have heard him. They drug the monkeys, so they don't scratch your face, he added pointlessly.

A young boy of eleven or twelve emerged from the group of older dancers now and the men formed a circle around him. Some played instruments – hand drums and boxy guitars – and others clapped and stamped in time as the boy spun himself quickly to a frenzy, his blue silk robe swirling around him, working the crowd section by section, trembling, sometimes grasping himself through the flimsy costume and rolling his wide eyes, jerking his hips wildly towards the watchers.

Good God! Phelps yelled in her ear. Come on, let's go.

She nodded, expressionless, and they pushed clear of the tight ring of watchers just before the shuddering boy reached them.

They drifted aimlessly for a while, avoiding the knots of tourists and Marrakechis surrounding the story-tellers, the troupes of players and the dirty blankets spread with remedies on open patches of ground. Are you ready to eat? he asked at last, and she nodded, leading the way at once towards the smoking ranks of the food stalls. She slid onto one of the narrow, rocking benches of the first stall they passed. The night they'd arrived, Phelps had insisted they hold out against the hailing and sleeve-tugging of the waiters until they'd seen what every long avenue of kitchens had to offer. It had been a trial even to Phelps's cool blooded patience and by the end of their wandering through what felt like an entire city within a city of smoke and bodies and noise Rachel had been almost too vexed to eat or speak.

This place only does soup, she announced flatly now, surveying the chalked up menu board.

He shrugged. Let's have soup here and then go on somewhere else later. It smells good, anyway.

Before she could answer him an open-mouthed, sleepy looking boy presented himself in front of them. He held up two fingers and Phelps nodded. Almost immediately he returned with their wooden bowls of lumpy, orange-coloured soup and a few wedges of bread on a plastic dish.

This is okay, she said, tasting a little and then churning the bowl's contents from the bottom up with her spoon. It's like minestrone.

He soaked a segment of bread and chewed it down quickly. The flavours were sharp and simple. Already he could feel his mood begin to lift. We're having a better time today, aren't we? he ventured.

It's been fine.

Phelps looked at her, his brief optimism already draining away. She was tapping her spoon dully on the rim of her bowl, watching the cook and the boy waiters all busy at their work. He took another chunk of bread, dipped it and filled his mouth, his face still turned to her and hers still turned to all the quickness and liquid bustle of the stall. He chewed slowly this time before swallowing. You haven't liked anything, have you?

Still absorbed, she gave a small shrug. That's not true. I like this soup. And I'm glad I saw the tombs, she said.

He grunted. The Saadian Tombs had been depressingly dull. The carved archways and cool, gloomy chambers had been impressive enough, in their way, but everything was railed off and the graves themselves had seemed wretched to him: low, tiled platforms interrupting the chamber floors, like empty pedestals waiting for fitments in a vast, unfinished bathroom. When he'd tried to take a couple of photographs, more from a sense of obligation than interest, the flash on his cheap camera had taken so long to recharge that a squat, fierce-eyed Frenchman in the queue behind him actually began elbowing him aside – a sharp, painful jab on the bone of his hip.

Even after he'd retreated alone to the scruffy gardens surrounding the chambers there were more of the same long, tiled slabs ready to trip him up amongst the stringy weeds and yellow grass. He'd found a fig tree at the back of the tombs, in the shadow of the old palace wall, and had thumbed open some of the fruits to suck on while he waited for Rachel to find him. A dusty, wrinkled gardener had looked on solemnly from a narrow wooden bench. Phelps had wondered why no-one else ever thought to take the figs – not even the ancient little gardener. They were delicious.

It took a while for Rachel to appear and by the time she did his fingers and lips were coated in a strong, clear glue of fig juice. She poured some of her bottled water over his hands and offered him a tissue for his mouth, then watched him steadily and silently from behind her sunglasses. I feel like a fly cleaning its legs, he said. A middle-aged English woman must have overheard him speaking because she turned abruptly off the garden path and approached them through the long grass. A younger woman, her daughter, Phelps guessed, trailed a little way behind her. It's all very beautiful, but I wish there was some *information* around, the woman confided at once, glancing towards the nearby gardener. Even if it was in French. At least then I could *try* to read it. We don't know what anything *is*, do we Lizzie? The pretty, long-legged daughter agreed. Her white cotton wrap was almost transparent in

Fiction/029

the bright sun. Rachel made polite small talk for a while and Phelps took a snap of them as they stood there, the three women, knee-deep in the weeds beneath the fig tree.

Phelps finished his soup, scouring the bowl with the last of the bread. You want to try another stall? he asked.

Rachel shook her head. Let's have another helping of this and then go back. I'm tired of the square.

He shrugged. Okay, he said. Fine. He caught the waiter's eye and held up his bowl, then pointed to Rachel's.

The heavy-lidded boy nodded in reply and took their dishes back to the cook.

If you can't relax why don't you just call the hospice? he said abruptly.

The question seemed to take her by surprise. She stared at him as if from far away, as if he'd somehow made a fool of himself, of them both, in company. I've called him every day, she said at last.

Oh, he said. Well that's good. How is he?

The boy brought back their bowls, filled again and steaming. They ate for a while in silence. Listen, let's not keep bitching about it, Phelps said at last. I'm sick to death of it. I offered to cancel but he wouldn't let me. He told you that, didn't he? He *wants* us to be here. Can't you just accept that and try to have some fun now?

She swallowed her mouthful and set the spoon down in the bowl. Don't tell me what my own father wants, she said. And don't tell me to have fun. Then, in a sudden burst of anger: You didn't *help* me. You didn't take my side and do the decent thing.

Phelps glanced around, nervously, but no-one at the stall seemed to be paying much attention. The boy was holding out menus to passing trade. The chef was watching the boy with an appraising eye as he worked the crowds. The decent thing? Phelps said sharply. What about us? What about life muſt go on?

You don't know what decency is, she broke in. That's what you are – indecent. Selfish and indecent. And if my father's right about heaven and hell then that's what you'll have to live with for all time, all eternity – your indecency.

She took up her spoon again though her hand was trembling.

Phelps shook his head. She was her father's daughter, that was for sure. He was a tough, stubborn old raptor, a missionary all his adult life for some strict evangelical sect Phelps had never heard of before meeting Rachel. He'd been widowed for years and maybe that was why, even though his daughter had backslidden almost completely from her childhood faith, he doted on her and kept his disappointment well hidden. He'd taken Phelps aside once, solemnly, just before the wedding, and explained calmly, man to man, that he had always prayed for Rachel to marry "in the light", and to not be "yoked to an unbeliever", because the Bible was clear in forbidding that. He'd had his big household Bible open at the relevant passage and pointed it out to Phelps, the two of them stooped over the big open book like scholars. But he would accept Phelps as his own son for Rachel's sake, and pray that the light of conscience within her – that was hidden now for a time – would show forth again as the years went by, and lead them as a couple one day into the gracious and forgiving arms of the Lord.

Well, thank you, Phelps had said dazedly, finding himself shaking the old man's firm, dry hand. There'd been an awkward silence then that Phelps had had no idea how to tactfully break until Rachel had tapped on the study door, calling them both through for coffee.

Now the old man was just weeks away from death, eaten up by cancer, still hoping against hope, Phelps supposed, for the light to shine on them both, or at least on Rachel again, before he went. Not that you'd know she was all that backslidden, he thought now, picking out the tough stem of some herb from his soup and laying it to one side on the plate. She rarely drank, never smoked or swore, had only ever slept with Phelps, or so she said, and basically seemed to live her emotional life inside the same armour of religion she'd started with, but without the faith. It was still there, the tough shell of it, like the safety glass of a museum case, and even if you couldn't tell from what she said or did, day to day, you could walk right into it. Oh Christ, yes – you could smack right into it and not even know what you'd hurt yourself against. You could do that over and over again.

Anyway, Phelps was in the right about the holiday, he was sure. It was like a point of honour with the old man not to make a fuss about death, to welcome it, in fact. Phelps was sure that was why he'd insisted they go ahead and take the holiday. And besides, there was every chance he would last until Rachel got back.

Opposite them a tall, elegant Moroccan woman in a Western dress suit had settled herself alone at the table. She called on the waiter for something and he ran off eagerly to one of the neighbouring stalls. The woman gazed around, alert, while she waited, smiling faintly and nodding to the chef when he noticed her, then making eye contact with Phelps and allowing the same smile to remain on her perfectly painted lips. Within moments the boy was back, presenting her with an egg. She set it to one side until the bowl of soup was served, then tapped it smartly on the wooden rim. The egg white dribbled between her fingertips into the soup and she let out a quick cry of surprise. The boy turned to see and clapped a hand over his mouth, then laughed. They'd both thought the egg was hard boiled, Phelps guessed. She scolded him rapidly in Arabic but Phelps could see she was amused too. While the waiter brought her a fresh bowl of soup and a paper napkin for her fingers she smiled ironically at both Phelps and Rachel. She even rolled her eyes for comic effect as the boy set a replacement egg in front of her, giggling. The little drama cheered Phelps. He glanced sidelong at Rachel but she seemed oblivious to the whole thing, and that cheered him too. He felt a sudden conspiratorial bond with the attractive, ironical woman sitting opposite him. He wished he could speak to her and discover something about her life in this hot, smoky city, and about the other kinds of things that amused her. Her smile and her long delicate fingers were wonderful. She was peeling the shell from the egg very quickly and deftly.

A knot of tourists, three young couples chattering loudly in Spanish, pressed up along the bench to them. The chef called out roughly to the waiter and the interruption of his voice drew Phelps's attention away from the woman and to the man's tall, lean presence instead. His pockmarked face was sweating above the great drum of soup. He stirred it continuously with a steel ladle as long as his arm. A sudden childish impulse to stand and measure himself against the tall sweating man in his stained white overalls and wilted white cap came over Phelps, and he wondered at it.

I'm ready to go, he heard Rachel say.

I wish I could buy a drink, he replied. I'm sick of orange juice. I couldn't live here.

No-one's asking you to. And if you want a drink so badly just go to one of the expensive places, in the modern quarter. They all have bars.

He shook his head. Let's just go back, he said.

Their small, stifling hotel was beyond the *Djemaa*, tucked inside the elbow of the medina's crooked northern arm. They were almost clear of the food stalls when Phelps felt the first tug at his sleeve and looked down to see a very small, urgent face staring up at him, its loose, mobile lips streaming an incomprehensible torrent of French. The little boy's teeth were yellow and peg-like at the front, much too big for the delicate, rapidly moving mouth. The kid was darker skinned and more brightly dressed than the locals, maybe a Somalian, Phelps thought – attached to one of the bands of desert traders.

Hello there, he said, beaming down. No *parlez Francais*. Sorry, *mon ami*. He waved his fingers and strode on to catch up with Rachel, who hadn't paused.

Poor scrap of a kid begging, he said as he reached her shoulder, but was immediately interrupted by another series of tugs, more forceful now, at the back of his shirt.

This time the boy had something to show him: a darkly varnished box, the size of a cigarette packet, introduced with another long, breathless volley of French. Suddenly a black, worm-like neck and head, crimson-eyed, mouthless, lurched up out of a hatch in its top. *Voila!* the boy exclaimed.

➼

Fiction/031

Despite himself, Phelps laughed. Ah! A snake! *Tres mal!*

He felt Rachel take his arm, drawing him on again, and turned to go. But the boy was unshakeable now. He slipped between them and presented himself to Rachel, insisting again on demonstrating the box. The more he sprung the painted wooden head out of the dark hatch the more it seemed to Phelps comically phallic and obscene. He laughed each time, provoking the boy into ever more excited monologues.

*Non, merci,* Rachel said without breaking her stride, ignoring the rest of his tireless, quickfire monologue. He spun back to Phelps who widened his eyes in mock warning to him. Then he darted forward to block Rachel's path. No! Phelps heard her scold, real anger sharpening her voice. Leave us alone! I know you understand. Go away. Go back. Go!

We've finally been blessed with a child, Phelps called to her. What'll we call him?

Rachel trudged on, not bothering to turn.

How about Persistence? That sounds like a good old fashioned missionary name.

He saw her back stiffen, though she kept walking, and suddenly he was sorry and felt a quick spark of impatience at the boy for leading him on into cruelty.

They were inside the medina now and buzzing mopeds and scooters wove past them constantly from in front and behind, sometimes beeping, sometimes brushing their sleeves at speed. Hey! Careful! Phelps shouted above the din to the boy. He was still prancing from one to the other of them, still flicking the ridiculous, ugly wooden head out of its chamber at them, completely careless of the traffic in the tiny street. He bumped heavily against a hand cart and staggered, but his eyes stayed locked on Phelps's. Christ, Phelps moaned. Careful! he shouted again.

Well stop *encouraging* him! Rachel called back, almost desperately.

A rasping, antique scooter revved and popped noisily behind him and Phelps cupped his body sideways to let it pass. The old man riding it, his colourless burnoose billowing around his skinny body, tooted the horn at Rachel's back and she sidestepped heavily, as if dazed or drunk, before swaying back into line behind it and tramping on again. Phelps could no longer see the child but he knew by the continuous rise and fall of his chattering voice that he was still with them, trailing behind.

At last they were on the steps of the hotel. Suddenly, without warning, Rachel swung herself around and took hold of the boy's narrow, chicken-bone shoulders. *S'il vous plaît!* she commanded. *S'il vous plaît!* Spinning him away from the steps she pushed him smoothly but ruthlessly back into the road. A moped scraped to a halt, inches from the child's small body. The rider, a young local woman, stared up at them, astonished, before carrying on. To Phelps's surprise the boy simply recovered from his initial stumble and then, without a sound or backward glance, drifted away into the crowd.

I learned that in India, she said blankly, not meeting Phelps's eye. From the missionaries. Something happens in a kid's mind if you do that. The actual physical push. Her face was white and shining with sweat.

Phelps followed her into the dim reception area. Nobody was at the desk though a well-thumbed Superbikes magazine lay open near the phone. He followed her heavily up the stairs and into the stale warmth of their narrow room.

I don't know what's wrong with you, he muttered, dropping onto the unmade bed.

She stooped to unfasten her sandals, then padded to the corner basin to wash her hands. Don't you dare criticise me, she said flatly. You led him on. You liked all that. You liked that he *chose* you.

Phelps snorted. She'd finished washing now but was still standing at the basin with her back to him, hands gripping the taps. Her calves looked pale and heavy above her bare ankles, the muscles bulging under the skin as if she were squatting or climbing. Anger, he supposed, or maybe just the angle of light from the weak bedside lamp. It repulsed him a little. He lay back flat and closed his eyes. You could have killed him, he said simply.

Eventually he heard the soles of her feet slap faintly across the tiles to the bathroom. He heard her rummage amongst her toiletries and then snap off one of her disposable capsules of eye-wash. She'd become morbid about her eyes recently, he reflected. Always examining them in the mirror. Always dropping something into them. Why the eyes? he wondered. He rubbed his own closed eyelids, tiredly, realising they were dusty too. Opening them and turning to his side he watched her brush past the bed, still teary from the eye drops, and stand at the washbasin mirror again for a final inspection. She cleaned her teeth, swilling her mouth with bottled water. Finally she slipped out of her thin dress and unclipped her brassiere before switching off the lamp.

In the darkness the sounds from the medina seemed magnified, as they did every night, though it was getting late enough for most of the scooters, carts and shoppers to have finally emptied from the souks. Sex was out of the question, Phelps knew. Apart from the troubles of the evening it was hopeless in the heat. The first night, the only time they'd tried since arriving, he'd been unable to finish. God, I'm sorry, he'd gasped, wilting out of her, his whole body slippery with sweat. Drink some water, she'd gasped back, but even then he'd been too sapped and self-conscious to get started again.

He rolled over and kicked his burning feet free of the cotton covers. Rachel, asleep at last, champed her mouth stickily. Phelps stared at her upturned face in the faint light from the window. The coloured glass cast a yellowish, unhealthy stain over her skin. Her left arm was flung up to the side of her head, the fingers curled to a loose fist. She made another noise far back in her throat. When he closed his eyes he saw the boxed snake again, lurching up towards him. Then he saw Rachel, very clearly, turning the boy like a peg in the ground before thrusting him away. He reached for his shirt, lying where he'd dropped it on the tiles beside the bed, and wiped the sweat from his face and neck. Before tonight he'd only once seen her behave so strangely, so unnervingly. She'd pushed *him* then, he remembered now. The office girls where she'd been working had taken her out on some kind of surprise hen night – it was the week before their wedding – and had spiked her drinks. Around three or four she'd somehow found her way home, blind drunk, sick and raving, mostly against him for some reason. He'd tried to clean her up and quieten her down because the whole tenement must have been disturbed by the din, but she'd wrenched away from him, flailing her fists at his head, then lurched away so that he had to chase her in circles round the couch. Get your big, fucky fingers off me! she'd screamed, over and over again. Don't touch me with those fucky fingers!

Fucky fingers. He'd have laughed if she hadn't been waking the building. And when he'd finally taken hold of her, desperate to hush her, that was when she'd pushed him, hard – catching him off balance – and he'd toppled as if pole-axed over the back of the couch. By the time he'd picked himself up she was locked in the bathroom, unanswering, and he'd had to kick through the lock to see that she wasn't lying there unconscious or worse.

He swabbed his face with the shirt again. She always claimed she could remember nothing of that night, and he'd never told her about the grotesque chase around the couch, or the push, or what she'd been screaming, disgusted, as she struggled away from him.

Somewhere nearby in the ancient tangle of the medina a scooter's engine gave out a hard, rising moan before fading away into the distance. *All éternity*, he thought suddenly, and tried to recollect their quarrel at the table, to make better sense of it, but all its bizarre details were a blur now. He got out of bed and clattered noisily in the bathroom, hoping to wake her, but when he returned to bed she was only mumbling in her sleep. I know you; I know you, she said thickly, without any human sense or emotion.

*Furnace* by Wayne Price is now available from Freight Books

# Excavating The Heaney Machine
## Dearman McKay

"I'll dig with it," the machine reads, "Between my finger and my thumb." And I'll dig with it.

The machine stutters, "The squat pen
rests" but it is not rested- there is a "grandfather"
but the turf is shallow,
not cut curt,

just a beefy ridge,
the verbs swung low.

The Heaney Machine digs for words but there is no "good turf",
no "potato mould", no "squelch and slap".
There is "no spade".

If there had been a "thumb" there may have been a weft,
but now
not a single swing to raise and drop.

The Heaney Machine says, "I'll dig" but it does not–
the "living roots" in its sunken head
a different sort of memory.

# This Is Not A Translation
## Dearman McKay

This is not a translation of potato, patata, buntata, aardappel
or the Huckleberry Finn song you used to mow the lawn to.
Don't believe in Billy Connolly
or the fake Scots Scots speak to pretend they speak Scots

or the blunt Gaelic Aunt Julia might speak if she spoke
Urdu very loud and very fast.
I do not answer it
but she should understand it.

Chan fhaca Tu i, you wandering bard without bardachd,
she was hiding in the station her
boy a deer, his broken words a landscape,
the songs not White Heather but brittle Heathens on fire.

This is not a translation of how Scott candied the North,
nor how the North sent treasure sou'westerly
a catechism for a pillow, a Hi-ri-ho-ro to Bheir mi o.

This translation is not a colour or creed or memory.
It is not a tongue, or race, or national team.

It is not a translation.
It is not a refutation.

# The immaculate speech
**Nick Brooks**

The essays and the pamphlets
the politics and the poetry
the immaculate speech
the tongue now languishing
the voice a whisper
no more rants on unruly wine-waiters
no paeans to oral sex
no more the Larkin in the long grass
the importance of Orwell not quite as important, perhaps
as all this remaining now left to live
the hope that it will be love that outlives us
the knowledge that it will not
that it will be your words
your words alone
and so again
the threat of silence, at once unkind
the silenced words
the epiglottis
*that roaring old speedbag!*
hanging limper than this pen.


# Post-Revolutionary Poets of the Future
*an Ode to Modernity, i.m. Christopher Grieve*
**Andrew McCallum**

They constantly enter their poems, day and night.
They do not wait for the works' gates to be opened
by literary criticism, by refined and delicate thinking.
They enter their poems as they enter factories, plants,
full of energy, noise and anger.
They churn the sirens, switch on the machinery, start work.
The façade of the poem dirls with drills, with lathes.
The grey metallic air shudders with vibrations.
They mount the scaffolding of their stanzas.
With welding-torch in hand they fuse rhythms
and tender rhymes, testing with micrometers
the calibres of their thoughts and passions.

# Women's Secret Language in China
## Tessa Ransford

Secret language
for women, for only
women, mother to
daughter over and under

How we enjoy and how
we adapt, what children need,
when to hold on and
when to let go, what the body
knows, where we are strong,
why we live long

Renewable wisdom: endure,
listen, hear, wait, watch,
welcome, encourage, restore

Spindly signs like needle marks:
share, safekeep,
embrace, praise

Fury, mercy, laughter,
laughter, will soon
all die but
our language will
surpass itself

# Hum Int
## Andrew Philip

*There are spaces*
*where infringements are possible.*
Norman MacCaig

The great men looked at each other.

On the table in front of them lay a note
setting out credible intelligence

that, somewhere in the dark –
in the minds of the angry, the awkward,
the unemployed –
                        a poem was growing.

They shifted in their chairs.
                              The poem
was not amenable to measurement
against capital or revenue budgets.

Their Italian suits began to chafe
at the crotch.
                The poem was known only
to say: *Trespassers will be wélcome.*

Their chilled wine could not take away the taste.

# Look North (and North Again)
## Andrew Philip

      Since the result of
           the referendum on
returning Berwick-upon-Tweed,
there have been increasing reports that adults

      throughout North England
           are spontaneously
becoming Scottish. Doctors state
that the condition does not seem infectious

      but they are baffled
           by its rapid spread south
and the fact that most patients show
no previous connection to, or even

      predilection for,
           bold Caledonia —
sorry, no idea what came
over me there. The Scottish Government is

      said to be working
           round the clock in order
to isolate the cause so that
the effect can be sold in tourist hotspots.

      Claims that the disease
           originated in
a particularly fine batch
of Aberdeen Angus immediately sent

      sales skyrocketing
           in North America,
but European agencies
are considering bans on Scots food exports.

      Meanwhile, Number 10
           is said to be sair fashed
about the menu for the Queen's
official banquet in Holyrood the morn.

# Tae a Lousy Piper
*on seein him crawl up the Royal Mile*
**Andrew Philip**

Mishanter faw yer crabbit face,
great golach o the pipin race.
Afore St Giles ye tak yer place
wi ither gowks
there for tae blaw an pech an skraich
for furrin fowk.

When you stairt up, the lift shuid fill
wi groans fae them that has tae thole
yer total want o tunin skill,
yer connacht reeds,
the mankit time ye stamp out ill
wi muckle feet.

But naw: it's photaes taen, siller skailt
intil yer gantin case that waits
for unsuspectin tourist bait
that cannae tell
gin whit ye play is worth its weight
or straucht fae hell.

I'v never heard sic constipation,
sic wersh, wanchancy emmanation
fae this braw emblem o ma nation
as you purvey.
Nou, this micht come as a revelation
but—ye cannae play.

The ugsome din ye pass for pipin
wid fleg an fash the fiercest Viking.
Nae maitter that he's yaised tae skitin
gleg throu battle,
the pair auld craitur wid gang gyte an
sned his thrapple!

O wid some pooer the giftie gie ye
tae hear yersel as ithers hear ye!
I threap it wid dae nocht tae free ye
fae yer glaikit notions.
Truth is, I wid prefer tae see ye
faur ower the ocean.

Sae listen here: enough's enough.
I dinnae hae tae thole sic guff.
An nou thir lines has caaed yer bluff,
juist haud yer wheesht.
Pack up yer pipes, syne bummle aff
an gie us peace!

# I was like, oh my God, I was literally
## Gordon Legge

'...THE BLUE FOUR and a half, the left, the peep toe, it was the same, looked great, but only on its own, only on the left...'

'I go between a three and a five and a half.'

'...so blue, no; red, no. Now...'

'Those guys, look, they're creeping me out.'

'– they're not doing anything – ...now, come the day, she'd four to choose from: the red, the blue, the white and the brown.'

'Brown?'

'You don't wear brown to your wedding.'

'Only boys like brown.'

'Well, they weren't really brown, more... chestnut. Size 5. Pointed...'

'Then why are they wearing suits then?'

'...toe!!! Brown can be okay. Cindy's got mules, they're brown, ochre. They're lovely. She was...'

'Cindy?!?!? What happened to Holly Two Bras?'

'Cindy's Amy's new besty.'

'Okay, Holly then. She's actually really nice when you speak to her. She's not that keen on Skelly Bob. It's not what you think.'

'She the one that does sports?'

'The one that's rubbish at sports. She's just big. She just barges.'

'Holly's alright.'

'Holly's problem is she wants to be successful. See if you fancy freaking her out, tell her you've got an uncle that works in TV and he's going to fix you up.'

'That's not nice.'

'True. She's not that bright either. Skelly helps her.'

'Skelly worships her.'

'Skelly snogged Jordan.'

'You met Jordan?'

'Think so. I think he spoke to me...'

'Really?'

'Yeah, I was reading a book, and he came up and went, What you doing? Eh, reading a book. He went, Cool, touched my arm, and walked away.'

'That's Jordan.'

'He touched your arm?'

'Is Skelly still getting copies of your notes?'

'...'

'That's shocking.'

'What's this?'

'Skelly copies Cassie's notes.'

'You're kidding?'

'It's what I do. After the 'mystery virus', Mrs Wilson goes, Cassie, can you help Shona, show her what we've been doing? But it's not stopped. Have you got the stuff from this morning? Have you got Tuesday's? She's clever enough, too, but she'll be like, Oh, I don't understand this, pretending she understands the rest. And I'm like, well, that's cause, admit it, go on, just admit, admit you weren't paying attention, you've a lot on your mind, you can't be bothered. And please don't cry.'

'She's always crying.'

'Then you explain, and she's like, Oh, that was really easy. D'uh. Then she starts laughing.'

'Then Skelly helps H2B.'

'They study like crazy, too. Come in early. Stay late. Ask questions.'

'You notice how it's the same ties they're

wearing.'

'Sure sign they're up to no good.'

'Listen, we're fine. There's a squaddie along there. I've gave him the signal.'

'...'

'How d'you know he's a squaddie?'

'Squaddie bag. Looks like a squaddie. That fit, bendy look.'

'...'
'...'
'...'

'What d'you mean you gave him the signal?'

'... ... ...'

'Amy!'

'My cousin's into squaddies. You know what she says? She says, great bodies, can take a telling and away half the time. Between that and keeping themselves clean, what more could you want?'

'She the one that lasted six months?'

'No, that was Suzie. Suzie's into doctors.'

'Amy's family picks its partners from Yellow Pages.'

'I'm going for a vet.'

'...'

'Don't look at me like that. If you're after a certain type of person, chances are a certain type of person is going to have a certain type of job. Simples.'

'It's not about being after a certain type of person.'

'Squaddies have ten different handshakes.'

'...'
'...'
'...'

'So they can gain advantage. That's nearly all what they talk about: violence, how to break bones.'

'Eh, how d'you know this?'

'Read it in a book.'

'...'

'Was that the book you were reading when Jordan spoke to you?'

'...'

'Do you think squaddie'll do anything if those guys start?'

'Start what?'

'They keep looking over.'

'Maybe cause you keep staring at them.'

'...'

'My dad says guys with suits can be the worst.'

'So, did everybody enjoy themselves?'

'Yeah, it was great. Thanks.'

'Met some nice boys.'

'I'd a great time.'

'You spent most of the night playing with your phone.'

'I was telling everybody what a great time I was having.'

'I got a number.'

'They weren't boys, they were old.'

'I got invited to a party.'

'Did you tell them you were still at school?'

'Yeah, I said my uniform was in my bag. Alongside my knickers.'

'Did you enjoy it, Celia?'

'Yeah, they're my favourite group. I just think they're so clever, they're just...'

'Would you marry a musician?'

'...'

'Would you marry Ezra?'

'Yes.'

'See. Told you. Short girls, famous boyfriends.'

'Rubbish. Famous boys go for TOWIE blondes with...'

'Ah, but their psycho stalkers are teenie-toaties.'

'Did you stop growing when your mum and dad split up?'

'...'

'Did your hair stop growing?'

'...'

'Mine fell out.'

'!!!'

'What?'

'You're joking?'

'True. I'm going round picking up clumps before they've the chance to see it. Hoovering the pillows.'

'That's sad.'

'That's when I started tying it back.'

'And, Celia, you have your mum staying one week, then your dad the next?'

'...'

'That's weird.'

'It's called nesting.'
'I know but – so your mum's got a house, your dad's got a house, and you've got a house?'
'...'
'And their houses are empty when they're staying with you?'
'...'
'You know what you should do, you should leave brochures lying about. Oh, dad's taking me to the Maldives.'
'You should. We'll help you.'
'You should copy keys and we'll party at their houses. Say you're on a sleepover. Invite boys.'
'Should tell them lies about each other. Tell your dad your mum's seeing a geriatric millionaire.'
'Tell your mum, Dad's really happy, I've never seen him so happy, you should see him.'
'Tell them the other's won the lottery, but you've not to say.'
'Tell them they're getting fat.'
'...'
'D'you get twice as many holidays then? Does your mum take you away and your dad take you away?'
'D'you do anything special?'
'Must be joking. White water rafting...'
'Oh, no! Not white water rafting!'
'Celia'd a great time. Celia really enjoyed herself. Celia made loads of pals.'
'Dragged round the rellies, that's what I get. Here's Cassie. Top of the class again.'
'You top of the class?'
'...'
'...'
'Sorry.'
'Were you top of your old school?'
'No. Well... no.'
'I don't understand relatives. What's the point of them?'
'And do your mum and dad go holidays without you?'
'Yeah. Me and Claudine are off to the Gambia. Just a few days.'
'My mum went to Paris and never even told me.'
'Really?!?!'
'I love Paris.'

'I'd love to go to Paris.'
'You okay, Celia? You look knackered.'
'Yeah. I'm glad you all had a good time.'
'I'd a great time.'
'It was fab.'
'Yeah, but... but you're not really talking about it.'
'It was great. We came through for your little group. We danced. We sang. We flirted. What more could you want?'
'...'
'Joking. You know what it is? You've got a post-high low. It's like when you wear a new outfit and nobody mentions it. Or you send out a funny mail...'
'...and nobody responds.'
'Snap out of it, girl! You're two thoughts from the huff.'
'Hit the huff!'
'Hit the huff!'
'Hit the huff!'
'Know what I think: I think maybe you fancied Tony. Wanted him for yourself. See, you're into a group he's into. Something in common. You want his number?'
'...'
'Look, quick, creepy blokes are passing round a phone. Is there not somebody supposed to be checking tickets?'
'My dad says you never see a guard after football.'
'Was there football?'
'Would you marry a footballer? ...Hold on, message. It's mum. At Waverley. Nice PC Brian has allowed me to park illegally. Train on time. Celia, prepare yourself, you're about to meet my mum.'
'Amy's mum's amazing.'
'She is.'
'How far gone is she?'
'Seven months. She just smiles and pats and rubs herself. She glows. She's like... ... ...'
'...'
'No, it's like... ...... ...'
'...'
'That policeman, he'll have fallen for her. She'll've had his life story.'
'Amy's mum gives off some kind of happy

Fiction/043

gas. It's like, nothing's ever a problem.'
'You fancy my mum.'
'No, I don't. I just...'
'Warning but – you'll get, Celia, darling, love, I've heard so much about you, you poor thing.'
'...'
'We told her everything stopped growing when your mum and dad split up.'
'...'
'You'll get the cuddle.'
'...'
'You'll start crying.'
'No, I won't.'
'Bet you your red top you will.'
'Celia, I understand. It's okay.'
'So there's police at Waverley?'
'My dad says dodgy guys get off at Haymarket.'
'What you doing?'
'Texting to say Megan's pleasuring a squaddie in the toilet.'
'Don't!'
'Say she went to a party with guys we met. Tell her we said, Megan, don't, don't do it, but we couldn't stop her. She beat us off with her shovel fists.'
'Don't!'
'Okay, I'll say you're staring at dodgy blokes.'
'...'
'Did your hair really fall out when your mum and dad split up?'
'...'
'How old were you?'
'Twelve.'
'Was that when you were wearing the beret?'
'A total stranger even asked if I'd a serious illness. They noticed. Mum and dad never noticed.'
'Did you tell them?'
'...'
'You mean they still don't know?'
'...'
'And Celia's mum and dad split up in February. You poor thing.'
'Mum was going to wait till I left school. In the end, she said she couldn't.'

'Bitch.'
'I've not got shovel fists.'
'She waited till my brother left.'
'Big bitch.'
'Do you think they split cause they didn't like you? They could only handle you one week at a time?'
'...'
'I used to think that. I used to think everything.'
'So you had to move?'
'...'
'That's not fair.'
'That'll be Amy. Peep toe brown shoes, 'I do', then twenty years of a loveless marriage.'
'Ivory!!! Pointy!!!'
'Amy'll be lucky to last six months.'
'Whatever. Marriage, three or four babies, then a highly acclaimed career in water colours. Hubby can do what he likes. I'm taking a lover.'
'You going to get celebrity shag cards?'
'What?!?!?'
'!!!'
'Is that when...'
'They're not actual cards. You nominate celebrities you can get off with.'
'Mr Johnstone.'
'Mr Johnstone's not a celebrity.'
'Can it be anybody?'
'Rosies are red/violets are blue/I'm getting banged in the bushes/by you know who...'
'We could make conference shag cards.'
'Amy's got a thing for conferences. She keeps...'
'D'you not think they're sexy? Everybody dressed up and smelling nice and... Hey, you could get them in your welcome pack: sponsor's bottle of water, map and timetable, and shag card.'
'Open days are sexy.'
'Megan got a snog at Stirling.'
'Open day shag cards.'
'You could get holiday shag cards.'
'Hotels!'
'Hotels are sexy. I was...'
'His n hers!'
'Mr and Mrs!'
'Collect the set.'
'Shag Card Monopoly.'

'How would...'
'Message from mum. PC Brian says he'll look into it.'
'What?'
'Said you were getting off with the squaddie in the toilet.'
'Did not!!!'
'Will she really cuddle me?'
'Smother. She'll smother you. She'll find out more about you in two minutes than we have in two months.'
'Got your work cut out, girl.'
'Has your dad got a new girlfriend?'
'...'
'Has he?'
'And, guess what, she looks and acts exactly like my mum.'
'Joking!'
'Never!'
'And it's not what you think. It's somebody that works with my dad. Think she's had her eye on him. She dresses like my mum. Has her hair like my mum. She...'
'Stalker!'
'...asks all these questions. She gets the photos out and stares at them.'
'Is she teenie-toatie?'
'...'
'Stalker!'
'Has your mum got a new boyfriend?'
'Hundreds. It's like, This is my friend Derek. This is Andrew. This is Dimitri. I'm yeah, okay, get it, this is the guy that's going to be sticking his thing into you. Yeah, like, I really want to shake that hand.'
'What sort of music d'you like? What's your favourite subject? You got a boyfriend? ...'
'Pervs.'
'My dad says with the boys he's only got one cock to worry about; with the girls, he's got hundreds. When I was wee, I used to think I was going to start growing them all over me.'
'Does your dad make the tea?'
'Yeah, chilli with everything.'
'Same as mine! Mine's does that. Makes something, screws his face up and adds loads of chilli.'
'That, or cumin and coriander.'
'They think you should like what they like.'
'I know, it's...'
'Who would be the worst sort of person you would marry?'
'What, what sort of occupation?'
'!!!'
'!!!'
'!!!'
'!!!'
'Can squaddie not just batter them?'
'...'
'Ignore them.'
'My dad says that's the problem with going out. You have a nice time, and then it gets spoilt by ARSEHOLES!!!'
'Cassie! What you all doing at the weekend?'
'...'
'I was thinking of going to see my pals.'
'Nah, dump them. You're hanging with the cool kids.'
'You're one of us.'
'What?'
'One of us!'
'One of us!'
'One of us!'
'Come round. Roland's coming over. You want me to fix you up? I'm good at that.'
'Can just imagine your house. Wedding photos, hundreds of them. Everywhere.'
'So, what's yours? Homage d'Ezra?'
'...'
'Do you still keep pictures of your mum and dad together? Or is it just pictures of your mum and pictures of your dad?'
'You know who you'd like?'
'Is there anybody you fancy?'
'...'
'Just don't be too needy. And wear that red top, the nice one.'
'Do you have a boyfriend at your old school?'
'...'
'Is he fit?'
'Is he bendy?'
'Does he have a nice smile?'
'He's quite funny.'
'Anybody can be funny. You need a smile.

Roland's got a nice smile.'

'Mr Johnstone's got a nice smile.'

'No, he's not, he's like... ... ...'

'No, he's not.'

'You know who's got a really nice smile? Graham Saunders. Listen, I know he's fat and disgusting and smells of wet farts, but he's got a really nice smile.'

'That's cause he's farting all the time. You ever tried...'

'None of his pals smile.'

'I know, they're like... ... ... ... Ryan Stobley... ... ...'

'Rhys Fulton...... ...'

'Jamie Bradshaw...... ...'

'Celia doesn't smile.'

'...'

'You don't.'

'You've got nice eyes.'

'I do so smile.'

'Show us.'

'... ... ...'

'...'

'...'

'...'

'What?'

'You know what you do, you... ... ...'

'I do not.'

'You seen Holly smile?'

'That's Page 3. Hand on hip, launch the tits and... ... ...'

'There's nothing wrong with my smile!'

'Nothing wrong if you want to terrrorize Gotham. Oh, message from mum. Peter's been showing me his handcuffs. You call them bangles. Train on time. How often has Megan said, Where are we?'

'...'

'Will she really cuddle me?'

'It'll be, Celia, if you ever have problems, don't hesitate, come and see me. There's always room at ours.'

'Amy's mum's got short hair.'

'She says it's the fourteen year old boy look.'

'She can't look like a fourteen year old boy. She's really old.'

'She thinks she does.'

'She does.'

'She's really pretty.'

'She is.'

'Is that the look you're going for?'

'...'

'Are we going to Sick Note?'

'Celia, oh, you have to come. It's brilliant. Everybody goes. We all get dressed up. They play good music. You want to be a DJ, don't you?'

'Thought you wanted to be a vet?'

'I'm hoping to do both.'

'You know what I think you should do, I think you should be an MP.'

'Yeah, we'll be your campaign team.'

'I'd vote for you.'

'Do Holly and Skelly go to Sick Note?'

'Holly and Jordan go to George Street.'

'Skelly came one time...'

'That was totally embarrassing.'

'She was with this old guy...'

'Who she promptly ditched...'

'Skelly gets really drunk. I've always liked you, Amy. You and me...'

'Guys like her.'

'Oh, er, mm, let me think... wonder why that could be.'

'She doesn't?'

'She does.'

'Allegedly.'

'Has anyone ever actually spoke to her?'

'She takes everything so seriously. That time she got 52% and ran out crying.'

'That was funny.'

'And see if she sees you talking to anybody, she's straight in, and all over them. She's as bad as my wee brother. You're playing with a rubber band, and it's, That's mine, give me it.'

'Hold on. Squaddie's putting his jumper on.'

'...'

'...'

'...'

'And for handsome squaddies like yourself/ my fee's reduced to zero.'

'Eh?'

'It's a line of poetry... I can be your pin-up girl/ your bargain playboy bunny.'

'Is that from the squaddie book?'

'Megan, you're missing it, creepy guys are

getting off.'

'Haymarket. Told you. Taxi to the West End. Dicks.'

'You know how squaddies are so fertile? It's cause they hardly ever do it. When you do it all the time it waters it down. You have to save it up and then it comes out as the good stuff, like squishy cream.'

'...'

'That wasn't in the book I read.'

'Can I get a loan of that, the squaddie book?'

'Maybe Jordan'll speak to you.'

'Did he really touch your arm?'

'...'

'Oh na na/What's my name?'

'Oh na na/What's my name?'

'What's my name?'

'My phone.'

'About time. You've texted twenty people.'

'Mum.'

'What's she saying?'

'She's wanting to know what time I'm getting the train.'

*What meanings do you find in the title and how are these related to the story?*
*How, precisely, does Célia help establish flow and tone?*
*In what ways do Megan's contributions impact the others?*
*Discuss fully the expression 'shovel fists'.*
*Why is there little information about the setting? What happens to point of view in such a treatment as this?*
*Identify some of the means used to achieve the mood of the story.*
*Does Amy contradict herself? If so, to what extent? Which word best describes Amy?*
*Is it a revelation that Cassie is 'top of the class'? Cite examples. Explain Célia's reaction.*
*What, if anything, is the significance of the end of the story?*

*Choose one of the following:*

*At one point Célia expresses disappointment. Recall a time when you felt disappointment with your friends. How did this make you feel?*

*Célia has read a book about squaddies. Write about a book you've read.*
*Imagine yourself as Holly Two Bras/Skelly Bob/ the squaddie/a suit guy/Célia's dad's girlfriend and describe an incident involving the element of surprise.*

Fiction /047

# After the Dance
## Carl MacDougall

IT WAS AFTERWARDS, when everyone was hanging around, she noticed Jamsie Fallon. He was on his own, away from the crowd. She remembered feeling sorry for him, the lost way he had about him, as if he knew there was something missing, but he didn't know what it was or how to find it. That sort of thing was always more noticeable in big men, their bits of awkwardness and difficulties seemed to stand out more.

She never thought. He didn't live up her way, but he tagged on with Fraser while she and Annie walked together as far as McArthur's Field. When Fraser stopped to light a smoke, Annie held her coat open against the breeze, though there was hardly any wind, and they sort of paired off, walking in front and bumping into each other, nudging, the way you do to get the thrill of a touch, or so she imagined for she had never wanted that or even thought about it, but afterwards it was the most obvious thing.

Nice night, he said.

She asked where he was going and he said he was just seeing Fraser back, for it was a long road to be walking on your own. And it was a grand night with a good full moon and he liked that, liked watching the shadows and the changes in the land, the way trees looked different, the way you could hear the rush and tumble of a burn, but the water was unusual, darker in the moonlight.

She said Goodnight at the road end, but he followed her up the path and over the cattle grid to the house and when Annie and Fraser went round the back, she stood awkward for a second or two, his face long and pale and shadowed and she thought she might ask him in for a cup of tea, when he said, We could go round the other side.

And she turned. She didn't say anything, because the idea had never occurred to her and she didn't know what to say, so she just turned away when he grabbed her arm and said, So you don't think I'm good enough, do you.

And while the words and the breath stuck in her throat he swung her round, hit her and ran her into the barn at the side of the house and with the cows in their stalls and the smell of the place around her he threw her onto the cemented floor and put his hand over her mouth and she kicked and pulled at his hair and face because she couldn't breathe and when at last the breath came to her she took it in handfuls, big gulps of air till she felt the pain of him inside her and she screamed, so he put his hand over her mouth but she could breathe this time, so she grabbed his hair and tugged his head back and spat at him, spat into his face, though by now he was finished and he rolled away and she put her heel into his face as he was bending forward and pulling away from her. She thought she might have caught his eye for he let out a yell and grabbed her leg, but she jerked herself free and ran into the house and up the stairs and into the bathroom where she looked at herself in the mirror and though her clothes were filthy and she looked the same she knew he had changed her.

Five months later when she began to show, her mother put her on the bus to Glasgow.

The nuns took it from her. She never held

the baby.

They took it while it was wet and red and dripping and the nun's apron was shining with her blood even though there was only a wee light bulb, she could see the red glow on the apron and hear the baby's cry.

They never told her, but she knew it was a girl.

She stayed in the hostel, working in kitchens, making soups and stews, some sandwiches and cakes to pay for her board. She never saw anyone except the nuns and the other girls: You've to hide your shame, the sister said.

Then her place was needed and with the baby gone, she was told to leave.

Of course, there's nothing to stop you going home, the sister said, but if you want to stay here we can help find you work and a place in a good, steady home.

Next morning she cleared her plate and left it on the trolley by the serving hatch, beside the teacup and plate for the toast. She collected her bag and left. She told no one she was going.

Out in the street, it was a clear, bright day. The wind was lovely, the clean, fresh smell and the feel of it full in her face, but she would have to move. She stood by the gate and the city moved around her. She knew she'd have to be quick because the van that took them to their kitchens would be leaving after the register check, when they'd find her missing, after the sister had been sent for and she'd asked if anyone knew where Catherine Morrison was and if anyone had been speaking to her. When the van left the sister would phone the police, then tell her family she was missing.

She got on a bus that said City Centre.

She was lucky. Looking back, she tells herself, she was lucky.

She got off the bus at Central Station and stood outside because she had no place to go and thought she might have to go back home.

A woman asked if she was all right and took her to the chapel house at St Bartholomew, where the woman at the door smoothed the front of her housecoat and looked down the street. You'd better come in, she said.

The house smelled of stale air freshener and polish. There was a bouquet of artificial flowers on the table beside the phone. The woman showed her into a side room.

Did you get tea? the priest asked.

I'm fine, thanks.

No, sit there and we'll fetch you in a cup of tea.

Three days later she had a place in a lodging house in Hill Street. On Sunday she went to the chapel at St Aloysius.

She wrote to Annie and told her she was settled, told her she'd got a job in the college offices and was managing fine.

Annie told her she and Fraser were engaged. She gave her the date of the wedding and told her to put it in her diary because she wanted Cathie to be her bridesmaid.

It was a hard letter to write. It took her three nights and when she'd finished it she put it straight in the envelope and phoned Annie's mobile: There's a letter in the post, she said.

*I cant do it. As much as I would love to and as much as I want to and no matter what I do to try to help me make myself do it, I know I cant. It isnt you and it isnt Fraser and it isnt the wedding. You must know that. Who doesnt want to be at her sister's wedding. Not me, I can tell you. But I cant come home. Not yet and you know why. It's not that Im scared of who I-ll see, though I dont want to see him, no it's not that it's just that I am not ready, not ready to come home or do anything yet. I am settling here and Im trying to settle here and its ok. Its not like home but its ok and works fine and everything. I cant write and I want to talk to you to tell you what happened and even though what happened happened she was still my baby and they took her. But youve to send me the pictures and tell me what's going on. You could come to Glasgow for a honeymoon though I know youve always wanted to go to Spain. Maybe you and Fraser could fly from Glasgow and I could see you then. I want to see my Daddy in a suit and tie with a flower in his lapel ready to give you away and even Mummy in a flowery hat and a new coat would be good. For God's sake Annie,*

Fiction/049

*please, please forgive me* for not coming.

Her daughter would have been 18 months old when Fraser and Annie were married.

She stood on the bridge and looked at the water and thought of what it would look like in the moonlight, though she knew this place would never be without light.

Three months later she went back for her father's funeral.

So you've come and see us, her mother said. Why weren't you here for your sister's wedding? It was a disgrace, and everyone asking where you were.

Mum. I told you about that, Annie said.

Some daughter you turned out to be, running away with your shame and thinking all you have to do is come back here to bury your father. You killed him, her mother said. He was never the same after you left.

You've no right to talk to Cathie like that, Annie said. You of all people.

She didn't speak to her mother, never said a word till after the service when the house was full of mourners.

He was there and she knew he was there. He had a scar on his forehead, running from his brow to the side of his eye.

Her mother was standing by the sideboard talking with Father McDowall and Mrs Gillies who arranged the flowers. There was an awkward hush when Cathie came into the room. She went over to Jamsie Fallon and she spat in his face.

You're not welcome here, she said. Get out.

And she turned to her mother.

Unless you invited him, of course. He can stay if he's here on your invitation.

It would be better if you left, the priest said. You can pay your respects another time James.

But he sat there, her spit drying on his face.

Annie ignored him when she went round with the tea.

Come on, Fraser said. Don't be such a dick. Get out of here. You shouldn't've bloody come in the first place.

Jamsie Fallon stood and surveyed the room. No one looked at him as he moved towards the door. He stared round the room again, turning towards his chair as if there was something he'd left.

We'll need to be going soon ourselves, Mrs Gillies said when he'd gone.

Her husband nodded.

It's getting late, a woman said.

Andy the postman stood up and looked out the window. I'll just see that everything's okay, he said.

They left as they'd arrived, trickling out in ones and twos, hugging and shaking hands.

And with everyone gone and the front room cleared, when the chairs had been put back and the extra food packed in the freezer and the sandwiches thrown in the bin for the hens, they sat round the kitchen table, the way they'd always sat, with Fraser in her father's place and Cathie facing her mother.

You'll have to come back, her mother said. Annie's going to have children and she'll have her hands full and I'm getting on, so you'll have to come back to look after me.

She never spoke, but lay in the bed where she'd slept for most of her life, staring at the ceiling, watching the way the light dimmed behind the heavy curtains, faded but did not disappear, stayed bright.

I'll look after you the way you looked after me, she said when she left next morning. She hugged her sister and kissed Fraser's cheek.

He walked her to the road end.

I'll come back to bury her, she said. And I'll send money to help pay for whatever she needs.

She might have to go into a home at the end, he said.

Then put what I send away. It'll help pay for it. I'll write a note to Annie. But if it gets too much you can let me know. We'll settle this place up when she's gone.

Things change, he said. You might want to come back and you'll surely be here to see the children. We'll see how it goes. Let us know you've got back safe.

I'll be all right, she said. God knows, I've waited here for a bus many's the time before now. You get back on up to the house.

Be sure and write, or you could phone, he said. It would be nice to hear your voice.

She waited till the sound of his boots on the gravel faded as the wind rolled over the crest of the corn, occasionally green but mostly yellow with poppies and a scattering of cornflowers, the red campion and scabious in the sheuch where she'd played. She had gathered these flowers and pressed them for a Blue Peter project, knew their names and habitation. In the afternoon the butterflies would be out and the bees would bump round the place, the swallows diving and the blackbirds loud at twilight.

She had loved it, loved it and thought she would never leave, would marry and live here forever, bringing in the winter coal, watching the spring seeds sown, that they would carry her down the lane the way they had carried her father. She and her man would maybe buy another field and get some more cows and her children would fetch them home the way she had fetched them and she would stand at the kitchen window and watch them stagger up the road in the evening.

When the bus came she sat at the back, the other seats taken in ones and twos. She knew no one and looked out the window as a chill settled inside her. It was a new feeling and it made her anxious; she knew her time here was over, not just the dream, but all of it. And as she looked at her reflection in the fading light she saw herself years on, coming home from work or going to the chapel to pour the tea.

# Knife
## Andrew McCallum Crawford

THE KNIFE SCREAMED when I pressed it into the grinder. I soon had it squealing. 2000 rpm, that's what it said on the plaque next to the On button. There was nothing I didn't know about this sharpening business. I'd been doing it all week, since they took my driving licence off me. I told McCabe straight away. I think he appreciated it. Maybe he forgave me, although it struck me that he didn't quote a line of scripture. He had a verse for every occasion. So did I. It was usually a total non sequitur, but it managed to shut him up. I knew he liked a drink. Perhaps there's something in the Bible that says too much whisky is good.

Another perfect job. I pressed the Off button and laid the knife on the pile. Someone was standing in the doorway. I couldn't make out who – sunlight was streaming over his shoulders. He just stood there, perfectly still, the silhouette of a statue. At first I thought it was McCabe, or that mate of his, Sergeant Bilko, who was always turning up unannounced.

'Alright?' I said.

The figure stepped inside. It wasn't McCabe. It wasn't Bilko, either. I didn't know who it was. He looked like Jack Nicholson – no, younger. Oddbod, but taller. That was it, a tall, adolescent Oddbod. His eyes roamed the workshop and fell on the pile of knives. He licked his lips.

I was sweating.

'Is Mr McCabe here?' he said, slowly. He sounded like he had memorised the question.

'He's not in here, mate,' I said. 'Have you tried the house?'

He came closer and started prodding near the grinder.

'You'd better not touch that,' I said. 'It's a hair trigger.'

'Is Mr McCabe here?' he said.

I gathered up the knives and placed them behind an oil drum in the corner, taking care not to damage the blades. We'd had a few Youth Opportunities kids coming round. Time wasters. This boy was something else entirely. I'd noticed the lump in the top of his forehead. It was like a baby's fist with a ladder of stitches in it. Post-op. I wasn't taking any chances.

'Have you tried the house?' I said. The door was on the other side of the workshop. Having put the knives out of reach, my aim was to get to it.

'I'm here for a job,' he said. 'They told me about a job.'

What were those fuckers down the DHSS thinking about? Fair enough, everyone was supposed to take care of everyone else, but what were they doing sending the likes of this to a farm? Didn't they realise it was a hazardous environment?

'The laddies are up the field,' I told him. 'Maybe Mr McCabe's waiting for you.' I managed to get to the door, and air. 'Come with me,' I said.

McCabe was round the side of the big shed, fixing a window that had recently had a ball kicked through it.

'Mr McCabe,' I said. 'Someone here to see you.' I didn't bother hanging around to explain anything. I knew nothing, and that's the way I wanted it to stay. I went back to the workshop. A minute later, McCabe marched in and started poking about on the bench.

'Dang things,' he said. 'Where are those blessed knives?'

'Eh?' I said. I'd just put them on top of the oil drum. McCabe spotted them. He picked one up and ran a thumb across the blade, like a true professional.

'That's a bit blooming sharp,' he said. 'I've told you before...'

Oddbod was in the doorway. McCabe handed him the knife.

'You have got to be joking,' I said.

'Folk come here to work,' said McCabe. 'Not to footer about.'

Oddbod began slashing at shadows. I gave him plenty of room. 'Mr McCabe,' I said. 'I really think you should reconsider.'

'Not at all,' he said. 'He'll be careful. Look, he's a fully grown man.'

I was left to get on with it. I leaned on the oil drum, thinking. I heard the Subaru getting fired up. A couple of seconds later it flashed past the window. I went outside. The yard was empty.

I'd been keeping myself to myself in the workshop. There was a lot of stuff that needed fixing, a lot more stuff than there had been the previous week. The summer was only three months long, and I knew it was in my interests to make myself invaluable. Unsackable. A lot of broken machinery was lying around. I'd broken most of it on the Monday when everyone was up at the field. McCabe just nodded when I told him about the dire state of affairs. 'It's a good job you lost your licence, then,' he said. 'Don't worry, I'll get Chas to do the driving.' He had warned me about oversharpening the knives; they were for cutting cabbages, but the laddies knew the risks. Chas, the only one who had facial hair that didn't look like a burst cushion, had shaved his chin with one of the thinner blades as the boys looked on jealously. They were more impressed with Chas's stubble than with my skills at the grinder, but that's teenagers for you. Working on the farm was something to keep them busy. More than that, it gave them thirty two quid to blow in the Auld Toll on Friday nights.

I was bored. I looked at the machinery.

There was a lawnmower that I'd told McCabe was well and truly knackered. All that was wrong with it was the spark plugs – I'd unscrewed them. And there was a disc harrows that needed greasing. As far as McCabe knew, the discs needed replacing. I'd told him I would save him a packet by sharpening them. His face had lit up. I still hadn't worked out how to remove them from the frame.

I was turning into a compulsive liar.

So what? It was only for the summer. Next year I would be in full time employment in a bank somewhere, wearing a suit and making a fortune. But there was something going on in the back of my mind, something to do with conscience. I didn't like lying. It had nothing to do with damnation and Hell, which were McCabe's points of reference, but I knew it wasn't right. Maybe I had spent too much time studying Philosophy; Philosophy loves hypocrisy, and McCabe was full of it. You could find him and his crowd down the precinct every Saturday morning outside Boots, giving it maximum New Testament Repent to the shoppers. It was difficult to tell who was the leader, McCabe or Sergeant Bilko. You wouldn't have wanted to sign up, it all looked very curious indeed. That was the point, though. It was a strange kind of proselytising. They were spreading the word, they were telling everyone about the Way, the Truth and the Life, but they didn't want you in their gang. The Bowhouse Brotherhood, that's what they were called. I don't know if that was their real name, but everyone in town called them that. They were famous. Notorious. Of course they were – the precinct was stowed at weekends. They used to bring their kids to work beside us. I'd been coming here since my first year at Uni, and there were always new faces. Young faces. They brought them here to instil the work ethic, while in the evenings Sergeant Bilko introduced them to the adolescent delights of Famous Grouse at McCabe's house, a grand old pile round the back of the workshop. An infidel breaking bread in front of them was not to be countenanced. They ate on their own at dinnertime. McCabe once went into a spasm

Fiction/053

when I opened a crisp poke next to him.

The Subaru was back in the yard. McCabe came into the workshop. I was blowing on a spark plug I'd just had time to pick up.

'How's it going with the repairs?' he said.

I tutted. 'Bit difficult, chief,' I said. 'But I'm getting there.'

'Good,' he said. 'Eh, can you come with me a minute?' He took me to the far end of the yard. 'There's something wrong with this,' he said. It was the John Deere. Nothing to do with me, nothing malicious, at least. It needed diesel. It had been needing diesel since Friday, when I parked it. I climbed inside and turned the key in the ignition. The fuel gauge said 'E'.

'Just leave it to me,' I said. 'I'll fix it.'

The laddies were playing football next to the shed. It looked strenuous. The grass was up to their knees. I noticed that iron bars had been fitted over the window. Chas was sitting on the roof of the diesel tank, smoking.

'You want to watch that,' I said.

'What?' he said. 'Diesel isnae flammable.'

'Not that,' I said. 'You're supposed to be driving.'

Chas laughed. He put the spliff to his lips and toked hard. He held it. He looked at the sky. It was getting cloudy. 'I think I'll take the afternoon off,' he said.

'Where's the new guy?' I said.

'What new guy?'

'The boy that came round this morning. I thought McCabe took him up the field.'

'He must have taken him up the Overflow,' said Chas. 'He didn't bring him anywhere near us.'

He had been left up there all by himself. He was probably one of those slow lunatics who did whatever you told them until you told them to stop. Or broke them. Like a machine. Whatever. It wasn't my problem. I went back to the workshop. I was flicking through an old copy of the Sun when Chas staggered in, giggling. He sat on the floor in front of the oil drum and got his tobacco pouch out of his trousers.

'Two spliffs at dinner time?' I said. 'Are you going for the record?'

'Me?' he said. 'No, I'm a Scotsman reader, me.' He burst out laughing then got back to building his joint.

Footsteps in the yard. I looked out the window. 'Hey up,' I said. Chas ran into the toilet and stuck his head under the tap. McCabe was examining the Subaru. He gave each tyre a perfunctory kick, then looked over at the workshop. At me. I turned to see Chas lying on his back in front of the oil drum, his arms and legs splayed out. He was making stuttering noises in the back of his throat.

McCabe walked in. 'What's wrong with you?' he said.

'I had a dodgy Pot Noodle,' said Chas.

McCabe looked at me. 'A what?' he said. At first I thought he was joining in the banter, but banter wasn't his style, not with the likes of us. Maybe he was, actually, unaware of the existence of Pot Noodles. I knew televisions were anathema to him, he'd probably never seen a commercial in his life. Well maybe accidentally, down the precinct; Radio Rentals was round the corner from Boots. But didn't his lot go shopping? Right enough, shopping was women's work. They seemed to have that kind of thing worked out.

'It's dehydrated food particles,' I said. Chas made a small yelping noise. He tried to turn it into a groan. I managed to keep a straight face. 'Loads of salt,' I said, 'something which, as you know, is really unhealthy.'

'It jolly well looks like it,' said McCabe. 'He'd better take the afternoon off. Clear a space for him up the back there.' He looked at his watch. 'I haven't had my dang lunch yet,' he said. He looked at Chas. 'Don't worry,' he said. 'I'll drive the laddies back to the field.'

Chas coughed at the ceiling. 'Thank you, sir,' he said.

I ducked into the toilet and turned on the tap. Hopefully, it covered the sound of my laughter.

I didn't clear a space for him. I watched him skin up. We spent the afternoon shooting the shit, until we heard footsteps in the yard. We knew it wasn't McCabe. He didn't drag his feet. It was Oddbod. He stood in the doorway. He was grinning. He had the knife in his hand, buffing it up on the leg of his jeans. 'I cut myself,' he said. He showed me. The back of his left hand, all the way across to the base of his thumb, was hanging open like a tin of salmon. A ripe bead of blood plopped onto the workshop floor. The dust hissed.

'Jesus Christ,' said Chas.

'You shouldn't say that,' said Oddbod. Metal scraped denim. 'You shouldn't take the Lord's name in vain.' McCabe had wasted no time with the brainwashing, it seemed. Whatever, I wasn't going to argue with him.

'Have you looked at your hand?' said Chas. 'The Lord would be taking his own name in vain if he saw that.'

'I cut myself,' he said. He sounded proud, like he'd just passed an induction test instead of proving what a useless bastard he was.

'You'll be needing a jag,' said Chas. I was impressed. Despite the two joints, he was still capable of connected thought. Oddbod raised his hand to his nose and sniffed the wound. Then he licked himself. 'I've seen dogs do that,' said Chas.

'If you want to lay the knife on the bench,' I said. Oddbod did as he was told. Of course he did. 'Come on,' I said. 'We'll see if McCabe's in. He'll take you up the hospital.'

'Aye, get it seen to,' said Chas. 'Before Lobotomy sets in.'

'Eh?' said Oddbod.

'Come on,' I said. Oddbod was smiling a lot, but I didn't want to find out how far his sense of humour went.

We walked round to the house. I'd seen lots of cuts on the farm. I'd suffered a few myself. I knew the score. The dull thud, the shock, then, after a few seconds, the blood. It was when the bleeding stopped that the pain started. His hand must have been gowping.

A car passed us in the driveway. It glided to a halt in the parking space. Sergeant Bilko got out. He clocked the boy, then the hand. 'What the blazes happened to you?' he said.

'We've had a bit of an accident,' I said, and was ignored. Oddbod's shoulder was gripped and he was pushed up to the door. Bilko rattled the knocker.

After a moment, McCabe's head appeared, immersed in a halo of soup fumes. 'Alec!' he said. 'Blessings to ye.'

'And to you, Graham,' said Bilko. 'Sorry to get you up from your lunch. Scotch broth?'

'Aye,' said McCabe. 'The woman makes a rare pot.'

'Though not Pot Noodle,' I said, and was ignored.

'Anyway,' said Alec. Sergeant Bilko. He jerked a thumb at Oddbod. 'Have you seen the state of this?'

McCabe stepped outside. 'Aye,' he said. 'It's another of these DHSS referrals.' He shook his head. 'One tries to do the decent thing.'

'It's Brother Daniel's laddie,' said Bilko. 'Didn't he phone you?'

It took me a second to get it. McCabe seemed to be struggling. He scratched his head then patted the linen napkin that was hanging from the throat of his shirt. There was still no mention of a first aid box. Protection from soup stains and positive employee identification seemed to be more important than industrial injury of a criminally negligent bent. 'Well, I'll be...' he smiled. 'The last time I saw this yin he was sitting on a po!'

Oddbod raised his hand to his mouth and licked the flap of meat.

'Holy God in heaven!' said McCabe, and reeled back against the door jamb. It was at this point that my presence in the company was acknowledged; my employer's eyes.

'Now, now,' I said. 'No need to take the Lord's name in vain.' Oddbod nodded, which I found encouraging. I was in need of allies. I could see where this was going.

'You cheeky...!' said McCabe. 'I... I told you about those knives. I've been telling you for weeks!'

'Oh, come, now, Mr McCabe,' I said. 'I've only been on the grinder since Monday.'

'You know what I mean!' he said.

'I take it you're the student,' said Bilko. 'You mouthy young so and so. I've heard about you.'

'Indeed,' I said. 'And we've all heard about you.' I swear his glasses steamed up when I said

Fiction/055

that. Maybe it was the soup fumes.

McCabe made to put his hand on Oddbod's shoulder, but stopped short before contact was effected. His front teeth were nibbling furiously on a stubborn grain of barley. 'Suffer the little children to come unto me,' he said. 'Mark 10:14,' he added, his voice trembling.

Sergeant Bilko Hmmm-Hmmm, Hmmm-Hmmmed his endorsement.

'Aye,' I said, 'And too many cooks spoil the soup.' It wasn't quite the non-sequitur I was going for, but it did the trick. The conversation was over. McCabe, his napkin flapping, ushered Oddbod into the sanctuary of the house, and Savlon. Bilko followed. The door slammed shut in my face.

McCabe knew I was lippy. That's why he employed me. I was a foil for his biblically barbed comments, he regarded me as a challenge. But was being cheeky a sacking offence? It all came down to who exactly Brother Daniel was, and McCabe's relationship with him. Could he risk sacking me? Any idiot could learn how to sharpen a knife, maybe even Oddbod, but I was the only one on the farm who knew how to fix the broken machinery. By the end of the afternoon, there was a lot more of it. Most of it was lying in bits, strewn over the area in front of the oil drum; Chas had, in the end, decided to go home. The damage was rather more substantial than loose spark plugs.

Who was I kidding? The problem – the real problem – was that I was beginning to believe my own lies.

Oddbod's knife was on the bench. I gave it a good wash under the tap. I pressed On and pushed the blade into the wheel. It didn't scream; it didn't even squeal. It whined. It was still sharp. Sharp as a razor. Too sharp by half.

# Extract from the novel *Ramshackle*
## Elizabeth Reeder

MONDAY

'I tried to wake you,' Linden's note reads in the morning. 'I've got an early class, but I'll pick you up from school.'

The rug just inside the door is wet, like she's gone out and come back and the snow-shake off her boots has melted. She's been down to the lake. The new snow, the wind, the rough water. All of it icy and unhelpful.

There's a pot of coffee waiting for me.

'P.S. Don't forget to eat something.'

Food is the last thing I want. But I know she's right. It's what you do in the morning. I make two BLTs. I slide one into my school bag for lunch and take the other one with coffee to the living room so I can watch the lake. The bread sticks to the roof of my mouth, the coffee helps, its bitterness is just right.

In Chemistry I'm stuck with spotty Scott. He sits too close. Food in his teeth. Breath rank with breakfast and dinner and plaque. Big spots, pus-heads. He's ugly and that's gross, but the problem is he's dumb. With a capital D. Dumb.

I try not to talk with him at all. I'm aware that last year he evacuated the building with his mistake in biology. I can't even comprehend what you could do with a dead frog that would cause mass hysteria. He managed it. He's a mistake of biology.

His stiff fingers crowd the test tubes. His grin has a bit of bread in it.

I try not to breathe in but I do try to stop him from pouring the contents of one tube into the other. When I don't succeed, I'm the first one to the door.

There are no flames but plenty of smoke and fumes and the main alarm goes off. Four fire engines arrive. We're out back on the track field. Freezing. There's got to be some law against this. But it's not a drill. It's the real thing. A few kids nip down to smoke some cigarettes by the train station or swig from hipsters behind the goal posts. The explosion has flushed Jess out of gym and she's standing by the corner of the building with her hips pushed right up close to Kevin. I don't see his girlfriend but I know exactly where this is headed. Jess is always the other girl. It's almost like she seeks it out. Like it's a requirement. 'Boyfriend wanted, must have sexy car and blond girlfriend. Catastrophic break-up imminent.'

I scan and find Quiz, he's standing with some rugby buddies.

'Hey, Roe.' He's non-committal.

'Hey, Quiz.' I give a single sway to my hips, raise my hand towards his pals, 'John. Chris.'

'Hiya, Roe.'

Quiz reaches out his hand. I take it. He rubs my arm with the other. 'See you later guys,' he says. And we walk out towards the far side of the field.

'It was my lab partner who did this.'

'No kidding?'

'I couldn't stop him. He guarded the phials with his zits and laughed this hideous, maniacal laugh.'

'Well, you got me out of Math. So I thank you.'

The bells ring, on and off, and we have

to go back in. We can't go back to the lab, it's still a bit too toxic. They herd us would-be chemists into the auditorium and we get an ad hoc and non-specific talk about safety. About one partner looking out for the other. I shove a finger up and down first towards spotty Scott and then towards Ms Clunes who really should know better than to chastise her strongest student in front of the whole class for the quite reasonable action of not putting herself between her psycho lab partner and his death wish.

'Okay kids.'

We all hate it when he calls us that. Today Mr R pauses, looks at us. I wonder what he sees. He's looking like he's been dragged through shrubs backwards.

'Today, we're going to talk about...' He licks his lips, runs his hands through his hair, when his fingers get jammed a bit, he pushes on through. Second time they run smooth. 'I've been thinking about space. About how every space, every place, has its natural order. Where the molecules are in their natural state. Every time you or I move in space, we displace the natural order. Every time you move, you stir things up.'

Mr R has a theory for everything, it's not really a Communications class, it's a make it up by the seat of your pants philosophy class.

'What about light? Does that change the natural state?' Overenthusiastic Freddie doesn't raise his hand, just jumps in. Today Mr R doesn't mind. We're witnessing a new world order.

'Good question.' He pauses, his eyes steady on us all, yet flicking, absent between words. 'Let's say a room is dark. A light slices across. What is displaced?'

Silence.

'Has anything physically changed?'

'Yes. The whole room is transformed.' Freddie again.

'But physically altered?'

Sandy, the science geek, 'Yes, light is energy.'

'Sure,' says Mr R, 'Yes and no. It passes through but does not take up any room. Any space. It simply affects the molecules that are already there.'

'But it alters our perceptions.'

'Exactly.'

'What if it heats them up?' Sandy again.

'Well, then I suppose that's a bit different. The same molecules get excited, then calm down. But once the light, the heat, is gone, they remain the same as they were before.'

Place. Space. Displacement.

So I'm sitting there thinking that everything we do is bound to upset this world. To throw out of whack what is perfect without us. What a load of crap. Natural order has to be active, to account for all the life about us.

'Aren't presence and movement part of order, a living order?' I suggest.

'In an ideal world, Roe, that might be the case. The truth of the matter is that absence is presence. That's the reality of it. It restores what has been upset and disrupted. What has become disrupted. Sometimes for years.'

'So if we all left right now,' smart-alec James, 'then it'd be okay because it'd be the way things are supposed to be?'

Mr R looks out the window, at an unpeopled expanse of mazed sidewalks and frozen grass, his hand plays at the muscles of his jaw and then follows the bone and then the red brown wiry hair to the end of his lumberjack beard. He twirls some beard-hair between his index finger and thumb. His eyes, well, they're not here anyway.

We're all silent. I've never seen an adult come apart before. But this is it. His actions are empty and watery.

'You know people who never just stay in one place? Those people who never try to work it out but they just flee? Well, it's better that they go. It replaces the natural order.'

I look at his left hand, an indentation at the base of his ring finger. The ring gone, he's had his natural state reinstated.

It's just like with keys. Lock and key and how we think they make things whole when they come together, but what if it's just the opposite, the lock is whole, a complete entity on its own and the key invades, pushes the molecules into unnatural spaces, tumbler and pin, and turns it.

But what if the natural order is with the two of you there? Right there. And when one goes, the air invades, displaces and everything is off kilter, unnatural. Space as the invading presence? As the opposite of the state of grace?

'Hmmm,' starts sweet-faced, but tricky as a fox, Missy McLaughlin who leads the field hockey team to victory after victory with her underhand tactics, 'What does this have to do with communication?'

'It's about its breakdown,' Mr R says.

And before the bell, which is just sound and not presence, invades this space, and before this opportunity reverts to the reality of a normal class, all twenty-two of us slide out of our chairs and into the perfectly balanced, waiting hall.

My locker is a mess. My jeans are too tight, my hair just looks like shit. My locker has one pile of papers and hard folders leaning to the left, on top of that another leans to the right and then my running gear is crammed in the mini-compartment up top, my shoes bending unnaturally every time I have to shove the door closed. I lean my head against the chaos. The bell rings and the world is loud behind me. Everyone moving. I can't get my feet to go. Who cares?

I spend lunch in an empty classroom and then it's onto history. My maps suck and at the end of another class full of dates and mind-numbing facts, Mr Pavich hands out the tests we took on Friday. Every test but mine. The bell rings. 'Miss Davis, will you stay after class please? The rest of you can go.'

Jess elbows me on her way out, her A+ test smug in her hands. 'Uh-oh.'

'Up to my desk,' he says, pointing a finger at me and then crumpling it in towards his nasty little chin.

'You can't seem to see the boundaries, Roe. It's a real problem.' He pauses, for the drama of the moment, 'It's easy, these countries are one thing and then they're another. They can't be more than one thing at time.'

That's me all over. A problem with borders, with boundaries.

'You can't just make it up,' he continues, small pinched face, greasy grey hair, linear pea-brain.

Why? Why can't I? This isn't history. It's making silly lines on a piece of paper. Where's anything that matters? Where are the people? The passions? Where's the history?

He turns the test over, slowly, like a flag unfurling.

F —. In red. Nearly covers the whole page.

His mean beady eyes on me, creepy, full of misplaced power: I'm not just bad at this, I'm atrocious; I don't even belong on the academic scale. It's on the table between us. He's relishing it. Stating the obvious.

F —.

A made-up grade for a girl who makes things up.

'You'll need to have your parents sign this, to prove to me they know exactly what you're up to.'

'I don't have a mom.'

But this doesn't faze Pavich. He doesn't want to hear it. Doesn't matter. Countries go to war, entire towns wiped out. A line moves. What do my petty problems matter? These maps are important. I should prioritize.

I want to say, my dad's missing. I can't get you the signature you want. I want it to matter, make a difference. But it doesn't. Things explode, wives leave, teachers go off the rails, dads abandon their posts.

The former Yugoslavia, the former USSR, the former me.

'Sure thing.'

'You better study extra hard for the test on Wednesday.'

'Harder than I've ever studied for anything in my life. From this point on my life is empty of everything but lines on a map.'

'Glad to hear it.'

Irony missed.

As I leave the room, I feel him watching my ass, the nazi, fascist perv. Outside the door, Jess leans with her back against the row of lockers. Her legs crossed casually at the ankles, her stomach bare. I flip the test paper out towards her.

'No way.'

Fiction/059

'Yes, way.'
'I didn't know you could get an F minus.'
'You can't, Jess. He's just making a point. The creep.'
'He's not that bad.'
'Your talent blinds you to the facts.'
'You want to ditch 9th period and go to Carl's?'
'Can't. My aunt Linden's picking me up and we're going shopping.'
'Is she still staying at your house?'
'Yup. Her pipes burst. She needed a place to stay until they're fixed. Can't get a plumber until Thursday.'
Dad will be back by then.
'Call me later.'
'Of course. What are you going to do?'
'Nothing.'
And I know this nothing is called Kevin.

Linden has tried to clean herself up. I know that. Beneath her parka, which she opens as soon as we're inside the police station, she's got on black baggy trousers, a push-up bra, a small sweater and the ends of the shirt hang down below it. Her hair smells of smoke when I hug her. And her fingers are a mess. Black underneath the nails. I hold one hand, turn it palm up and then back again.

'I forgot my nail brush sweetie. Surely it won't matter.'

As soon as we enter, Quiz's mom, Officer Berg crosses the room towards us and I know the chain of events to come. She looks stiffer in full police uniform, a lump of panic sticks in my throat. Linden has no idea who she is.

'We'd like to file a missing person's report,' Linden says.

'Who's gone?'

'My brother, her dad.'

Mrs Berg looks at me. I smile. Inanely. How inappropriate can my responses be? 'Linden, this is Quiz's mom. Mrs Berg, this is my aunt Linden.'

'Quiz didn't mention this to me.'

Linden looks at me. Mrs Berg looks at me. 'He doesn't know,' I say.

Her tone softens and she becomes more business-like and yet more like a mom, more like the woman I've met a few times before, usually in the Berg kitchen. She directs her questions at me, which I'm grateful for. 'Since when?'

'Since Friday night.'

'Who saw him last?'

'Me.'

'What time?'

'Around midnight. He kissed me goodnight.'

'Anything strange about that night? Or the week before? Has he seemed under stress or done anything out of character?'

My chest is clasped hands. Sudden.

I raise my eyes slowly. 'I didn't notice anything.'

I will not cry. I will not cry. Linden weaves her hand through mine. Lock and key.

My dad knows how to make the spaces within locks fit into any shape, he can change the shape at will. My hands slot into his perfectly anytime. *Berwyn. Doors open on the left at Berwyn.* Which state is the natural, the right state?

'Did he leave a note?'

'Nope.'

'What did he take with him?'

'Boots. A big coat, a hat. His wallet. His lockpicking equipment, I think. Some keys.'

Mrs Berg leans over in confidence, smiles. 'I locked myself out of the car once, and was late for my after-school run. On his way to help me, he picked Quiz up from school. He's good at what he does,' she says.

'He often goes out after dark and practices picking these difficult old locks he keeps just for this purpose. He practices opening them without light. He says it keeps him sharp.'

Mrs Berg smiles, but it's a short one. Then she turns to Linden. Sharply. Both hands flat on the counter, all business.

'Is this the first time he's done something like this?'

'Of course it is.' I say.

Linden shifts. Unfolds her hand from mine. Looks at me and then at Mrs Berg.

'No, it isn't. He's done this before,' says Linden. I see the side of her face, it's crumpled up.

'What?' My voice is shrill. Loud. 'What are you talking about, he's never, he's always been right here. This isn't like him, not at all.'

Linden steps in closer, all her attention on me. I bat her hand away.

'Roe, honey. He used to. In his teens and twenties. I've not known how to tell you.'

'What? But I've never... That doesn't matter. It doesn't mean anything. He's not done a thing like this since he had me.'

'That's not exactly true.'

My lips are a hard-line. My arms crossed.

'When you were small, a toddler, he brought you over to my apartment. Middle of the night, with an overnight bag, diapers. I mean, you were still small, a baby. He handed you to me, and put the keys to his house on my hall table, in case I needed anything.'

My chest isn't tight, it's a fortress.

'He said he'd be gone a day. He was gone nearly two weeks.'

I don't believe her. Can't believe her. 'My dad never did that.'

'Sweetie. I'm not saying this to hurt you.' She doesn't move any closer, but her tone is more apologetic, intimate when she continues, 'Roe, that wasn't the only time.'

I can't think. Not just one time? Other times? What other times? I blink. Look from one face to another. I'm sweating beneath my coat, my hands are stiff, a muscle running down my back is burning, throbbing.

Linden continues, 'The police need to know this, the more the police know, the better they'll be able to do their jobs. The sooner he'll be home.'

Linden's never been anything but honest to me. Her tells: when she touches her face, when she takes an extra second and breathes deep. She does neither.

'Roe, honey. Why don't you go get a soda? I'm going to talk to Linden for a while.'

'Or you can stay Roe. It's your choice.' Linden doesn't look at Mrs Berg, she looks at me. She isn't a mom. It's not her role to protect me from the facts, she knows this. 'I'm sorry Roe. I should have said earlier. I didn't know how.'

My head goes down, my hair in front of my face. Something's damaged. He's gone and we need to find him. The metal edged counter, the sound of phones, the cleanness of the lines of the uniforms, Mrs Berg's good intentions, Linden's guilt and worry. I don't want to hear anymore.

'I think I'll go to Carl's and get something to drink.'

Linden gives me no warning and has me in a hug. Light and quick so I can't react. Photo chemicals cling to her hair. I hear her rough hands on my coat. I unfold her arms from around me, hold her hands.

'You need to take care of your hands,' I say. 'They're a mess.'

'I know.' She smiles and tells me what I know she has to: 'Roe, I've had to call Duncan and Mel. They'll be at the house when we get back.'

My Uncle Duncan, the world's most anally organized oaf and his slow food gardening wife, the lovely I-had-a-lapse-in-judgment-when-I-married-him Mel.

'You sure are on a roll with the bad news.'

She laughs. 'I promise he won't be there for long.'

My buttons slide one after the other through the eyes of my coat. I pull up my collar and walk out into the cold.

*Ramshackle* by Elizabeth Reeder will be published by Freight Books in April 2012

# Watching Wild Parrots in San Francisco
**Brian Docherty**

*'Autumn in California is a mild*
*And anonymous season'*
(Kenneth Rexroth)

In this quasi-Mediterranean Autumn,
tables talk to trees; trees call to fishing boats,
Bermuda-rigged yachts, or any other vessel
not made of fibreglass but honest wood.
According to the latest tele-historian,
America is the world's 68th Empire.

He does not explain how he counted
those flourishing before the last Ice Age,
just deploys the logic of late capitalism;
if we can see it, count it, expropriate it,
the world must exist for our benefit,
but as Pliny the Elder learned in his trireme

off Pompeii, perspective is what matters
when you interpret the bigger picture
as waves or hills; if you are safely ashore
observing waves through a window,
or glimpsing hills through a dancing porthole,
either way they should be blue & smooth.

Either or both will change if you get closer
to that distant ambiguity or ideal form;
but once you get up close and personal,
perspective & objectivity vanish like the birds
sporting themselves among the wall of green
promising Summer will stay a little longer this year.

Then I remember I am in North Beach;
the natives think July & August cold here,
December is wet enough to mime Glasgow
where that red & green explosion of parrots
would be a mere mirage, not the local fauna
defending their territory or advertising for a mate.

# Summer
**Julian Colton**

Summer is not the black crow's natural habitat
More the Black-headed Gull

Returned from breeding grounds
Black Sea and Volga

Winter's brittle grey trees
Thickened by green landscape brush

Slow to leaf
Uncertain, tremulous patches

Hover flies with ink
Spot laden heads
Bear no decipherable text

But circle above the dewy grass
Revel in the moister heat

Where spring and summer
Have no clear demarcation

This smudged Scottish season
A matter of a few raised degrees

Tilting of the Poles
Earth's latitude sun proximity

Light the bats' eyes impulse to mate
Crucible smelt possibilities.

Animal, vegetable and human
Cannot resist the temporary inward draw

June's fully-opened solstice lens
On to Autumn's squinting aperture.

# Sour Jewel
**Andy Jackson**

*i.m. Billy Mackenzie*

I think it was the bustle of the place
that did for me, the record shop
oblivious, impersonal, that voice
above the local noise, here a joyful skip

and swoop, there the grating edge of teeth.
*Billy's gone* I heard. *The stupid sod
has done it.* No doubting such a truth
when all you knew of him said

this was how he'd always meant to go.
Surely he was asking for it, crooning
*Gloomy Sunday* down at Fat Sam's, grey
clouds round the baby grand, brewing

retribution in the belly of a double bass.
He'd done the city thing, there and back,
and back again. He left behind the house
he'd never known, the loaded deck

that dealt him aces, all of which he'd fold.
Somewhere there must be that feral
out-take from the studio, the wild
and lonely *dies irae* sung as a recessional,

his steep falsetto rise let off the leash,
foreshortened by the accidental melting
of the precious piece of vinyl, out of reach,
a limited edition, perhaps the only pressing.

# Dignity
**Andy Jackson**

Give me a pear from the blue bowl, Jane.
Give me five a day, for old time's sake.
Peel me a grape, disembowel a fig.
Let fruit be waiting when I wake.

Pour me a glass of the finest, Jane.
Wine with the strength to dismember the speech
We need them to know our intemperance.
A glass of Ribena. Sex On The Beach.

Play me a song from your canon, Jane.
Strum like you strummed on our days on the loose.
Sing of the world we found no way to live in,
songs of the shotgun, the razor, the noose.

Write down the words we agreed on, Jane.
Remember, they'll look for the flaws in your hand,
so keep it compact, don't sketch in the margin,
and never give reasons. They won't understand.

Hold onto my hand. It is time, Jane.
Set down your drink. It will never grow cold.
Our eyes may stay open. Our lungs may not rattle.
No closing music. No credits to roll.

Give me a pear from the blue bowl, Jane.
Give me five a day, for old time's sake.
Peel me a grape, disembowel a fig.
Let someone be waiting when we awake.

# Extract from *Buddha: A Novel*
## Kevin MacNeil

1

I offer at the end of this, my last human life, the story of how I came to reveal the nature of the universe for the benefit of all sentient beings.

Truth takes many forms; the road of truth has but two pitfalls. This is the tale they tell of my conception. My mother, Queen Mayadevi of the Clan Sakyamuni, had a strange dream the night I was conceived. She dreamed that four kings from other clans entered her bedchamber and with a solemn bow raised her bed to shoulder height and carried her off towards the Himalayas. When they reached the Manosila tableland they lay down her bed and their own clan queens led her to the glittering lake called Anotatta. There they bathed my mother in its refreshing waters; it is said that the waters in this lake are wondrous and can remove all human stains.

The four queens dressed my mother and anointed her with sweet and subtle perfumes and placed yellow flowers in her hair. My mother, whose name Mayadevi meant 'goddess of illusion', so radiantly beautiful she was, looked about her. She saw a bal tree seven leagues high and a silver mountain on top of which sat a golden mansion. And she saw a golden mountain from which a gleaming white elephant descended.

The queens prepared an ornate bed for my mother and she lay down upon it. Approaching from the north, calm and steady in its movements, came the great elephant, with a smooth dreamy clamber, a perfect white lotus clutched in its trunk. The elephant circled my mother's bed sunwise three times, trumpeting with a huge and majestic roar. He locked eyes with my mother for a moment then gently penetrated her side with a tusk, which did not pain her at all, but suffused her body with a feeling of warmth and completion.

The road of truth has but two pitfalls. This is the story they tell of my gestation.

My mother had no morning sickness. Indeed, so unusual was my gestation that to some who gazed upon my mother's swollen belly I was visible like a jewel in the twilight. Others went further and said they could see me, all of my limbs formed, for the full nine (some say ten) months. My mother bore me with great tenderness, like oil in a bowl.

The road of truth has but two pitfalls. This is the story they tell of my birth.

My mother, Queen Maya, asked my father if she may travel to the city of Devadaha, so she could give birth to me in her hometown. The journey was long and hot and my mother had her retinue stop awhile at Lumbini Park so she could rest in the shade of the sal trees. In a grove thrumming with bees and burbling with birdsong, she reached up to a branch – which bent down to meet her hand. As she touched the tree, or the tree touched her, she felt deep pangs within and soon she gave birth to a son. Two sparkling waterfalls – one warm one cool – rushed gently down from the sky and cleansed me. Just as a gem will not smear a cloth nor a cloth smear a gem – why would they? – so my body was naturally unsullied. Before any human hands could touch me I stood upright on a lotus flower that had miraculously sprung from the earth.

So they say. Well. Question everything, I say. The story I offer you here is true and I transmit it with words, symbols, silences.

Question everything because three things cannot be hidden for long: the sun, the moon and the truth.

Why do I offer you my story? To reveal here and now the truth. Of the nature of the universe. For the benefit of all sentient beings.

2

Question everything. With truth there are only two mistakes one can make. Yes; the road of truth has but two pitfalls: not starting and not going all the way. (The last time someone said to *me* 'Question everything' I gave a half-smile and said: 'Why?')

I questioned the stories people told of my birth and gestation. What I know for certain is that my mother bore me with great tenderness like oil in a bowl and she gave birth to me in Lumbini Park on Friday the 15th of June, being that month's Full Moon Day.

My father, King Suddhodhana, was as delighted at my birth as he was soon to be heartbroken. He believed, even before the old ascetic Asita told him so, that I was to be a great figure in history. He was confident I was destined to be a great warrior.

I am not a great warrior. I love peace. Serenity. Compassion. Freedom. Wisdom. And as for death; I have overcome death.

Give me any reasonable person who is honest and decent and straightforward and I will give him or her the truth. Of the nature of the universe. For the benefit. Of all. Sentient beings.

3

They say even as a newborn child I was lustruous and steadfast as the sun, that I held people's gaze like the moon. My father, King Suddhodana, named me Siddhartha, meaning 'wish fulfilled'. Prince Siddhartha Gautama. Back at the grand clan residence, my mother and father doted on me. I was a little miracle, with a radiant gravity of my own.

Well, this is true of all children.

Meanwhile that strange old ascetic descended from the hills to which he had long since retreated. When he reached Kapilavastu, he begged to see the newborn child. The proud King and Queen granted Asita his wish and when he set eyes on me his reaction was not at all what they had expected.

He burst into tears.

My mother and father exchanged glances as the supposedly wise man howled and shuddered and wept.

At last Asita regained some composure and my father demanded to know the meaning of his impertinent behaviour.

'King Suddhodhana, Queen Mayadevi. My eyes flooded with tears because your son will be the greatest being this world has seen.'

I can picture how my father beamed. How his eyes glinted with a hungry pride. 'Yes,' he said. 'My son shall rule the world. Armies will tremble at the sound of his name.' His tone changed. 'Why,' he barked, 'is that a cause for sadness? You ought to be showering blessings on my son, not crying over him like a crazed person.'

'I am crying,' said Asita, 'because your son will attain Buddhahood, Enlightenment shall be his, and I – I shall not live to see it. Mine is the grief of an old man who will not hear the teachings of this *Buddha-to-be*.' He flung himself to the floor. 'I do not bless the child, I ask the Buddha-to-be for *his* blessings.'

'My son shall be a great warrior,' said the King. 'An emperor!'

Kapilavastu was a minor territory and 'King' really meant 'Chief'.

'King Suddhodhana,' said Asita. 'Your son will be more than a mere emperor. He will escape samsara, the cycle of birth and death. He will transcend suffering. He will find and reveal The Way to Enlightenment itself. He will reach the shore which has no other shore. He will unlock the secrets of the universe, he will embody ineffable wisdom and infinite compassion and he will offer to show others The Way. I will not be alive to see such a marvel in this lifetime.' A fresh burst of tears broke through Asita and shook him bodily.

'Dry your snivelling face,' said King Suddhodhana. 'The Prince, just as my Brahmins have decreed, will be a great emperor. His name will live forever. He will enjoy a reputation that is feared from horizon to horizon.'

The Queen said nothing. She took my little finger in her hand and kissed it. She had a smile on her face which some say was the blissful indulgent smile of a first-time mother and which others say was the smile of one who knows a great secret.

Seven days after she gave birth to me, my mother died.

4

Seven days after she gave birth to me my mother who bore me with great tenderness like oil in a bowl collapsed and died. The entire clan plunged headlong into sorrow, much of it genuine.

The loss of his favourite partner stultified the King. My father's grief was like a sickness of mind and body. He took to his bed for three days and nights. Sometimes he lay motionless like the corpse of an elephant neither eating nor blinking. At other times he thrashed like a young tiger that has been speared multiple times. He clawed at the pillows and he scratched at his own face and he flailed as if he were fighting himself.

Just when his Brahmins were beginning to fear he had lost his mind, he hurled the bedcovers away and leaped out of bed. He had about him a refreshed air and a sense of purpose as when a village emerges gleaming and resolute, washed clean by a terrible storm. In a loud, steady voice he announced that his late wife's sister, Maha Prajapati, would now assume the role of mother to me.

They say when she heard these words her breasts at once grew swollen with sweet milk. (How do they know the milk was sweet?)

'My son,' King Suddhodhana declared, 'shall be spared suffering. His mother's death shall not be in vain. She has suffered that Siddhartha may not. The Prince shall have a carefree childhood. You will see to it that he is joyous.' He looked around meaningfully. 'Joyous. Or else.'

And so with servants and jewels and silks and all sorts of freedoms and confinements my father, filled to bursting with the kindest and proudest of intentions, almost ruined me.

5

My father tried to ruin me with kindness and ambition and anxiety. He announced: 'No harm shall come to my little boy who shall one day be feared and respected by friends and enemies alike. The Prince will bring everlasting glory, his achievements will illumine the Sakya clan, people in lands yet unknown will tremble at the very mention of Siddhartha Gautama.'

Poor Dad.

He created three lily ponds for me at his main residence. Blue lilies flowered in one, red lilies in another and in the third white lilies blossomed. Their lovely colours and shapes transfixed me and it is a wonder to me that I never fell into the water and drowned. Looking back, I see that even then these astonishing flowers were seeding themselves in my contemplations.

My tunic, cloak and undergarments were made of the finest Benares cloth. Day and night, a white sunshade was held above me so that heat and dust might not inconvenience me. I was not allowed to leave the palace compound. My father had his men build three houses for me – one for the Winter, one for the Summer and one for the monsoon season. I dined on the best meat and rice and the servants made do with thin lentil soup and broken rice.

Time passed as a jug fills, drop by drop, and in these overprivileged circumstances I grew and despite these overprivileged circumstances I grew tall and handsome and well-mannered and thoughtful. I endeared myself to everyone.

Almost everyone. I had a cousin whose hatred for me was like a fire that constantly threatens to blaze out of control, deceptive even when simmering quietly warm as true friendship.

I did my best to ignore his half-hidden

contempt and concentrated instead on my education. I excelled at all the traditional arts and sciences: astrology, archery, horsemanship, mathematics, languages, wrestling and charioteering. I surpassed firstly my fellow pupils and latterly my teachers themselves. I never failed to pay my teachers due respect. I began to feel wise beyond my years.

My father's pride in me was a comfort and an embarrassment. I craved his approval and yet when he boasted about me in public it was as if a brief fever flushed through me.

Furthermore I sensed my cousin Devadatta's jealousy as a force that wanted to leap, like a destructive fire, from one place to another. I decided to be vigilant around him. He cast me baleful sideways glances when he thought I wasn't looking and even when he smiled at me I could see the latent animosity in his features. His uglymindedness threatened my serenity. I wondered how to remove this strange poison from my life. From his.

Thus what peace of mind I had was like the sky, deep and beautiful and blue and endless-seeming or it was like the sky, deep and dark and blank and endless-seeming.

6

When I was seven years old my father took me to a ploughing festival. The horns of his oxen were garlanded with white blossoms. As king, he made the first ceremonial churn of earth, his back gleaming in the sun. At midday a ploughing competition got underway. I laughed when one of the oxen sat stout on the cracked earth and refused to budge, blinking placidly at the farmer's frustrated pleading. But my interest began to wane in the heat. My attendants led me to a tree in whose shade they had prepared a couch. I sat down to rest.

After some time I realised that I was blending gently into a strange harmony with my surroundings. My breathing was slow and steady. I breathed in, my breath somehow knew it must turn, I breathed out. I had never thought about breathing before, what it is or why. I breathed in, my breath was neither entering nor leaving, I breathed out.

My body pressed down on the couch which accepted this human weight quite naturally. As my legs felt the silk in my tunic and the silk in my tunic felt the fabric of the couch, my legs seemed to be aware of themselves for the first time. I thought: *I am connected to everything. My leg connects to the tunic the tunic to the couch the couch to the ground the ground to the tree the tree to the sky the sky to the earth itself. What of everything above the sky? I am part of everything. I connect to everything. Everything connects to me.*

The question arose: *Who then am I?*

I did not know who I was. I sat there breathing steadily with my eyes half open. My mind was like a vast still lake which reflected slow clouds as they came and went, drifting in the blue. I did not know who I was and instead of frightening me this realisation afforded me a great sense of inner peace.

Time itself seemed to have floated away. When my attendants returned, they informed me that the ploughing festival was finished.

Shadows stretched over the park and it seemed to me the park had no more substance than the shadows. I smiled. I knew I had accomplished something, though I did not know what.

I had been everything and nothing at once. Curious.

# Windows
## Alison Irvine

MY HUSBAND HEARD it first. In bed one morning he said, 'Did you hear our new neighbour?'

'No.'

'Really?' He closed his eyes. 'Oh my god, oh my god, oh my god!'

'Loud?'

'Loud? It was incredible. You're a light sleeper, I'm surprised you didn't hear it. I mean she really went for it. What on earth was he doing that was so special?'

'Who knows? She might have been faking.'

He looked surprised. 'No, it didn't sound like she was faking. But she's certainly a screamer.'

He seemed a little awestruck, a little wound up.

That wasn't the end of it. As we ate breakfast I decided to ask if he'd ever been to bed with a screamer.

'Yes,' he said. 'As a matter of fact I have.'

This surprised me. It just did.

'What was she like exactly? How did she scream? Did you enjoy it?'

'Well,' he wriggled his eyebrows and pursed his lips, 'Well, the minute I entered her –' Did he say entered or did he say put it in? 'The minute I... she just went wild. Shrieking and screaming and moaning and thrashing about.'

I listened with interest.

'Actually, it was a bit distracting. I couldn't concentrate. It put me off my stroke.'

I tried to picture it.

'But let's not talk about past conquests,' he said. 'You're the one for me now. You're not a screamer are you darling?'

I shook my head and said, 'No, I don't suppose anyone hears us.'

Sex for us – we did do it – was like painting an egg. It became tricky, precise, dare I say it, functional. I never wanted to end up on my back on the bed afterwards, legs in the air, letting gravity help things along while he put the kettle on or read the newspaper. But I did. I used to call out 'bring me in a couple of biscuits with my tea, will you darling?' I also criticised him a lot. I used to study him and wish he'd take the scissors to his nose hair.

I heard the screamer too, that night. I don't think I'd been asleep for long. I woke to her plump cries, her ripe shrieks and clearly saw a tree in my head, its branches stretched wide, stark against a purple sky. Sometimes her screams were regular and rhythmic and sometimes they were long, bumpy, ghost-ride cries that jiggled and bounced and stopped and started again. She made a tremendous performance of it all. Beneath those cries I heard his voice and it was a smooth sleek polished boot of a voice; young, full, puffed, pleasured. They went at it, the two of them, however they were doing it (I had the missionary position in my head but I suspect it wasn't that), and they sounded like music, like television; she screaming, he urging, she profaning, he grunting, until suddenly they stopped. Footsteps above. Murmurs. I rolled over and went back to sleep.

In the morning I asked my husband if he'd heard the screamer.

'I think they heard her in the Trossachs,' he said.

'Perhaps she has a new boyfriend, if they're doing it so often.'

'Well, it's heartening to note he doesn't last much longer than me,' my husband said.

Then he said, 'Did you find it erotic?'

I paused. 'Yes. Yes I did.'

I thought about what I'd said.

'Did you?' I asked him.

'Yes. Yes I did.'

We lay there, facing each other – his breath smelt, I'm sure mine did – until our dog scratched at the door. I got up to feed her. He got up to shower.

It was a Saturday so we decided we'd take a stroll then call in to the chemist. I needed more sticks to pee on. A friend said the sticks had worked for her but my doctor was sceptical. She said a sperm's journey to an egg was the equivalent of my husband swimming the channel and if we waited to have sex until the stick gave us the go ahead, the sperms might arrive too late and miss the egg altogether. Might they? I decided we'd get the sticks anyway. What did she know? She probably had kids. She probably got pregnant tying her shoelaces.

So we were leaving the flat, shutting the door to the block behind us.

'I want to get two newspapers this morning,' my husband was saying, 'because there's a free DVD in one and...'

And then we saw her on the street coming towards us. The screamer. In white furry boots. Her hair was black and she had a thick fringe that leaked below her eyebrows. She was so slight I wanted to feed her. She was a baby giraffe, a colt, a tiny young woman.

'Good for her,' my husband said.

'He must be her boyfriend.'

A young man walked alongside her with his arm around her shoulders. He wore a striped hat that slouched on his head. His hips were slim. He carried a newspaper. She carried a pint of milk.

'Do we say hello?' I asked as they approached.

'If you like.'

I smiled with my lips closed. They passed in their louche intimacy.

'Good for them,' my husband said.

'They look so... nubile,' I said.

We walked quietly to the shops, holding each other's woollen-gloved hands.

'Get off me, I'm not ovulating,' I said as my husband stood behind me in the bathroom, running his hands down my thighs.

Above us I heard noises. 'Oh for God's sake, not again,' I said.

'They're only singing.'

They were indeed singing. Perhaps it was fun time in the shower.

My husband's hands continued their journey over my thighs. I bent forwards to splash my face with water and he pressed himself against my behind.

'It's not the right day,' I said. 'If we do it now you'll use it all up.' I straightened and reached for a towel to dry my face.

'You are joking.'

'No, I am not joking.'

'You're denying us sex – I can tell you're in the mood – because it's the wrong day?' He leaned back against the towel rail. I motioned for him to move over and hung the towel back on the rack.

'It's not just about being in the mood any more. It's about making a baby. Nothing's worked before so we're trying it this way this month. We need your sperms for when it really matters.'

'I think you're becoming obsessed.'

'Of course I'm becoming obsessed!'

'Why don't you just relax about it all?'

'Now you're putting me under pressure.'

'You're not supposed to be getting stressed darling.'

'Don't stress me out then darling!' I raised my voice.

'Stress is bad for my sperms too.' He raised his voice.

'Shove your sperms up your arse.'

He stared at me then walked out of the

room, dislodging the towel from the rail.

You see, it turned us into children this trying for a child. I re-hung the towel, put the failed ovulation stick in the bin and glanced in the mirror at my tense, strange face.

It wasn't long before we heard the screamer again. I opened my eyes in the early hours of one morning and listened in the darkness.

'Can you hear them?' I heard my husband say.

So he was awake too. His voice was thick with something.

'Yes,' I said.

We lay like bears in the dark, facing each other, foreheads touching. We listened to the knocks and creaks of their furniture; sex's percussion. We listened to her cawing, gull-like screams, her agile crescendos, her frantic grace notes, his staccato, rhythmic bursts, we listened to the whole piercing, popping score of the sex upstairs. When they were done I heard footsteps again, a toilet flushing and the murmuring of voices and practicalities.

'Do you think they're on drugs?' I said.

'Shush,' my husband said and kissed me. His lips felt soft.

'Erotic,' my husband said.

'Isn't it.'

We took off our nightclothes, put skin to skin and got back to, rather rapidly, something of the old days. When it came to putting it in, I thought about the dates and saving it up but I didn't stop us. And as were doing it and coming to our own conclusions (he before me – we still remembered that necessary part of the procedure) I let out my breath harder than I usually did – I saw that tree with its spread branches in my head – and I remember much more than a small sound passed across my lips and out into the bedroom's grey air.

I would like to say we conceived that night but that would make too neat a story. We did conceive; I am big with child, as they say, but it wasn't that night.

For a few more weeks the screamer screamed. We got used to it and often joined in to get the block rocking as my husband liked to say. He changed, as if he was having an affair; the best kind of affair – one in which his wife is complicit and present. I changed too. I loosened up, so he said. That first night we listened to them served as a bookmark: there was what came before and what came afterwards, which was in the spirit of the screamer. I threw my ovulation sticks away. We no longer fought in the bathroom.

But then one day I saw her. It was the first time since the day on the street when she'd looked so young and slight. She was crying. She wore a scarf, despite the warmer weather, and her hair wasn't black any more, it was red. She was alone. A day later I saw two men carting boxes and bin bags from her flat into a car. They drove away and came back again, making several journeys and many trips up and down the stairs. Finally, she got in the car and never returned. Later, a To Let sign appeared in the street outside our block. I often thought of her.

I already know what kind of mother I'll be. I'll be terse and harassed. I'll learn to butter bread more quickly and I'll push my hair behind my ears, even when it doesn't need getting out of my face. I'll give hugs and wipe noses but I'll be worn out and I'll wish for solitude. Then I'll have moments when I'll be flooded with remorse and love and urgency and storm from the bedroom or the bathroom or wherever I've been hiding and join in. My husband will put up with me. He may or may not have an affair. We'll have sex from time to time.

And our child – this child that I'm growing – will be like us – it won't be able to help being like us. It'll loathe us for being so like us; it will wonder how we ever came to have it. But I hope that given the spirit of its conception, our child will have a little of the screamer in it. I really hope so. All you want is for your children to be like you but a little bit different, a little bit better too.

# The Umbrella
## Regi Claire

'THERE HE GOES again,' my mother said, jerking her chin towards the window.

Out on the street in the driving rain, his closed umbrella tucked under one arm, I saw my father pause to adjust his hat and put up the collar of his coat. 'Never uses his brolly if he can help it. "So nice and cosy in its sleeve," he says, "so neatly folded. Seems a shame to disturb it. And then it would need drying out again – too much trouble altogether."' My mother shrugged, shook her head and glanced at me.

I had another sip of coffee. *He is obsessed, or mad*, I kept thinking, before trying to push the thought out of my mind. He was my father, after all. It wouldn't do to call *him* mad. But the thought wouldn't budge; it puffed itself up and I remembered how I don't water the plants on a new moon. Don't walk behind an old woman with a humpback and a stick. Don't answer the phone if it rings on the full hour. Because bad news bleeds – it bleeds into the morning, into the afternoon, bleeds into the evening.

That night, after my parents had gone to bed, I fetched my father's umbrella into my room. *Don't be silly*, I told myself as I slid off the sleeve, which was still faintly damp, and undid the strap. *You're a grown woman, ready to start your own life under your own roof, once you have saved enough money.* But I hesitated. Then, holding my breath, I grasped the leatherette crook in both hands and pressed the push-button.

The umbrella sprang open with the sound of a muffled gunshot, making a black halo above me. *Bad luck*, I heard someone's voice say. Mine. I refused to listen. Never again would I let myself be terrorised by old wives tales. And so, with the biggest, sharpest safety pin from my sewing kit, I set to work. Again and again I plunged it into the umbrella's taut fabric.

At first, the puncture marks were almost invisible. Until I started to ram the pin home with a tearing, retching twist. When I finished, half an hour later, I was hot and sweaty. And proud of myself: the umbrella looked like a sieve.

Just then, my mobile rang. I picked it up. 'Hello,' I said. But the other person had already hung up. A wrong number, no doubt. I smiled to myself as I saw the time: eleven o'clock on the dot. I was beginning to grow up.

Standing in the centre of my room, I raised the umbrella towards the dim ceiling light above my head and looked up. For just a moment it was like catching a glimpse of the night sky with its galaxies of stars, or perhaps even of what lay beyond it all, beyond that silky, glittering blackness. I thought of my father then, wrapped in the duvet beside my mother. Imagined him overcoming his reluctance and opening the umbrella at last. The rain would come scissoring through the holes, glorious, cold, vindictive rain.

And suddenly I could feel it myself. Could hear it falling all around me, faster and faster. I could see the drops now – they were bleeding into a pool on the polished floor.

# Edwin and Federico: A Fable
**Andrew McCallum**

*Then I realised I had been murdered.*
*They looked for me in cafes, cemeteries and churches*
*... but they did not find me.*
*They never found me?*
*No. They never found me.*
(Federico Garcia Lorca, 'Fábula y rueda de los tres amigos')

Edwin found you in a fruit shop in Rutherglen, fingering the strawberries
he wanted you just for your summer lightning on the Kilpatrick hills
he used you
I did not want to be the one to tell you this

        pero, tú va a ser mio esta noche, Lorca, mi fantasma – mi pesadilla
        pues, ponme frio

he sang that on the street, the way a lovelorn loun might sing to you

tonight I dreamt you bloody on that fence
*cogido,* within your death

        how dare you wake me up in Spanish?
        I have things to do
        ghosts to meet, nightmares to ride
        what do you want of me?
        sing it out

that picture of you, one of the only ones, in best bib and tucker...

I saw them kill you tonight, the *Nationalistas*
they laughed at you
you smiled at them
they gambled for your clothes
the pain made everything bearable, insensible
you were thinking of Granada
you kissed your cross... before you knelt for the bullet, in best bib and tucker

I breathed your last breath tonight
I picked you up and carried you off
later I looked for you in cafes, cemeteries and churches... but I did not find you
nor could I find the fruit shop from which you rushed with Edwin
to eat strawberries whose like there never was that sultry afternoon

# Hero
## Andrew F Giles

Cocking a blown-up head from a war grave marked Trimble
& faltering, a fingerless touch, slowly slipping his dry skin up

& over, Jimmy scrapes phantom teeth down Gore's fly. The hard
muscle undoes him. Vidal bleeds History, but this poor guy –

he's a patchwork of heroism & the locker-room, all-thrusting,
all-blond. This sub-story is another palimpsest, America's last

scourge trumps himself up on romance & perfection, so quick
to say the past is the past. Jim's eternal Death is like a couch, the cut

up landscape of yesterday seems overworked, feathery, too trusting.
Can it be that greedy war & a husband-toting mama sucked Gore

so very dry? Only *this* revealed to him that America was a whore?
Kerouac, wriggling under Gore's masterful loins, a beat-up dunder-

head brought up in shit & poison, shape-shifted quickly from sex
to sex. Imagine those two clever boys sweating it out in the thunder.

It seems all America, the truth, was born in that suck, fuck & tussle.
Making a monstrous child, nobbing a speed-freak with hate in his veins

& an ice-livered King. Gore. Piling on layer after layer, is this cold hustle
the only answer? You wander the streets tucked up warm anyhow, bright

eyes fixed to the end. Flesh by night. You make me miss myself, as if curled
up in the shell of a giant's ear I slept & drifted into the lug, finding myself

the cause of deafness & as indistinct as a foetus. The giant streetwalks some
more, wrapping up losers state by state, starting with Martha's Vineyard.

One helluva funeral song, sang to the tune of Marilyn's *happy birthday*, makes
his lips twitch. Note: America has been sent to the abbatoir, must send a card.

Gore Vidal is haunted by that sweet blood that ran between his thighs, slightly
hard of hearing now, there's a distance in his ear falling, falling, falling & the echo

of his heartbeat is doubled, like gunshot. Thinks: *but still he does not love me.*

# The Songs of Kirilov
*after Dostóevsky, The Devils*
**Niall Campbell**

"There's no ground for resentment in all
this. We've entered into a world in which
these are the terms life is lived on. If you're
satisfied with that, submit to them, if you're
not, get out, whatever way you please"
Seneca, Letter XCI

"Kirilov was sitting on the leather sofa
drinking tea, as he always was at that hour."
Dostoevsky, *Demons*

Rain in the air, the smoke rose and rose smoke;
the wife of the small town's perfumer dead,
how he burns her last clothes in the garden.
Their red hours he spent redressing the air
around her. Tonight, when she's missed, the night breeze
although so painfully sweet, is still sweet.

\*

And there I was in Grez, the artist's town,
Rue Victor Hugo, Rue Larson, the deep river
that had won the body rather than the name
of a novice painter. The thronged riverfront
turning home, pale. But even in this, there was
how his rushed breath sent small waves to the shore.

\*

These carefree hours no less impressive
than my cold apartment floor in America.
A month into my secluded famine,
your letter still to arrive from Moscow,

the water cup and water bowl grown strange
and deep as the wellsman's first ever well.
With hunger aches, I think of my best days:
her kiss; my brother's death; the day in question.

\*

My favourite thing: to go in the storm
to a town plantation, and watch the peach trees
suffer the gale coming for their soft worlds.

Sat, soaked through, pocketing the rain,
knowing for the walk home there'll be bruised fruit.
Unred, unripe. Just one will fill the palm.

\*

As though it matters in the end,
whether yours' was the hooded crow
or the dove hot in the cherry tree:
no song but *caw*, or none but the softest.
With the strange fruit that ripens into
darkness, pitted in the leaves.
Does it matter if it was the cloud filled,
or a night sky, that took it as its own,
camouflaged the pale or inkset bird.

## After the battles of Camulodunum, London & Verulamium
**Andrew F Giles**

Your embezzled queen sinks this fermented dram down her neck
to end the strategy her lord Prasutagus brought with Iceni coin
to the promoters of rome & faces him in the otherworld with lore
of oakgrove & sorrel & brose. I sink it like I swig the sour swipes
at table & the biscuit & brewis down my gullet, at the end of long
days of prayer & campaign. You fear the bane mixed with blood
at my mouth, so pale-faced are you, driven Iceni? So many
of your unlicked whelps saw the romans at my daughters'
cunts & at mine, they took at us like worms at meat, slow &
pushing their backs at us. The worst was not these men, their fists
& whips & close teeth, but the dead king Claudius who policed
strong Iceni coin to pay his temple at Camulodunom which
offends the holy places of my lady Araste, my lady who noted
the sunwise running of the hare & gave the Iceni license to war
& the bodies of rome & for her sake your queen sinks this dram.
I drink because thieves have taxed & levied my hearths & fields -
& deep hills where even the Iceni dare not. Paullinus is at us with
a valleyful of dogs, they say all the barefoot elders with deep
eyes who read the trees & hills have gone to the knife. My gods
now we have snarled enough & can no more against such military
might & coin. I hold the stone head of Claudius in my hand. His dead
heart is stuffed with Iceni credit & his unfit laws churn up my land
into patterns & weird oversea shapes, that is all. It is finished, drink.

# Issy[1] on Odradek[2]
**David Betteridge**

Listen. (This is Issy's lesson.)
"Odradek": is it Czech?
or germane, perhaps?
or Mick's 'n' Mac's?
Check.

"Means *dissuade*," says one.
Dissuade? From what?
we wander. Check.

Odradek: a name, forsure,
a made thing's handle.
Made by whom? and named?
Self-maid 'n' named?
Mm, could be.

What like? What look?
A Woden star, a spiel,
a rood out-rigged,
a fank, a clitch, a rainbow's ruck
of teatered yarns...

Onetime fell, we know –
a relict, bust past best –
but still can stand,
rod's end, on tippitoes;
can speak, or whwhssprr, rather.
(Shsh, don't sigh, don't say!)

*Odradek, be héld!*
*Be śtayed!* But no,
too skittling, vagaring butt of stick
for that! An all-evader,
dearth- and death-evader,
it is aim-loose, asking-proof,
and ever quick.

1. For Issy, see James Joyce's *Finnegans Wake*.
2. For Odradek, see Franz Kafka's *Trials of a Family Man*. (See through a gloss darkly.)

# How long
**Mark Edwards**

how long you gonna nurse this
   despite my best advice
knowing full well what was lost will not return
   is further from here than whoever you're wishing
would chap the door to pass on news more urgent
   or that rarest of things a song weaved so tight
the very ground begins to shudder
   at this point surely you'd pause to consider
then again if I was in the vicinity somewhere
   along the road up the brae early
making the rounds shuffling past the greasy papers
   the usual chill plus last night's chips repeating
what you need to do is carry your arms in silence
   trust your own wounds believe certain waiting rooms
given time will allow the leaves to turn and no doubt
   the sweeping can commence
surely you'll recall
                        at a stretch
                                3 decades back
when tricks of the light blinded your eyes
   a glancing header too fast and wide
this cold hearth creeping steadily forwards
   scratching itself muttering next to one last sinkful
of somebody's dirty weekend dishes
                        you meet him there
your jack the lad
your spitting eldest best dressed uncle
   the man you promised the world
some would say you murdered

# Are you sure you want to talk to me?
**Dilys Rose**

THE BIG GUY ahead of me, with body odour which punches above its weight and a T-shirt bearing the rollicking slogan *Murderers' Row*, lollops against the aisle seats and squeezes towards the back of the bus.

You retract your legs, I stuff my bag under the seat and settle down beside you. It's the only empty seat apart from the one which the big guy is aiming for. If we're both careful we won't have to make too much body contact, though this is no luxury coach. After your casual opener about having already travelled over three thousand miles by bus – three thousand miles! – you can still opt for silence. Considering the distance you have already covered, your ability to maintain a neutral tone is impressive, though you roll your bus ticket back and forth like a cigarette you're itching to smoke, and murmur about making your final connection.

Are you sure you want to talk to me? The thing is, if you do, I will pay closer attention than you might expect. Or want. When you repeat the number of miles you've already chalked up, I note your red-rimmed eyes, like scallops prised apart with a shucking knife. After already four days in transit, why don't you just press your face into the donkey jacket which doubles as a pillow and doze away the hundred miles we'll spend in close proximity?

Before departure, the bus driver instructs us, for the benefit for other passengers, to silence our electronic equipment and phone conversations. He takes his time over the announcement, relishing his moment of glory, his power of office and his ability to intimidate us. If he had a mind to it, his deep, assertive voice suggests, he could leave us stranded at some nebula of nowhere, the rain falling steadily on our heads and not a soul on the road finding the pity in their hearts to stop and offer us a ride. When we are all chastened and muted, the driver's heavy gold bracelets clink against capable wrists, he buckles up and power steers us out of town.

Like the driver, I am all for a quiet ride but it's not going to happen. Not that you are loud, no, you're soft-spoken, low key and unsmiling so I can't comment on the condition of your teeth but doubt you have a decent deal on dental insurance. On the subject of dental work, I'm reminded of a story I heard the other day. In a country still picking itself up from its time beneath the Soviet hammer, a poet was tipped for the Nobel Prize for literature. Anticipating glorious photo opportunities and not wishing to be shown up as the poor man of Europe, the authorities decreed that the man's teeth should be fixed by the state, so that he could smile widely and evenly when the flashbulbs popped. Work commenced but at some point during the drilling, the filling, the crowning and bridging, news got out that the poet had been pipped at the post by a writer from a wealthier country with, we can probably assume, noticeably better dental treatment. The orthodontic work was halted, leaving the Nobel manqué with a half-gleaming, half-crumbling folly of a mouth. I don't tell you this story. I can't be sure it would make you smile.

You say you are going to visit family who live in upstate somewhere. I don't know the place but the name is familiar: an old name transported from the old country, on a brisk clipper or a rackety coffin ship. I imagine it's a rural area though not in any plush, lush way; more hard-pressed dirt than prime real estate; peeling wood shingles; a porch stacked to the eaves with a guilt trip of recycling and several generations of machine parts which might but never do come in handy. There will be animals: a tick-ridden mutt or an edgy, loose-jointed hound; a slink of feral cats in knee-high grass, a snake coiled in the basement like a garden hose, to keep down the rodents. This may be nothing at all like where you're going but it's what happens: you tell me stuff and I make up the rest.

Your hair is the warm, woody colour of a field mouse. You are by no means wee or sleekit or cowrin, but perhaps there is something tim'rous about you. You haven't seen your family for several years and plan to spend a month out east. The prompt for your visit is an aged, ailing grandma who may not last another winter. As it is barely spring and the greening of the trees has been arrested by recent storms, floods and prolonged low temperatures, attributed to the cloud of volcanic dust which has already spread around most of the world, you are thinking ahead. Going while the going has a purpose.

This is not your first trip back. Done the journey several times. Clocked over thirty thousand bus miles. Had you flown, you'd have earned enough air miles for a freebie but no such reward is offered to the frequent bus traveller. And even though you've dozed on the coach or passed restless nights on waiting-room benches, pushing down the crap fast food which is all that's to be had, your budget is already strained. Not that you put it like that.

Cost a lotta money, you say, a lotta money.

The mention of money so soon makes me wonder if this might be your lead-in to a sob story, if you'll wind up hitting on me for a tap. Have you been doing a similar number on each stage of your trip; bending an ear, elaborating or editing details as you saw fit? I don't think so. Wouldn't you at least have mastered the name of your grandmother's illness?

It's not eczema, you say. She been on oxygen for two years.

Emphysema?

That's it. I ain't dumb, you add, then break off and gaze out at the bare trees and yellow earth sliding by. High above the highway, without the need of a single wingbeat, a hawk turns a slow circle. And another. The sky is piebald, a drab blue daubed with dark, shifting cloud. You flatten out your bus ticket. From days of handling, the inkjet printout is beginning to smudge. You ask to borrow my pen, draw on the back of your ticket.

My house, you say, holding up an archetypal kindergarten dwelling: a block topped with a triangular roof, four windows, a door with a handle, a scribble of smoke spiralling from the chimney.

And this is me, you say, pointing to a stick person floating stiffly in mid-air. I ain't no good at drawing.

As with most life stories, the order of your telling is roundabout, repetitive, full of holes. Your immediate concerns are grandma's advanced age and infirmity, and meeting up with the extended family. Your tone remains neutral, deadpan. No charge of anticipation. You don't say, for example, that you can't wait to see your mother, your aunt Pearl, cousin Rodney, to hold in your arms the new baby of your second cousin. On the subject of new arrivals, you are adamant:

I ain't looking after nobody's baby, unless there's a emergency involving the hospital. Or somebody pays me to babysit.

Though I've known you for less than an hour, this sounds rehearsed.

I ain't no good with babies. I've applied for a course in Culinary Arts Plus. Know what I mean by Arts Plus?

You outline the course content, how many hours of this or that, each possible step of a possible career ladder, in what quickly become tedious detail. It's as if your brain has blocks of information stamped on it, facts to be retained and retrieved exactly as given. You reel off the layout of the building in which each class will take place; where cake decoration sits in relation to cooking a charity meal for two hundred or working in a pizza joint; exactly how much you have to pay for meals at the college – twenty cents for lunch, twenty cents! – how much financial support you're due because you are disabled – you mention a bad knee – and how you won't have to do the usual killer shifts of the catering trade.

At your age – forty – it seems late to be starting on a course which at best will offer minimum wage for the first so many years and then, if you're lucky, up it a few more dollars an hour and possibly throw in a slightly nicer, smarter uniform, with epaulettes and a ceramic name tag rather than a card plastic one, a canvas hat with the restaurant logo on the brim. But there's a reason. There's always a reason. I make positive noises, contribute a few anecdotes from my own memories of the catering trade but you don't pick up on anything I say. We say stuff but don't really get any dialogue going.

I offer you a cereal bar which you accept with alacrity. And thanks.

That's the turnpike, you say, pointing to a sign on the highway. It means we've crossed the state line.

Crossing the state line sounds more dramatic than merging with a more or less identical stretch of tarmac but after a while a few hills rear up, small ponds glint, a broad slow river cuts through the valley. Little about the scenery interests you until we pass a monumental angel standing by a pond not far from the road.

Must have beeen a graveyard there, you say. My grandma's got a graveyard on her land. She got a memorial stone for a girl named Thankful Williams. Twenny five when she died. Dunno what she had to be thankful for.

With no glimmer of a smile at the sad irony of Thankful Williams but a stolid confidence in your facts, you talk on for a while about graveyards and the civil war, how important it was for a family to bring home their young men and women, to bury their dead on family soil.

When you dry up on graveyards, I ask whether the state you've travelled from is very different from where you are going.

It's a different shape. State I'm in now is nearly a square, you say, then pull up the sleeve of your T-shirt and point out a nasty bruise. A woman attacked me, the other day. One street over from mine. I didn't do nothin to her, was mindin my business but she hadn't taken her meds. I was in her way and she lashed out. Police say she'll be okay if she takes her meds. Me, I won't be walking down that street no more.

The bus bounces along. The view is pretty much as it's been for the last half hour.

I'm going to sleep for a bit, I say.

You go right ahead.

Nudge me if I snore.

I'd be the last person to care.

I close my eyes, to give you a chance to keep the rest of your story to yourself, and to decide whether I want to hear any more of it. The motion of the bus rocks me into a doze. I jolt awake when the guy in the *Murderers' Row* T-shirt rumbles down the aisle.

Is the big guy asking about transfers? you ask. Maybe I should ask about my transfer. I didn't catch what the driver said at the last stop.

No talking to the driver while the bus is in motion! the driver tells the big guy, loud enough so everybody else gets the picture. The big guy growls and lumbers back up the aisle, jerking his head like a hornet's at his ear.

The driver rattles his bracelets, switches on the fan.

I hope we don't run into traffic, you say. I been snarled up in traffic a few times already. Almost missed my last connection.

You check your ticket again, turn it over, study the house on the back, make the stick person flitter about.

My daughter will be twelve tomorrow and I won't be there for her birthday. I missed the last six birthdays. She don't stay with me no more. She's with her father. And his new girlfriend. I had to give her up. For adoption and... and now I don't get to see her no more. When she's sixteen, I'm pretty sure it's sixteen, she can come see me. If she wants to. Long as I ain't a convicted felon. If I ain't got in no trouble with the law. If I try to see her before that, even just to give her a birthday present, the new girlfriend will call the police. And then I won't get to see my daughter for even longer.

The new girlfriend lies about me. Tells bad lies. Real bad. But she's right about one thing. I ain't no good with babies... In four years I should have finished Culinary Arts Plus and likely I'll have a job, maybe in a pizza restaurant, and I'll be able to visit my daughter...

That's a long time to wait.

I dunno about the restaurant hours. I get a lot of pain. My knee. And then... I don't always see things right... I ain't dumb.

Thirty miles to go and we've hit a traffic jam. Defying the driver's instructions, people on the bus begin to fiddle with phones, iPods, electronic games.

Thirty thousand miles, I say. You could have travelled right round the world!

I guess... There's forms I have to fill in for the college. I don't like forms. Used to get all kindsa forms from the clinic and the school about my daughter but they got me mad, the forms got me so mad I didn't fill them in. I looked and then... I have to fill in all kindsa forms for Culinary Arts Plus. I ain't dumb.

You give me a sharp look, and suddenly we are too close for comfort, close enough to see each other's pores, blemishes, stray hairs, to feel the heat from each other's breath and it's as well we're at the front, near the assertive driver who surely wouldn't allow anything bad to happen on his shift. But I can't help wondering what you did to have your daughter taken away and what's behind that sharp dark look in your eyes. I was wrong about tim'rous. You're far from tim'rous.

It ain't dysex... lex... dyssexia, it's hyperact. *Hyperact*. Filling in forms makes me hyperact and... and then the meds, the meds... I ain't dumb but I ain't no good with babies neither.

There are holes in your story. Traplines have been laid.

Nearly there, I say. And only a few minutes late. We should make our connections.

I sure hope so. If I don't make my connection, I dunno where I'm gonna sleep tonight. I ain't got money for no motel.

It all works out. We collect our luggage from the hold. Your final bus is ready and waiting, engine running. No time for protracted farewells. We say goodbye. No smiles, no handshakes but we wish each other luck. Sincerely. Luck matters.

You will remember next to nothing of me – perhaps the colour of my hair, my light Anglo-Saxon eyes, the name of my homeland, my unfamiliar accent. We haven't exchanged names and your lack of curiosity about who you've been speaking to will protect me, if not you.

My train is standing on the platform. It's fairly full and due to depart shortly. I nip into a vacant double seat and spread out my coat, hoping to keep the spare seat to myself and have a quiet ride when you, the big guy from the bus, sweating from the exertion of hoisting yourself up two high steps and manoeuvring your bulk through the doorframe, stop and say:

Is this seat free? You going all the way to New York City?

All the way, I reply, hoping you'll look elsewhere for a seat.

Me too! you say, plumping down and instantly overflowing into my space. Well, hey, we can get acquainted. You were on the coach, right? Man that was some goddamn quiet journey. I was just thinking to myself all the way and you know what I was thinking? I was thinking that I really wanna talk. Some stuff I been carrying around way too long, you know. Gotta get some stuff out, share it around you know, let it breathe some fresh air, give it an audience, know what I'm saying? We got plenny time to get acquainted. I mean, sometimes you wanna be quiet and sometimes you just gotta tell somebody your story, right?

In a few hours, if the train runs on time and no unexpected delays occur at the airport, I will fly over the Statue of Liberty and under the cloud of volcanic dust which for the last week has brought air traffic throughout much of the world to a standstill. I will fly – unless the volcano spits out more dust, or its bigger more dangerous cousin wakes from his slumber and wants a piece of the action – towards my own story; its gaps and elisions, its traplines, its random acts of violence and love. In the meantime, Mr *Murderers' Row*, are you sure you want to talk to me?

# The Judge
**Roddy Dunlop**

START WITH THE law. How the law works in places like this. I had a friend Mathew who turned out to be a homosexual and he explained to me about the law once. It was years ago. Law here is based on precedent and precedent is based on reason. We are a secular country. We pretend we don't have a shared sense of morality because that would mean there would have to be something mystical at the root of it all. So what do we have? Reason, precedent. He was almost sixty, the judge. He was not a religious man. He was a scholar. But it seemed to him increasingly these days, as he read and reposed, that that which one could hold in the hand and call absolute knowledge, this thing he had forever sought to hang his soul upon was, somehow, an illusion. He adjusted the weight of his buttocks on the thin pillow and looked down at Jock. I am to represent Reason, he was thinking. It can be channelled in a million directions but takes root nowhere. He'd seen a lot of the law.

He hated anything to do with animal rights. With people it was usually cut and dried. If you leave your first born in a pool of urine for two weeks then it's wilful neglect. A gentleman who forgets for a while that he has a dog, on the other hand, is not an uncommon thing, and it can be put down to absent mindedness or the onset of dementia. In the Lammermuirs they kill animals as a matter of course. In the hills that flank East Lothian, there are traps everywhere. Traps like oversized comic-book mousetraps on planks of wood laid from bank to bank on every bend of every burn. Little square trays of poison pellets in the heather for raptors, stoats, crows and foxes. Trap your next door neighbour's dog in a spiky iron trap though and its wilful cruelty, or wilful neglect if the defence lawyer is sufficiently charming and persuasive.

The problem, he reflected, in a quiet moment as the jurors pored over article six from the 1998 amendment of the 'Revised Bill for the Treatment of Animals Engaged in Agricultural Occupation Act', was that he was on Jock Feeney's side, because Mr Feeney really did love that bull.

Jock's face was red from having been shaved. A couple of his neebours were in the gallery by the door. Wullie Lamb, the landlord of the Long Bar, had minded and gave him a wee wave with the racing post. A lassie from the Evening News was down, in Haddington District Council Sherriff Court, on a sunny, crisp spring morning, with cracked pale-green emulsion paint and a feeling halfway between a community centre and a church.

–Can you confirm your name please? Are you mister John Feeney?

–Aye Jock, Jock Feeney your honour.

–Your date of birth?

–Eh, seven, eleven, thirty-five.

–And it says here that you are resident at Seton Mains Farm?

–Aye, sortie. Ah've aye bided roon aboot Hawdintin, ken, diffrint fairms. Thon wiz the last yin ah wiz it.

–So you are currently of no fixed abode?

–Aye sortie.

This was the big one for Jock. He was sombre and alert. They couldn't fine him because he didn't have any money, and it was unlikely that they'd throw him in the pokie. He was an old man. There wasn't much left they could take away. He understood this. But it was the big one anywey.

–Mr Feeney, do you mind if I call you Jock? Okay Jock, it's alleged that on the third of February this year you dragged a bull, with a rope around its neck, into the middle of the river Tyne and let it drown. Tell us what you remember about that day.

–Ah mind it wiz bucketin doon the rain, and me and Seamus wur gaun ower fae West Saltoun te the Crosby's fairm ootside Begbie, tae inseminate some coos.

–And the bull?

–Seamus, aye. Hud um six year.

–You were the owner of this bull?

–Aye. Ma only yin. Ah stairted wi yin and ended up wi nowt, your honour.

–He was your only bull?

–Aye, but he wiz gid. Ah mind it the first tappin, he done sixteen Ayrshire in twa days.

–I'm afraid I don't understand you Jock. Can you speak more clearly please?

–Sorry aye, well, ken the tappin? They pit the tappin oan the bulls privates, like paint ken, blue stuff, and then ye kin see what coos have been seen tae. The furst yin, fur Seamus, he done sixteen in twa days. Eighty pounds ah made. Ah've got a photie if ye like?

The prosecutor for the crown looked over to the judge and they both shrugged. Jock fiddled with the top button of his faded suit jacket. He was a wee man. His boots were polished but they hadn't quite worked things out with the bottom of his trousers. His eyes had gone a little watery from life. The judge studied him. The newspaper lassie studied him. It seemed everyone in court wore the same kind of smile as auld Jock fiddled with his buttons, even the suits from the SSPCA. He reached into his breast pocket and pulled out a small photograph, folded down the middle. He unfolded it and looked at it for a second, made a short clicking noise with his false teeth, then handed it to the QC who looked at it briefly and passed it to the Judge. It was a portrait of a sandy coloured bull. A big, virile bull with ears like handlebars. He had a mop of curly hair on his big meaty head and beneath the fringe his eyes were askew. Strikingly askew. Both looked into the centre. The judge smirked then immediately composed himself. This, he thought, was a bull that had done a great deal of inseminating down the years.

–So, you were going from West Saltoun to Begbie?

–Aye, an what ah mind aboot it wiz, thur wur fower big motors, a black yin, then a white yin, then a black yin again, aw big fancy motors, then anither white yin. Like piany keys.

–You were walking along the road, the old B16?

–Aye. Pairt ay the wey. It started buckitin rain, oot ay naiwhare, so ah stoaped under a tree and hud a wee smoke ay ma pipe.

–Jock, how did you end up downing your bull?

–Ah nivur. He jist drownt.

–But how?

Jock needed a pee and so a recess was called. The lawyers and the judge went backstage for a cup of tea, and Jock made his way to the lavvy. It was a guid question. Aw he could think o wis the wey the rivur seemd tae huv changed. But how kin ye explain that to thon, that dinnae ken naethin aboot coos. The journalist and Jock's supporters, the four of them, went outside for cigarettes.

George, Dode, wiz in a spot ay bother umsel. He could feel for Jock and he wanted the auld gadgie to win. Buckin scoundrels, as wee Joke would say, the loat ay thum. He walked outside and the sunshine hit him and this was it, there was nothing else to do. He'd been laid off at the garage, fifty, nae chance ay any other joab except cleanin the public lavvies. If that's the way it goes that's the wey it goes. He was still a guid car mechanic.

Backstage, the Judge and the lawyers were discussing whether or not they believed a cow could swim.

Jock was still shaking himself off when Dode came in, the big galoot.

–Is it no aboot time they wur geein ye a colostomy bag, or whatever the yin fur pee's cried?

–Ah'll tell ye Dode, it's when ye cannae hae a pee thit ye huv te start worryin.

–Yur right, listen John, Ah seen ye the night eftir Seamus died. Ah seen the nick ye wur in. Ah ken ye nivur meant nae herm te that bull. Ivrybody kens. Ye ken Willie's pittin oan some sandwiches in that the night, whatever wey it goes?

They tucked thumselves away and walked out into the corridor, Dode wi his hand oan Jock's shoodir. Then Jock went right, back te his seat, and Dode went left.

–Guid luck auld freend.
–Thanks Neebur.

And the Judge was thinking – here it comes, the line about the river changing. He'd seen the papers and that was the only line submitted. It wasn't any kind of line of defence at all. Still he knew it was probably the truth.

–The court is reconvened. Welcome back Jock. Was your bull, Seamus, a good swimmer?

–Ah dinnae ken your honour, but he aye managed.

–What were the conditions like?

–Normul. Naithin oot the oardinary. Bit rain like.

–Seamus, was he displaying any signs of fatigue or injury?

–Seamus? Awch a wee bit ay arthritis in his knees. Foreby that he was fine ken.

–So how did he drown Jock?

–The river hud changed, your honour. Rivers are always changing.

And Jock wouldn't even have mentioned it if the river had gotten broader or narrower, shallower or deeper. What he meant he couldn't explain because he didn't know, had no way of knowing that the river actually had changed. It was sediment from the Langholm mine that had killed Seamus. There was a small scale mine, seven miles upriver from Begbie, towards Whitadder. It was owned by Gatsberg Industries, and they were digging out a hillside in the Lammermuirs and selling it as aggregate for motorways. They'd had a big order to fill in the winter. There had been a lot of digging and blasting. The thaw and the spring rains brought all of that fine thorazite dust down into the river Tyne and when Seamus crossed that day it stuck to his hooves like wet cement. But neither Seamus nor Jock nor the Judge knew this.

–So in summary, Jock, you were aware that the bull in question was ageing and arthritic. In spite of this you led him into a deep stretch of the River Tyne on a day when, as you observed yourself, it had been raining heavily, and this to save you a five mile walk. The bull drowned. And in your defence you claim that 'the river had changed'.

The judge paused. He paused for a long moment, an uncharacteristically long moment thought Dode who himself was thinkin

–This isnae lookin gid.

It wiz nae trial at aw. Ye nivur goat tae ken nuthin aboot Jock nor Seamus, the wey they wur, the wey coos ur. No thit Dode kent nixie aboot how coos wur, bit how kin ye judge a case aboot coos if ye ken nuthin aboot thum. An foreby aw that, ye nivur goat tae ken the actual story – the wey wee Joke jumped in the Panny umsel, the wee man wi aw his claes oan, in triet tae pull the per beast oot. The wey he wiz in the Long Bar that night, seventy year auld and greetin. Quiet like ken. Undemonstrative. Sittin quietly greetin tae umsel wi eis bonnet in is hands. Buckin scoundrels awright.

Ye coudnae argue wi thum. They hud aw the wee fiddles. A five mile walk? It wiz five mile one wey. An rainin heavily doesnae make nae difference – raining continuously diz. A wee bit ay the arthritis? Whaes no goat a wee bit ay the arthritis? An what's the furst thing the doacter'll tell ye? Git yersel doon the swimmin pool.

There wis wee Jock oan the stand, heid forret, noddin like a boxer, tryin ae hink ay what tae say tae defend umsel and no able tae find a thing and the moment awready past. Yet aw ye needed wis twa minutes in his company tae ken he wis a true gentleman and thit thur wis nothin cruel and nothin willful aboot um.

The judge was telling himself
    –Be Reasonable. Look at the facts as they have been established by this court of law and pass sentence.
    –John Feeney, as much as I admire your honesty, the weight of evidence presented to this court today leaves me with little choice but to find you guilty of wilfully neglecting an animal in your care, resulting in the death of the foresaid animal. I sentence you to six months in prison, suspended for fifteen years on the grounds that you swear to have no contact whatsoever with animals engaged in agricultural occupation. On behalf of the court I'd like to express our sympathy for your bull, Seamus, and to wish you all the best young man.

# Poem I
**Ross McGregor**

Ah kicked a dandelion clock
it flapped unner the sole ae ma shoe
flexin like a hollow limb
wi dark pink skin

The flight ae the white floss
deid in the breeze ower-by
The bald heid wis left but
waitin tae see oot the summer

# Poem II
**Ross McGregor**

It was the time ae year when the colours bleed
the last ae life afore the winter smothers them deid

an auld Mercedes abandoned
its metallic grey paint evaporatin intae the night

the man taped black bin bags
ower the caved-in windaes

he was fair fightin against the bluster ae plastic
blawin wet in his face

# Poem III
**Ross McGregor**

Ah see you
emptyin yer bin
at nicht in the dark
when yer face is hidden

Ah see you
openin the ootside cupboard
and placin the bag intae
further hidden darkness

Ah see you
lukin oot tae the street
unner the sky
shiverin black

Ah see you
wide open and unseen
but yer face isnae light
by bein unseen

Ah see you
and yer face isnae light
by bein unseen


# Poem V
**Ross McGregor**

Sometimes ah'll wauner tae the far corner ae the field and find ma spot aside the river, unner the bypass where the road stretches oot fae the toon

The trees are stunted there wi low hingin branches for shelter. Ah'll mibbe have a can in ma pocket and ah'll sit and drink it while the sun goes doon tae wherever it goes

The beer tastes fine in the damp cauld and ah'll watch the river drift by like a secret and feel the droplets ae moisture cling tae ma een and freshen ma nostrils

Then when ah luk aboot me at the grass turnin night-time blue ah'll imagine whit it'd be like tae still be sittin here listenin tae the birds screamin ower the rummle ae lorries right early in the morning

# At Balmaha
## AC Clarke

Sometimes a day will fall just so,
as if we'd tugged a crucial thread
clear of the snag and tangle.
Once we'd have called it grace
and even now a subtle shift of air
the turn of a smile, the sun breaking cover

to gleam on a wet road – even the simple
rightness of a choice – feel as though
*given*. Take us, this morning, here
where a few boats in the lochside harbour
are in their winter drowse already
and the tree-crowned island – a place

we're always meaning to visit – stays
just out of reach: it's touch and go
our happiness, but as real
as the sky, the water, the bright, not-quite-dead
leaves. I could believe another
presence – presences – of such rare

substance the least touch would shear
them like cobwebs, dip and hover
above us, so strong the hope of a good will
at watch, beyond our reckoning. I know
this day will build on memories
– enough, perhaps, when all is said

to keep us from the undertow of fear,
reminding us of what was possible
and may again be. And although
the world of timetables and diaries
is pressing in, the day holds steady,
sheds not a drop, though ready to brim over.

# Extract from the novel *The Year of the Whale*
## Simon Sylvester

EXTRACT 1

'This is the River Kent,' I tells em, having a quick head count. There's seven chaps, three ladies, one nipper and one puffing dog. We're short a hound, but he'll be fine. Mist has plastered hair to their heads, beads of it bright on every brow. Grand weather for walking. Much of them looks glum.

'It rises in the hills, and flows down through Kendal and Milnthorpe to the bay. With the tide out, it's only a foot deep. Or maybe two. This is the part,' I grins, 'when we get wet.'

'Wetter,' mutters one of em.

'Come on. Off with your boots. No sense wading with them just to walk the rest of the way in wet shoes, now.'

When I leave the house, Lizzie ties the knots to make it easy on my creaking metatarsals, and I set to hauling off my boots, a slow burn warming in the elbows wrists knees and hip. The group follow suit, some having a grumble, one or two of em chirping. The little lad is standing by his dad, bright as a button, starts to paw at his shoes.

'You leave that, Andy,' says father. 'I'll carry you.'

He looks at me, and I nod back. The right thing to do.

'All set? Aye?'

Blank faces.

'Grand. Now, listen. Feel with your feet for ridges in the current, as they're higher and a touch firmer. It's cold, but take your time, be sure of your feet.'

Trousers rolled past the knee, I set off. Water's icy cold as always, same all year round, grit sharp or sludgy in the toes, current feeble and constant, a trickling thing in a weak and tugging channel. Shallow today, and only three or four dozen yards across, but the other side plays a hide-and-seek in swirls of fog. Crossing a river of forever, walking in my own head, walking always walking. I am a man of three legs, two of bone and one of hawthorn. Makes me think of the riddle of the sphinx. Ice dulls the flame burning in my knees, and the missing hound waits for me on the other side, head cocked and happy wagging.

'Good lad,' I tells him, 'you don't mind the water, now, do you?'

His tongue lolls. Aye, a grand day to be a mongrel. A grand day. Looking back I can see the group as milling ghosts, greying shapes on the other side. I holler at them, wave, and there's nothing, nothing, and slowly dark shapes cross the river, lurch toward me in pairs, holding onto one another and cursing. I give em a hand out of the river, and they stand shivering. The nipper rides atop his dad's shoulders, giggling.

'Good lad,' I tells him. 'You too, Andy.'

Standing on one boot to dry my foot and fit the other, the others hopping and cursing, dropping boots and laughing. Crossing the Kent is a bit of fun. An ice breaker. A head count, seven three one and two. Arse flat on the ground, I tangle the laces together just as best I can, my fingers arguing with the string.

'That's the worst of the wet stuff,' I says. It's

just walking from here. 'Reckon we'll stop soon for a bite to eat. Half an hour, mebbe.'

Confidence grows after crossing the Kent, the pace picks up. The punters start to know what the firmer bits of sand look like, feel like, start to better judge the placing of feet and the length of stride, feel the wonder of the walking. They relax to my pace, ask questions, take pictures and whoop, write quick names in the sand with birch twigs. The mongrel dog patters and sprints on the sand, loping paw prints scatter mud, come back to find us, sprint off again. I give him a twig to keep him quiet, let the youngster sink a couple more, there and there, that's the lad. Mun be eight or nine year old, and all the makings of a proper walker.

We walk and I tell em, should they ask, of the monks at Cartmel priory and the Romans stationed far from home, the freak tides and mad storms, the Celts and Vikings, the Normans, shipbuilding in Glasson Dock, a hundred years exactly of the old coach service, the proposed bridge and tidal barrage which shouldn't ever happen, if you want my opinion. There was Saint Patrick stormtossed in his coracle, bird watching in the estuary, even the chance of a hoopoe. All the folk who drowned at Black Rock and beyond. Victorians, smugglers and slaves, poor old heartbroken Black Samboo who they say came all the way from Sri Lanka, like as not, and how tractors break down in salt water, how a jumbo works, the day Robert the Bruce and his ragtag army crossed the bay and sacked Lancaster in the space of a single tide.

'There's a lot of ghosts in this little patch of land,' I tell em. 'A whole great weight of history. Everyone that's ever lived leaves a bit behind em. Just a little bit. It was round here,' I say, 'that I saw the ghost ship.'

There'd been little pots of conversation, but that shuts em up. All folk love a good ghost story.

'You didn't really,' says the nervous chap.

'Oh, happen I did, sir. Right round here it was, down toward Humphrey Head, out on my own. Must have been more than ten year ago. I was walking about, minding my own business, looking for a good spot to lay some nets. It were just as foggy as today. Just like this, come to think of it.'

They have a good look around em, a long hard look.

'And I heard it, first. There was this noise of creaking, and gulls, and when I turned to see, there was a bloody great ship going right past me, barely a stone's throw away. Coming right out the fog. Only it were low tide, folks. That's the thing. The tide had been out for hours. I were standing on the sand, just like this here. And no ship's got business in the bay anyway. Too shallow for a big ship. And this was a full square-rigger, three-masted. She had no sail, everything stowed sloppy along the yard arms, but she moved over the bay right slow and steady.'

I can sense em drawing closer to me as we walk.

'I looked up, and there was a gang of black fellows on board. They was gathered at the edge, staring out. And they were all of em stark naked, begging my pardon. They was pointing my way, and I thought at first it was me they was looking at. Scared me witless.'

Fog turning wheels and lazy draughts.

'But it weren't me. There was something out behind me.'

It takes em a moment to see I've finished the story.

'Is that it?'

'That's it.'

'But what happened?'

'Well, they went thataways into fog. I hightailed it home to my good wife, and I had a bloody big brandy, excusing my language.'

'But what were they pointing at? What was it?'

'I've never known, miss. They was all pointing the same way, back behind us, over to Priest Skear.'

They all turn to look east, see nothing but blank and bright and white.

'I know there's one or two other old timers seen the ship, too. The local thinking goes that it's a wreck from the slaving days, or perhaps a mutiny gone wrong. They were given short shrift in those days. It was a tough business. Hung em from the yards. Left em for a day or two, then cut em down. Left em for the fish. And then there's the others.'

'There's more?'

The nervous fellow almost moans the question. I wink at the nipper's dad, and he grins back.

'Good Lord, yes. It's a very big bay, sir, and very old. On days like today, when the fog is thick and a man can't see the shore, there's plenty of folk come across horses and carriages running on the sand like it were two hundred years ago. Foam in their mouths, all frantic to beat the coming tide. I know another chap saw these two legionnaires sitting on quicksand, rolling dice. And there's some has seen the monks at Cartmel, walking in a row, just like we are now. My old mucker Lawrence saw em up on Chapel Island, near Flookburgh, over where them boys drowned at Black Rocks.'

There's a silence.

'They wear dark hoods. Walk barefoot in the sand.'

Lord, I enjoy this.

'Oh, and then there's Rabbie's army. Robert the Bruce. Can't forget them. I used to shrimp with a lad who's uncle said he'd seen the army marching on to Lancaster. The bay was a shortcut from Scotland, see. They burnt half the city to the ground, but the story goes most of em drowned on the way back, trying to race the tide.'

The footsteps of the walkers, walking. We could be a marching army.

'How much longer is there still to go, Henry?'

'Oh, there's a wee while yet. Another couple of miles, maybe less. No rush.'

'Right. No rush.'

'Should we stop here for lunch?' I asks them, bright as can be.

'Maybe not right now,' says one.

'It's rather damp here, isn't it,' says another.

'Fair enough. Best stay close, folks. There's a lot more quicksand towards Humphrey Head. You'll get stuck fast. You won't want to stay behind in the bay with weather like this, I'd warrant.'

Having a chuckle inside, I lead em through the fog in a tear track labyrinth, hop across the maze of little currents, climb atop the rippled sand bars, salt water in scattered pools, the mark of the worm, fresh water in veins and forks and tiny tributaries, rushing out to sea.

The ground is getting soft. I pause, study the sand. They slow at my shoulders. Something gnaws in my knees.

'Watch it there. No, come over this way,' I says, and we cut a sharp dogleg to the north.

'Are you sure you know where you're going, Henry?' asks yon snooty wench.

'You'd best to hope so, eh?'

'What?'

'This is my home, miss. I'm what we call sand-reared, born and bred round here. Sixty year and then some. Fished here a long time afore the walking. Still go out fishing most days I don't walk. I know where I am.'

Step careful through another dozen paces and the sand flattens and firms, the unsteady ground left behind us. I dogleg again, turning back to westward.

'See? Just a little detour.'

'Henry,' says the nervous one, jogging a little. 'Henry.'

'Yes, sir.'

'Were you involved with the cockle pickers?'

I go a little cold inside, walk a little more. If I keep walking, it don't hurt so much as if I stop and start again. Arthritis, says the doctor. Old Man Arthur is a rat. The teeth are always growing, the dentine's always soft, ground away, whetted and sharpened.

'You know, those Chinese ones who died.'

He makes it sound so easy. Like a man might forget.

'Aye,' I says, 'now you mention it. Happen I was.'

'What happened with all that?'

Man was made to walk. We're all nomads, whether we know it or not. I shrug. 'It was a bloody bad business. Like enough you saw the news. Immigrant workers come over here and used as slaves, near enough.'

There ain't no more chattering. Everyone is listening. Know the end of the story already, keen to hear the start.

'Them poor silly sods get put to work all hours. All over the country it is. Picking cabbages down south. Packing salmon in the islands. Come here thinking it'll be better than back home. This particular lot worked in the bay. They worked all hours, worked like devils for a pittance.'

A pittance, fifteen pound a year.

'Didn't see the tide coming in. Or mebbe they did, thought they could beat it.'

Reckon the fog is thinning.

'But they couldn't. Not even a good horse beats the full bore tide. It comes in a rush, like a wall, sometimes a full foot high.'

Aye, it's thinning alright. Burning off. There's the palest disc of a small low sun, somewhere beyond this cloud, worming into us from the outside.

'There was a lot of talk in the papers about them having trouble with the locals, but it was local lads tried to tell em about the tide that night. They didn't listen. There was twenty-two died, I think, in the end. Might have been more, but we'll never know for sure, for we never knew how many went cockling in the first place. The helicopter did a couple of runs and found one lad still alive. He was standing on his tiptoes on a sand bank, sick with cold. The others had been washed off it, or tried to swim for shore and drowned.'

Gulls, herring gulls, wheeling blank faces.

'Soon as we could, next morning, soon as the tide allowed it, we went out to look. Had to wait all night. I found two of em myself,' I says. 'Barely a stone's throw apart. Back towards Jenny Brown's Point.'

I fling a finger behind us, off towards the east. They turn to see.

'Oh, look.'

I turn, too, we all look, surprised to see most of a murky shore, the grey weight of Arnside Knott and the ragged forest of Silverdale. The fog is dying. The spell is broken, the cloud bound for elsewhere.

'It were seven years since,' I says. 'No, six.'

'Well, they shouldn't have been here in the first place,' she says. Them new boots of hers is mucky now, the way all good boots should be. 'Should they.'

'Aye. Happen I heard that said afore today,' I say. 'But I tell you what. They were people, miss. Actual people, real folk. And they all had sons and daughters and brothers and sisters and mums and dads. Some of em didn't even get found. Never got buried. Left for the crabs. You got a mum and dad, miss?'

She's quiet, the gull.

'Reckon it don't matter where they come from,' I says. 'That's no way to go. They shouldn't have died like that, not here. Not here.'

And then there are no more questions on it. We walk. Maybe I was a bit hard on her. And then again, maybe I weren't.

'That's quicksand,' I tell em. 'Shallow, but it'll stick hard. Mind your way.'

They drift apart from me, lag behind, talk amongst themselves. Mist in glue and reeling patches, a sometime hint of a sun, the ghost of distant shore. It's thinning, a blank nothing that squirms. Things I see that come and go in charcoal pieces. Two of them I found, two of the poor sods. Ebb, flow. My feet treading into a hundred square miles of mud and blank blank sand, wiped clean twelve hours at a time. The rhythm of walking is good for the spirit. These folk spend all that time sitting or their backsides or beating about like flies. Sometime it's simply good to walk, with a knapsack and a compass and a pocket knife and a good stick and a thermos full of soup. Even the fire in my hips and knees is dulling, lulled by the music of a journey of a thousand miles, a journey such as starts with a single step. All is well.

All is well.

There was two of them.

Two of em, drowned and turning over. Twenty-two of them. You should have been there, Henry. That's your job.

Calm, Henry. All is well.

Walk.

EXTRACT 2

And then my eyes start to fail me, see a shadow of something, a few hundred yard ahead. Must be a hound. But no, both are behind me with the group of walkers, tired and muddy happy hounds. And happen when I look west again, the shadow has gone. Blank and white, a shifting swirling wall, sand underfoot snaking into grey, ripples of it like the end of the world. The tides will tug forever. There's a lot of ghosts in this land. And I'm a daft old man who needs an eye test.

A shadow.

A dark shape, swimming in the fog. And I'm thinking, no.

Not again.

Don't let it happen again.

Not in my bay.

The lump shifts in the mist, swims away, swims back again, another soul hiding in the fog. Sudden it's more there than not there, flat and lumpen, laid out flat on the sand. A boggart, a banshee. Dream or no, that weren't a gull this morning. Knew I heard it. Banshees hanging off the steeple. Bloody Celts. Banshees are a sign of death. All them slumped stones in the priory graveyard. All the barrows in the valley. Wights chewing on the bones of dead kings waking up.

'What's that, mister Cowx?'

It's the first thing the kid's asked me, his mittened hand pointing at the dark lump.

'Good question, lad,' I murmur to him. 'Why don't I go and have a look, eh?'

And now the grown-ups have seen it, too.

'Rest here a moment, I reckon.'

'What is it?'

'I'll go and take a look. Stay here, please, folks. Have your lunch, a good spot for it.'

'A rock.'

'No rocks in the bay, he said.'

'They're called scars in the bay.'

'Skears. You're not saying it right.'

I leave them wittering on the sand bar, voices fusing in fog as I approach the little lump in little steps. Don't bother with the birch twigs when it's only me, thinking only not again, no, not again, no, no, no. Not another one. The bay's had enough already, and that's the truth. Another waterlogged body to heave-ho over, scoop a finger of sand from the eyes, pointless check the pulse, another little ghost walking with me in the sand, the fog, the bay, the sea. But I draw closer yet, and it ain't a person, is it. Relief floods through me, getting near. It's a lump is what it is, a hessian lump of something big. A broken-up crate, maybe, tumbled off a tanker. An upturned boat, washed up the coast. Some numpty's car, caught by coming tide. Sticks and tarpaulin. A broke-down tractor, decades old, long hidden and revealed overnight. A lost kite, that'd do me.

And then the fog clears afore me, and I see it clear and entire. Walk on regardless a few steps what don't make much sense. And then I stop, stop walking.

I stop walking.

My old eyes can't see the whole thing at once. It's huge. And it's a whale. A great whale. Wisps of cloud roll behind it in a flurry. Standing near a barn door tail of barnacles and piebald patches, I screw up my eyes, look at my feet. This ain't real. Tide-washed ridges of sand ripple away from me. It's not real. It's a ghost. Look again, Cowx lad. It's a sodding great whale, bang in the middle of the bay. And the journey starts with a single step. I walk up to it, walk around it. Can't quite grasp at the sadness of it, the size. The knotted line of spine, weed caught on a flipper like a dinghy, patches of white scattered on the grey, ash on charcoal.

I walk to the head, grooves in the long fluted head. My feet in the sand standing looking, soaking it in, wondering. Coils of fog that reel and drift around me. The ebbing tide has sucked the sand out from under it, left it in something of a puddle. Lying deep in a bed of mud and sea and still taller than me by far, by double or more, mebbe. The body is a drumlin, a dome, a burial barrow. Kings of old, a king of the sea. You've come a long way to get here, mucker.

What to do. Could leave it to the sea to wash away, to come and claim its own. Should probably call the council. How many miles it mun have travelled. Where it was born, where it's been and what it's seen. The tug of the currents, places I will never go. I haven't left my home in ten year. Whole days I can't feel my knees for the grinding. There's a rat always eating from the inside. Barnacles, everything in grit and flakes. How are they going to get rid of it? It's too big to carry out, even with yon bloody great digger from the quarry works. Can't bury it, no time between tides to dig deep enough. Maybe they'll ignore it, wait for the sea and gulls and fishes to clean it up, and take the bones one at a time on the back of Stephen's tractor. Or burn it. Health hazard. Picture the whitened stack of ribs clattered about in his flat bed trailer, bound for the tip, a tugging wake of landfill gulls churning after him in protest. The bones of kings, the barrow wights are cold and old, hunched up. Clinging to the steeple. There's a sadness in me like the end of the world. The size of it, too big for living.

And then it groans.

And then a tiny eye rolls at me.

And then there's a puff of air somewhere, somewhere atop that great smooth back. There's air. There's a lowing of cattle, lost and stuck. There's life. Life. It's alive. Alive, tiny slap in the sand, a flipper shifting. There's an eye watching, sees me clear, sad dark little deep down inside. Reach out. Pull off my glove, drop it. Stretch across the pool to touch the skin, lay a hand on the slick skin, palm flat, fingers spread, and press. The callous from my walking stick. Deep within, furnace bellows flutter, air hiss in and out. Something rumbles. Life. Spume in a trickle.

It is alive. It is drowning in the bay. My bay. My eyes prickle.

I am the Queen's Guide.

I'm the walker on the sands.

Swing my knapsack from one arm, ignore the rat that crickles in my elbow. Kneel beside the poor bloody thing. I fish about inside my bag, find the phone. You have to carry one, they said. It's Health and Safety, Henry. Alright, I said. I'll take one. Arm's length, I peer at the keypad. Nine, nine, nine.

'Which emergency service do you require.'

'Coastguard.'

'Connecting you now.'

Fuzz.

'This is the UK Coastguard. State your name and location and the nature of your emergency.'

'My name is Henry Cowx,' I says, and I am the walker on the sands. 'Morecambe Bay, to the north, about a mile due east from Kent's Bank. And I've found a whale.'

The phone hisses a moment, clears again.

'A whale.'

'Yes. Beached. It's alive.'

'A whale?'

'Aye, and a big one at that. Can you put me through to the Morecambe station, please, miss? I'll have Phil, if he's there. Or young Adam.'

'Uh, one moment.'

The whale moans, lows, stuck and lost, calling out forever. Mist gathers on its skin, runs down in glassy drops. Crick and crane my neck and look up at it, left and right, take it all it. It's a bloody whale. Gurgles, heaving. All dying things need company, ghosts that need the living now and then. Happen no-one should take the last walk on their own. You say your farewells before a journey, and well met on the other side. Flippers slapping sand, the daft great puddle he's landed in. The tide carved him out a grave.

'Steady, mucker. Steady.'

My phone yaps.

'Hello?'

'Who've we got here.'

'Hello, Henry. It's Adam.'

'How do, Adam.'

'What can we do for you today?'

'I've found a whale.'

'A whale. I thought that's what she said.'

'Aye. And it's a bloody big one.'

'Right, then. Whereabouts are you.'

'Near the eastern sand bar, mile from Kents Bank, mile from the river. Got eleven walkers and two dogs with me.'

'Grand. Reckon I'll send out Stephen and his tractor for your lot, first.'

'Aye.'

'And I'd better call the RSPCA or summat.'

'Better had, aye.'

'And then we'll come.'

'Right.'

'Grand day for walking.'

'That it is.'

'Haven't seen a fog like it since last year.'

'No.'

'Righto, Henry. See you in a bit.'

'So long, Adam.'

The phone dies with a long low steady tone which is not in keeping with the situation. I turn it off. Adam's a good lad, as Lancastrians go. I'd just as soon've had a Cumbrian. They get on with things, don't faff. But, still.

'Beggars and choosers, eh mucker?'

Stroke the whale again, skin like glass, a callous to be proud of, a lifetime of polish in the ocean. Smooth and salty as the grip on my old hawthorn. Never seen a whale before, the weight of it humped huge as Arnside Knott, the sand rinsed away around it. There's the odd dolphin washed up round the coast. Once, a porpoise in the Leven. Let nature run due course. Bird tracks in circles, waiting. Gulls and banshees, vultures. Sometimes the council come to burn them. Barrow wights.

'You're lost right bad, old son,' I murmur.

The great whale grins ten foot wide at me, agrees. He don't need telling. The mist is thinning still in growing day, breaks in the fog banks showing distant shore. In flat bright winter sun, windows glitter all along the shore. Watched on every side.

'Look, I'd best get back to my group.'

The whale watches me.

'But not for long. I'll be back for you.'

He don't want me to go.

'I hate to walk away, mucker, but the job has a duty of care.'

All for fifteen pounds a year and a cottage not worth the cost of demolition.

'So I'm coming back, alright. Soon.'

His careful eye, the great swell of body.

'Well met, mucker.'

A single step. A thousand miles. The fog dissolves as I draw towards them, the seven three one two sculptures on the sand bar. They look at me, watch me walking right close. I stand beside them, and they seem very small. A handshake like a butter pat. Metatarsals grinding. Flippers slapping sand. Handwriting, write names and wait for the sea what turns a new page every tide.

'Well, then,' says I. 'Well, then.'

'Henry?'

'Is everything okay?'

'What was it?'

'Well,' says I. 'It was a whale.'

'A what?'

'A whale. It's a beached whale.'

Pause.

'A real whale?'

The question don't seem stupid. Somewhere I can feel the coldest winter sun shining side-on blinding.

'Yes.'

'Christ.'

'A whale.'

'Is it still alive?'

'Aye, it is.'

'Can we go and see it?'

He's too eager, flapping at his camera.

'No,' I says, never in my life more certain. 'Best to leave it. I've called for a tractor to take you home, and the coastguard are coming out to see to the whale.'

'Why can't we see it?'

I glares at her, her in her snooty haircut and her job in the city and her boots bought once and never used again. 'Because it's alone and dying, that's why. And it don't need the distress.'

She glares back.

'But maybe we can help,' she sneers.

'Aye? That's right big of you,' I say. 'And what if it comes from China?'

Her mouth opens and closes shut. She crimsons, looks down. The group bubble down, but still they peer around me. The whale is cloaked in mist but coming visible, my tracks to and from it slowly sinking away. The sand takes the ocean, the ocean takes the sand. The scrap for all time. All of life is carried on the tide, one foot high and rushing. The fog is drifting back into the Irish Sea, takes the boggarts with it, takes the bloody banshees. Bloody Celts and all their little folk. The wights go back to their barrows, chew on the bones of kings long dead. Rats.

'Have your lunch, I reckon.'

But they don't believe me, so I set to my lentil soup, and then there's a reluctant shift of bags and Tupperware, sandwiches, tea in a flask, chocolate biscuits. I sit apart from them, half an eye on my whale, half an eye on the distant Kent. The mist is clearing. Sometimes the whale is in view altogether, and then more often than not, and then just there for the world to see. The curtains of fog draw back on my whale. The curtains draw back, drop him on a stage.

'Bloody hell. It's huge.'

All good things mun end. Them clever electric cameras purr and click and zoom in close.

The group are gawping, pointing, taking pictures, all but the nipper and his dad, who are drawing whales in the sand with a birch twig. Stephen appears distant in his tractor, churning sun through fizzing spray, the mist in only low small patches where there's still a shadow, clinging to the drowning pools. Lizzie'll want me home for a hot bath and my tea. Courage, Henry, and have some soup. It's only after unscrewing the thermos I feel the rust tweaking in my wrist. Old, and sudden tired, and riddled with holes. I'm part woodworm, part sawdust. I'm made of iron filings.

The youngster pats in the sand with his twig. It's a pretty good drawing of a whale.

'Why's it here, dad?'

'It's got lost, Andy.'

'Oh. But how did it get up and onto the land.'

'It didn't. Remember I told you about the tide?'

'No.'

'How it goes up and down every day?'

'It comes and goes, yes.'

'You remember?'

'Yes.'

'Well, it would've swum here when the tide was up,' and here he draws a wavy line above the whale, 'and then the tide went out, and it got left behind.'

A second wavy line, this one drawn beneath.

'Oh.'

'Yes.'

'That's sad.'

'It's very sad.'

'How will it get home, dad?'

Gulls, the sky in gold and brighting blue, blinding light of wet sun on winter sand.

'Dad?'

A long way south, two mile or more, way down on Cartmel Wharf, tiny black specks pick at the cockles. Same distance again, the dark lumps of Heysham.

My group take their pictures, try to get reception on their mobile telephones, chatter. Stephen's tractor draws closer, gets bigger, flays the sand, drags attention from the poor bloody beached thing. He carves a big circle around us, turning, the flatbed trailer clattering in protest, brings the cab round to point back at Arnside. He kills the engine and hops down from the cab, gumboot flops towards me.

'How do, Henry.'

'Hello, Stephen.'

He looks over at it, two hundred yards hence.

'You don't see that every day.'

'No.'

We look at it. From here, it could be an island, a skear. Whale Scar. A knott. Whale Knott. None of em sound right. It don't belong here. But it is of the bay regardless. It is of the sea. Living in a halfway place. Threshold. Anything can happen out here.

'Well then. Reckon I'd best be getting this lot home.'

'Aye, if you don't mind.' I step to the group. 'Folks, this is Stephen. He's taking you back to Arnside. This is the end of the walk.'

End of your walk, but not of mine. A thousand miles, a single step. Farewell, well met. They grumble but they go, Stephen giving hands up onto his flatbed. The hounds are picked up and bark uncertain, skitter at the trailer edge, ears flopping over eyes. The nipper's dad walks over to me.

'Thanks for the walk, mister Cowx.'

'Aye, fine. Thank you.'

'Andy thinks you're great. He said to say your joke was very funny.'

The lobster blushed.

'Aye, well. I'm sorry today's turned out like this. Shame not to finish the walk.'

He shrugs. 'The bay's not going anywhere. Maybe next time. Maybe later in the year. It's a shame about the whale.'

'Aye, lad. Aye, it is that.'

We look on it.
'So long, then, Henry.'
'Bye, lad.'

The nipper is waving at me. His dad hauls himself onto the trailer, settles down and puts the youngster in his lap. Stephen guns the engine, tractor turns a tight loop, herring bones carved into the mud. Mongrel yips. Most of the group are taking last pictures of the whale and talking on mobile telephones, but the nipper is still waving, his dad watching me, nods. Aye, so long. Well met, and so long. He was a decent one, that lad. Both him and his boy.

The sun is low and glaring in the clouds, the last of the fog filming pools and hollows. In every freezing pool there's a body, hunched over, hugging to its knees, neck twisted back and upwards, staring with white dead fish eyes. I see them all over.

Wait till the last sound of the tractor has been taken on the ragged wind, and I turn. It's me and the whale left alone in my great bay, my bay, all the little pulses of land and sand and water, fresh or salted, the currents and the quicksands, the mud and rivers and fish and gulls and little cockles and an old man shot through with arthritis and a bloody great sodding huge beached bloody whale.

Two hundred yards, a single step. Creak and crack, and go to find my fellow walker in the fog.

# El Café de l'Opera
**Cat Dean**

THE DAY AFTER the *Teatro Liceo* burst into flames, Luis and Paco greet me like an old friend, kissing me on both cheeks.

'*Siéntate! Siéntate!*' says Paco, white-haired and wearing a cream suit.

'He means "Please, sit down,"' says Luis, tipping his elegant fedora.

I squeeze behind the tiny marble-topped table and order a *café con leché* from the handsome beak-nosed waiter who usually ignores me. Above me float green *modernista* murals of thick-ankled girls bearing fruit on platters.

The musicians arrive; they speak of lost lovers and children: violins engulfed in flames, smoke-damaged cellos and of Ramón who is deep in wordless mourning for his bassoon. The talk bounces over the tables. Javier, *él trombonisto,* describes how he fought his way past the emergency services to rescue his trombone.

He pats the hard case.

'I never let her from me. *Nunca.* You understand?'

I understand. I look at the case and wonder how many women have envied it.

'I only eat *las frutas*. You understand?' asks Alejo.

'Mmm,' I am sucking a lemon *granita* through a straw.

'*Sólo las frutas.* Only fruits. *Sólo* – only. *Las frutas* – the fruits.'

'I know. I understand. Only fruit.'

'You are thinking "Why?" Why does this man only eat the fruits?'

I shrug. I am not thinking that.

'*Bueno, las frutas*, the fruits, they have many, many, many *vitaminos* and *nutritivas*. And look,' Alejo bares an arm, 'I am strong. I am the biggest in my family. I have four brothers. I am not the oldest. But I am the biggest.'

'Because of the fruit,' I say, nodding. Alejo is not tall.

'Yes. The fruit. *Exactamente.* That means 'exactly' but here we can say '*exactemente*'. You say it.'

'*Exactemente*,' I say. I look at my watch. 'I have a class.'

I end up in bed with some English teacher from one of the other language schools.

'Let's have a boff,' he says.

I giggle. I've never heard it called that before. Maybe he is very posh. Or maybe he is older than he looks.

'No thanks,' I say, and he gives up, after a while.

Hello everyone! This is a pic of Café de l'Opera, my 'local'. Why didn't anyone tell me teaching is hard work?! Has anyone else entered the murky world of employment yet? Does everyone still go to The Green Tree? And when are you layabouts going to come and visit? Isabel x

'Now you sit with *él astrólogo* but we met you first,' says Paco. His voice is petulant.

'You are so pale,' he continues.

'I am from Scotland.' I know what is

coming.

'Maybe you have the *problemos* only women have,' whispers Paco. 'I was a doctor; you can tell me.' He pats my hand and leaves his heavy on top of mine.

Sergi *el astrólogo* scribbles exquisite copperplate in a hardback book three, maybe four, inches thick. Every day he wears a dark red cardigan, a white shirt and a striped red-and-navy cravat.

'Read it,' he says one day, and pushes his book across the table.

'*No puedo*, I can't,' I say. 'I can hardly speak Spanish.'

'Read. Read!'

I am surprised; I get the gist of it: spheres, music, harmony, patterns on earth reflected in the sky.

'So, what is my sign?' I ask when I finish.

'Aquarius,' he snorts. 'What else?'

Then he takes my palm and tells me about myself.

'Come home with me,' whispers Javier, nuzzling the top of my head.

'*No gracias*,' I say.

A discussion starts.

'I just bought you dinner!' shouts Javier eventually. People look at us as they stroll down the Ramblas.

It's like being adrift in fast-flowing water: by the time I've grasped a phrase, more have swept past and the phrase I am clinging to doesn't seem important anymore. I let it go and reach for another.

'I don't understand,' I say. I can't explain that the water is flowing too fast; that I am drowning.

He keeps shouting. I pretend that he is talking about food.

'Why don't you want omelette! You're the type of girl who loves eggs! Or do you just pretend you love omelette? A little girl's game? I know you want omelette!'

When he is finished, I shrug in what I hope is a nonchalant Spanish fashion.

I pay Javier back by going to Bar Pastis with one of his friends, Henrik, a quiet Swedish guy with pale eyes and clammy hands. I make my excuses early and go home. Alone.

'I invite you to my house,' says Alejo.

'I don't think I should come to your house, not alone.' There is only so much talk of fruitarian diets I can take.

'*La casa de familia! La casa* – the house, *de familia* – of the family. Come *esto Domingo*.'

The last words persuade me. Everyone visits family or friends on a Sunday. Men, always men, carry patisserie boxes by their curled pastel-coloured ribbons through the quiet streets.

'Ok,' I say.

Next time I go to the café after the drink with Henrik, Luis and Paco raise their eyebrows; Javier is nowhere to be seen.

I don't go again for a while.

'Welcome!' says a voice as I step through the doorway.

I look around. I can see no-one. Then I look down. I am only 5'3" but in front of me is a woman who just reaches my breasts.

Alejo's mother sits beside me on the sofa with the see-through plastic covers. Her little thigh presses against mine. I am a giantess.

She keeps reaching up and squeezing my cheek, saying '*Nena, nena.*'

All the family are there; five brothers and the parents.

'Aha! *La vegetariana. Las frutas. Sólo las frutas y verduras!* Understand?' says Alejo's beaming father.

One brother makes a strange hand movement; he puts both forefingers together then rubs them lengthways against each other.

I cannot stop staring at his fingers; they seem so lewd but everyone laughs, even Alejo's mother. I look at the clock.

I don't say 'Give me an all-over boy-crop,' but that is what I get. When I come into my 8 pm class, there is silence. My hand drifts up to the back of my neck.

'It's short,' I say.

'Aii!' says Josep.
'Ay mi Dios!' says Nuria.
'You look like a boy!' says Ignasi.

There is a torrent of noise. Hands are raised, voices are raised, heads are shaken.

'Where is this *péluqueria*? How you say in English? Hairdresser?'

'Close to my flat,'

'Where you live?'

'In the *Barri Gótic*, near Café de l'Opera.'

'Ai, ai ai,' breathes Mercé.

Heads are shaken again and there is another silence.

'This is not a good place,' says Josep.

'This is not a good place for a foreigner,' says Ignasi.

'Or a woman,' says Nuria.

'Especially not a foreign woman,' says Josep.

'It is full of, how you say, people who take things?' says Mercé.

'Thieves?'

'Yes, *exactemente*, it is full of thieves. And gypsies!'

'And *las putas!*' says Nuria.

'That means whores,' adds Ignasi, helpfully.

Cousins who know the renting business are discussed. Friends who may have a free room are mentioned.

'My flat is fine. Now,' I turn to the whiteboard, 'who can tell me the difference between 'alone' and 'lonely'?'

I get a lot less bother from men.

When I look in the mirror, my face seems huge.

I miss the bother; more than I would have thought.

It could almost be a different café at night. I feel dowdy beside the slim-hipped Catalan girls and choose a table at the back.

A girl with white-blonde hair and red lips smiles over to me. She is with a black, muscular guy with a broad white slash of teeth.

'May we join you?'

She is German.

'Of course,' I gesture to the seats opposite. Maybe we will become friends. We chat. I keep running my fingers through my short crop, willing it to grow. After a while, a look passes between them and they disappear into the night.

I wonder if they were trying to pick me up. I drop by the café in the evenings from time to time, wondering if I'll bump into them again.

I don't.

I hear shouting, English shouting, on the street below. I push the doors open and step onto the balcony. Below are three men, early thirties, falling around and laughing.

'Hello,' I say. It's only 11PM, early for here. I am wearing a white cotton nightdress; it's tight over my breasts, flattening them completely.

They look up; their faces open with surprise.

'You're an angel,' says one. 'An English angel.' I don't correct him.

'How old are you, love?' asks another.

'I'm twelve,' I say, on a whim, and wait for the banter.

'Where's your mum, then?' asks the third. They really think I am a decade younger.

'Oh, she's out,' I say. 'She's an artist, she's got an opening.' It must be the short hair.

'Anyone in the house with you, darlin'?' asks the third again.

'No, I'm here alone. She'll be out for hours,' I say, for fun.

There's a scuffle of movement below. I lean over the cold railings to see. One of them is climbing up. I can see his shoulders heaving. His thick fingers grasp the balcony railings. His knuckles have black hairs on them. If I was wearing shoes I could stamp on them.

'Paul, you fucking nutter!'

'What are you doing, man?'

'I'm going to fucking get her!'

His friends try to pull him down. I step backwards into the room. I close and bolt the outside doors. I close and bolt the glass doors inside and sit still and small on my bed.

The blunt sound of him falling to the

ground.

Silence.

Then a massive crashing to the doors downstairs; I can feel it through the floor tiles. The whole building trembles. The battering goes on and on and on. Eventually there is shouting, angry Spanish shouting and then angry English shouting and then more angry Spanish shouting, and eventually, silence.

Instead of going to the bathroom during the night, I squat on the red tiled floor and pee into an empty Volvic bottle. When I wake in the morning, the sun shines through the gold liquid, pale as cava.

Coming up the Ramblas: Javier, wearing pale baggy trousers and a familiar-looking older man. Not Paco. Not Luis. He is wearing a denim shirt, a silver skull nestles on his chest, his hair is slicked down.

'You don't recognise me?' asks Sergi *él astrólogo*. '*Mira, mira,*' he says, holding out his hand so I can admire the raft of silver rings across his knuckles.

'*Que pasa?* What happened?' I asked.

'I finished my book!'

'*Félicidades!*' I go to kiss his cheek. He pulls me close and presses his stomach against me. His breath is heavy and rank; I can smell his sweat.

'Now I have money! Money for drink, money for women!' he says. Sergi lets me go and links arms with Javier, dancing around like an overweight satyr.

The beak-nosed waiter brings over my *café con leché* and stands by my shoulder, opening and closing his hand without looking at me. I pay; he leaves.

I look up at the murals and imagine one of the thick-ankled girls taking a peach from her platter, pulling her arm back and aiming it straight at me. My hand shakes slightly as I pick up the *café con leché* and I slosh coffee across the table. A fat brown splash lands on the postcard I have just written. I wipe it with a napkin but it smears my words.

It is stained but readable. I will still send it.

Hello everyone! At Café de l'Opera again. Here is the Sagrada Familia; it's very moving. Decided to teach in Tokyo after the summer, so come and visit soon! Isabel x

# Sandra Alland
## Air

'REMEMBER THE FLIGHT to Costa Rica in '96 when we toured the cockpit twice? Amazing.'

Sasha and I always took tours of the cockpit in those days. You just asked a flight attendant and they took you up to see the sunset or mountains or whatever, and you chatted up the pilots about the importance of their job. In '98, Sasha broke her leg roller-blading just before we left for Iceland. She was so charming during the cockpit tour that the captain decided to let her land with them. Since she was already in there and her leg hurt, I was sent back to my seat.

'I remember smoking on the plane from San Salvador to San José,' she says now, buckling her seatbelt and placing her seat into the upright position. 'That was amazing.'

'It was disgusting and we didn't,' I tell her. Sasha always has memory problems with anything related to health. 'We both smoked, but the 'smoking section' two rows behind us was so full I puked and you had an asthma attack.'

'Amazing,' insists Sasha, then goes quiet for a while. She's back in Costa Rica, probably smoking.

As the plane starts to move, I remember the clouds of smoke floating around us as we floated among real clouds inside a hunk of 1970s metal. It had indeed been amazing. We had been shocked by videos of people back in the '60s smoking at universities or in hospitals. Yet cigars on a plane were still normal.

'What about the machetes?' she asks. 'Those were truly amazing.'

The machetes. We'd gone to Costa Rica for four months to work for a volunteer program called *Youth Is Great!* I blush every time I think of my stupidity in 1996. I was only 22, and like everything it was Sasha's idea, but neither is the best excuse. I thought I was helping build a school dining hall in a tiny Latin American village that didn't have school dining halls or electricity. *Youth Is Great!* thought I was 'developing my character' and raising $4000 for them to spend on anything but Costa Ricans or food for volunteers. They turned out to be more right.

Sasha and I did build a dining hall, sort-of. But we also mutinied from *Youth Is Great!* and our 20-year-old Australian group leader, Tracy Without An E. We became friends with some local farmers, and when the rains came early they asked us to help pick the bean crops before they rotted. Because we were considered delicate females at the construction site, we were only allowed to develop our characters by throwing buckets of water on the walls to keep the concrete from cracking. Sasha was a carpenter and we were both feminists, so we didn't need much encouragement to go AWOL.

Don Licho handed us machetes and Sasha went at those beans like Tank Girl. I took a slower approach, talking with Don Licho in the rain, asking in my limited Spanish about his farm and how exactly one uses a machete. Despite her complete lack of Spanish, Sasha managed to tell him I was a poet, so it was instantly decided that I would recite while we worked. Don Licho had a respect for poetry that I'd never seen in Canada; it was like he thought it was a necessity.

The rhythm of the rain and machetes was the perfect backdrop to my poem about hating Tracy Without An E and how this experience had changed my life but not how I'd imagined. I felt fantastic speaking angrily into the clouds. Don Licho seemed to dig it, too, as far as you can dig poetry by a 22 year-old in bad Spanish. But I'm pretty sure the whole town hated *Youth Is Great!* so I was bound to be a hit.

The next day I got stung by a scorpion and almost died. The nearest doctor was an hour by a bus that came only on Tuesdays, no one had a car, the one bicycle *Youth Is Great!* had supplied was broken, and I didn't see any horses nearby. I was furious that I would die in the service of *Youth Is Great!* So was Sasha. She had decided I would be a famous poet that very morning, and saw my impending death as a slight to her genius and financial security.

'The world wasn't safer then,' Sasha interrupts sleepily. 'Machetes!'

When I didn't die from the scorpion bite and the beans were all picked, we went back to watering the walls for another few weeks. But we were different people – thinking about dying does that I guess. Also Don Licho had given us both a gift for helping: a large bag of green beans and shiny new machetes. Though we were severely emaciated, the machetes excited us more than the beans. They gave us a sort of magical power over the dread that was *Youth Is Great!* We didn't care anymore that the water filter was broken and we probably had parasites and impending dengue fever. We went wandering off into the forest whenever our foreman wasn't looking, and slashed gleefully at giant ferns and banana leaves.

No one blinked when we boarded the plane back to Canada, machetes gleaming from their place tied to our carry-on knapsacks. We took a tour of the cockpit with our machetes. Sasha showed hers to the pilot, told him how she decimated the scorpion that tried to kill me. How now the future of literature was safe.

'Amazing,' Sasha says into my hair as we rise heavily into the air.

I nod and breathe her in, staring at the sealed cockpit door.

## THE UNIVERSITY of EDINBURGH

**Scottish Universities' International Summer School**

Creative Writing and Literature Courses

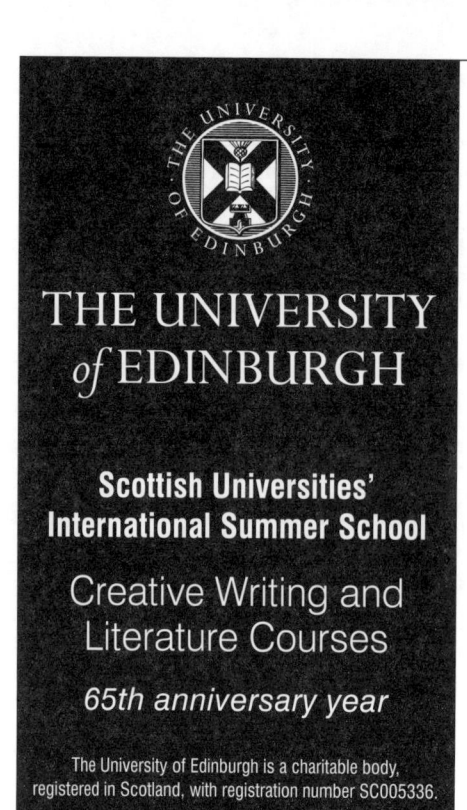

*65th anniversary year*

The University of Edinburgh is a charitable body, registered in Scotland, with registration number SC005336.

**Creative Writing** 31 July–18 August 2012

An intensive Creative Writing course with a difference in the beautiful city of Edinburgh. This is an accredited course. The programme includes: masterclasses; small-group seminars; individual one-hour tutorials each week; morning lectures in Contemporary Literature; events at the Edinburgh International Book Festival; a social and cultural programme and the bi-annual publication of *Northern Light*.

**Text and Context Literature Courses**
9 July–18 August 2012

Courses consist of morning lectures followed by two-hour seminars. Accredited at two levels. Residential and non residential places. 2012 literature courses:

- Modernism            9 July–21 July
- Scottish Literature    23 July–4 August
- Contemporary Literature   6 August–18 August.

For further information please check our website, where you can download the brochure and the application forms for Creative Writing and the Text and Context courses: **www.summer-school.hss.ed.ac.uk/suiss**

---

# Ramshackle
## Elizabeth Reeder

'Original, moving and insightful... A beautiful book.'
Anne Donovan

Released 23 April 2012

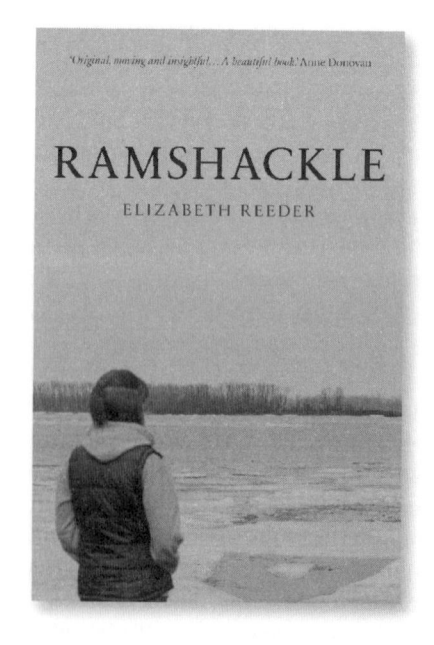

**FREIGHT BOOKS**

freightbooks.co.uk

# Truthful Fiction, Narrative Truth

Villa Pacifica & Twelve Minutes of Love: A Tango Story
**Kapka Kassabova**
*Alma Books, RRP £12·99, 320pp &*
*New Live Portobello Books, RRP £18·99, 323pp*

However tempting it is to read a novel as the author's true self, we must be cautious not to imagine too much truth in the fiction construct. But with the parallels between Kapka Kassabova's first UK novel and third memoir – as well as their joint publication – we are positively encouraged to draw parallels between (so-called) truth and fiction.

In *Villa Pacifica*, 39 year-old Ute is travelling with her husband, Jerry, through a remote and exotic part of the South American coastline. Ute is used to travelling for her job as a guidebook writer, but unseasoned traveller Jerry joins her to work on his stalled novel. They stumble across Villa Pacifica, an almost-empty hotel beside a national park. It's 2009, but the guestbooks are only filled in up to 2006 – which is the beginning of the time-slips, confusions and overlaps. More guests arrive, the sexual tension builds, the weather threatens, and it's not long before someone ends up (literally) inside the tiger's cage.

On the surface, the non-fictional *Twelve Minutes of Love: A Tango Story* seems very different. It's a personal chronicle of the author's 10-year obsession with tango, as well as a history of the dance and its music. Kassabova's intense prose and emotional distance create an odd contrast, as the narrative feels simultaneously sparse and lush – rather like tango itself, perhaps. Even those with little interest in the technicalities of dance steps will appreciate how Kassabova's ennui turns to a gradual kindling of passion for dance, for love, for life.

Reading *Twelve Minutes of Love* after *Villa Pacifica*, I felt like I was seeing childhood photos of acquaintances, or old pictures of buildings before they're renovated. Look, there's the ruggedly sexy man with his maté gourd! There's the tsunami, the political upheaval, the snapshots of exotic but disappointing places! And of course, Ute/Kapka, the wandering woman with her Eastern European hangups, repressed desires and confusion about love. It may sound like it would be dull to read the same characters in two different narratives, but in practice it's quite the opposite. It's fascinating to trace the lines of truth in the fiction – as much as memoir can be truth, that is – and to see how authors continually spin their lives into narrative.

For me, *Twelve Minutes* had a far more satisfying narrative than *Villa Pacifica*, and it's only when reading the former that I realised what was lacking in the latter. I wouldn't want to give away *Villa Pacifica's* ending, but to be honest I couldn't if I tried; even weeks after reading it, I still don't see how all the little mysteries tie together. It reaches no conclusions, touching on many possibilities but committing to none. And maybe that's the point: it doesn't all tie together, just as in life. But a novel is not a life, it is a narrative – and while ambiguous endings aren't necessarily a bad thing, here it felt unsatisfying after such an intense and lushly-described buildup. *Twelve Minutes*, on the other hand, wraps everything up beautifully. Perhaps because it spans a much longer time period, Kassabova is able to step back and see the route of her journey: not just where she's been, but where she might go next. It even has an epilogue to conclude the stories of each of the principle characters. And of course, there's a happy ending.

Both *Villa Pacifica* and *Twelve Minutes of Love* stand up perfectly well on their own, but reading them together gives a much more enriching experience. The joy for me as a reader was in the blurring between fact and fiction: the echoes of people; the intensity of place; the protagonist's desire to find herself, to lose herself, to capture some intensity of life that constantly eludes her.
**Velveteen Rabbit**

# Blue Notes

Furnace
**Wayne Price**
*Freight Books, RRP £8·99, 176pp*

*There was no depth to life, I remember thinking suddenly, and it seemed like a moment of final clarity and truth to me, the great lesson of my long, trivial summer. There was a shifting, fascinating surface to people and the things they felt and said, but underneath it all was just a stony simplicity.*
'Underworld'

The award-winning, Scotland-based short story writer Wayne Price is no stranger to *Gutter* magazine, having seen two stories published within its pages, in its first and fifth issues. The latter, 'The Wedding Flowers', is reprinted in this, his first collection, which – it must be noted, in the literary equivalent of a declaration of interest – comes from the same publisher as this very literary journal. Collecting together a baker's dozen of stories, standing tall without the increasingly-obligatory introduction by a recognisable author, *Furnace* quickly shows that Price is a measured, meticulous writer. This is both the collection's strength and its potential weakness.

In one sense at least, his stories cross the world, with locations ranging from Edinburgh to New Hampshire, from a down-at-heels Welsh fishing village to the dusty Chilean countryside. As for his central point of view characters, he seldom repeats the same gender, age, class or cultural characteristics, although it's fair to say that their sexual orientation is invariably heterosexual. That said, in 'Rain', it's arguable that the strongest, albeit passive, presence in the narrative is an injured racing pigeon.

By bringing these stories together, however, *Furnace* also shows just how similar Price's writing can appear on first reading. Images and tropes pop up repeatedly, such as unseasonably hot weather, insects on flesh, fish, and characters named only by what they do – the fisherman, the slaughterman, the manager. Characters are invariably mired in the memories of past actions, marred by the wisdom of hindsight. Perhaps most important of all, regardless of whether the story is being told in the first or third person – or who the pivotal character actually is – Price's cool authorial voice remains clear throughout. And it is the kind of voice that ensures, however much you might sympathise with his characters' confusion, sadness and loss, it's generally difficult to care much about them.

Yet these are not stories that fade quickly in the memory; despite a lack of any flashy writing, these are tales which can linger, unsettlingly, in your quiet moments. Given that Price first came to Scotland in 1987 to begin a PhD on contemporary American fiction, it's not stretching credulity to suggest that he is consciously following in the footsteps of Raymond Carver, who was at the height of his powers at that time. Yet Price's work isn't simply a hollow copy of Carver; he has found his own voice and expression of Henry David Thoreau's much-quoted "lives of quiet desperation".

If you are a reader who habitually jumps around collections and anthologies, choosing what to read first on length, title or other such criteria, it's worth pointing out that *Furnace* offers real rewards to those who read the stories in the order in which they are published. Thematic variations flow from story to story – from uncooked fish in one to cooked fish in the next, and then on to a story called Salmon. Price is like a cool jazz musician, using his familiar tools and idiosyncrasies to improvise subtle variations in colour and tone in each piece; building from one story to the next is a subtle strand that pulls you through the collection. Optimism may not be obviously on show, but there are moments of real pleasure to be found within these pages. *Furnace* is a startlingly confident and powerful debut.
**Yeti**

# Politics, Politics

The Bees
**Carol Ann Duffy**
Picador, RRP £14·99, 96pp

In every collection, a reader learns about the poet's life. In the case of Carol Ann Duffy's *The Bees*, her first collection since becoming Britain's poet laureate in 2009, we learn of the responsibilities of her job. From what can be gathered, it's mildly soul-destroying. An authorial and politically-conscious voice rises from *The Bees*, which, due to poems about the Duke and Duchess of Cambridge and David Beckham, feels more serviceable than personal.

To begin, one must understand Duffy's broad metaphor of bees. Bees represent people at work, language and virtue. "I became a human bee at twelve", Duffy narrates in a poem about an early job picking fruit. Bees also represent the sound and structure of language. Duffy describes the qualities of bees in the opening poem: "brazen, blurs on paper, / besotted, buzzwords, dancing / their flawless, airy maps". Duffy mimics these attributes in her work. Media buzzwords sting in the poem entitled 'Politics': "to you industry, investment, wealth; roars, to your / conscience, moral compass, truth, POLITICS, POLITICS." Duffy also conveys the erratic motion of bees with staccato beats, jazzy rhythms and mid-line drop offs. In 'Echo', the disjointed yet repetitive lines on the page successfully create a swinging motion:

> "when your face...
>        when your face,
> like the moon in a well
> where I might wish"

However, the bees in these poems also represent purity, a metaphor that puzzles. Is she commenting on the purity of poetry as the highest art form? Perhaps, as in the poem 'A Rare Bee' where a bee blesses a poet with inspiration: "and that this bee made honey so pure, / when pressed to the pout of a poet / it made her profound..." Romantic imagery of bees as munificent creatures is evident in this poem and in many others.

Poems about 'bees' aside, the remainder of the collection is a blend of civic-duty poems and those which shed light on Duffy's life. To her credit, the royal wedding poem 'Rings' is a gentle, lyrical poem which celebrates marriage in general, and does not specifically mention the royal couple. However, the poem about David Beckham entitled 'Achilles' loses its appeal when the reader realises it's about the football player and his injury. As laureate, Duffy also includes political poems such as 'Big Ask', which addresses government secrecy in a series of rhyming questions. The answers provided are deliberately evasive and ironic: "Guantanamo Bay – how many detained? / How many grains in a sack?" Though sharp-tongued and timely, the long pairs of q's and a's take on a flippant tone after a while.

It can be concluded then, that Duffy is best when she has no agenda. We start to hear her personal observations and naturally majestic voice in the poem 'Drams'. The lovely, wintry three line stanzas create a pleasing rhythm: "Barley, water peat, / weather, landscape, history; / malted, swallowed neat". Other soft-toned poems include a poignant tribute to her mother entitled 'Water', where Duffy describes their final moments together: "Your last word was water, / which I poured in a plastic hospice cup, held / to your lips – your small sip, half-smile, sigh". But despite these gems in between, Duffy ends the collection on the subject of bees. Returning to 'A Rare Bee', the narrator goes in search of a mystic bee that inspires artists, and prays: "Give me your honey, bless my tongue with rhyme, poetry and song". This parting line from Duffy makes it sound as though for Britain's poet laureate, writing has become work.
**Puss In Boots**

# Trapped on the Tide

The Blue Book
**A L Kennedy**
*Jonathan Cape, RRP £16.99, 384pp*

Physically, *The Blue Book* is beautiful. It has an attractive Prussian blue hardback cover with gold trim and lettering, the pages have the same blue edging, the paper is of outstanding quality, the whole thing has a pleasant heft to it. As Kennedy says "blue books keep the privacies of trades and crafts", which in this novel is the craft of being a dodgy psychic. Open up this wonderful object and you will not find the element of 'readability' so desired by Booker prize judges, but an extremely challenging read.

*The Blue Book* concerns the story of Elizabeth who, while waiting to board a luxury liner for a trans-Atlantic voyage with her partner, Derek, is accosted by an intrusive man and his magic tricks. We later learn that the intruder is Arthur Lockwood, Elizabeth's former lover and ex-stage partner in a psychic double-act. Once on board, Derek quickly develops chronic sea-sickness and is subsequently side-lined from the plot and any further character development. The narrative then takes up the possible reconciliation of Elizabeth and Arthur until their arrival in New York and the final twist in a very simple and straightforward story.

There is no doubting Kennedy's talents as a writer. When she stays with Arthur, when she takes us into his childhood and adolescence, when she keeps to a non-tricksy writing style full of wit, rhythm, sharpness and insight, she can be a real pleasure to read. She is particularly good at describing Arthur's uncanny ability to inhabit the loves, fears and desires of the clients he is reading. The book is probably at its most interesting when she reveals many of the trade secrets from the world of the professional clairvoyant. It was not surprising therefore to see Derren Brown cited in the Acknowledgements.

However, it is in the voice of her main character, Elizabeth, that Kennedy is at her most infuriating. First off, she delivers this character in three different fonts – plain, italic and bold. Authors resorting to visual tricks are a bit like film directors using voice-overs – it probably means the text or dialogue is just not good enough to support the narrative. Then there are those lists that read like Thesaurus entries as in "someone goes to see a card-reader, palm-reader, aura-reader, colour-reader, I-Ching reader, psychic, obeah man, medium, santeria wise woman, healer, crystal gazer, cyber-witch, someone who claims to be a gypsy on a seaside pier." There is the tautology and endless repetition as in "Elizabeth concentrates on biting, chewing, swallowing, biting again – on bread and meat and meat – while Bunny and Francis continue to be cleanly and plainly and purely just what they appear to be." And those words that run into each other for no reason at all, like 'everyfuckingwhere' and 'blacksuitmen.' The reader is not only trapped inside a listing vessel desperate to get to the end of the voyage, but also inside an over-elaborate writing style desperate to get to the end of a sentence.

Conversations between Elizabeth and Arthur are consistently intense and unnatural, while those between Elizabeth and two elderly passengers, Bunny and Francis, seem an irrelevant distraction. We spend an inordinate amount of time staggering along tilting corridors and assembling food from the buffet bar. When we do get taken on a journey into Elizabeth's subconscious, invariably we end up with hardly any greater insight than when we started.

*The Blue Book* is a curate's egg of a novel albeit a very pretty ultramarine one. No doubt reviewers and prize-givers will love it for its challenging nature and its slick and crafty use of language. While this reviewer could not help but admire this novel's aloof intelligence, overall this was a frustrating read.

**Tarka the Otter**

# Teenage Kicks in Shetland

The Roost
**Neil Butler**
*Thirsty Books, RRP £7.99, 208pp*

Neil Butler's *The Roost* – his debut collection of short stories – is set in Scotland's northernmost outpost. Ever since Alasdair Gray's breakthrough with *Lanark*, Scotland in literature has become inhabited by the imaginations of those who live in it, as opposed to views imposed from outside. Now here is a new version of a part of Scotland to add to the panoply of writers who have re-imagined their own locations.

Escape, or the lack of it, is at the heart of Butler's work, which has some of the depth of a novel through its linked set of characters. A bit like *Trainspotting*, although without the impact of that whizz-bang of a book, *The Roost* takes us on a tour not of a landscape but of a sub-culture, in this case a set of angst, sex, drugs and games-ridden teenagers permanently exiled in a place that offers them either their whole lives, or nothing at all. In this place, like everywhere else, the possibility of love, friendship and aspiration exists, and so do beatings, drug deals, blackmail, rape and exploitation. Butler shows us a territory that is neither a rural paradise nor a backwater, following his group of wild children as they grow up simultaneously shepherded by and completely unknown to their parents.

He handles it for the most part with verve and skill. He seems able to inhabit his characters, almost to creep inside them. We can relive, if we want to, the pitiless glare of puberty, its deep cruelty and complete lack of any concern for anyone else. Hormones, bottles of booze and pills pop as Butler reminds us how scary it is to be that age. That his young players lack compassion, like the vicious Ellie, or are marginalised, like game-boy Simon in 'Rage Quit', brings back the full horror and seductive joy of teenage kicks in a deliciously disgusting cocktail.

When these stories are at their best, the comedy and terror of adolescent existence is captured completely. Ellie's inner torment as she's taken on a tour of relatives and the local wildlife when she'd rather be ruining the lives of her drunken pals, for example, works well, maybe better than her eventual shallowness. Similarly, Simon's isolation at school, home and in his head – except when he plays on his Xbox – brings out the true awkward, gangly, physical pain. Other stories in the collection manage this less well. Butler's lightly sketched style is effective, but one or two episodes seem too flimsy for their cargo and founder under the burden he places on them.

But where he's good he's very good, and the sharp-cracking dialogue and hard-nosed sarcasm of these lost souls whip through the book like lashes of Atlantic wind. Local culture and dialect are relegated to second place, seen as pretensions rather than anything to do with the lives of these young people, while Butler places new media at the centre of his characters' lives without ever pretending that it has replaced their hearts. They might communicate in all sorts of new ways on their laptops, consoles and mobile phones, for better or worse, but their real hearts can still be broken, and usually are.

Maybe the most interesting device is the mixture of legend and reality: a selkie as one of the young girls, a dog that can change shape. But these excursions into the fantastic, although they work well, are not taken any further, as if the author has toyed with them before deciding against. There is a growing sense of confidence through the collection and by its end it is the realistic picture of the awful transience of adolescence that strikes the reader most strongly. This is an assured debut by a new voice that for the most part says what it sets out to. But the best is undoubtedly still to come.

**Marvo the Wonder Chicken**

# True Lies

My Mother's Lover
**Urs Widmer**
**Translated by Donal McLaughlin**
*Seagull Books*, RRP £12·00, 127pp

These days literary biography is becoming an increasingly popular diversion for novelists. Think of John Burnside's acclaimed *A Lie About My Father* (Cape 2006) and *Waking Up in Toytown* (Cape 2011) and Janice Galloway's award-winning *This Is Not About Me* (Granta 2008) and *All Made Up* (Granta 2011). One suspects these departures are partly to pay the rent, partly to generate a wider readership. But biography must also be liberating for novelists, allowing them to play with the reader's obsession with 'real truth' against the perceived untruth of fiction.

The idea of a story being true has always delivered humankind a delicious frisson. Culturally, truth is very now. It's at the heart of the inexplicable popularity of sub-reality TV shows like The Only Way is Essex. And misery lit. And *Heat* magazine. We love so-called truth. We gorge on it.

In *My Mother's Lover*, Urs Widmer, one of Switzerland's most acclaimed and prolific writers, draws on his own life and family to create a beautiful and heart-breaking story of unrequited love. As with Burnside and Galloway, the book is one of a number by Widmer that explore his own biography. Delicately and elegantly translated by Scotland's own Donal McLaughlin, this is a short but complex and enthralling read.

It begins in the present with the death of the eponymous lover, Edwin, a now famous composer, wealthy industrialist and undisputed national treasure. Widmer's mother, Clara, is long dead, driven mad by her unreciprocated passion. She'd first encountered Edwin as a penniless and humourless young man, in the carefree days after the Great War, when she'd attended concerts performed by his shoestring orchestra, specialising in the exciting new music of the time, Bartók, Stravinsky et al. As an heiress, dominated by her self-made father, she hardly notices him, but becomes embroiled in the running of the orchestra. Eventually, despite her natural reticence, they become lovers.

However, Clara is only a waypoint on Edwin's voyage to success, and she is soon discarded. She's made penniless by the Crash of 1929, and whether by fortune or design, Edwin marries into the business that was once hers, and through a talent for profiteering during World War Two, Edwin becomes one of the richest men in Switzerland as well as an acclaimed artist. The small kindnesses that keep Clara's love alive turn out to be mirages, and despite marriage and a child (Widmer), she slowly loses her mind.

It's been suggested that the character of Edwin is based on the Swiss conductor and businessman Paul Sacher. When Widmer discusses this book in public he states categorically that it's the story of his mother's ruined life. But one suspects that the author of over thirty books, as many radio plays and the translator of amongst others, Joseph Conrad's *Heart of Darkness* (another story presented as reportage), is playing with our obsession with truth. Widmer delivers his tale poker faced, and his skill as a writer has you flicking through looking for family photos. The powerful anger at the heart of the novel is reminiscent of Hanif Kureishi's *Intimacy*, another allegedly autobiographical novel. But while the personal story resonates, I suspect the target of Widmer's opprobrium is not Edwin/Sacher, but the culture and society that created him, and the story is that of a nation jilted by those who once promised so much. But, deliciously, the question remains, is it true or is it 'all made up'?

**Behemoth**

# What Dreams Can Do

As Though We Were Flying
**Andrew Greig**
Bloodaxe Books, RRP £8.95, 64pp

*As Though We Were Flying* begins with what amounts to a chilly shock in 'The Tidal Pools of Fife', a fond reminiscence of the lost (and hard-to-believe-it-ever-existed) culture of Scottish coastal outdoor swimming pools. To a carefully-set stage of "rough concrete walls" and "long pastel beaks of diving-boards where folk dared or did not", Greig invites us to immerse ourselves in the logic of his book, like the poem's "loons and quines" do in Fife's icy salt water. It's a canny start to the collection, the metaphor of diving in cold and waiting for the body to adjust to the water's temperature a suitable analogy for the experience of sharply recalled memory, but also of commencing reading, gradually tuning into the book's rhythms and textures.

And just as I imagine the waters of the coastal pools must have, Greig's writing resists total adjustment. Like his friend and mentor Norman MacCaig, the subject of Greig's last book *At the Loch of the Green Corrie*, Greig's writing manages to be both forthright and subtle, direct and aslant. Ranging between Edinburgh, Spain, Orkney and Fife, the poems in this, his eighth collection, seem permanently caught in the enjoyably sudden, alert wooziness of waking up and not knowing at first exactly where you are. Less jetlag, as the book's title might lead you to suppose, than the sense of returning home after an absence. It's not unfamiliarity that causes the collection's dominant atmosphere of faint disorientation; rather, it's familiarity itself, a sense of uncertain recognition, or as he puts it in 'The Natural Order: thrush': "Such an old thing new, / pine needles sprung / sharp on fading sky / as missal thrush hits topmost twig, / clings on, sings –".

Sensing the old anew is also the subject of 'Edinburgh Coliseum', in which Greig sees the violence, debauchery and spectacle of ancient Rome re-enacted in Scotland's capital as "footpads, dossers / and night patrols scuffle behind the museum, / and the consuls carriage glides by the Coliseum / while drunks screw in the dried-up fountain / in the moon-drenched Princes Street Gardens". If there's awkwardness in the proximity of 'dried-up' and 'drenched', it's that I mean by the collection's subtle disorientation, its air of confused coming-to, as if from a dream.

Dreaming is at the heart of *As Though We Were Flying*, the title seeming to refer to the commonly reported dream sensation of flight. But Greig is no surrealist, and his attitude to dreams is less that of blurring the distinction between dream-life and reality than marking it out, stoically shaking it off. He describes waking beside his wife who recounts her dreams of the night before and immediately his attention diverges to the here and now: "her moving lips, throat, those slim shoulders / draped in a shawl of light". One of the most formally interesting poems of the collection, 'The best thing a dream', is built around a short sequence of variations on that phrase, winding intestinally around its theme: "no the best thing a dream / can do is remind you / it's not true".

Less successful is 'The Luncheon of François Aussemain and Erzébet Szántó', in which Greig borrows Don Paterson's alter-ego of Aussemain and introduces him over a glass of Pernod to the romantic interest of his own satire of a public intellectual: tweed-suited Erzébet Szántó, who "strides Princes Street Gardens in Doc Martens." The poem lacks some of Paterson's wit, and I hope I'm not being too prim when I consider its gags as puerile, relying on the idea that the couple might have "got it on in Edina". That poem aside, the collection is a delightful mapping of arousal in its least suggestive sense, a suite of sensory awakenings to sit up and take notice of.

**General Woundwort**

# On Two Sides

Across The Bridge
**Morag Joss**
*Alma Books, RRP £12.99, 300pp*

The premise for *Across The Bridge* is an intriguing one. A woman, unhappily married and recently pregnant, is on holiday near Inverness. When a local bridge collapses her car is plunged into the river and everyone, including her husband, presumes she's been killed. The fact that she was not even in the car provides her with a means for escape. She lets everyone believe she is dead and begins a new life on the other side of the river: across the bridge.

Three narrative strands follow the three main characters, with most time being spent on two women: Annabel, as the mother-to-be renames herself, and Silva, a young, Eastern European woman who has been living with her husband and daughter in a trailer on the banks of the river. What only Annabel knows is that Silva's missing husband was driving her car – and it's this knowledge that leads her to Silva's trailer, where the women form a surprising, if secretive, friendship. And so, in some respects, this is a book about redemption, about working through loss and being given a second chance. This is particularly evident in the third strand of the narrative, which follows Ron, a modern day Charon seeking redemption for his role in the fatal crash of a busload of children.

Ron is not so much a character but a symbol as he ferries people across the water, from town to forest, from one life to the next. He is haunted by guilt and searching for purpose, which he finds by helping Annabel and the bereaved Silva build a new home in an abandoned cabin in the forest. While the women clean and wash curtains, Ron clears the gutters and does other manly things like sorting out the plumbing. It was around this point that I began to wonder what the message of the book was meant to be. If you're a woman and you want to start a new life, what you really need is a man around to help you? But thirty pages before the end the tone changes completely, from meditation on rebirth to fast-paced thriller complete with buckets of tension and torture.

I like a thriller as much as the next reviewer, and the writing in these last chapters leaps off the page. Joss's status as an award-winning crime writer is evidently well deserved: the horror is undeniable and I raced to the end of the book. The trouble is it felt like the end of an entirely different book to the one I had been reading; the message less that it is possible to find redemption, more that pregnant women had better not depend on other women for help, because underneath their suspiciously efficient skin they are vicious unhinged psychopaths.

The fourth character in the book is Annabel's husband Col, and he's my favourite – not because he's nice (he's not) but because he surprised me in a quiet and very believable way. At first he seems dull and cruel, and it's his insistence that Annabel get rid of her baby that prompts her to disappear, convincing herself that he will forget all about her. But he doesn't forget. He haunts the book, returning to the collapsed bridge day after day and turning to Ron for support. Whether he really does love Annabel after all or is being driven by a mixture of guilt and loneliness it's hard to say but, like all the characters, when he is left alone, he is left lost and searching. Perhaps his haunting presence is supposed to be creepy, but it's not. It is sad and poignant. What lingers after finishing the book is not the brutal finale but the behaiour of these two men. It may not be the message intended but for me the real core of the story is this: it doesn't matter what side of the bridge you are on, or how many times you think about crossing over; at the end of the day, the human need for a bit of company is pretty universal.

**Golden Monkey**

# Fiction and Football

Bring Me The Head of Ryan Giggs
**Rodge Glass**
*Tindal Street Press, RRP £12.99, 288pp*

Sport and art never seem to have the easiest of relationships, particularly when it comes to football. It can be depressing to count the number of awful films involving football; likewise, you don't need too many fingers to count the times fiction and football come together with any outstanding results: David Peace's *Damned United*; Irvine Welsh's often overlooked *Marabou Stork Nightmares*; and most recently, Alan Bissett's *Pack Men*. To this canon, not quite a first eleven, more an aspiring five-a-side team, can be added Rodge Glass's new novel *Bring Me The Head of Ryan Giggs*.

Glass's novel isn't the story of Ryan Giggs, so those expecting an exposé of the superinjunction scandal will be sadly disappointed. It's the story of Mark 'Little Giggsy' Wilson: a footballing prodigy destined for great things as part of the now iconic Manchester United team of 1990's, 'Fergie's Fledglings'. His life is defined by the highs and lows of his team; he's a boy who never fitted in, never understood the world around him, and his only guidance and solace is his father and football. But when both of these are wrenched from his grasp, Wilson is unable to cope, turning into a sociopath, an obsessive and a fantasist, unable to deal with his failure or the success of others. Success epitomised by one Ryan Giggs.

The backdrop of this novel is the story of Manchester United's meteoric rise from the barren years of late eighties to the constant success of recent times, reaching a pinnacle within the novel with the 2008 Champions League Final. The book's emotional heart however is the story of Mark and his father, Gregory, who is an alcoholic and a gambler, but also the person from whom Mark most craves love and respect. His father sees escape through Mark's footballing skill and obsessively drives him forward, to the detriment of everything else in his life. But when his father disappears just before Mark's United debut, the point of it all disappears. With the addition of Mark's brother, Guy, this is very much a book about men and masculinity, symbolised by the male dominated world of football supporters: craving success, seeking escapism, deluded by hope, their sexuality repressed, their love defined by hatred. Overall it's not a pretty picture.

In telling Mark's story, Glass captures a period of great change in both football and British culture; how football moved from 80s hooliganism to 90s hedonism, the Age of 'Golden Balls'– the marketing and media saturation, the glamour and cult of the celebrity. A world which, in Mark's eyes, is inexplicably forever out of reach.

An obvious Man United fan, Glass writes convincingly about football from both sides of the white line, capturing the psyche of the footballer and fan alike. He combines fact and fiction with finesse, with cameo roles from Ferguson, Beckham and of course Giggs, alongside the obsession and absurdity of the average football fan.

Three interwoven narratives give the book momentum, the first two documenting Mark's rise and fall, the third focusing on the 2007-08 season. And it is here that Glass is most influenced by David Peace: the fractured chronology; Mark as an intensely unreliable narrator whose grip on reality loosens as the story proceeds; the changing font style to denote change of voice; the changing perspective. While one narrative tells the objective story, the parallel is the personal version, the voice of the dark subconscious. Glass uses moments from recent history, moments from our popular collective consciousness as his creative starting point, proving that literature is still hugely relevant, and agile enough to respond to our contemporary world.

**Houyhnhnm**

# Dirty Yet Hopeful

**Wasted in Love**
**Allan Wilson**
Cargo, RRP £11·99, 194pp

Allan Wilson's collection of stories is described on the inside cover as dirty realism, and the influence of the style's father Charles Bukowski is acknowledged by a character reading a book about "sleeping with lots of women and working in a post office."

The settings are similar: pubs appear in almost every story, and if not, alcohol is usually involved. Characters work dead-end jobs, often in supermarkets. Stories take place in the eerie, regret-filled light of early mornings, after binges and all-night parties. Wilson's stories feature not-quite-ended relationships, straggly and frayed around the edges but with the potential for a warm, beating heart underneath the despair. The book's epigraph from Pedro Calderon de la Barca ("when love is not madness, it is not love") reminds one of Breton's 'l'amour fou', though these stories depict love less as mad than mundane, which is no bad thing.

There is a problem, though, of voice: Wilson's is not as strong as those of his idols, and as a result not all of the stories succeed completely, particularly in their use of dialogue. Annie and Alex, a couple who recur throughout the collection, epitomise the struggling souls of Wilson's characters as well as this issue of technique. The intimate settings suggest a portraitist's eye but their everyday conversations – particularly in 'Day 19' and 'The Marijuana Room' – risk banality.

Better are the two stories featuring an Elvis impersonator, refreshingly not the symbol of dejection often associated with such figures. In 'Her Last Night' he takes centre stage in a story that pairs atmosphere with acute characterisation, particularly the pitch-perfect sense of elation mixed with fear in Liane as she marks the closure of her burger van by making Elvis take repeated photos of her. 'Sharkman #1' is an unflinching story of a graduate supermarket-worker whose boss shares with him his life's work, carried in an Ikea bag: a comic featuring a human-shark superhero. It is a tale of thwarted ambition nicely contrasted by Elvis's success – both musical and romantic – at the supermarket's Christmas do: "There was an Elvis tribute act playing and this checkout girl Lynne got caught shagging him in the toilets. When he came back out for the second half somebody shouted, 'Elvis, gonnae play Love me Tender.'"

Best are the wonderful lines scattered throughout these stories. The sibilance of "when the man's hand falls onto Susan's thigh she stays still" perfectly captures the sleaziness of Colt in 'Dangers Far Worse Lost than Run,' while 'Lost in the Supermarket' features an old customer, bewildered by life, whose "eyelids drooped so far it was like he was displaying the inside of his face." Wilson is funny too, drolly remarking "oh to have someone ignore your emails via proxy" in 'Important Things To Do.'

These stories are really vignettes, and occasionally Wilson's sentences have an almost imagistic quality, a few words holding within them an entire story: "eyes touching like fingers," "laughter like vomit." This crystalline quality appears too in the repeated motions of human bodies in different stories. Compare this line, for instance, from 'A Couple' – "She was scrubbing her hair. The movements caused the towel around her body to unravel, sliding into a heap on her lap" – to this from 'Boiler' – "As she sang, she swung her head from side to side and the towel fell to the floor." It is here that the reader gets the sense of lives overlapping, of Glasgow's residents existing in the same place and time, struggling with similar problems and sharing familiar moments of intimacy. These moments find Wilson at his strongest, showing the interweaving of the particular and the universal. Focusing more on these powers of description and less on humdrum dialogue would make him a writer to watch.

**Mr Mistoffelees**

# No Ground Wasted Here

Working the Hill
**Jim Carruth**
*Mariscat Press, RRP £6·00, 36pp*

This, Jim Carruth's fifth collection since 2004's *Bovine Pastoral*, cements his place as Scotland's laureate of 21st Century country life. Not since Gibbon has a Scottish writer captured its people, labours and livestock with such utter contemporaneity.

These poems present a spare, honest but heartfelt series of insights into the modern farmscape for a society that has lost sight of where its food, bristles, shoes, footballs, handbags and milk come from. As 'Uses' neatly illustrates, using as its narrator a backyard pork butcher: "Yes – you can find a use / for every part of the pig / except the squeal. / ... / it's the squeal, / that stays / piercing my summers."

From the romantic movement onwards, the "timelessness" of the rural has been a trope and a trap for urban poets infatuated with green and pleasant lands; but, coming from a farming family himself, Carruth eschews such sentiment. Rather, his forensic poems eye the country with all its joys and hardships intact, and are thus firmly in the tradition of Clare, Hardy, and to an extent Burns (who is himself lampooned as "nae farmer" in 'Different Fields – v. ploughman without honour' for making "Sic a waste o / aw that guid grund / He didnae hae the hairt / fir the sair won hairst.")

But there is a subtler link to Burns in this collection, and it is to be found in the sense of a wider perspective, the allusion to greater human themes. These poems may have their roots in rural Renfrewshire, but they give no sense of being parochial, referencing as they do art, music and poetry from sources as diverse as Brueghel, Van Gogh, RS Thomas, Michael Jackson, the Ulster poet Art McCooey, the oral history of West Africa and the field hollers of American slaves.

To this reader, there is a trans-atlanticism in much of Carruth's compositional approach that greatly enhances his poems' communicative power. Where deployed to full effect, it imbues the poems with crystalline brightness. This fresh and distinctly un-British quality brings to mind the work of Americans such as Creeley and Williams (whose work is given a nod in the excellent 'Landscape with Fall of Icarus – after Brueghel'). And in the conventional syntax, sincerity, clarity of line-meaning and emotional resonance of poems like 'Spade' and 'The Back End', can be found striking resonances with the objectivist tradition of Charles Reznikoff and Louis Zukofsky.

The poems are well-selected, and prove the ongoing vibrancy of the short chapbook anthology form. Elegantly produced by Mariscat press, this book is a pocket-sized treat. A nice touch is the replacement of page numbers with footers detailing the different tools of the farmer's daily tasks: sickle, flail, pitchfork, graip, spade etc. Great attention has been paid to the arrangement and running order of poems, and the book seems to be intended to be read at one sitting.

That said, it is easy to dip in and out of. Stand-out pieces include the two-part poem 'Working the Word', and the aforementioned sequence 'Different Fields', in which Carruth interrogates the value of artistry as found in sheep shearing, the abstract shape of a salt-lick or a Henry Moore, the poetry of RS Thomas and Robert Burns, or the landscape painting of Van Gogh in the later stages of his mental illness. It finishes ('vii. poor harvest') with a knowing warning to the poet as referencer: "Seeding your verse with epigraph will never green your barren land".

As the book's jacket quote from Douglas Dunn points out, Scotland sairly needs writers like Carruth to provide a counterweight to a national literary narrative that has over-identified itself lately as being from an urban nation.
**Moby-Dick**

# A Timeless Ensemble

Spellwinders:
poetry from the Clydebuilt Jazz Ensemble
**Jim Carruth (Ed.)**
*Dreadful Night Press, RRP £7·00, 64pp*

In addition to his talents as a poet, Jim Carruth is also the convenor and general lynchpin of Glaswegian poets' collective St Mungo's Mirrorball, under whose auspices he edits this splendid short collection of jazz-inspired verse commissioned for the silver jubilee of the Glasgow Jazz Festival.

Since the Beat era and even before, jazz and poetry have always been bedfellows. But please dispel right now any comic thoughts of goatee'd men in black polonecks clicking their fingers and syncopating a sonnet – yeah – this is a carefully conducted anthology with more female contributors than male jazz afficionadoes (who find themselves gently mocked in Claire Quigley's 'Fake it in Private'). Each poet takes the role of an instrument in a virtual jazz orchestra, the Clydebuilt Jazz Ensemble, named after St Mungo's Mirorball's poet development appreticeship of the same name.

The range of possible approaches facing these writers must have been daunting, given the vast hinterland of jazz and poetry available for exploration. Many poems take the obvious starting point of rhythm and most use it effectively either to create new possibilities, as in Evelin Pye's poem 'Todd Gustavsen Ensemble', or to confirm old certainties, as in Chloe Morrish's 'Pete Johnstone plays Take Five'. Other poems explore the art of composition and the questions of posterity common to both art forms, whether through Christie Williamson's ethereal 'Writing a Standard' and its philosophical impermanence: "Artists do not give birth / to the timelessness / ... / ... / It gives birth to them"; or playful examinations of the vocabulary of jazz and its relation to everyday speech as in Gordon McInnes', 'I prefer Cerulean to blue'.

In fact, it is the sheer diversity of ways in which the poets engage with their subject matter that make this little anthology such a pleasant and often surprising read. "Whether they are taking song form themselves, as in Alexander Hutchison's 'What catches the light' and Gerry Loose's 'Abdullah Ibrahim'; playing off on a wild solo, as in Clare Quigley's "Sextet"; or recording the confusion of the contemporary scene (Amy Anderson, ' New to Jazz'), each of these poems takes a fresh look at its musical brethren. Nice.
**Moby-Dick**

# The Classification
**Li San Xing**

THE FIRST THING we noticed about the creature, aside from the fact that it was like nothing we had ever seen, was its extraordinary tameness. We had come almost face to face with it in the thickly wooded mountain path, brunching its solitary way through a patch of pungent cress, and where a more cautious vertebrate might have sought the security of the undergrowth, this beast seemed content to pay us as little regard as the overhanging cedar branches prodding its peculiar coat, or the crows carousing down in the gully.

'Is it a goat, uncle?' whispered my nephew.

'I'm not sure,' I said, slipping off my sandals in order to approach the creature as discreetly as possible. It did possess an unquestionably goatlike frame, and the goat was the only mammal known to reside at this altitude. But its neck was far too long for a goat and its hooves too broad, features which, together with a thick white mane covering its eyes and neck, lent it the appearance of a diminutive horse. Then again, I had never seen a horse with such an outrageous coat. Each strand of olive-brown hair was as long as a cob of corn and as wiry and thick as a twist of tobacco, and no sooner did this cumbersome fleece suggest a member of the yak family than both the mane and tangled coat acceded to a sudden and premature thinning at the rump, where a short, neat and thoroughly unyaklike stump of a tail flew firmly in the face of categorisation.

Though we still had a few hours of daylight left, and my wife would be furious at us for returning for the third day in a row without a new goat stud, I decided to bring the creature to the town for further inspection. The townspeople's initial reaction to the creature was one of great hilarity, and my nephew and I were swiftly accused of costuming one of our regular goats in a tragic bid for celebrity. Luckily any notions of a hoax were soon put to rest by the town doctor, whose brief examination of the creature quickly confirmed its authenticity. People's attentions now turned towards identification of this strange beast, which, I felt, had maintained a promisingly goatlike placidity throughout the proceedings. Unfortunately, it seemed every farmer hoping to lay claim to the beast could identify at least one attribute to back up his case, and by the end of the meeting the creature was beginning to resemble a compendium of all the different species known to the town.

While the doctor and his assistant retired to the surgery to carry out a more thorough examination, all across town theories abounded as to the origins of the creature. Those who had nothing to gain by the identification dismissed it as the unfortunate offspring of two different species, or an animal that had been born as one species and was merely in the process of metamorphosing into another. The pastor attempted to resolve the farmers' quarrelling by alleging that the creature had been sent by God as a symbol of their faith, 'which may take many shapes but in which every man may find his own truth'. It had been sent, he said, not to divide the farmers but to unite them. The farmers finally agreed to unite, but only long enough to physically eject the pastor from the inn.

In the end it was the doctor's announcement that the creature was equal parts sheep and horse that united the farmers, in a collective din that was equal parts mirth and outrage.

'Mother Nature has presented us with a challenge,' said the Mayor, 'and we shall face this challenge as our town always does: with a solid fibre of fairness.'

In accordance with the doctor's classification, it was decided that the creature's time should be divided equally between the service of the shepherd and that of the horse farmer by way of alternating three-day shifts. The sheep flatly refused to tolerate the new addition to the flock, maintaining a constant wide berth and reducing the sheepdog's coordination of the herd to an exercise in futility akin to the pressing together of two positively-charged magnetic poles. A further problem was posed by the creature's wiry fleece, which not only took twice as long to shear but resulted in clothes too rough to wear. And just as worthless was its milk, a thin, acrid concoction completely repugnant to the senses and all the more insulting for the fact that the creature produced such a staggering quantity of it; the shepherd's attempts to persuade the townspeople that it contained healing properties meeting with little success. But if the creature unimpressed as a sheep, it was an unqualified disaster as a horse. Subjected to the arduous physical labour expected of any other workhorse on the ranch, the creature's feeble frame was barely capable of dragging the titanic metal plough a few feet a day and was regularly found collapsed in the field from exhaustion. Nonetheless, rather than assign a less strenuous post to his new charge, the horse farmer persisted in the conviction that a lifetime of idle grazing had made a thorough sheep of the creature, and that regular ploughing was the only way to 'awaken' its dormant horse genes. The creature would work, he said, until the last drop of sheep's blood had been wrung from its bones.

Despite the farmers' efforts, the creature remained hopelessly incapable of fulfilling the most basic duties of a sheep or horse, and to those of us sceptical of the doctor's verdict this was more than sufficient grounds for reclassification.

'As soon as a man can present me with concrete, educated medical evidence to support his argument,' rejoined the doctor in an official statement, 'I will be more than happy to consider re-examination.'

Nobody was more determined to disprove the doctor's judgment than I. We were still yet to find our goat stud, and having spent several weeks struggling with my own dual roles of scouring the mountains and managing the farm, I had no choice but to join the crowds routinely gathered on the fringes of the neighbouring farms in the hope of discerning some irrefutably goatlike behaviour that would tip the creature back into my custody. It was astonishing to see how much the beast had changed since our first encounter with it in the mountains. Not only had its drowsy disregard for the world around it been replaced with an air of watchful apprehension, but while it had once appeared entirely comfortable with every inch of its disputable figure, it now seemed no more certain of what it was, and where it belonged, than the rest of us.

It was only when the creature passed within reaching distance of the fence one day that we discovered the horns. They were just growing in, and so densely hidden by the fierce confusion of fur on the creature's forehead that it was possible their emergence had eluded the doctor's analysis. Most significantly, the horns bore no resemblance to those of a male sheep, and when the doctor confirmed that he had detected no horns upon examination, the town hall ordered an immediate and conclusive reappraisal of the creature.

The nature of the previous classification meant that even farmers of hornless livestock had something to gain from the doctor's verdict. Once again homes and workplaces were alive with speculation. 'Half bull half cat' was a popular combination among those who discerned an unmistakably feline carriage in the creature, and where I saw the emerging horns of an adult goat, others saw not horns at all, but an extraordinarily durable pair of rabbit ears, or the mutinous teeth of a young shark.

The news that the physiology of the creature had been established as equal parts deer and bear was received with immense excitement. On the one hand this classification placed the creature squarely in the camp of wild animal and therefore officially belonging to no-one; but at the same time, as it was open season on both deer and bear, this opened the possibility of owning the creature from the narrow avenue of the town's farmers to anyone who happened to possess a gun. I for one found this classification even more dubious than the last. Aside from a conspicuous dearth of any features which could be considered remotely bearlike, there was something remarkably convenient about the creature boasting the genetics of not one but two huntable animals. Nevertheless, my suspicions were not shared by the rest of the town, and scarcely had the Mayor ordered the immediate removal of the creature to the lowland woods when people were already scurrying home to prepare for the hunt, exchanging theories as to the flavour of its meat and arguing over the most lucrative use for its carcass.

The shots could be heard long into the night. Having lain awake for several hours, I crept through to the kitchen to warm some milk and found my nephew sitting in the dark, his hands cupped to the window.

'Look,' he said.

I cupped my hands to the glass. Now and then, against a canvas of inscrutable black, the furtive flare of a shotgun blast traced the fragile outline of the lowland forest in the distance; but as hard as I tried to imagine the creature running for the safety of a ditch or thicket, all I could muster was the graceful sprint of a startled deer, or the clockwork hobble of a billy goat.

'We shouldn't have brought him,' said my nephew.

I placed my hand on his shoulder. 'I don't want to have to carry you up that mountain tomorrow,' I said. 'Get some sleep.'

The following morning the whole town had turned out to watch the horse farmer and his son parade the carcass through the town, but instead of the cheers, congratulations and applause that typically followed a successful hunt, the proceedings were accompanied by an unprecedented, funereal silence. Most people could barely bring themselves to look at the creature, tied to a branch by its oversized hooves, its coarse fleece sodden with blood and mud, for more than a few seconds; even the captors themselves could only focus on the next shameful steps ahead of them as they shouldered the burden of their prize. When it was alive, when any man could have owned it, the possibilities of what the creature could have been had seemed endless. Only now that it was dead could the townspeople see what it really was. It was utterly and unequivocally unique.

# Critic's Corner
## Alexander Hutchison

1. FROM THE START

Poems are about
wonder and terror.

Wonder's too strong;
terror's too strong.


2. LETHAL

I heard a singer
the other night who
would have had
Jim Joyce (the fellatelist)
clawing up the floorboards
with those long *durty* fingernails of his just to get
within earshot of her
dulcet *vibrato*.


3. NO DISPUTE OVER TACTICS

'Chopped up prose,' 'blocks of stone'
may have prompted satisfaction in some
quarters, to people on the *qui vive* for that
kind of thing. As for myself, I would never
seek to irritate this particular party – not least
because he is my own true friend, but mainly
because he could slice clean through any gloss
or flam you wished to advance, and do it in
the classic way: smiling straight into your
face as his hand went to work. And that,
I confess, would be my own choice too.


4. SUNSET OVER HACKNEY

Well, at the end of the day
you can't say fairer
than that – let's face it.

## 5. RAMSHACKLE

Ramshackle
is certainly

the word to
describe it.

Clear design
or pride in
appearance

not high on
this agenda.

Homely and
functional
maybe – but

not enough
door knobs

not enough.


## 6. MERCY

Two-dimensional
antiqued claptrap.

*Trysts*
my arse.


## 7. NEITHER DEEP, NOR CHARITABLE

'Give you the whole
history from "tossed"
to "toast" – yes
the whole thing
all over again.'

'But this is *now*.'

'Not for me it's
not – not if that
is what it is.'

8. GOMA GOMA GOMA

(*Young people who gathered around the Gallery of Modern Art in Glasgow have been moved on, and the area is now monitored by security guards.*)

They've vandalized the Goths.
The market has had its say.
Concerted material interest
has driven the Goths away.

A little bleak denial does
nobody very much harm.
Spiked hair and deathly pallor
can sometimes pass for charm.

To congregate is human;
to diss the world divine.
But the traders want silver to jingle
And customers toeing the line.

They've vandalized the Goths.
The merchants have entered the fray.
Concerted material interest
has driven the Goths away.


9. THERE YOU GO

He always aimed
for the top;

but the top
never wanted him,

never showed
the slightest
inclination.

He had to go
round or sap:

tunnel through,
setting charges.

10. SPOILSPORT

Lord, not another
wee dead surprise in halting
Japanese measure!


11. NAE HERE, NOR ONY PLACE NEAR

Airless antipathist, skimping for wit.
Nasty, obstreperous, nose-thirling nit.
Doggy, diffident, dry-rotted shit,
Resile, resign!
Embittered, envenomed; endogenous blister.
Wittering lightweight; clogged-up clyster.
Occluded wart-suck; putrid impostor –
Huffy humbug's ensign.
Absolute twat.
Graith-grasping prat.
Arse splitter-splat.
Necrotic nithing – on the Picadilly Line.


**Notes:**
**Lethal**
The singer's name eludes me now; but what Nora Barnacle and James Joyce got up to on their first date is a matter of record in Ellmann's biography.

**Nae Here, Nor Ony Place Near**
This unpleasant, and doubtless unworthy, piece was prompted by a review in the LRB which described ideas contained in the final paragraphs of a book by a writer I admired as "foetid;" and did so unfairly, it seemed to me, and mostly for show. "No," I thought, "you want *foétid? This* is foetid." There appears some separation between the title and the body of the poem, and also in the final line; and if there is, it must be for good reason.

# Extracts from the novel *Claustrophobia*
## Graeme Williamson

ONE

Frank is on the internet when the doorbell rings. He pushes back the chair, stands up, walks to the window, squints down onto the step. McCollough's broad shoulders and crew-cut cranium swivel in the shelter of the doorway. A decrepit 50 watt Marshall amplifier sits beside him on the step. A stubby finger emerges from a jacket sleeve and pokes for a second time at the bell. Frank steps back as McCollough looks up even though he is entirely aware that evasion is futile. His visitor's psychic sensors will have already penetrated the aluminium cladding, the brick, lathe, plaster and wallpaper and detected his presence in the house.

Outside the sun shines through the branches of the little gean tree and a slender spiky shadow stretches across the green. It's four in the afternoon. There is no sound but the idle scratch of McCollough's heel on the cement doorstep. The world appears to be at a standstill. Frank holds his breath and hovers by the curtain, his fingers resting on the window ledge beside the hyacinth pot. Above his head the sun beats on the tin roof and despite the lateness of the year the house simmers like a cauldron. A drop of sweat slides from his forehead into his left eye. The muscles in his chest tense, his lips grow moist, a painful warmth ignites in his mind. The air about him grows misty with androstenene as he recalls the images from his favourite website. He wipes his damp face with his sleeve, tiptoes back to the computer, sits down, clicks on a key. His face grows serious. He hears the letter-box clatter then the sound of retreating footsteps and his mood turns to anger and guilt. Who does that bastard think he is? Why should he always be at McCollough's beck and call?

An hour later, on his way out Frank looks in on Janine. As usual her room is in darkness and she is lying fully-dressed on the bed. The nurse rises from her chair in the corner and flickers like a ghost through the stripy shade cast by the Venetian blinds. She observes warily as Frank approaches but her flawless porcelain face shows no expression. Janine's eyes are open, her pupils dilated. A pair of green low-heeled shoes have tumbled from her feet onto the floor. The room smells of humid warmth, chemicals, stale breath, freesias. He walks to the bedside, stands and watches her breathe. A lock of fiery red tumbles over her eyes as she turns her head. He leans down to brush away the fringe and wonders how it is that regardless of the temperature in her room his wife's skin always feels cool.

'I'm going out,' he says.

'Where to?' Her voice is expressionless, an aural black hole.

'McCollough's.'

'Will James be there?'

'Yes, possibly.'

'I haven't seen him all week.'

'He has his own life now.'

'Well, if you see him, tell him to visit.'

'I will.'

'Was that someone at the door earlier?'

'No.'

'Are you sure? I thought I heard something.'

'I don't think so.'

'It might have been James.'
'He has a key.'
She looks past his shoulder towards the shaded window, smiles.
'It's sunny.'
'Yes.'
'And Suzanne?' Will she be there?'
'Probably. She does live there.'
She reaches out her hand and Frank clasps it in his own. The stone on her wedding ring digs into the soft skin of his finger joint.
'You seem tired,' Janine says.
'Yes.'
'How can you be tired? What have you been doing?'
'Maybe I'm just bored.'
'Remember when we used to go hitchhiking?'
'Yes.'
'The lorry drivers used to tell us their life stories. You couldn't stop them. Do you remember that?'
'Yes.'
'Well, you can look on your life as a boring lift. It doesn't matter what you feel about it you'll get wherever you're going whether you like it or not.'

When Frank turned eleven his mother began to warn him against women. 'I'm a woman Francis, so I can tell you, I'm up to all their tricks.'

Any student of the scriptures, she explained, knows that insane jealousy is as hardwired into God as vanity and weakness are into a women. From His divine hand alone God dispenses whatever modicum of happiness is available in this world, according to His own imponderable whims. Women are always trying to usurp this miracle and employ it for their own frivolous, self-gratifying ends. Driven by vanity even the best woman's love is a tawdry facsimile of God's authentic, terrifying affection.

A day or two after Janine's accident his mother phoned him:
*You have to get on with your own life. Janine isn't your responsibility.*
She did not want her son's future blighted by his unmanly tendency to self-sacrifice.
'We're getting married,' Frank said.
'You're a fool,' his mother said. 'It's a mistake.' And later the same evening, after he'd returned home from the hospital she phoned him again.
*I curse you, Frank. I curse you.*

Frank reaches down and strokes the skin of Janine's cheek. 'I agree,' he says.
'Drive carefully,' she says.
'I'll drive how I like,' he says, but the old joke doesn't raise the hoped-for smile. He leans over, kisses her on the cheek, wipes the unexpected accumulation of saliva from his mouth, goes to the door.
'Can I bring you anything?'
Her pale eyes turn to him and she smiles. 'Yes, as you're asking. What about a beach?'
'A beach?'
'A nice big beach. Full of Italians and loud, spoiled children. Girls going by on pedalos and handsome boys flying those parachutes.'
He smiles at her but his fingers tap impatiently on the door frame.
'I don't blame you,' she says.
'Don't blame me for what?'
'Anything.'
'Everyone blames someone for something,' he says.
He steps outside.
The nurse turns, picks up her magazine from the chair, sits down. Janine lies back, crosses her slender legs, gazes up at the ceiling, shivers, reaches with her right arm, pulls her dead left arm over her breasts.

TWO

Frank sets off for McCollough's, farting along in the white Fiesta with the broken exhaust. The road climbs out of Tintown and he glances back and forth, taking in the foreign neighbourhood. Crisp packets and plastic bags scratch idly around the empty streets. He is searching for roses. The only place that has them is the corner shop near the pub. There is a flurry of movement at the corner of his eye, a scurry of footsteps into the shadows of a side street. A doleful, inquisitive dog darts from a close mouth, pauses, sniffs, pisses against a stank and trots away. A few of the newly-rehabbed cream and terracotta stucco flats already have steel shutters over the doors and scorch marks around the windows. The local Teams have tagged everything in sight. Some of them aren't bad; exotic scripts and runes signifying primal municipalities and sometimes the outlines of a beautiful palimpsest, violence worked into colour. I Am Here, you bastards. Pigeon Man bustles by, huddled up in his tarpaulin coat, the right arm knotted, Daddy long legs, one false the other prosthetic, white plimsolls flashing over the pavement as he motors up the hill on his daily perambulations around the city. James swears he's a saddhu but Frank's not sure what that is. Pigeon Man doesn't look Indian.

A flash of crimson catches his attention. He pulls up outside the shop, gets out, looks up and down the empty street, selects a bunch from the bucket by the door, sniffs the scentless blooms, takes a note from the pocket of his jeans and peers into the obscurity of the shop's interior.

Shelves with bread and biscuits, tins and jars, cigarettes and sweeties emerge from the murk. There is a furtive movement behind the fenced-in booze counter. A pair of eyes blink loris-like from the gloom.

'We're closed,' a voice says.

Frank waves the roses in the doorway.

'Just put them back,' the voice says.

A coldness seeps out from the darkness like a sick breath. Frank shivers in the shade. After a moment's hesitation he replaces the dripping bouquet, stuffs the note into his back pocket and steps back into the street. The loris-eyes blink as he retreats to his car. 'Never mind,' the voice says, 'we'll have plenty of lovely flowers tomorrow.'

Frank restarts the car, cranks up the tape and resumes his journey to Mitre Hill. The street widens into an avenue, divided by grass islands, beds of parched shrubbery and gangling cherry saplings. No shops around here. He pulls down the visor as low sun slips beneath the branches of the plane trees and blinds him. He drives slowly, squinting at the dazzling, overexposed thread of tarmac. A scattering of dried out blossom drifts across the road.

Spewing smoke signals into the baking air he passes the clapboard Evangel Hall and the red-gravelled football pitch. The road winds east along the escarpment, the vertiginous edge of Sugartown. Far below lies the Mitre Hill dump. Beyond, fields of grasses and scant coverings of wild flowers stretch towards mountains. A faint skin of snow still covers the summits. The sky is the blue of a baby's eye. At the centre of the football pitch five squeakies are gathered around a burning car drinking from a ginger bottle and laughing. This year there's a fashion for bare bellies and Frank thinks some of these lassies would be doing the public a service if they wore those Arabic things and kept some of that off-white flesh under wraps.

The gardens on either side of the road are deserted. The Mary Celeste atmosphere is disconcerting. On a Sunday afternoon there ought to be people outdoors, waxing cars, mowing lawns, building walls. Must be the heat. The place reminds him of the Greek cemetery he and Janine slept in once, where the mausolea were laid out in streets just like houses for living people.

He turns the corner into a cul de sac shaded by lime trees and pulls to a stop. He turns off the tape player and sits at the wheel tapping his fingers urgently on the steering wheel. McCollough's van isn't there, in fact the street is empty apart from a single 7-Series BMW pulled up on the opposite kerb. Midnight blue, tinted glass; impossible to know if there's anyone inside. Not from around here anyway, whoever they are.

Frank climbs out and casts his eyes over the arrangements of pots and slabs in front of the house. The plants look so fresh they might have just come out of a fridge. All Suzanne's doing. If it was up to McCollough the green would be a landfill, buried under half-welded cars, industrial salvage and crates of empty bottles. Frank pities Suzanne. According to some book Frank read years ago one of the Popes kept a rhinoceros in his castle in Marseilles and cohabiting with McCollough must be like that. Living with the ever-present threat that one day, maddened by his captivity, he'll take a flaky, smash his way through the living room wall and run amok through the leafy avenues of Mitre Hill.

A curtain flickers at a neighbour's window. Frank's hackles rise at the invisible watcher but he shoves his hands into his pockets and takes in the view. It's nice up here. The air is fresh and there's a big sky. Between the trees, visible far below, there's a skyline like a mouthful of broken, rotten teeth. Red and honey-coloured tenements with windows full of sunlight, cranes and high flats, the thread of river winding to the West and that white block on the south side perched on a hill like a statue of a gannet.

As he walks to the gate resin from the trees sticks to the soles of his trainers like chewing gum. Every step makes a sucking noise. He trips over a mountain bike lying half-hidden behind a pot, regains his balance and crunches up the path. There is a roar of vacuum cleaner. The door opens.

Suzanne is wearing jeans and a thin top held together at the neck by a little 12 carat gold Ankh brooch. No makeup. Her left breast brushes against his shoulder as he passes her in the doorway. He avoids catching her eye but flashes a tense grin as he squeezes past. Musk and citrus float in the air of the hallway, a cool breath in the desert of the day. His mouth is dry and his face reddens with the effort of concealing desire.

'Like my new motor?' he says, nodding over his shoulder.

'It's been there all morning,' she says.

'Anyone inside?'

'Not sure. Some kids checked it out early on and kept away from it since.'

They pause, give each other an appraisal.

'You look a bit hot,' she says, leaning down to click off the Hoover plug.

'I could murder a glass of water.'

He lets her pass, follows her through to the kitchen and watches her fill a tumbler from the filter jug on the counter. He's excited by their proximity, their shared solitude, by the fact he has no idea what is going to happen.

A long time ago the four of them, he and Janine, McCollough and Suzanne, were saying goodnight after seeing a film. Janine was still well then. They were all drunk and they started kissing. First the women kissed each other, then the men kissed the women. As Frank leaned over to give Suzanne's cheek a quick peck his hand rose instinctively, past her shoulder, its intended destination, and rested against her hair. Not like Janine's, which was fine and soft as silk, but heavy and brittle with hairspray. As soon as this accident happened Frank realised he'd broken a taboo he'd never heard of before. Something about hair. It's just there, on people's heads, you wouldn't think twice about it, but then when you touch it it's an intrusion, a very personal form of contact. His hand paused, transfixed by the sensation under his fingers. He closed his eyes, drew in her smell and let his fingers curl into the profusion. No one noticed but the recollection lingered with him for days, the exultation of a newly-discovered sin.

'I hate the heat.'

'It's bound to rain sooner or later,' she says. 'You're never that far away from a spot of rain.' Sometimes she sounds just like her old man.

She hands him the glass. Frank drinks the water, walks to the sink, rinses the glass under the tap and lays it upside down on the draining board.

'You're well trained,' she says.

They make eye contact.

'The perfume smells nice,' he says.

She leans towards him and gives him a sniff.

'You could do with a shower, actually.'

The only thing that's missing from the exchange is the subject matter. Frank is trying to sound her out. It would be a disaster if he got it wrong. This is the sixth time he's been here, but he still doesn't trust his own judgement. The world's too small. There's no witness protection programme for guys who fuck other men's wives. But Suzanne's gaze is unreadable and all of a sudden the thought crosses his mind that she might be myopic. Women with those

➵

Fiction/129

chocolate-coloured eyes are often half blind. Perhaps she can't even see him properly.

He doesn't want to miss anything but the fact he's stopped blinking is conspicuous. His vigilance is threatening to kill the atmosphere.

'I wanted to get you some flowers,' he says. 'But something was going on at the shop.'

'Oh?'

There's a noise from the hall. Suzanne's attention drifts away to a point behind Frank and to his right. A boy about eleven years old in Reebok and Hilfiger steps out from behind the kitchen door.

'Just the man,' Suzanne says, and she pushes between them towards the door.

'Hi Stevie,' Frank says.

Stevie looks at him blankly and says nothing.

Suzanne returns with her purse. 'We need a couple of things,' she says.

'I don't want to,' the boy says, though he doesn't move. His eyes are still on Frank.

Suzanne fiddles with her purse. 'Get a DVD,' she says, 'and we need bread, and food for Max...' She recites a short list of staples.

Before he has time to think better of it Frank takes the note from his back pocket and offers it to the boy. 'I'll pay,' he says and he adds hurriedly, 'And get a bunch of roses.'

'I'm not buying flowers,' the boy says.

'No roses, no video,' Frank says. He winks at Suzanne, 'That's commerce. I'm surprised your Dad hasn't taught you that already.'

The boy snatches the money and makes for the stairs. Frank goes to the window and looks into the back garden. A strip of dull, yellowed grass with a stained clapboard hut at the end. Dead borders on either side. A single dishtowel hangs limply from the neighbour's line. He hears the sound of a cupboard door opening and closing and overhead the low level mayhem from Stevie's room as the boy gets ready to go out. When he turns back Suzanne is mopping the floor.

'It's funny,' he says.

'What is?'

'I never imagined you doing housework.'

She raises an eyebrow. 'You thought Jon did it?'

'No. Obviously not.'

'You thought we had a maid.'

'A cleaner.'

'No,' she says. She looks thoughtful. 'You can't trust them. If they're not breaking your stuff or stealing things they're talking to the neighbours about you.'

'I thought your Mum was a cleaner.'

'She was an office cleaner,' she says, frostily, although Frank doesn't understand what this means.

He turns back to the window, glances up at a stranded cloud, closes his eyes and imagines floating away in the high altitudes, to a land far away from Mitre Hill. A beach might be OK but not Italian, thanks all the same. The Mediterranean would be too hot. A cool place would be nicer. A long, empty shore in the north where the air smelled of cedar. Scandinavia perhaps, that sort of place. Lying on a towel with these women on either side of him. Food for mind and body. That would be fine.

He feels Suzanne's breath on his neck.

'He said he dropped by to see you,' she says quietly, 'but you didn't answer the door.'

'Well, if I'd heard him I would have answered.'

'I said that. He was angry though. He wanted to drop off an amp. He was doing a favour for James.'

'That's a shame,' Frank says.

A smile flickers at her lips.

There's a clatter on the stairs and Stevie lands heavily in the hallway outside.

'Chaos on legs,' Suzanne says, as the front door slams.

'Aye.'

'Was James like that?'

'Like what?'

'Wound up. Speedy.'

Frank laughs out loud. 'Hardly, no. Not James. He always kept his light under a bushel.'

She frowns. 'Under a what?'

They are now standing face to face and toe to toe.

Five minutes later they are in the shower room next to the kitchen. A pale blue plastic soap dish in the shape of a dolphin tumbles from the edge of the basin as Suzanne grabs at the rim. The soap slips out and skids across the tiled floor. Frank's balding pate moves rhythmically at her shoulder and in the mirror he catches sight of the tiny dogbite scar at the edge of his hairline and the two dark discolorations beside it, side by side like a snake's fang marks. He's noticed them before and he wonders if it's liver disease. His father's skin went blotchy like that from cirrhosis.

Frank's having a good time generally speaking although he's a little too wound up to be completely comfortable. Not so much passionate as ravenous. No one could accuse him of lacking enthusiasm, however. He tries experimenting with the position of his feet so as to take some of his weight off Suzanne. God knows the position he's in is uncomfortable enough but it must be worse for her. Of course Suzanne does Yoga, and that does seem to keep her agile. Maybe he should take up Yoga too. It might give him some extra flexibility for these close encounters in cramped places.

This is the way it's gone every Friday for the last two months with two weeks off when the band wasn't playing and McCollough stayed in the house. Sometimes whole minutes go by in which he can nearly relax. For at least a year, ever since that accident with Suzanne's hair, the idea had been there in his mind; he'd hoped but hadn't really expected it would happen, but now it does and each time Suzanne gets a little more under his skin and his curiosity is further aroused. Who is she, under her affectations? Fucking may not be the most efficient system for finding out, but you can trust the body. Even while he's thinking his thoughts and she's thinking hers, if she has any, their bodies are trading information back and forth through nerves and flesh and skin at the speed of light.

Suddenly his attention has wandered. His head disappears from the reflection in the mirror and he is gone from inside her. There is a crash as he falls backwards, his feet flying from under him, and he lands heavily on the toilet, breaking the plastic lid and plummeting to the floor. He comes to rest wedged between the bathtub and a bleached pine towel rack. There is a long red scratch down the length of his arm. Suzanne kneels beside him and puts her hand over his mouth to stifle the threatened laugh.

'Fucking soap,' he says, pointing to the far corner.

'Shhh...'

She stands up, turns on the tap, wrings the edge of a towel in hot water and bathes his arm. The damage appears superficial, although a tinge of purple hints at a developing bruise. 'You shouldn't get yourself so worked up,' she says, and rests her forehead against his. Her long hair veils their faces and they kiss. 'It's frustration,' he says. 'It's just frustration. I'm so clumsy.'

'No,' she says, 'it's OK. It's always a bit like a Steven King film with you, you know. Quite enjoyable in a perverse sort of way. Not what I expected at all. A bit scary.'

'Thanks.'

Frank pulls on his clothes and listens. At the very moment he opens the door and puts his head out into the hallway Stevie passes on his way to the kitchen. They exchange glances. The boy's eyes are unoccupied as if he's been stunned by the hypersonic, ear-splitting electronic high hat in his earphones and he seems oblivious to the man in his mother's wetroom. He raises a bunch of red roses and thrusts them in Frank's face. Frank takes them and slips back through the door as Stevie continues on to the kitchen. He turns back and draws the door shut behind him.

'I think it's safe,' he says, laying the flowers in the washbasin and running in a splash of water.

Suzanne laughs mirthlessly. 'You must be joking,' she says. She reaches her hand up to cup the back of his head, leans into him and kisses his ear. 'There's nowhere safe in this world, honey.'

# The Quadrangle
## Michael Owen Fisher

6 FEB 2009

Iain is washing up when a light comes on across the quadrangle. He sees a smudge of movement in the window opposite him and reaches for his glasses. A young woman is clasping a towel to her chest. Iain drops to the floor, scurries on all fours across the lino, and flicks off the kitchen light. The woman pauses in the centre of her bedroom and pads herself dry. Iain's mouth lolls open as he shuffles on the draining board, attempting to find a clear line of vision through the candles on her windowsill. The rubber gloves trail suds across his fly.

Rachel pulls the duvet further up her body and twists onto her side, so that her head rests a metre from the screen. The TV licks her face with red flecks. 'Finished?' she asks.

'Yes, all done,' Iain replies, moving from the doorway of their marital bedroom into the en suite bathroom. He cleans his teeth every morning and evening in their en suite rather than the larger bathroom at the end of the flat. 'You looking forward to seeing your mum tomorrow?'

Rachel's eyes laze on the TV.

'Rachel?'

'Mmm?'

'Should be fun. The trip with your mum. Tomorrow.'

She closes her eyes. 'Yes.'

'We've reached that time again,' the host announces over the game show's incidental hum.

Iain reaches across the bed. Rachel's nose twitches, as if she were able to sense her husband's hand hovering above her arm.

'Goodnight,' he says. 'You sleep well.'

7 FEB 2009, AFTERNOON

Iain listens to Barbara's footsteps echoing up the block. She stops on the third floor landing and drops her head to one side, feigning exhaustion.

'So many stairs,' she says, 'don't know how you do this every day.'

'Good journey?' Iain asks. He bends forward to kiss his mother-in-law. Her cheeks are pink, downy, and cold.

'Not too bad. Slight hold up around Crowborough.'

They look at each other, then at the hall floor.

'How's she been?' Barbara asks.

'It's okay.' Iain puffs out a cheek and focuses on the space beside the front door. 'You know. We're doing ok. She's been drawing a lot, really got into it. As the doctor suggested. Little sketches of buildings. Skyscrapers. Which is good, I think. A good hobby.'

Barbara opens her arms. She has dyed her hair late-summer brown this morning. Iain smells a trace of ammonia as he presses against her soft pastel wools.

'Little Eiffel Towers,' he says, laughing.

Rachel fumbles with her jacket as she enters the hallway. She looks up and her mouth curls into a rictus. 'I'm ready,' she says, 'if you are mum.'

Iain drowses on his bed, and the damp winter sun drops low. He thinks about the woman in the window. Her shallow curves and her skin, mannequin smooth. Stray light from the quadrangle wisps across the ceiling and hangs over the black of his eyes.

### 18 JAN 2008

Rachel is home. She is Iain's wife of nineteen years. Rachel is a retail consultant for a large pharmaceutical firm. She plays the clarinet, but less often than she would like, watches legal dramas, and enjoys reading novels by Maeve Binchy and Alan Hollinghurst. She is E(xtroversion), (i)N(tuition), F(eeling), J(udging) on the Myers-Briggs Type Indicator. When she is confused her eyes circle round and round like a child's toy. She loves cuddles.

Iain forms a letter T with his forefingers, which is the couple's shortcut for 'do you want tea?' Rachel sits on their sofa, caressing the underside of her chin and staring past him into the plane-scarred sky. She fails to see her husband's question.

'Any tea?' he asks.

'I'm okay for now.'

'Sure? We've got some Lady Grey in, or builders' tea.'

'I'm alright.'

Beside Rachel is a family photo in which Adam has shoulder-length hair. Iain wears an iron grey sweater, the one that made him look thinner but later began to unravel at the sleeves. Rachel wears a skirt that lets through sunlight. She is leaning into her son's shoulder, laughing.

'Adam's going to phone this evening,' Iain says.

Rachel moves a hand up and down her cheek. The sun crawls from behind a small cloud, setting off slow-motion explosions on the steel and glass of the office block across the road.

'Good. That'll be good.'

### 7 FEB 2009, EVENING

Here is Iain at his desk, wearing a smart black shirt. Outside is dusky. The windows around the quadrangle glow solar yellow, as if they were soaking up the sunset. A baby's cry thrums, hangs, and distracts Iain from the parity product graphs on his laptop screen. The girl hurries into her room and tosses her hat onto the bed. Her hair tumbles across her shoulders. Iain scrolls down the jags and spikes of the graphs and pretends to make notes in his writing pad. Her face is flushed. She removes her jeans and heavy winter coat and disappears into a wardrobe. Iain presses his pen to his lips and stares academically into the night sky, his eyes squinting and unsquinting as if he were zeroing in on a thought. The girl emerges from the wardrobe holding a green dress, and her eyes skip across the quadrangle. He exhales. Sighs jesus. His flat door clicks open.

'We're back.'

### 15 MARCH 2008

Iain watches Tod Browning's 1931 version of *Dracula* late at night and is taken aback by the similarity between Dwight Frye's unhinged expressions as the dark prince's servant, Renfield, and his wife's smile.

### 9 FEB 2009

Iain rummages in his clothes cupboard. Water runs and stutters into confluences down to the towel around his waist. The young woman is curled on a chair in her dressing gown, eating from a bowl. Her bedroom is lit in muted yellow, but brighter light pulses from a TV in a hidden corner of the room. Iain dabs his hairy torso with the towel and waters a plant on the windowsill with his free hand. His midriff has the firm, buttery swelling of middle age. The woman removes her dressing gown and moves about her room in a knee-length negligee, which gleams like sun-drenched fuel. On Iain's desk are the latest pupilometrics data for the prototype *Eos* double-page spread, which features every colour in the *Eos* range: chocolate, crimson, caramello, mother-of-pearl, ivory, coral/aqua. As Iain suspected, crimson and coral/aqua elicit the strongest responses. He holds one of the data sheets, his eyes narrowing in faux-concentration. The towel has made his skin pink. The girl stretches forward to close her curtains, allowing Iain to see the swell of her breasts. She smiles and produces an equivocal movement with her hand, which Iain interprets as a wave. Her curtains close.

15 APRIL 2008

Dr Gianakos edges the acetate sheet across his desk and waves his pen over Rachel's forebrain. 'It's here we've seen... where we have found something of note. The forebrain, here,' the doctor says, lifting his long fringe and massaging his forehead, 'exposed to the bony ridges inside the skull is, I mean, it's probably the most vulnerable part of the brain.'

Iain nods, his eyes fixed on Rachel's indigo brain, which the doctor has illuminated on a mobile electronic tablet.

'Rachel has damaged a specific part of these frontal lobes. It's easy for this to happen in a crash. I mean, the effects are varied, but some damage, temporary or otherwise, is common.' The young neuropsychologist draws a squiggle in the air over Rachel's frontal lobes. 'There is such a high chance of—'

'So...'

'Yes.' The doctor shifts upright in his chair, and now he nods, encouraging Iain to speak.

'So this part of her brain is affecting her emotions. Has changed her...'

'Yes, exactly. Damage here explains this... this emotional void she has developed.' Dr Gianakos pauses, anticipating another question, but Iain has glazed over. The doctor's hand fans and contracts on the desk. His tone becomes more subdued. 'You mentioned Rachel's outbursts. I mean, this is an associated sign. The frontal lobes, one of their jobs is censorship. Screening out this aggression and certain... primitive urges.'

On the doctor's desk, beside the brain scan and propped on the rear of a framed photo, is a wide-eyed, white-coated bear holding a stethoscope in its paw. Iain leans on the desk and toys with the bear's fur.

'And.'

'Yes,' Dr Gianakos says.

'And in the long run?'

11 FEB 2009

Behind the frosted glass of their flat door is a tall silhouette. Rachel is motionless on the marital bed, except for micro-movements of her eyes across the TV screen. The bell rings for a second time and Iain opens the door.

'Hello sir. I was wondering if I could come in for just a brief moment.'

'Yes, yes, come in,' Iain says. His voice rises an octave mid-sentence. 'Tea? Can I get you some tea?'

'No thank you. It's just a brief visit actually sir.'

Rachel stands in the bedroom doorway, tugging her dressing gown across her chest. The policeman nods hello to her before turning back to Iain. 'Is there a room we could pop into briefly, sir?'

21 JULY 2008

Iain has been with *Cook & Magris*, part of the *Praesto Group*, for eighteen years, for the previous five of which he has been a creative director. He is respected within the company for his understatement and gently-delivered assessments, especially of product life cycles, and for his analyses of parity products. Today Iain plans to commute to *Cook & Magris's* London offices once Rachel and he have finished at the Centre for Clinical Wellbeing. He holds his briefcase between his feet. The cognitive therapist's room is stuffy even though she has left open her awning window. Through the window waft summer scents: dead air, clean grass and the soapy, carnal smells of plants yielding and opening.

'Rachel, do you feel as though any changes have taken place in you since the accident?' Dr. Leighton asks. She has the poise of someone trained to avoid unnecessary movements and maintains her expression of professional sympathy while she waits for Rachel's response.

'The main thing is, I don't worry about things.'

'And is that a good feeling?'

'Yes.'

'It is good?'

'Yes. I only worry about how I feel in the morning. Sometimes I feel... bored. I think that's it. Bored. Or restless.'

Dr Leighton writes in her notebook. Iain watches the trees rustle outside and pictures the doctor, in black spandex, ordering him to remove his trousers.

'And Rachel, when you say you don't worry,

does that mean you don't care about anything?'

'That... I think so.'

'Do you care about Iain?'

Both the doctor and Rachel glance at Iain, who is knifing his nose with his fingertips.

'I suppose so.'

'Do you love him?'

'Oh yes. Course.' Rachel's lips contort into another Renfield Smile. Over the preceding weeks it has dawned on Iain that, although she spots cues and produces appropriate and well-timed facial responses, his wife has forgotten why she smiles.

'And what does the love feel like?'

'I don't know. It's good having him around. We've been together so many years.'

Dr Leighton's hand whirrs across her notepad. She nods encouragement, her head sweeping down in slow arcs. Her hair is fizzy red. Iain imagines how it would feel on his skin.

'I don't know.'

11 FEB 2009

A wedge of amber light shines from the top of the girl's window, where the curtains have failed to meet. The policeman leans from Iain's bedroom window, nodding to himself, satisfying himself with something or other.

'Can I ask,' Iain says, 'who reported this... what would you call it? Display?'

'Public indecency is the term that tends to be used.' The policeman plays a couple of scales across the sill. 'And I think we both know sir, for me to reveal that sort of information is a hostage to fortune.'

15 MAY 1987

*Gianni's* lighting is low. Rachel and Iain sit opposite each other on a small table near the window. Every curl of lip, change of timbre, and head movement is precise and measured. The restaurant is busy. They watch their waiter hurry back to the kitchen.

'He's funny,' Rachel says.

Iain imitates the waiter, dipping his head with exaggerated deference, and they both laugh. 'Yeah, he sounded like the skeleton from the Scotch tape ad.' He begins swaying his head to a private rhythm.

Rachel raises an eyebrow.

'Tape what you want both night and day,' Iain chants, tapping out the beats between lines in the air. 'Then rerecord, not fade away.'

She grins.

'Rerecord, not fade away,' they repeat in unison. Rachel rocks back in her chair, giggling, hitting an angle where her filigree broach reflects the candlelight onto her face. 'He does.'

Iain wears chunky-rimmed Cazal glasses. His hair is wiry and big, and he has a habit of stretching his facial muscles by flexing his jaw to his chest, which action refreshes his eyes but results in his mouth opening in the style of a horror film still or the figure in *The Scream*.

Rachel tells him about her cat, how she loves that almost every meal in South America is served with popcorn, and of her fascination with tall buildings. Whenever she struggles to remember a name, her nose crimps and puckers, and the small muscles above her eyes knot so that she resembles a person trying to scratch their head without using any hands. Iain steals looks up and down her purple dress and makes an effort to avoid stretching his facial muscles. *Gianni's* empties around them.

18 FEB 2009

The exposure data from 2007's *Maia* campaign falls into the range Iain envisaged, and, in his opinion, justifies the ramped-up DAGMAR he has been pushing for *Amy's* new *Eos* range. He scrolls down the spreadsheet on his laptop one more time. An architect's lamp illuminates the prototype *Eos* spread beside his computer.

*To bring a Smile to Your face, and His*

Most of the windows around the quadrangle are asleep, but Iain's attention is caught by a fourth floor flat in the opposite block. In the curtains' slight opening he sees a shift in the varieties of black, a shadow of shadows forming, then stillness. Iain stands and tilts forward over his desk to improve his view of the window. Seconds later the curtains ruffle and close.

The young woman's curtains are closed too.

They have been for several days, ever since the policeman's visit. Iain feels beneath the folders and papers in his desk drawer. He pulls out a jiffy bag, on which he has scrawled the woman's address in thick black felt tip. Inside the bag is a mother-of-pearl *Eos* bra. The new *Eos* range has embroidered tulle and a high cotton percentage for maximum comfort, no underwiring, and a macramé lace balconette. Iain runs one hand across its surface and rereads the note he has paper-clipped to the strap. He puffs out his cheeks and reburies the jiffy bag at the bottom of the drawer.

Iain pulls on his pyjama bottoms and leaves the room. The door to the marital bedroom is ajar and from it light leaks into the hallway. He pauses by the door, bends forward and peers through the gap, which is no more than a pupil's width. Rachel is standing in front of the mirror, examining her body, lifting and kneading her heavy breasts. She mumbles as she jerks a comb through her hair. Iain watches with one eye pressed into the thin band of light. His face hangs post-coma blank. Rachel sets down her comb on the dressing table and turns to face the quadrangle. Her nose crinkles, and she presses herself up against the cold window pane.

## all the time billions
**Chris Powici**

all the time billions of almost nothings passing right through us it would take four light years travelling through solid lead for a neutrino to notice anything else in the universe actually existed so this holy palaver of skin bone hair etc is less than mist and the migrations of geese plato's head bach fugues aspirin the difference engine rainforests and the paris metro barely more than the sheen of dust on a bat's wing who knows maybe even you yes *you* with your blue northern eyes and memories of the sea are flowing through this poem rapt and quantumly beyond its trembling nest of sounds and are wrought of the very stuff of light improbable and utter

## Graviton love
**David Eyre**

We detect its presence
for a chest-pounding nanosecond
before it escapes
to a tightly-wound

unkent dimension
coiled around itself
like a spiral
carved in rock

the absence of its energy
the proof
that it is now
somewhere else.

# Nothing
*(after Vasko Popa, 'He')*
**Lindsay Macgregor**

In this game of hide-and-seek
there's nothing to be found.
The players search so earnestly
hefting bluejohns, scouring Anapurna
puppeteering on the moon
but everywhere they look
they find something.

They lie awake at night
trying to crack
the kind of place that
nothing might hang out.

There's a formula in alphas
and omegas and tiny
superscripts describing
latitudes of nothing
should it actually exist
but it cannot be applied
because they don't know
what it means and all along
nothing stares them
blankly in the face

## You can see light. What's it like?
**Nuala Watt**

heat                                             silence

the right response

stays                                                                    i n v i s i b l e

but the question                                                     glows
                                    between us
a small sun


it has disappeared


her face and i have twisted
my head away                                                         a f r a i d

that her query could
                                    blind         me



## Sometimes I forget
**Stav Poleg**

You ask me if I miss him, but haven't you read the book?
He cries for me by the sea, he tries on silhouettes and moon-shaped
sirens, he's always coming home behind this island's pulsing
mountains. I drink coffee at night to keep me fresh and ticking.
There's a storm to come, a goddess to confuse me, a raft
to launch and crash, a story to retell until I hold it by heart.

The first years are sort-of celebrations, everyone offers
something to drink. *We know it's painful Penélope*, they play
with my name, *you look pale Penélope*. Sometimes I forget
to wash the dishes, to call on birthdays, to look for a job.
Then, quiet thunderstorms. I'm ticking, ticking
with my fingers on every upturned stone, and sometimes happiness,
sometimes, for a while. But every bloke carrying himself
from the waves, turns me into furious gods, foreign cities, open hands.

# Returns
**Judith Taylor**

You accepted love, and wore it
as you wore the giver, lightly on your arm
a whole season
before you tired of it
and tried to send it back again,
saying you'd changed your mind.

There was a family
where I used to live, notorious
for the same thing. They'd never pay
more than the first instalment
and return the suit, the coat, the expensive car
after the wedding

or the funeral.
People used to point them out
to one another, not to forget
what like they were.
And I'd love to know
what you think you've deserved.

# Tinderbox
**Jim C Wilson**

Just in case his hotel caught fire
Hans Christian Andersen carried a rope,
his means of escape from the nightmare pyre
if, sometime soon, his hotel caught fire.
Each day he expected something dire
(though snow queens and mermaids helped him cope).
So, just in case his hotel caught fire
Hans Christian Andersen carried a rope.

## Last Night
**Jim C Wilson**

Last night in bed
your breathing sounded
oddly like the chiming
of a distant clock;
not digital
or electronic –
more like the one
in my parents' house,
which ticked and slowed,
forever losing minutes.
So what could I do
but listen and listen
as night turned slowly
towards the dawn?


## Apple
**Christopher Crawford**

Remember, after sex
we went to the coffee and cream cake
you say you will not always give yourself

but do, and enjoy. It was Sunday, so why
not go to the orchard. The way the field,
when we opened the gate, leapt

from the sparrow
and nailed itself to the trunk
of an apple tree.

Apple, we can hear.
I know why
the bird went to the song, which is why

he was nailed there, sparrow, so that others
do not do this.
So that they understand.

# A Modern Melodrama in V x 53 words.
## Penny Cole

I
He pays for everything, from the child's education, landscape with monkey puzzle trees, her cars and much else between. But the small deposit of love they began with, spent across this vast property, gives rise only to the occasional fart of feeling; not of love, really, but something lower to do with money.

II
On Christmas morning, no playful things but commodities braced in hard paper which lies stiffly, a bright contrast to the child's pale feet. Gifts with a quality of pure worthlessness, striking in itself, but also offering a glimpse of an unimagined future. All day the rooms are close and heavy with unsatisfied hunger.

III
An encounter at a play, he gleaming, with tailoring even darker; a General off duty, eyes so black she was drawn right down. She asked "Why does Jamaica need an army, who will you fight?" From then on, each time they met he declared war on England and won victory after glorious victory.

IV
She had no interests, only driving. Suspended high above the road her thoughts would slip downwards, through strict leather gloves, down the steering column to the road, leaving no trace or wrinkle until one day a closing frame, a black and white film, leapt into her mind with the word "Fin" in red.

V
He said, to give bad news I wear my white coat and speak slowly. Death cannot be explained at speed even when it has arrived that way. I realised early in my career that if you do not say the word 'dead', clearly, at least three times, they watch the door for hours.

# Holding A Cord
## Patricia McCaw

It was very good of them, really.
A time of terrible grief for us all
but he was their son, and I
was someone he'd always love,
he told me
lying on one elbow before the fire
in his place—he always burned coal
where I was electric.
Thirty years the same place. Me too.
We had coincidences like that all along the way.
Two big men we were, each a moustache
at varied times. Taken for twins more than once
though I had six years on him.
That made it worse.

I half-expected to be discouraged,
let down gently, told 'It's a family affair, Sam.'
(some guff-- the da wants it small, close relatives)
But they took the ground from my feet when
he pulled me to him like a long-lost son,
never said a word that made sense but
held out a cord to me, and the six of us
lowered away, one black back.
I wanted to jump in after him.
It took the death of him to light the life in me.

I didn't go to the funeral tea, out of respect.

# Earthquake
**Deborah Moffatt**

Perhaps it was the crowing of a cock that woke me,
or the honking of horns over the constant roar of traffic,
a morning like any other, noise never-ending in Mexico city.
You slept soundly, as if nothing could ever happen.

I couldn't understand how you could sleep like that.
I was raised on fear and terror, on warnings and threats.
Danger was everywhere. My family never slept
and always kept one eye on the door, every sense alert.

We had gone to a *bris* the day before, a family affair--
your family, not mine. The men had drunk good whisky
to settle their nerves, (though the father, your brother,
was afterwards rather green in the face, for quite some time),

while the women, stiff with hairspray and heavy with gold,
babbled careless vapidities and eyed one another's clothes
with open avarice, and the older ones spoke only Ladino,
to hide their unkind words from my ears, I imagined.

I have always imagined the worst; it's easier that way.
They would have seen the fear that I wear
wrapped about me like an old worn overcoat,
a dirty secret I couldn't possibly hide.

A cock crowing, cars honking, whatever: something woke me.
I left the bed, went to the window to inspect the day,
taking nothing for granted, looking for vital changes
in a city where nothing ever remained the same.

The Hasidim were leaving their homes, tidy and smart
in their hats and curls, as joggers ran laps around the tiny park.
I envied the joggers for their diligence, the Hasidim
for their faith, their customs, their daring to be different.

I turned away from the window, and noticed the paper lampshade
swinging gently in an imperceptible breeze. Dizziness and fear
made me weak at the knees. Nothing was as it seemed.
Somehow I had never imagined that was how it would be.

I stood in a door-way, as you had told me to do,
although I didn't believe it would do the trick,
and I left you there asleep in the bed;
as good a way to die as any, I supposed.

I could always imagine worse things;
certain things, I don't even have to imagine.
I know the worst; it's in my blood,
and nothing I do can ever change that.

In the kitchen a pot fell from the stove with a clang;
there were bangs, rattles, shuffling noises.
You tossed uneasily, but never woke
until just after the shaking had stopped.

"Earthquake," you said, smiling at me where I stood,
as if it hadn't occurred to you that you might have died,
or that I might have tried to wake you to save your life;
in your eyes there was only unquestioning kindness.

I didn't want kindness; I didn't want your trust,
if that was what it was. Trust is fatal. "Good-bye,"
I said, although I couldn't tell from the way you smiled
if you understood that I was leaving for the last time.

# Dundee wedding
**Deborah Moffatt**

The tattered petals of crocuses, like spent confetti,
litter the grassy banks of the city's roads,
scattered by a relentless wind.

Among the reeds that fringe the Tay
she lay, mud oozing through her toes,
a baby's head emerging through the blood.

At high tide the mud and the reeds are hidden
beneath the quicksilver gleam of a dead-calm river.
Deep down, the dark water washes away her tears.

The wedding never happened. You see her now
tip-toeing round at the back of the Overgate
wrapped in a plaidie and wearing no shoes.

Along the river side, broken-backed daffodils
nod their shredded heads, wiser now, after the fact,
their beauty fading fast, their time past.

# The hour lost
**Stav Poleg**

We travel north.
The sky, Lorca's primary colours:
blood and moon and green.
All sorts of green.

I'm having dreams, you say,
as if it were impossible. I'm falling
in and out of boats. Planes.
All sorts of.

And since you never talk
like that, I can't respond. Instead,
I turn the radio on and off. Too much
politics

"and don't forget to change
the clock tonight". The final early sunset
of the season starts at six, like an April
dress-rehearsal.

I think of how it always
leaves me with a sort of jetlag, days
of relocated breakfasts, dinners,
sleep,

until it's settled and midsummer,
until the days are so long I can't remember
it was any other way. Perhaps
it wasn't.

You never visit us, you say,
it makes no sense to see you once a year,
and only in the spring, as if you're
some kind of bird.

The road enfolds the mountain.
The sky's misleading shades of plum,
the foothills, coffee. It makes no sense,
you say again,

and I can't tell if it's your fears, the hour
lost, or that in spite of all my efforts
I feel at home in here, just here.
But I agree.

# Extract from the novel *Wider than the sky*
## Pippa Goldschmidt

FOR JEANETTE'S THIRTEENTH birthday, her parents buy her a camera. It's a proper SLR, and it makes a satisfying thunk when the shutter is released. She spends hours outside, taking photos with different settings. She learns that when she increases the f-stop to reduce the size of the aperture, the resulting photo is darker, but more of it is in focus. There is a tension between clarity and light.

She takes pictures of starlings perched on telegraph poles, and of fish lying on slabs in fishmongers.

'Very nice,' says her mother, 'Why don't you do people?'

So she offers to take photos of the school play. This year the play is 'Mother Courage.' Jeanette doesn't know the story before she goes to the dress rehearsal. As she sits watching in the school auditorium, she realises it's about death. Mother Courage drags her cart and her three kids through endless battle zones to make money, but she can't protect them, and they all die. The two sons' deaths are pointless, but the silent daughter, Kattrin, dies saving the lives of a family caught in a fire.

The rehearsal proceeds in fits and starts. Lights go on and off at random, regardless of whether anyone's on the stage. People appear in the wrong places and have to disappear. The two sons have to die over and over again because neither of them can remember their lines. The universe is supposed to go like clockwork, but this one is flawed. Eventually it reaches its conclusion, and Mother Courage shackles herself to her cart yet again, and goes off to yet another war.

At the beginning, Jeanette takes loads of photos, but by the end she's simply holding the camera up, to stop people from seeing the tears running down her face. Death by water and now fire. She wonders how her parents can stand watching all those TV programmes full of bodies.

'You've been working hard!' Her teacher, Miss Nightingale, is silhouetted in front of the stage.

She nods.

'Are you going to develop them now?'

She nods again, and stumbles off.

The school darkroom is in the basement of the science block. When she tries to open the door, it's locked. Someone else is in there.

When she rattles the door handle again, a voice squawks from inside, 'Hang on!'

And the door opens slightly, just enough for a cross face to peer out, flushed red from the safety light, 'I haven't finished, actually.'

'But I booked it for this afternoon.'

'Oh,' and the face looks a bit doubtful now. Jeanette recognises it; Alice Airy from the year above, 'Sorry.'

'Is there room enough for both of us?' she asks.

The door opens a bit wider, 'Suppose so. Come on.'

The most difficult part of the process is at the beginning; getting the film out of the camera and onto the developing reel. That has to be done in complete darkness, without even the safety light. As Jeanette slowly guides the

Fiction/147

beginning of the film into the reel, she's aware of Alice, silent and invisible, on the other side of the room.

'Won't be long.'

'Doesn't matter,' says Alice, out of the blackness, 'I'm not in a hurry.'

But something goes wrong, the film tightens itself into a knot and won't wind on properly. Jeanette has to start all over again. It's like learning to see with your fingers. Everything you do has to be guided by what you can feel.

Finally she gets the film into the developing tank and is able to turn the safety light back on. Alice is sitting on one of the benches, perilously close to the sink, swinging her legs. She has short tufty hair and large eyes, with lots of black eyeliner crayoned on, making her look younger than she is.

'Why are you staring at me?'

'I'm not,' Jeanette concentrates on shaking the developing tank. It's important to keep the liquid moving. She looks around but she can't see what Alice is working on, 'Where are your photos?'

'They didn't come out properly. I threw them away.'

Jeanette waits for her film to dry and wonders why Alice is still there.

'I don't want to go home yet,' Alice says. 'Do you ever feel like that? Home is piss, really, since my mum had my baby brother. It's just baby baby baby. It's really embarrassing too. Fancy having sex at that age.'

As she sets up the enlarger, Jeanette watches Alice out of the corner of her eye, 'Yes.'

'Yes what?' Alice is still swinging her legs.

'Yes I feel like that too.'

She holds the negatives up to the light, and squints at them. Impossible to see, at this stage, whether they'll make good photos. But she likes looking at negatives, at the world transformed into bone-white and coal-dark. She offers one of the strips of film to Alice, 'Careful. Don't touch the surface.'

Then she notices that the bin is empty, 'Thought you said you'd thrown your photos away.'

Alice doesn't reply. Jeanette lays the wet contact sheets on the counter and inspects them. This time she doesn't get emotional. The world seems more manageable in shades of grey. She can even examine the photo of Kattrin standing on the roof of the burning building, just before she plunges to her death.

Finally, the contact sheets are done, the tanks are all cleaned and stacked against the wall, the enlarger's back in its box. Jeanette's ready to go.

'You coming?' she says to Alice.

Alice slowly eases herself off the counter, 'Suppose so.'

When they leave the darkroom, Jeanette's eyes are so used to the monochrome red safety light that everything seems larger, lighter. Through the windows the sky looks bluer than she ever thought possible. She laughs, and so does Alice.

'Wow,' says Alice, 'It's like being in a cartoon.'

It's late now, all the other kids went home ages ago. As they walk down the long corridor, Jeanette says to her, 'You never took any photos, did you.'

And Alice shakes her head, not looking at Jeanette. 'It's nice and quiet. No one bothers me there.'

Jeanette feels a small splutter of annoyance. 'If you're going to hide in a darkroom, you might as well learn how to use it.'

Alice grins, 'Are you going to teach me, then?'

Jeanette brings Alice home for tea.

'What's in there?' Alice asks as they go past the closed door on their way to Jeanette's room.

'Nothing.'

At teatime, the two of them sit waiting at the dining table. It's sausages, they could smell them upstairs before tea. But when her mother brings them in, on the old tin baking tray that's always used for this meal, Alice says, 'Oh.' A small sad sound.

'Oh?' her mother echoes.

'I don't eat meat. I'm really sorry.' She

looks it too. Her eyeliner is smudged, as usual. It makes her look like she's been crying, even though she hasn't.

'Why didn't you tell me?' Jeanette's mother turns to her, exasperated.

'I didn't know.'

Her mother sighs, 'How about an omelette, then?'

'That would be lovely. I'm so sorry! Thank you!' Alice smiles, hugely, brilliantly.

Her mother smiles back. 'More sausages for Jeanette, then. Lucky her.'

But Jeanette is remembering that Alice ate a chicken sandwich for lunch. 'You do eat meat,' she hisses, when her mother is back in the kitchen.

'Not sausages,' says Alice. 'Not processed meat.' She looks sad again.

Her father arrives home halfway through their meal. 'Well, well,' he says. 'Hello.'

'Hello,' says Alice. She's only been picking at her omelette and Jeanette's mother is looking exasperated again, 'I'm Alice.'

'Very nice to meet you.' And he leans forward to shake her hand. Jeanette stares at her father. He doesn't usually talk like that.

He's wearing a short sleeved shirt and Jeanette can see the old burn scars on his arms, the landscape of gouged and contoured skin. She wonders how visible the scars are to other people; if you didn't know about them, would you be able to see them? 'Sausages!' he says, and smiles at Jeanette and Alice. Jeanette watches Alice smile back.

'I once knew a dog who could say sausages,' Alice says, 'It was a poodle,' and Jeanette's father laughs.

When Jeanette returns to the table, after helping her mother clear away the first course, she realises there are four of them. Two to the power of two. The family's been lopsided for so long, like a broken chair, that she's forgotten what it used to look like when it was whole.

She pauses at the doorway to look. If she squints her eyes – but Alice doesn't look anything like Kate. Kate was solid, she could shovel in food efficiently and cleanly as if she were stoking a fire inside. Alice is too fragile, all eyes and skinny legs and leftover food. Even though she's three years older than Kate was, she's probably still smaller.

After dinner they go upstairs, past the door that never opens. Something's happened to the room behind the door, nobody's seen it for so long. There could be anything behind it. A whole new world. A vast dark space. Or just a narrow bed where no one sleeps.

As she promised, Jeanette teaches Alice how to use a darkroom. She gets Alice to practice winding film onto the spool with the safety light on. Even in the light, Alice keeps dropping things, 'Sorry,' as the spool hits the floor yet again.

'What's wrong with having a baby brother, anyway?' Jeanette's been to Alice's house and seen the baby, who sat in a mound of cushions on the floor, grabbing at people passing by. When Jeanette picked him up for a cuddle, he gurgled and smiled at her. The whole house was filled with noise. It seemed pretty good to her.

'We have chips all the time. Mum never has time to cook anything else. And she shouts. I wish she'd stop shouting at me.'

'At least she notices you.'

Alice has finally wound the film onto the spool.

'Right, you have to do it again, this time with the light off.'

'You are bossy,' Alice murmurs, as Jeanette snaps the switch off. She's used to the way darkness makes the room feel larger, makes you forget the edges of your own body so that you seem to merge with the surrounding air. There's the regular creak of the spool as Alice winds the film onto it. It sounds as though she's got the hang of it.

'Ready!' she sings out, so Jeanette turns on the light again. But something's happened to the geometry of the darkroom; Alice is much closer than she thought, close enough for Jeanette to reach out and touch her.

'What's the next step?'

'Sorry,' and Jeanette blinks.

In bed that night, she imagines stroking Alice's cheek, just making contact with the skin. Something takes up residence in her mind. Something whispers, *you want this*.

It becomes a habit for Alice to come back for tea at Jeanette's at least once a week.

'Poor thing,' says Jeanette's mother, 'Not a scrap on her. You do wonder what goes on in other people's houses.'

'It's alright. They eat plenty,' says Jeanette, but her mother just shakes her head, 'At least she gets a decent meal here.'

One evening she says to her mother, 'Alice is coming over next Friday.'

'Next Friday?' repeats her mother. And then Jeanette remembers. Next Friday is Kate's birthday. One of the days of the year that dumps them back in the past. No matter how many times the Earth orbits the Sun, it has to go through this same bit of bruised space, exposing them to the same pain. But it also reminds them how much has changed. The only thing worse than the sharp pain of grief is its numbing with time, because that dullness reminds you that the death, and the life it owns, is receding into the past, and you yourself are being swept away from it into the future.

That Friday evening, as they all sit round the table, the air is heavy with silence. Jeanette has not warned Alice in advance, has not been able to think of how to explain to her the significance of this date. Jeanette knows that Alice thinks of her as a lucky only child, in a blessedly quiet house with no noise or mess. This house is Alice's haven.

When Jeanette first started secondary school, she learnt to answer the standard question, 'Have you got any brothers or sisters?' with a shake of her head. No words were needed. No explanations were given. It was true, after all. Some other kids knew about her sister, most didn't. Because Alice was in the year above Jeanette and hadn't known her at primary school, she didn't know. It's better that way, Jeanette thinks, and it's beyond explaining now.

But on this Friday, Jeanette's worried. Silent words buzz around between her and her parents, words that have never been spoken. Words such as 'why did she have to die?', 'why her?', and sometimes Jeanette thinks she can even hear 'why not you?'

The words manage to attract energy to themselves as they fly through the air. Some of them are bound to crash into Alice, as she sits in the fourth chair, chattering about her baby brother learning to talk. The three of them are staring at Alice, as if astonished that she can be so ordinary on a day like today.

They finish their main course, and Jeanette's mother clears the plates. Jeanette, her dad and Alice wait. Sometimes this day is a relief, Jeanette has found over the years, the days and weeks beforehand getting more and more strung out, taut as a wire, before the final release of energy on the day itself. This year it's not like that, the tension has not dissipated. Something else has to happen but she can't imagine what, so she has to wait.

Ice cream appears. When Jeanette glances at Alice, she sees her running her left hand along the arm of her chair. Kate used to do something similar, and Jeanette blinks.

'Who used to sit here?' Alice mumbles through a mouthful of ice cream.

The three of them look at Alice and the silent words fall to the floor. Now they have to deal with reality.

Alice continues, 'It's all worn away here,' and she touches the patch of fabric made smooth by Kate's fingers.

Someone has to say it; 'Kate,' mutters Jeanette. Her parents just sit there.

'Who's Kate?' says Alice. But Jeanette has run out of words. She stares down into her bowl, not wanting to look at Alice's bright innocent face. Suddenly, Jeanette hates her. How dare she ask questions like that? How dare she use the present tense? Doesn't she realise you can't just say things in this house?

Jeanette gets up, still not looking at Alice, and slams her chair into the table. Her parents don't speak or move. They seem to have turned into statues. Perhaps they always were. 'I've finished,' she says much too loudly and walks out of the room, not bothering to wait for anyone's response.

As she runs upstairs, she hears Alice behind her, 'Wait for me,' and there is a sudden scraping noise as Alice falls over, 'Ow!' Good. Pain is good, especially physical pain, but Jeanette would rather feel it herself. There's no point in Alice getting hurt. So she waits for her. Grief is the same as gravity, the same heaviness. Grief sits on her chest and stops her breathing properly.

'What's going on?' Alice whispers. She's realised that today is not normal. Their house is not normal.

They're standing outside the closed door, and it finally seems possible to open it.

Inside. The room looks superficially like Kate's old room, in their old house. There is her bed, covered with her favourite duvet cover, the one with wavy blue and green stripes. Her swimming medals are hanging in a shiny clatter from her bookshelves. Swimming certificates are pinned to the wall, and Jeanette knows without looking inside, that the cupboard will be full of her clothes. She has an urge to open the cupboard door and rub her face in them, to smell the last of Kate, but she knows they have to stay innocent, blind to her grief.

Schoolbooks are piled on the desk by the window. Jeanette can remember her clear, round handwriting. The books will be full of it, but she's not sure she wants to see it. She's beginning to feel sick now. People are not like houses, or cities. They're not just collections of their own belongings. She could stroke the strands of hair in Kate's hairbrush, sitting on Kate's dressing table, and it would be no nearer to Kate than peeling a dead animal off the road.

It is utterly silent. Alice's eyes are even wider than usual as she watches Jeanette walk over to the window. The view here is slightly different to the view from Jeanette's bedroom, although you can only tell the difference over short distances. If you look at the flat line of the horizon it looks the same. And Kate never saw this view at all. Jeanette thinks of her lying in bed, waiting for the morning when she will get up, and go to the pool for her daily practice, and die.

She wonders when her mother carried out this recreation of the past, and whether it works for her, whether she's able to get any comfort from it. Does she come in here during the day when no one else is around, and pretend that she has two daughters? Is that why she always looks so unhappy when Jeanette returns from school and she has to return to reality?

She looks down and sees something dark lodged between the wall and the radiator. One of the swimming suits. She tugs it out, and it flops onto the floor at their feet. A pelt the colour of a starless sky, it lies separate from them, a portal leading down into the world of death. Jeanette's afraid now. She's disturbed the pattern of the room. She's even more scared when Alice bends down and picks the thing off the floor, scrunching it in her hands.

Jeanette touches Alice's arm, and they leave. As they shut the door, Jeanette realises that the room is like an event horizon showing the last remaining bit of ordinary life clinging to Kate, surrounding the black hole of Kate's death. Like death, a black hole is unknowable, shut off and unseen from the rest of the known Universe.

Back in the present, Alice sits hunched up with her chin resting on her knees, listening to Jeanette as she finally talks about her father setting fire to the garden, and her mother's anger. About the emptiness, the unspoken words, the 'why her' and 'why not you'.

Jeanette thinks she's never talked so much in her life. She looks down at her hands as she talks and she studies their surface, noticing how the skin seems to become more detailed, until she can see every individual freckle, and even the pores seem magnified. It is as if she is growing larger. Perhaps her talking has expanded her, made her occupy more space.

She stops speaking and lets a silence take over, but it is a nice silence. Nothing like the silences between her parents over dinner. She listens to Alice breathing, soft little puffs that dissipate into the air surrounding the two of them.

'What was she like?' Alice says.

It's difficult to distil Kate down into words.

She didn't have to describe Kate when she was here, and nobody has asked her about Kate since. Kate simply was, and isn't any more. She's too large for words.

Finally she says, 'She swam in straight lines and was proud of it, but she never looked down on me because I couldn't,' and Alice nods to show that she understands.

# A Walk Before Santa Soledad
## Conan McMurtrie

I WONDER WHERE the little beast has gone. Saying goodbye to his friends I suppose. The mosques are wailing for evening prayers. The van will be here any second. For God's sake, where is he? I wish that boy would learn some consideration.

Isa has been helping me to pack up the house over the last days. Bless him, he's been so much help to us in the time we've lived here in Alexandria. And just as well that he helped me pack, because John is a useless man. My husband falls apart when he's under any kind of pressure. Every time the same, he goes quiet and starts to blunder, then soon he disappears. He's always been that way, it doesn't surprise me anymore. But the boy worries me, he's started to show signs of the same weaknesses, small things that remind me of his father. For example, when I was taking down the curtains just the other afternoon, I overheard a conversation between him and his friend Ghassan when I stepped out into the patio to catch my breath.

Summer is creeping over Alexandria. The heat is fierce and the air tastes of dirt and rosemary. I stayed in the shade of the patio as I heard their voices from the window to his room. I can't say I caught everything they said, because my Arabic isn't as good as the boy's. And yes, it's impressive that he's so fluent with the language. In Turkey he was the same, speaking in months. Even in Greece, barely a toddler, I remember him catching some of their words. He's a sly little thing, adaptable and smart. In any case, I've managed to learn some Arabic myself, and although I'm not always comfortable speaking it, I can understand the gist of a conversation more often than not. And I certainly understood what was going on when I heard my son telling lies to his friend Ghassan.

Their voices came clear from his window. Ghassan said, 'what's the place called again?'

'Santa Soledad.'

'Santa Soledad. *Santa Sóledad*. What do they do there in Santa Soledad?'

'Don't know. Same as here. Lots of beaches. My mum showed me photographs, it looks a bit like here. Pretty much the same.'

'They speak *Arabi*?'

'Maybe. Not sure. Some people do.'

'What about girls? They got nice girls?'

'Yes.'

'Do they go to the beach too?'

'Think so.'

'In bikini?'

'Yeah, in bikini.'

They said nothing for a moment. One of them was kicking a ball around. I listened to it hit the bedroom wall and roll back across the tiles.

'Eid is next month,' Ghassan said finally. 'You're going to miss it.'

'My dad said we're going to come back for Eid every year.'

'James, Eid is next month. They're already preparing for it.'

'My dad said we can come back.'

'Nah. Impossible. You can't come back after one month.'

'Yes I can!' The ball banged hard against

something and the plants in the garden rattled.

They were very quiet then. I waited a minute but neither of them spoke. In a moment I went back into the clutter of the house.

Later that day, around sunset, I found a moment to speak to my son. His room was dark and cool and the air conditioner buzzed overhead. He was sitting on his bed against the wall reading a comic book. I switched on the light. 'That's bad for your eyes you know.'

He didn't look up. 'Wasn't reading it. Just looking at the pictures.'

'What comic is that?'

'Captain Majid.'

'Oh. Who bought you that?'

'Ghassan gave it to me.'

'Was Ghassan in the house today?'

'Yep.'

He still wouldn't look at me. 'Thought so,' I said. 'I heard you and him. Why did you tell him we're coming back for Eid?'

'I didn't.'

'I heard you. You told him we're coming back every year.'

'No I didn't.'

'Don't lie, I heard you.'

'I didn't say every year.'

I stepped closer to his bed. 'Yes you did. You know it's not nice to say things like that if they're not true.'

He didn't reply. I said, 'now Ghassan will think you're coming back next month. Then he'll be sad when you don't.'

'Dad said maybe we could come back.'

My voice rose. 'Dad can say what he wants. You shouldn't tell lies. You shouldn't make people hope for things that aren't true.'

He stared into his comic book. His hands gripped the pages, his fingertips were white. I took another step towards him.

Then he whispered, 'sorry mum.'

'Okay.'

His hair's a little long these days and he's caught the sun. I've got to say he's turned out a good looking ten-year-old boy. It's not an easy face to stay angry at. In any case I accepted his apology.

'Right, enough comic books. Come on, get up. You still need to decide which toys you're giving away.'

And now he's nowhere to be seen and the van will be here soon. I might have to go out looking for him. Surely he's had plenty of time to say goodbye to his friends.

Not everything he told Ghassan the other day was a lie. I did show him a book recently about Santa Soledad, and there are certainly a lot of beaches there. Although he wouldn't admit it – he's a stubborn child, very stubborn – he seemed intrigued by the photographs. As for myself, right now, I can't supress my optimism. After all, I am an artist. This is something I've been searching for my entire life. We are headed to a place where life can begin.

Past the Atlantic, past the Pacific, Santa Soledad is a long, curling city, winding through the coves and sounds of the coast. All around it the sea laps at the outermost streets, which are slim and white. The melodies of water drift through windows and gardens, under arches and pillows. Every night, when the sun sets, fulgurant light shimmers in the sea, melting to a dance of giddy stars.

Through the centuries, the city has stayed apart from civilisation, oblivious to the world's disasters. The tepid climate browns people's forearms and lightens their hair. The seasons are mild, days and weeks fall into each other, pushing gently forward. People there are tidy and solemn. Their eyes are small, and when they speak they are unobtrusive with their voices. Girls walk the streets in elegant dresses, red, yellow and blue. At night, in the bars and squares, men break into scenes of comedy and theatre, usually without preparation. They dance, drink and laugh, often for days on end, without ever falling into vulgarity. They have sensuality without vice. Santa Soledad is a land of poetry.

It will give us what we never found here in Alexandria, or in Istanbul or Thessaloniki. If I've learned something over the years, it is that art cannot arise from shoddy backdrops.

It just occurred to me that the boy might be upset about what happened last night. I wouldn't put it past him to have schemed this hassle for me. I'm loosing patience, I'll have to go find him.

Yes, last night. We've made a few friends in our years here in Alexandria, and we invited some of them round for food and drink, just a gesture of farewell. Isa arrived early, and he and John and I spent sunset in the patio. The night was hot and fresh and the mosques sang in the city. Nadia and Loubna and several others joined us soon.

Our Egyptian friends are not drinkers, unlike myself and John, who can get carried away on these sorts of occasions. In any case, we had a good time looking back on our better memories of Alexandria. We sat about with our stomachs full and some music playing. Loubna stood and did a short dance and we all laughed. I was filling John's glass, which he had drained a minute earlier. I was watching Isa's face as he spoke with my husband. Then he looked my way and something caught his attention behind me.

I turned. My son was standing at the edge of the patio barefoot in a t-shirt. His hair was a mess over his eyes and he looked confused. He was holding something at his side, a comic book I think. He came forward, rubbing his face with the back of his hand.

I started towards him, ready to lead him back into the house, but Isa spoke first. 'James, we woke you up with all this noise. Well I'm glad you woke up. Come and talk to me.'

My son made his way across the yard, sat next to Isa and raised his feet onto the chair. Isa began to speak Arabic. Because I'd been drinking I had trouble understanding them, and I went back to my seat and our friends.

In the meantime my husband was drunk. He stood, swayed, and stumbled across to the music stereo, then he tried to change the cassette. Loubna went to help him, and when the music started he grabbed her hips and wiggled his body in a vulgar dance. Loubna laughed and looked over at me. 'John,' I said, 'would you cut it out.'

He laughed and sang in tune with the music, '*John, cut it out, John, John...*'

I sighed and nodded an apology at Loubna.

John came back to his seat and yawned, the same loud yawn a dog would make, and kept with his ugly singing.

'John, please...'

'*John, please, ooh, John, John...*'

We all laughed at him. Across the patio, Isa and my son talked between themselves. Once or twice Isa patted my son's shoulder and ruffled his hair and the boy laughed. I tried to understand them. I made out some of the words, 'park', 'football', but not much else.

It was past midnight, and John's behaviour must have sobered our friends, because one by one they began to leave. My husband held them in long, sloppy hugs as they said goodbye. I accompanied them each to the door, but Isa stayed behind a while longer.

The night had turned thick and humid. I sat down next to my husband again, and he grinned at me when I looked at him. 'Good people. Good. Good people.'

I took a long gulp of cold wine. Across from me, Isa and the boy chattered and laughed. Their gestures swayed and their voices droned. As much as I love our friend Isa, he irritated me as I watched him laugh with the boy. I wanted to understand but their voices were distant and strange. The boy laughed away, so long past his bed time. When he speaks Arabic something whines in his voice and he giggles like a little girl. I slumped further back in my seat. I wanted to cut his hair, remove it from his face. Remove the whine.

I wasn't prepared at all when he looked up and attacked me. 'Mum, Isa says I could stay in Alexandria. He says I can live with him.'

'I didn't say that, James – '

'Mum, I can stay here. I don't have to go to Santa Soledad. I can stay here with Isa. Or Ghassan. His mom said I could. He's got an extra bed. Okay? I'll go to Santa Soledad in summer holidays. I'll go – '

'James, that's enough.'

My son leapt from his chair and scurried to the other end of the patio. His stare was fierce and he held his comic book tight to his chest. 'Mum, I don't want to go there! Santa Soledad is a stupid place! You and dad go. Please. I'll save up my pocket money to come to see you. I'll –'

'James.' I stood, took a step towards him and gathered my voice. 'Stop this now. Enough is enough. You're tired. Everyone's tired. Now say goodbye to Isa.'

Isa knelt and waited for him. My son's shoulders heaved and he groaned. For a second I thought he would continue with his tantrum, but he did as he was told and went to Isa, who reached out and hugged him. James seemed to go limp in the embrace, looking very tired, his arms dangling with the comic book hanging at his side.

Just a few minutes later I was saying goodbye to Isa. Soon enough, John and my son were asleep, and I sat alone in the patio for a while, staring up at the night sky.

This morning James appeared to forget the whole thing. He even seemed cheerful at breakfast, and later he helped me carry our stuff to the front room, getting ready for our departure.

Yes, he seemed cheerful to me. A little too cheerful. He spoke away as we worked. 'It's good that Isa came. I'm happy I saw Isa.'

'Good.'

'Are you going to write to him?'

'Yep. You can too. He'll want to know about your new school, your new friends.'

He grinned and said nothing. I wonder now if I caught something in his eyes, something he was keeping from me. In any case, for the rest of the day I attended to the final details. I had to collect our insurance papers and to settle some bills with our landlord. John was sick from his drinking and limped around the house looking wretched. I asked my son to take a bath and choose some clothes for the journey, which he did. Then he asked if he could go to see his friends one last time.

This is what I thought he'd been doing when I first noticed him gone. But as the hours passed I grew anxious. John hadn't seen him since afternoon. 'He'll be around, leave him be.'

'You idiot, we need to find him. Get a grip.'

At a quarter to ten I lost my patience and put on some shoes. The van was due to arrive.

I tried to stay calm as I went out the front door.

I peered into the dark starlight of the street. My heart thudded, my breath came fast and my fists were tight. I knew he could be anywhere in the miles in front of me.

Anywhere, but thankfully a small figure came walking from the shadows. I sighed and waited with my hands on my hips, and when he came close enough I said, 'in the house, *now*,' and went back inside.

My son stepped in after me. I turned and watched him. His face was lowered, he had something at his side, a comic book. I said, 'James?'

He gazed up at me. His cheeks were damp and reddish, he'd been crying and he tried to smile.

'James... were you saying goodbye to your friends?'

'No. Just walking around.'

'Walking around?'

He sniffed and looked down at his sandals. 'Just walking.'

'Okay. James, don't worry, I'm not angry anymore. Get your stuff, that's the van outside. We've got a long journey. James, stop crying, I'm not angry. Go tell dad we need to go.'

He shuffled out of the room and I went to greet the driver outside. There was banging and throwing and the engine's rattle. And now we're on our way to Santa Soledad.

# Viewing the Emperor
**AC Clarke**

The boy who saw the Emperor naked
had always been tiresome
like a mirror which won't forgive your flaws.
He wanted things just so. If bedtime was eight
it must not be a second before. If there was cake
it must be halved to the millimetre.
He liked charts, exact outlines, proof.

His sister, beside him, saw the Emperor
step out in all his finery, shirt rippling
supple as water over his breast, his cloak
trailing soft feathers. His eyes were topaz,
their narrow pupils black as obsidian.
She dreamed his talons digging for a hold
on her pale skin, his dipping beak.

Their nurse who thought book-learning turned your wits,
found both her charges troublesome.
The girl would scream herself awake,
the boy pelt her with stone cold facts.
She didn't see the Emperor at all.
She was exchanging gossip with the girl
behind her, who laundered the imperial smalls.

# Chimera
## AC Clarke

I saw the poetry god the other night:
squat as a Buddha on the chest of drawers
he manifested in a grubby robe
that wasn't tight enough to hide the belly
sagging over his thighs as he sat cross-legged,
hands folded. I didn't like his grin.

He thrust a bare foot out from under his hems
with the air of a bishop. I stooped to kiss a toe
worn as St Peter's in Rome: *just one poem*
I wheedled *after all these years of service*
*one true poem*. Thinking he hadn't heard
I tried again. A quiver shook

the folds of his being. *You want a poem?*
His voice was the size of a brass band. *I'll give you a poem.*
He pulled a sack with a paunch to rival his
from under his buttocks, gripped the cord at its neck
*Shall I, shan't I?* He tugged. Let rip a swarm
– a buzz of winged confusion, grab and slip

until my hands were black and stinging,
my prayers hoarse. He laughed so hard
the ceiling plaster snowed, the windows cracked.
I'll swear the temperature dropped ten degrees.
*Don't you know ANYTHING?*
He snapped his fingers. Before I'd begun

to stutter a reply (should I thank him or curse
the instant calm?) he started to fade,
first toes, then feet, hands, belly, shoulders
the last bit to go (what a prankster he is!)
his grin. It hovered in the air
crooked, a glint of gold in the left corner.

# Scrogs on a bush
**Bridget Khursheed**

Scrogs on a bush
by the river
in the hedge
reeking of fox.

Does fox eat scrogs?
They lie
spang-ed
by the tree.

A burrow through briar
stretches
to the kinnen field;
straight to scrogs.

Or scrogs to coney?
River treacles past
after flood
brown as rotten

scrogs on a bush
by the river
in the hedge
reeking of fox.

# Knife?
**Stewart Sanderson**

The soil spilled off it, showing unspoiled flint.
A nodule that could have been a knife
but with a hole in it the light fell through
so could have been a pendant; neck and tint,
this muddy samphire from a dead soul's kist
that my cold knife, my trowel, got me to.

Did it choose me – at random – from my friends
who worked and sifted with me in the trench
by nine dead cattle – cut by this *knife*? Strands
of Neolithic meaning stroked the thing
in contrast to the runnels, breaks and bands
which marked the walls' red paint in golden sun.

I thought I saw them for the first time then
and its
five thousand years, just waiting for my hand


# Wet Day
**Stewart Sanderson**

No good will come of us discussing this
but one wet day in Caithness we walk out
with sleek detectors on our rainproof backs
and by a flagstone farm my father shouts
*the batteries* – the laptop in his coat –
the rain had got to it and snuffed it dead
halfway across a pat thrown field of cows.

It died before the crest, the caesium
whose isotope we'd come for blinked away
and levelled out, still moving in the dark
of our machine, I think, and in the numb
dreich peaty soil between the Camster Cairns
and Fukushima; pent anent Dounreay.

# The gift from Cairo
**Rizwan Akhtar**

He tells me in Cairo the air is full of burnt sand
sends me an embossed camel skin rug
with Arabic calligraphy in curlicues
the narrow streets cradling
in the fumes of shisha
starkness of The White Desert
on men's ragged cheekbones
guides coddle the western women
sneak at their meniscus bodies
given to fits under its heat
the abrupt gusts airbrush
facile lines and histories
motes of afternoon dust appear
in their sleepwalk eyes
the armpits reek perfumed sweat
liquoring nights
in blue body of the Nile—
they say whosoever drinks its water
always comes back
like that desert-driven moon
gazes through the balconies of hotels
girdling nightgowns see the city
waning into darkness.

# Disaster diary
**Rizwan Akhtar**

                        One day it begins:
a pram scuttles in the Brokenhurst Gardens
the abrupt gales subsumes human voices

... (night a disconsolate sky with a single star
& a gibbous moon (like a chipped hazelnut)

... The Witch Hazel crumbles
in the garden's wet silence

... a pregnant cat
randomly thuds on the roof and limps away

... inside the family photograph trembles
only the children feel it, faces huddled
like frozen allusions, with a graveyard look
an old woman trapped among the grownups
and the frame

... mosquitoes drone, the shrivelled
dead moths drizzle from the dusty railings

... last year on Khartoum Road a man slipped
from the crusted snow, the place still look likes
a crime scene, there are other things too
                          a few find space.

# No me importa la lluvia
**Andrea McNicoll**

SHE SHUTS EARLY, gathering up the leftover carnations, lilies, roses, orchids and sunflowers. She snaps the stems, keeping the still-blooms at arm's length to avoid staining her clothes with the sap and pollen that can be such a devil to wash out, and delivers the flowers head first into the bin. She pushes gypsophila and aspidistra leaves on top, pressing the lid down. *What a waste*, thinks Laura, *I could have made at least another two hundred pounds in the evening rush.* Friday is her busiest evening; a time when men will pause as they rush through the station, suddenly remembering that to give a little to their wives is sometimes to get a little back. But tonight the men will have to do without because Laura has a train to catch, a plane to board and a husband to meet in Malaga.

Ewan went out to the apartment last week, and has been putting in the hours on the golf course. Unlike Laura, Ewan works for a multinational company and enjoys six weeks paid holiday each year. Laura's Blooms, he maintains, is just a wee hobby – it is Ewan, after all, who is the breadwinner. Whose money paid for the deposit on the Benalmádena apartment? Whose wages go towards the mortgage payments? Laura's Blooms barely breaks even most months – it's a time-filler, something to keep Laura busy while Ewan goes out to do real work. By the time he retires, 'Benalmádena', as he likes to say, will be paid for. They will rent out their house in Glasgow and move permanently to Spain. Imagine, Ewan often crows, never having to suffer a winter in Glasgow again!

Laura draws down and locks the shutters on her stall, then pulls her suitcase across the concourse towards her waiting train. She nods at the left luggage man (who always looks at her legs when she's wearing a skirt) and waves at the girl who runs the coffee stall. She boards and finds a seat, resting her head against the cold window. After a few minutes the train pulls away, chugging over the River Clyde towards Paisley, where she will take a taxi to the airport. Ewan will collect her in Malaga and drive them to the apartment in a rented car. Laura hopes that once she is there Ewan will spend time away from golf. She is going to suggest some day trips to him: Seville, perhaps, and Ronda.

She hopes to visit the Alhambra.

And that the apartment won't be too untidy.

*

Laura squats by the edge of the pool, staring at the frog floating on its back. Its belly is swollen, soft and white. She reaches out a hand, but the small dead thing is just beyond her reach. *Have I ever actually seen a real frog before*, she wonders, rocking back and forth on her heels, recalling stories about frogs on lily pods that turned into princes when appropriately kissed, pictures of cross-sectioned frogs from biology books, and Kermit the Frog. Her brother kept tadpoles for a while: Laura and he had watched legs growing out of the bodies. She remembers her mother, not exactly keen on wildlife, flushing the tadpoles down the toilet before they grew completely into frogs. Sitting down, Laura swings her legs into the water, easing her body in, trying not to disturb the dead thing. The water feels cold and a little viscous. As she moves towards it, the frog bobs away. She concentrates, managing eventually to get her hands underneath it, and lets out a small scream as she scoops the body out in one disgusted toss. It lands in the hedge. *Noone*, she hopes, *will find it there*. It will only add fuel to the fire.

She gets out the pool and heads for her sun lounger and towel. The tops of her wet thighs rub together as she walks. Looking down at her stomach, she wonders if a bikini is a good idea at her age. Laura lies down, waiting for the sun to warm her. She turns her head to gaze up at the apartments. The complex is nearly finished now; the hum and clatter of bulldozers and cement mixers has become distant, peripheral. Beyond the bright apartment blocks, ever more of the dry red mountainside is being churned and nudged aside to make way for holiday homes. In the evenings, Laura and Ewan often walk to the site edge to explore the half-built houses, tip-toeing through the shells as they count the number of bedrooms. A whole house! For them, one bedroom is enough. Even then, there have been sacrifices at home: they rarely go out now and have had the same living room suite for years. *Isn't it worth it though*, Laura thinks, as the sun starts to burn her skin. Everyone is buying a place in the sun: if not in Spain then in Turkey, Cyprus or Florida. One of Ewan's managers has a property in the south of Thailand.

Laura slips her bikini straps off her shoulders, doubling her chin to glance down at her heavy breasts, spilling out the scraps of bikini fabric. Some women sunbathe topless but Laura just can't bring herself. The sight of bare breasts embarrasses her. The German women seem especially comfortable with no tops on, striding around the pool with everything bobbing up and down. Ewan certainly doesn't object, although he thinks the older ones should keep their clothes on. There's no need for *that*, he said one day, frowning at an elderly woman on the other side of the pool. *What*, Laura worries, *will he think now that hers are going downhill too?* There's no money for surgery and it isn't as though she has the luxury of blaming it on childbirth and breastfeeding. *Feeding*, she thinks, frowning at her insubordinate chest, *the one thing that breasts are actually for*. It doesn't matter how much he insists that it's her great legs that turn him on: Laura knows from years of midnight nuzzling that Ewan's a tit man at heart.

She picks up her Spanish book. Laura decided last year when they bought 'Benalmádena' that she would make an effort. Sometimes, when the flower stall is quiet, she practises phrases under her breath. Speaking Spanish makes Laura feel more interesting. She uses her Spanish skills to book restaurant tables and shop in the local market. She loves wandering through the stalls, looking at the breads and cheeses, the cuts of meat and fish: it's much more *authentic* than the supermarket in town. Apart from when she's shopping, she rarely seems to meets any Spaniards, although she often passes the cleaner on the apartment stairs. She resolves to speak to the cleaner soon. Even *hóla!* would be a start.

*Patatas, cebólla*, repeats Lorna under her breath, *mayonesa y pimiento*. Ewan will take her to the market when he returns from golf. Lorna needs the *patatas, cebólla, mayonesa y pimiento* to make a potato salad for the barbecue, later, around the pool. Tony and Carole have organised it, putting up a poster in the lobby inviting everyone to come. Tony even drew a cartoon frog on the poster.

It was the rain that started it. The day Ewan came to collect Laura from the airport there was a huge thunderstorm. You've brought the rain, Ewan said, staring out the window at the sodden golf course. Then everyone started complaining that they couldn't get a good night's sleep. It was anyone's guess where the frogs were hiding until the storm, or what they got up to during the day, but since the storm the complex resonated at night with the sound of frogs. A child found one in the swimming pool. The boy had almost swallowed it, Laura heard, and could have caught a nasty disease. This provided the excuse people were looking for. Children, after all, are inviolable. Laura, however, doesn't mind the noise. To her the frogs make a kind of music that harmonises with the Moorish watchtowers, the old bull ring in the village over the hill, the palm trees, the bald mountains and the white tiles on their apartment floor, so cool on a hot day. The frogs are just another part of being somewhere *else*. Somewhere that *isn't* Glasgow. But others see the frogs as a problem, something to be fixed, and at the barbecue they will find a solution.

Tony and Carole are English, from somewhere like Essex, or Kent. They introduced themselves at the poolside. Ewan and Tony hit it off immediately and have been playing golf every day since. Laura knows that the Alhambra can wait. Carole wears a great deal of jewellery and has her hair done in a salon every second day. She has confessed to botox and a boob job. *She* bathes topless. Laura has seen Ewan peering hungrily at Carole's conveniently placed breasts. She declined Carole's invitation to go to the new English supermarket that afternoon, preferring to wait for Ewan.

Tony and Carole are just renting for now, while their house is built. They have two grown up children, Laura has been told: a son who is a successful accountant and a daughter who is married and has a baby girl. Her wedding cost the best part of thirty thousand pounds. Carole waved pictures of the granddaughter under Laura's nose but, as Laura had no glasses on, all she could see was a pink, blurry blob. Laura explained to Carole that she and Ewan have no children. It was never the right time. Work got in the way. The world is over-populated. Children are such an expense. And then there's global warming and internet grooming to worry about too.

*Special intransitive verbs,* reads Laura, *with the following verbs the Spanish construction is the opposite of the English. The subject in English becomes the indirect object of the Spanish verb, while the object in English becomes the subject of the Spanish verb.* Laura lays the book over her chest, wondering if Turkish would have been easier. *Turkish delight*, she thinks, *shish kebabs*. But Ewan ruled Turkey out because of the Muslims. *No me importa la lluvia*, she repeats, *I don't mind the rain – no me importa la lluvia – I don't mind the rain...*

\*

'Acid', Tony is saying to a group of men, 'I looked it up on the internet. It's been used on frogs in Hawaii.' He waves his beer bottle around. 'We could lay baited traps around the pool.'

The other men nod, murmuring. It is mostly British people who have come, and a few Germans. The children have eaten their burgers and are out of the way, playing in the pool, much to Laura's relief. No-one discovered the dead frog in the hedge. She sits down on a sun lounger and bites into a sausage. She needs to eat because the homemade tinto de verano is strong.

'Real Cumberland,' Carole boasts, sitting down next to her, 'from the new supermarket. They've got *everything*: Tetley's, baked beans, Marmite, black pudding...'

'Wouldn't that be dangerous for the kids?' one of the men asks Tony.

Laura smiles, chews and swallows, then washes down the sausage with another gulp of wine. She wonders if any of her *ensalada de patata* is left on the table. She had been about to put chopped olives in it but Ewan had moaned: he doesn't like olives. *How could anyone*, Laura laments, *not like olives?*

'We could lay the traps at night and collect them in the morning,' counters Tony, who thinks of everything.

'...of course, it's a bit pricey.' Carole refills Laura's glass.

'The other option is to poison the slugs the frogs feed on,' Tony adds, laying more sausages on the grill.

'I prefer the Spanish market,' says Laura, a little too loudly.

She sees Ewan frowning at her, or is he frowning at Carole's breasts? She can't be sure. She has made a special effort this evening, wearing a short, pretty dress that draws attention to her legs. Her only fear is that the dress is too young for her. Lately, Laura has caught sight of herself in changing room mirrors, finding a much older woman than she expects looking back, whilst in the background girls young enough to be daughters are trying

➻

on clothes.

'If you poison ze slugs,' interrupts a tall German politely, 'you vill disturb ze eco-balance.'

Everyone turns to look up at him.

'So what?' says Tony, barbecue tongs raised, 'who cares about *slugs*?'

'Yeugh!' Carole titters, looking around the group as she toys with the pendant that nestles in her cleavage, 'nasty, slimy things. Don't you agree, Laura?'

'But ze birds also eat ze slugs,' explains the German, 'do you also vant to kill ze birds?'

'Better that than kill a child,' says Tony, snapping his tongs.

'If I had my way,' Carole continues, 'I'd kill the whole insect world!'

The German clicks his tongue against his teeth. He must, decides Laura, be an environmentalist, a green. She tries to be green too, always putting the old newspapers, cans and bottles in the proper recycling bins. Ewan says it's a bloody waste of time. *The German,* Laura decides, stifling a giggle, *is a Green Giant.* Smoke curls up from the slowly cremating sausages. Conversations about the unappealing habits of spiders, bees, ants and cockroaches begin to flourish. Everyone has a story to tell.

*

Laura wakes up to a hot flush and leaves Ewan snoring in bed. They had intercourse last night and Laura feels hollowed out and sticky. She slides back the glass doors and steps on to the balcony. The sun is bursting over the mountain tops. At first, Laura didn't understand why the apartments were painted yellow and orange, but she knows now it is to blend in with the remarkable Spanish sky. They leave for Malaga airport at noon and will arrive in Glasgow when the Scottish sky is darkening and most probably grey with rain. Laura hopes there's something in the freezer at home for dinner. Their suitcases are packed and the apartment is tidy: she took advantage of Ewan's decision to play golf again yesterday to clean out the apartment fridge.

She looks at the perfectly still pool and decides to go down and break its surface, to bask for one last hour in the Spanish sun. So what, she thinks, *if another towel gets wet?*

She closes the apartment door softly, padding down the stairs in her bare feet, feeling like Juliette Binoche in 'The English Patient.' Laura has watched the film four times. Being a nurse during the war is a favourite fantasy. Other fantasies include opening a West End branch of Laura's Blooms, learning to dance flamenco, losing weight, writing a literary bestseller, working as a simultaneous translator for the United Nations, and giving birth to twins. She prays she won't meet Carole. Laura has avoided her since the barbecue, bumping into her only once since then, at the little shop on the complex edge. Carole was passing in her 4 x 4 as Laura emerged, clutching two bottles of wine and a family bag of crisps. Laura looked the other way but Carole slowed down, pushing her sunglasses over her nice hair.

'Not *more* tinto de verano,' Carole trilled, 'I'd have thought you had more than enough at the barbecue!'

Laura just laughed and waved. Carole, high on her seat, replaced her sunglasses, zoomed the window up and drove off. It was Tony's car, driven all the way from wherever it was they lived. It took three days to drive to Malaga, stopping off at Holiday Inns along the way. Carole said it was exhausting but Tony simply couldn't stand the rented right-hand drives. Lorna watched the back of the car as it sped off, noticing the pink sign bobbing in the back window: PRINCESS ON BOARD.

She didn't mean to get drunk at the barbecue. Ewan was cross with her the next day: she'd been rude to Tony about the frogs. What's your problem, Ewan asked, why the sudden interest in frogs? When're you going to grow up?

Today, Carole is nowhere to be seen. Laura spots the cleaner, who is polishing a mirror in the lobby. Now is her chance. Laura will speak to her in Spanish and the cleaner will be delighted and next time they come to 'Benalmádena', Laura and the cleaner will talk every day. She clears her throat.

'Hola,' she calls out, 'como esta? Como te llamas?'

The woman looks at Laura's reflection in

the mirror and sighs. She slowly shakes her head and says, 'no entiendo. I no understand Spanish.' She shrugs and carries on polishing. 'Polski,' she explains, 'I come from Poland.' Then she points outside at the pool. 'Problem,' she whispers, staring at Laura through narrowed eyes, 'at swimming pool.'

Laura blushes, hesitating for a few seconds before escaping through the door. *What's she on about? And why did she look at me like that?* Laura hugs her chest, wishing she didn't care what the cleaner thought, or what Ewan, Tony, Carole and everyone else thought. She wishes she didn't care about her breasts or her thighs. She wishes she didn't care about what's in the freezer, or whether another towel will get wet. The list of things Laura wishes she didn't care about goes on and on and on.

The air is fresh but the cobbled path hurts her feet. She stops short at the end of the path and covers her face with her hands. The garden around the pool is littered with little corpses. She vaguely remembers, through the usual fug of wine, Ewan going on about it last night: something about acid poison and Tony showing the Germans who was boss. Ahead, the pool beckons, still and blue and clean. She wishes she didn't care but simply can't avoid it. The sight of the dead frogs, their legs thrown out in gestures of surrender, is breaking Laura's heart.

# Bertolt Brecht in exile
**David Eyre**

I know it's an affront
to walk this same promenade
every day past pretty boats
tethered in a foreign harbour

a haven where they bob
in broken rhythm empty
and colourful despite the grey
winter surrounding the Med.

Last night we gathered again
and I sang songs satiric
and argued and fought
over pink wine and eau de vie

that didn't dull
the finality of failure
streetfights lost
and the impotence

of my never-ending words.
But what can you do
when a people burn
in thrall to hate

despite your every waking effort
but leave and take coffee
at the Hotel de la Tour
half-wishing half-dreading

that the well-dressed burgher
at the table behind
might start
whistling Mackie Messer.

# Autumn in Lahore
**Rizwan Akhtar**

The trees and birds
in Lahore's gardens
lose some leaves
some voices
stamped with dust
autumn-nudged silence
seeks space
on the stubbled faces
of old men
whimpering on sticks
fungal fingers
with children running
for their mothers
what was dear last year
is now unbelievably absent
cheeks
accumulate
eyes
extinguished craters
the evenings
as if on anodyne
bats cluster
in a web
of the dog-barked darkness
the city folds
like a bride
in its virgin embrace
I sleep in its lap.

# Lavender
## Graham Brodie

i found lavender
growing wild
by a gently flowing stream
darkly

i remembered you there
and thought of you
bleeding ever so slightly
out of your ears

we both held panic
in our hearts
as we wondered
what had happened

i checked your vision
which was fine, or
slightly off fine
but usual

you could still hear me
when i spoke with you
you said
and i believed

i saw you falling to sit
as i rushed back through the woods
to find help
as i saw it

my visions seem to fail
me here, alas
i just really remember the woods
your bleeding ears

and you, darkly

# Visiting Winter: a Johannesburg Quintet
**William Bonar**

1. VISITING WINTER

a wee bit frosting
by night
buys a wheen o
sun block
*Naw, ye'll no see me
back north*
he hoasts
cauld n beery


2. SCRAP

*Metal, we take anything metal, boss.*
they move slow through the garden   eyes
    raking

we clear out plant stakes   rusty brai   riddle
unnameable parts   your old netball pole —

later we drive out   they're still in the street
shopping trolley full   securing their score


3. BOY'S HOME

Although it's winter
this garden still blooms.

In a shady corner
an outhouse — one room.


4. SHEET METAL WORKER

Nineteen Forty-Six
Ah come oot here
frae Motherwell

when ah retired
Ah'd 243
blacks   37
coloureds

n 13 whites —
maist o thaim
Afrikanners —

under me


5. MIGRANTS

i

This strange winter, its low grinning sun
hot on my head, the houses cold

under clear skies, the hadidahs'
rooky clack as dusk takes hold.


ii

We drink in bars with wood fires
huddled close, my clothes too thin.

This strange city on its golden reef
cocks its alarms, locks itself in.

We make spoons in a narrow bed,
tomorrow we'll find your father's gun.

# FURNACE

## BY WAYNE PRICE

'This is a heraldic collection. The short stories of Wayne Price are of both incandescent restraint and dynamic range; many of these seemingly quiet tales, rise to that supreme level: namely some of the best short stories written anywhere in recent years.'
**ALAN WARNER**

'One of the few writers I know for whom the comparison with Carver is not fanciful – he really is that good' **ALAN SPENCE**

## RELEASED 20 FEBRUARY 2012
## RRP £8.99

**FREIGHT BOOKS**

www.freightbooks.co.uk

# Uptown New Year Transition
**Nicholas YB Wong**

For a moment we raise our heads
to see the fabric of fireworks and how its after-
glow outshines stars.

Then, we admit – briefly –
our insignificance.

Then the mother wildly nuzzles her baby,
then the boy grabs the girl's hand, smells her hair,
not letting go, to make his year complete –

Love, overused on days like this, is not festal
without the body of the other.

But how ironic that we welcome newness
by counting down the last ten seconds of the old,
already underfoot, trudging to escape from us.

Later tonight is still a night,
regulated by the same number of hours, hours
of numbness. When we wake up,

there will still be oxygen, the sky
equally infinite, so we can

breathe and go out, as usual, to plant
our hopes, year after year until

the seeds decide to sprout.

# Privilege of Morning
## Nicholas YB Wong

See, I'm a man who sits to pee to start my day.
My legs, bent more than ninety degrees, conjure more

inspiration than when straightened. I like it here,
naked, locked and clockless, like the subconscious,

but better organized. I twist and twirl my ionized
hair. Every strand of blackness shampooed into mind-lather.

The buck-toothed woman two floors above
screams from madness or boredom – She wants

to be heard. Hysteria is human inertia when
dreams hatch a plot for headlines. Astrologists discover

Orphiuchus, six days left of the Scorpion zodiac.
The North and South Poles grow bored, so they swap,

shifting the carapace of Earth to drift from faint latitudes.
Fast floods, fires fall, human offal swallowed. And in China,

herbalists urge using urine to cure osteoporosis. The world
too screams for remedies, while I, with my perfectly calcified

calcaneus and fibula, can sit, stand and walk my will
out to the streets, day after day, to the mesmerizing insanity

# neues Deutschland II
**Fiona Rintoul**

who are you
you Du Du you
and what do you do
für mich

you are cold eyes
like fishes
you are a black heart
bursting with bitter badness
you are a swastika, a jackboot
a bloodied face in the mud


(listen, it's quiet now)

you are a soft morning on the Elbe
a Virginia Woolf house
clinging to a Hamburg cliff
filled up with loved hushed words

you are a smile at the train station
a café by the docks
you are an opera from La Finece
bought in freezing winter

you are jokes
about the 9/11 bombers
sketching aeroplanes in the sun

you are this you are that
you are Du I am ich

# Auld grulsh, efter 'the poetry reading'
**Alan Harkness**

Rauk thochts o London first.
Here, slork that doun ye
– rum fae the Caribs –
noo pluff us oor ain philosophie,
tak waught an mak it seilfu!
Seilfu, lithe an hert-warm, pensefu
an vast lik yon lift, fur thonner
yer suithfast sel hearkens.

Aye, hir maks ye gowp, ye wi yer
threy scaurs – lyart lines –
juist lik Odysseus, ken,
strippit afore's cuttag nourice.
Hir ye luve, she's birks in munelicht
gin yon fortress voice o guff.
Hail warld's coil'd in southron souch.
Ach aye... coil'd in southron souch.


# Sunstruck
(After Alastair Reid's 'Scotland')
**Mary Wight**

I met the woman Alastair met,
still telling the world we'll pay for it

the sun shining on her face
as she reclined on a bed

and I wondered, if we pay at all,
do we pay ahead?

# Behind the Carpathians
## Svenja Herrmann

translated from the Swiss German by Donal McLaughlin

*God is the fact that we exist and that's not all.*
(Fernando Pessoa)

Behind the Carpathians Bucovina songs
I follow the crest of the hills and a melody
Rails hem the road and a dog
runs off its hunger

Look at this, I want to shout
when I see the dead donkey in the ditch
and how women get out of trucks
once their work on the men –
I say nothing

\*

Massive rose bushes on the path to the church
and the sounds of the toaca climbing
the steep, still wintry slopes
a rhythm so regular
you'd think there was nothing to fear

Frescoes flood the church wall
Five yards between Heaven and Hades –
the deadly sins the oxygen of Christianity
the nun will have none of it
she thinks she can convert me

In the dark interior
the rattling of the censer
and the whispering of faith
like the water splashing –
coming full circle, constantly

\*

Behind the Carpathians Bucovina songs
I follow the crest of the hills and a melody
Trees, like brush strokes – a child's hand,
and the last of the snow

Here's where I want to die
no bells, just the toaca: wood on wood
and I want to hear it

# My Father And Fishing
## Gordon Meade

My father was never happier than when
he was standing up to his knees in a fast-flowing river
fishing for rainbow trout. He had caught

the odd salmon in the past but it was
trout he loved. He said they made more of a game
of it. You could play them more. I could

not disagree. My idea of a day's fishing
was trying for an hour or two, hooking the occasional
eel and throwing it back. After that, I would

enter my own sort of trance. I would
drift off somewhere, no longer aware of my surroundings.
From time to time, I would come back,

just to check that my father was still there,
still reeling in or casting. When it was time to pack up,
we would dismantle our rods and head off

home. My father was never happier than when
he was fishing. And I was never more myself than when
standing at the edge and watching him.

# Life of Brian
**Graham Fulton**

Jesus at last it's Brad Pitt in his blue jeans
and all of the women and some of the guys
are going mental
and saying things like Oh my God!
and He's so cute! and
He's much smaller in real life!
and screaming and taking pictures
as he raises his arm and waves and smiles
in a meltingly friendly way
with his convincingly not-too-
long blond hair
and his reassuringly confident swagger
all the way back to his luxury trailer
for a cup of coffee, or a leisurely dump,
as soldiers
and SWAT teams
and a bearded trampy man
with a three-legged dog
wait about for the next take,
and a newly arrived wee woman
who's missed it all
says to her man Whit ur they dayn?
to which he replies Thur maykin a film
uh thu zombees!
to which she replies
Brian Pitt?
Who the fuck is Brian Pitt?
which is a really good question

# Four Kinds of Death
**Andrew C Ferguson**

**I: Dust**
(after Serena Korda)

Breathe in too quick, and you're sneezing philosophers.
In the old Victorian brickworks
heaps of the stuff rendered down
dust to ashes, ashes to mud,
brickfuls of the charnel house.

In Bazalgette's cathedral, the artist now
assembles her palette: the dust of foreigners,
dead gorilla hair, her mother's fingernails,
flesh made brick, a dance round the stack
then back underground.

A strange reinterment
for mute inglorious Miltons.

**II: Aspic**
**(for John Campbell Mitchell)**

Fellow artists collected in a cortege, then
his studio in Corstorphine
lay untouched for eighty years.

Rain, on a filthy night
clamouring at the window
to reach the dumb paintings.

Tsunamis of light on a summer's day
spent in emptiness
where only dust motes move,

till the housekeeper collected them,
wiping the frames
of forgotten originals.

The artist as genie, trapped
under the ouija glass, waiting
for his last family to die.

**III: Photography**
**(for David Octavius Hill)**

Fettered shadows, fading in the calotypes,
church schisms flaring
like a spread of chemicals
dealt by Adamson's expert hand.

Clergymen's lined faces,
serried ranks for your masterpiece
trophied heads, hunted across Scotland
by you, collector of the holy.

And you, stretching on a frontispiece
while pretty girls look on,
or the herring fisherwomen stare,
all fixed in a frame by Adamson,

before he dies, and your invalid first wife,
and then your daughter,
the studio on the fairy hill left untended,
as the shadows lose their fetters, and move in.


**IV: Living**

You don't know you spell
a Tarot for me,
the Crab card, the Demented Lady,
genes twisting like fingers
an incomplete calotype of you,
fading even in the digital.

The dream world, shadow chasing
- people that were here, plans to go
places only you now see.
You are the frontispiece
of a book I can never write,
a locked photograph

still living.

# The Optimist
**Graham Fulton**

in the corner of
the bookie's
doorway

trying to light his
fag in
the storm


# Slow Down
(After Jayne Wilding and after Henry David Thoreau)
**Larry Butler**

If I could write at a snail's pace
I'd leave behind all unfinished poems
complete each one
before I start another.

If I could slow down enough
I'd taste the words for things to eat
biting each damson, writing "plum"
with more relish than the last poem.

If I can go as slow as sky
day and night become different tones of blue,
     writing poems always fresh –
        they release our finest qualities.

For are we not all rushing through the hours
gulping too many damsons and plums
     eating our words to avoid the pain
        of remembering lost voices.

# Contributor Biographies

Sandra Alland is a Scottish-Canadian writer, performer and intermedia artist. She has published two books of poetry: *Blissful Times* (BookThug) and *Proof of a Tongue* (McGilligan Books); and one chapbook of short fiction: *Here's To Wang* (Forest Publications). She currently collaborates with the multimedia performance troupe, Zorras. blissfultimes.ca

Rizwan Akhtar is from Lahore, Pakistan, and currently reading for his PhD in postcolonial studies at University of Essex. His poems have appeared in *Poetry Salzburg Review, Poetry NZ, Wasafiri, Postcolonial Text, decanto, Poesia* (US), *Exiled Ink, Pakistaniat : A Journal of Pakistani Studies* (US), *Solidarity International, Orbis, The Other Poetry, South Asian Review, ScottishPen, tinfoildresses* (US), and a forthcoming Bloodaxe anthology.

William Bonar is a graduate of the Glasgow University MLitt in Creative Writing. He will make his Stanza Festival debut in the St Mungo's Mirrorball Clydebuilt showcase event in March 2012. His poems have appeared in numerous newspapers, magazines and anthologies and on the BBC Radio 3 programme *The Verb*. He lives in Glasgow and works in education.

Graham Brodie was born and lives in Edinburgh, Scotland. He has been writing and performing poetry throughout the British Isles since 1993. He has contributed in various ways to this world of poetry, and is interested in the creation of freedom in all forms. He tries to expand and express this belief through his life and work as a poet.

Nick Brooks is the author of two previous novels, *My Name Is Denise Forrrester* and *The Good Death*, and has just completed a third, *Indecent Acts*. He is currently at work on a fourth.

Larry Butler was born in USA and has lived in Glasgow since 1981; he teaches tai-chi in healthcare settings and leads life-story groups at the Maggie Cancer Care Centre; facilitates writing groups for Lapidus Scotland (creative words for health & wellbeing) lapidus.org.uk. Recent publications include Butterfly Bones (Two Ravens), and Han Shan Everywhere (Survivors' Press). He edits pamplets for PlaySpace Publications.

Karen Campbell, originally from Glasgow, is now based in Galloway, where she writes full-time. She has four novels about the politics of policing out with Hodder. Her new book *This is Where I Am* tells the story of a Somali refugee in Glasgow, and is published by Bloomsbury in spring 2013.

**Niall Campbell** (b.1984), from the island of South Uist, gained an MLitt in Creative Writing from the University of St Andrews in 2009. In 2011 he received an Eric Gregory Award from the Society of Authors, and a Robert Louis Stevenson Fellowship. His first pamphlet will be released by Happenstance in March 2012.

**Regi Claire** is Swiss by birth. English is her fourth language. Twice shortlisted for a Saltire Book of the Year Award, longlisted for the MIND Book of the Year Award and the Edge Hill Short Story Prize, she is the author of *Inside-Outside*, *The Beauty Room* and *Fighting It*. Regi teaches creative writing at the National Galleries of Scotland. regiclaire.com

**AC Clarke** has had three full collections published, *Breathing Each Other In* (Blinking Eye Publishers 2005), *Messages of Change* (Oversteps Books 2008) and most recently *Fr Meŝlier's Confession* (Oversteps Books 2012). Her pamphlet *A Natural Curiosity*, which includes the poem which won the Off The Stanza poetry competition, was published by New Voices Press in 2011.

**Penny Cole** lives on the southside. She was born in Edinburgh, lived in London and then moved to Glasgow two years ago. She is a journalist, reviewer and political activist. She restarted creative writing 5 years ago. As well as poems and short stories she has written and directed two one-act plays. She grows a lot of vegetables.

**Julian Colton** has had three collections of poetry published including *Everyman Street* (Smokestack Publishing, 2009) which was in the Hand + Star review website's top 5 books for 5 weeks over Christmas and New Year 2009/10. In 2008/9 he was CREATE Writer in Residence for Dumfries and Galloway. He continues to teach in schools, most recently as part of the Natural Identity project for the Tolbooth Gallery in Stirling. He lives in Selkirk in the Scottish Borders and co-edits *The Eildon Tree* magazine.

**Christopher Crawford** was born in Glasgow. His poems, fiction, translations and essays have appeared in *Agenda*, *Orbis*, *Envoi*, *Eyewear*, *The Literateur* and *The Cortland Review* among others. His poems have been nominated in the US for the upcoming *Pushcart Anthology* by RATTLE and *Now Culture*.

**Cat Dean** is an Edinburgh-based freelance website designer, tutor and mother of three. She is working on her first novel and blogs about writing and creativity amidst the chaos of family life at catdean.com.

**Brian Docherty** was born in Glasgow, and now lives in north London. He has been a civil servant, hospital storeman, warehouseman, market trader, lecturer and creative writing tutor. He was educated at Middlesex Poly, University of Essex, London University and St. Mary's University College. Two books, *Armchair Theatre* (1999) and *Desk with a View* (2008). *The 'If' in California* is due from Smokestack Books in October 2012.

The last time **Roddy Dunlop** wrote a bio for *Gutter* he thinks he was teaching at the high school in Niddrie. He quit his job soon after and walked to Switzerland where he lives, now, in a wee alpine village above Lake Geneva. It's a great place to contemplate all that is going wrong with the world without having to actually participate. 'The Judge' is from a novel he's writing at the moment called *Jock Feeney – A Story of Revenge*. What happened to the revolution?

**Mark Edwards** was born in Aberdeen, spent half his life elsewhere. His first book, *Clearout Sale*, was published in 2008. Hopefully, more to follow.

**David Eyre** is a journalist. He was born in Coatbridge in 1972 and lives in Glasgow's southside. He works as a Media Officer for Oxfam Scotland and was previously a producer/director with the BBC's Gaelic news service. He studied literature and Gaelic at Edinburgh University. Previous work has appeared in *Poetry Scotland* and *Irish Pages*.

**Andrew C Ferguson** is a Fife writer, performer and musician. He currently has a poetry collection under consideration, and a novel seeking an agent. He is one half of acoustic music duo Tribute to Venus Carmichael. He doesn't sleep much. Details of upcoming spoken word and music performances can be found at writers-bloc.org.uk

**Michael Fisher's** stories have been published in several magazines, most recently *Riptide* and *Bewilderbliss*. A graduate of the University of Glasgow, he now lives in Brighton. When he is not visiting the beach, bottle of factor 50 in hand, he is writing his first novel.

**Graham Fulton's** collections include *Humouring the Iron Bar Man* (Polygon) *This* (Rebel Inc) *Open Plan* (Smokestack Books) and Full Scottish Breakfast (Red Squirrel Press). New full-length collections *Brian Wilson in Swansea Bus Station* and *Please Wear Comfortable Clothes and Be Prepared to Discuss Suicide* are to be published by Red Squirrel and Smokestack in 2013 and 2014.

**Andrew F Giles** is a poet and translator with work in *Ambit, Gutter, Equinox, Poetry Scotland, The Nervous Breakdown* and *The Recusant*. He edits Scotland's online arts & culture journal *New Linear Perspectives*.

**Pippa Goldschmidt** is interested in using fiction to explore science. The extract published here is from her recently completed novel about a female astronomer, *Wider than the Sky*. She used to be an astronomer herself, and is currently a writer in residence at the ESRC Genomics Policy and Research Forum, at the University of Edinburgh. pippagoldschmidt.co.uk

**Dr Allan Harkness** is an essayist, poet and artist, and runs the art-environment-literature independent bookshop, The Forest Bookstore. His most recent essay accompanies the William Johnstone: Marchlands exhibition at The Scottish Gallery, Edinburgh (until March 3, 2012). His poem 'I like the unpath best' was a text installation & sound performance piece at Edinburgh University's 'Sensory Worlds' conference in 2011.

**Alexander Hutchison** is currently RLF Writing Fellow at the Royal Conservatoire of Scotland, and also the mentor for *Clydebuilt 5*. Late last year he shed his clothes for an image in a calendar from Wild Women Press to raise funds for type 1 diabetes; the best shots being taken in a bracken patch near Grasmere where Wordsworth composed *The Prélude*.

**Alison Irvine's** first novel, *This Road is Red*, was published by Luath Press in 2011 and shortlisted for the Saltire First Book of the Year award. She is a graduate of the University of Glasgow's MLitt in Creative Writing and was awarded a Scottish Arts Council New Writer's bursary in 2007. She lives in Glasgow with her husband and daughters.

**Andy Jackson** moved to Fife twenty years ago. His poems have appeared in *Magma, Blackbox Recorder* and *Trespass*. He won the inaugural Baker Prize for poetry in 2012, and is editor of *Split Screen*, an anthology of film & TV poetry, due out in March 2012. His debut collection *The Assassination Museum* was published by Red Squirrel in 2010.

Biographies/185

**Anita John** is a creative writing graduate from Edinburgh University and tutors for its Lifelong Learning department. She writes poetry and short fiction, is published in various anthologies and magazines and is a long-term member and Convenor of the Pentland Writers Group. More of her work can be found at: pentlandwriters.drupalgardens.com

**Bridget Khursheed** is a British-Australian poet and geek based in the Scottish Borders (poetandgeek.com). Good on mountains, bad on towers.

**Dearman McKay** is astray in translation. Recent work appears in ILK Journal and forthcoming in the pamphlet *Until This Horror, Cafe Sea*. He is a good smoker.

**Carl MacDougall** has written three prizewinning novels, four pamphlets, three collections of short stories, two works of non-fiction and has edited four anthologies, including the best-selling *The Devil and the Giro*. He has written and presented two television series and is currently working on too many things.

**Rob A. Mackenzie** is from Glasgow and has lived in Edinburgh for the last seven years. His first full collection, *The Opposite of Cabbage*, was published by Salt in 2009. HappenStance Press published an earlier pamphlet, *The Clown of Natural Sorrow*, in 2005. He is reviews editor for Magma Poetry magazine and blogs at Surroundings. robmack.blogspot.com

**Kevin MacNeil** is a multi-award-winning writer. A poet, novelist, playwright and cyclist from the Outer Hebrides, he now lives in London. Books include *A Method Actor's Guide to Jekyll and Hyde* (Polygon), *The Stornoway Way* (Penguin), *Love and Zen in the Outer Hebrides* (Canongate) and *These Islands, We Sing* (Polygon). His album with William Campbell *We are Visible From Space* is imminent. kevinmacneil.wordpress.com

**Kona Macphee** grew up in Australia and now lives in Crieff, Perthshire. Her most recent collection, *Perfect Blue* (Bloodaxe Books 2010), was awarded the Geoffrey Faber Memorial Prize for 2010. Some commissioned poems from Kona are featured in *Human Race: Inside The Science of Sports Medicine*, an exhibition touring Scotland in 2012. konamacphee.com

**Lindsay Macgregor** started writing at Dundee Maggie's Centre in 2008. She lives near Cupar, Fife and is currently working towards an MLitt in Writing Practice and Study at the University of Dundee.

**Iain Maloney** is a widely-published writer of fiction, non-fiction and poetry. Originally from Aberdeen, he now lives in a relatively safe part of Japan. He has an MPhil in Creative Writing from the University of Glasgow and a novel, *Dog Mountain*, available to a good home. He will be back in Scotland in May if anyone fancies a pint.

**Andrew McCallum** is one of 2,301 existentialia that reside in the antisyzygious town of Biggar, where Tweed and Clyde – like MacDiarmid's extremes – come dangerously close to colliding.

**Andrew McCallum Crawford** grew up in Grangemouth, an industrial town in East Central Scotland. His work has appeared in many reviews and journals, including the *International Literary Quarterly*, *Spilling Ink Review*, *New Linear Perspectives*, *McStorytellers*, *The Midwest Literary Magazine* and the *Athens News*. His first novel, *Drive!*, was published in 2010. His collection of short fiction, *The Next Stop Is Croy and Other Stories*, was released in October, 2011. He lives in Greece.

**Patricia McCaw** followed a varied career in social work with a Masters in Creative Writing at Edinburgh University, where she won the Grierson Prize. She has published poems in many literary journals and has recently finished a novel. Both Irish and Scottish cultures – north, south, east, west, past and present – inspire her writing.

**Ross McGregor** writes poetry and fiction. His poetry has appeared in *New Writing Scotland*, *Gutter* and *Tramway's Algebra* (Feb 2012). He lives and works in Ayrshire.

**Donal McLaughlin** (*An Allergic Reaction to National Anthems & Other Stories*) will feature both as a writer and as a translator in *Best European Fiction 2012* (Dalkey Archive Press). He is currently translating three books by leading Swiss writer, Urs Widmer. *My Mother's Lover* (Seagull) was published in June 2011. donalmclaughlin.wordpress.com

**Andrea McNicoll** graduated from Glasgow University's creative writing programme in 2006. Her first novel, *Moonshine in the Morning* (Alma Books 2008), is set in Thailand, where she lived for twelve years. *Moonshine in the Morning* won the Scottish Arts Council First Book Award in 2009. She is working towards a creative writing PhD at the University of the West of Scotland.

**Gordon Meade's** latest collection is *The Familiar* published in 2011 with Arrowhead Press. At present is one of the Royal Literary Fund Writing Fellows at the University of Dundee. Lives in the East Neuk of Fife where he divides his time between his own writing and running creative writing workshops for vulnerable young people and adults in schools, drop-in centres and hospitals.

**Deborah Moffatt** was born in Vermont and has lived in Fife since 1982. Her poems have been widely published, and her collection, *Far From Home*, was published by Lapwing (Belfast) in 2004. She has also published fiction in anthologies from Faber, Bloomsbury, HarperCollins and Virago. She plays traditional music on flute and fiddle, mostly in public-houses and village halls.

**Andrew Philip** recently read *Tae a Lousy Piper* and poems from his *Gutter 4* sequence *10 X 10* on Radio Scotland's *Christmas Morning with Cathy MacDonald and Ricky Ross*. He is now honing his second full collection of poems, which he hopes to publish in early 2013. His first book is *The Ambulance Box* (Salt, 2009). See andrewphilip.net for more.

**Stav Poleg's** poetry has appeared in magazines including *Magma*, *The Rialto* and *Horizon Review*, and her theatre work performed at the Shunt Vaults, London Bridge. A sequence of her poems, which follows the goddess Athena in *The Odyssey*, was recently performed at the Traverse Theatre as part of Words, Words, Words. She lives in Edinburgh.

A selection of **Chris Powici's** poems, *Somehow This Earth*, was published by Diehard in 2009. He edits *Northwords Now* magazine, teaches for The University of Stirling and The Open University and enjoys a happy addiction to cycling. Some of his cycling poems can be found at poetonabike.blogspot.com

**Tessa Ransford** is a poet and translator, and has been a cultural activist on many fronts over the last forty years. *Not Just Moonshine, New and Selected Poems*, was published in 2008 by Luath Press, Edinburgh. Two new books are due in 2012. One is poems and translations inspired by the Five Pillars of Islam with Iyad Hayatleh entitled *A rug of a thousand colours*. wisdomfield.com

**Dilys Rose** has published ten books of fiction and poetry, and has received various awards and fellowships for her work. Recent collaborations include the libretto for the opera *Kaspar Hauser: Child of Europe*, composed by Rory Boyle. She is programme director of the new online distance learning MSc in Creative Writing at the University of Edinburgh.

**Stewart Sanderson** was born in 1990 and is currently working on an mPhil in Scottish Literature at the University of Glasgow. His poems have been accepted by *The Literateur*, *Other Poetry*, *Erbacce*, *Lallans*, *The Interpreter's House*, *Bow Wow Wow Shop* and *Magma*. The Scots Language Society highly commended one of his translations in their 2011 Sangschaw competition.

**Simon Sylvester** was born in 1980. His stories have been published in *Gutter*, *Smoke*, *Fractured West*, PANK and other magazines. His flash fiction collection *140 Characters* is a print-on-demand ebook by Cargo Crate, and he writes new stories daily on *twitter.com/simonasylvester*. He lives in Cumbria with the painter Monica Metsers and their daughter Isadora.

**Judith Taylor** comes from Coupar Angus (somebody had to) and now lives and works in Aberdeen. Her poetry has appeared in a number of magazines, including *New Writing Scotland*, *Poetry Scotland*, *Smiths Knoll*, *Gutter* and *The Rialto*, and she is the author of two pamphlet collections: *Earthlight*, (Koo Press, 2006), and *Local Colour* (Calder Wood Press, 2010).

**Olufemi Terry** has published fiction, poetry, and nonfiction in *Chimurenga*, *Guernica* and *The American Scholar*, among other publications. In 2010 he won the Caine Prize for African Writing. He lives in southwest Germany and is at work on a novel.

**Nuala Watt** has an MLitt in Creative Writing from the University of St Andrews and is currently completing a PhD which aims to recast visual impairment as a positive aesthetic in poetry. Her work has previously appeared in *Magma* and on BBC Radio 3.

**Mary Wight** grew up in the Scottish Borders. She has an MSc in Creative Writing from the University of Edinburgh and her poems have been published in magazines including *Edinburgh Review*, *Poetry London*, *Poetry Scotland* and *The Shop*.

**Graeme Williamson** was born in Montreal and now lives in Glasgow. Originally a musician and songwriter he turned to fiction some time ago. When in doubt he is sometimes inspired by Flaubert's dictum: *Art isn't made with good intentions.*

**Jim C Wilson's** writing has been published widely for 30 years. His three poetry collections are *The Loutra Hôtél*, *Céllos in Héll* and *Paper Run*. He has taken first place in several UK competitions and was a Fellow of the Royal Literary Fund from 2001 until 2007. He has taught his Poetry in Practice course at Edinburgh University since 1994. Always available! jimcwilson.com

**Nicholas YB Wong** is the author of *Cities of Sameness* (Desperanto, 2012). His poems are forthcoming in *580 Split*, *American Letters & Commentary*, *Gargoyle*, *Interim*, *The Jabberwock Review*, *Quiddity* and *Upstreet*. He is the recipient of Global Fellowship Award at ASU Desert Nights Rising Stars Writer's Conference in 2012. He reads poetry for *Drunken Boat*.

**Li San Xing's** work has appeared in several publications, including *Gutter*, *Short FICTION*, *The Rialto* and *Brand*. In 2010 he was shortlisted for an Eric Gregory Award, and last year he was a finalist in *Glimmer Train's* Short Story Award for New Writers. He was born and bred in Edinburgh, lives in London and is currently working on a novel.